I lovingly dedicate this novel to the memory of my deceased husband, Aron Spilken, who is largely responsible for its creation.

Acknowledgments

Writing a novel is a long, lonely road, and I am grateful to the many friends who provided companionship and help along the way.

The following readers provided significant and repeated feedback and ideas regarding content and editing at various stages in the development of the manuscript, giving generously of their time and expertise: Lisa Zaslove, Ann Marie Yezzi, Margo Field, Leslie Goss and Michael Sweeney.

I want to thank my first editor, Paul Dinas, who continued to give advice and feedback long after the work he was paid to do was finished. I feel lucky to have had the benefit of his thirty years of experience in the publishing business.

Special thanks to the staff at Synergy Books, who have been ever patient and helpful. And thanks in advance to my publicists at Phenix and Phenix whose work is just beginning.

I want to acknowledge and thank all of the following people who read the manuscript at some point and provided criticisms and ideas, and/or helped in some other way with this project: Raul Diaz, Daniel Wile, Victoria Skirpa, Lior Katz, Roy Minet, Mary Miller, Robin Arie, Sharon Skonlnick-Bagnoli, Marianna Cacciatore, Julie Motz Peter Quince, Simon Jerimiah, Karl Kracklauer, Dana Levy, Beth Gailef, Jack Saunders, Bruce Wilson, Lorin Oberweger, Elizabeth Lyon, and Jayel Gibson.

I am very grateful, as well, to my deceased husband, Aron Spilken, whose idea and writing inspired me to take up this project. For a more complete description of his contribution, please read "About the Authorship of this Novel."

About the Authorship of this Novel

In Memory of Central Park was begun by my deceased husband, Aron Spilken, PhD, in the late 1980s. He created a vision of New York City extremely similar to the one presented here. The main characters, the Liberty Party, the Patriots, and a band of revolutionaries with many similarities to the group presented in the current version were included in his original manuscript.

Though terrorism was still rare and almost no one except Senator Al Gore considered global warming a legitimate issue, by the time my husband began working on this book, many people were concerned about overpopulation, the environment, and the loss of civil liberties. The novel was born, after all, during the Reagan years, a period similar in many respects to our current experience under George W. Bush.

My husband died suddenly and unexpectedly in November of 2003. About six months later, I decided that I'd like to revise and complete the book he'd begun.

From the very start, I loved this novel. Although it was not ready for publication, I liked it more than any of the other fine things my husband wrote. I found the writing exquisite, the characters exceptionally vivid, and the political satire wickedly satisfying. I felt I understood the soul of the book. And when I realized, in addition, that recent history had rendered my husband's vision of New York City more relevant today than it was when he originally created it, I was truly excited.

New York City as portrayed in *In Memory of Central Park* is a perfect symbol of the isolationism to which the current Bush has condemned our country. On almost every important issue, including climate change, the war in Iraq, and stem cell research, George W. has chosen to go it alone. And now that we have terrorism to worry about, now that the population of the planet has continued to grow exponentially, now that the rising waters created by global warming—barring some truly miraculous intervention—will surely flood the island of Manhattan, now that the world's water and air and food are even more polluted and our civil liberties are in yet greater jeopardy than ever before, this fanciful image of New York City in the mid-twenty-first century is an amazingly apt metaphor for our current reality.

In addition to the above literary and political motivations, I had personal ones as well. The loss of my husband was the worst thing that ever happened to me. It was quite frankly difficult to survive. I needed a purpose for my life, and completing this book provided that. Furthermore, my husband and I had always worked together on projects. I was his editor, carefully reading over his writing, making comments, discussing ideas, crossing out extraneous words, and rewriting sentences. We worked together, as well, on projects for the theatre, projects for the ranch where we lived, the design for a house we were building in Mexico. As a couple, we were constantly involved with one creative project or another. Picking up where he left off with *In Memory of Central Park* allowed me to continue collaborating with him despite his death. It provided a kind of contact I could not have had in any other way.

I also felt a need to express and honor the beauty of the relationship I'd had with my husband. I did this by developing and expanding the relationship between the two main characters, Noah and Margaret, which, though in part pure fiction, does mirror in important ways the relationship I had with my husband, both from his point of view and from mine.

While I have edited, cut, added to, and rearranged what my husband wrote, at least half of the words in the current version were taken directly from his manuscript. There are entire chapters that are pretty much the way he wrote them. Other chapters are jointly written; yet others contain my writing alone. Does this not make my husband a coauthor of this book? Certainly it does.

Nonetheless, *In Memory of Central Park* isn't the result of two people negotiating how it should be written or dividing it up between them in some arbitrary way. I inherited a manuscript, some of which I kept, some of which I threw out, all of which I edited, rearranged, and updated. Ultimately, I crafted the novel according to my personal vision of what it should be. I could never have guessed what Aron would have done had he chosen to complete the manuscript, nor did I try. This, of course, required that I write convincingly in the novel's original voice, which, for reasons I can't explain, I felt sure I could do. Since completing the book, I have asked numerous readers to guess which parts were written by Aron and which parts were written by me. Since no one yet has been able to identify who wrote what with any consistency, I assume I succeeded in this important task.

For a variety of complex reasons, my publisher and I decided not to list two authors on the front cover. However, I wish to acknowledge clearly and unequivocally that my deceased husband Aron Spilken and I are coauthors of this novel.

All my heart became a tear,

All my soul became a tower,

Never loved I anything

As I loved that tall blue flower!

From "The Blue Flag in the Bog"
by Edna St. Vincent Millay

🌸 *Chapter 1*

I grew up during the Interconnection of New York City. I remember it as a sudden, wrenching change, but that's because as an eight-year-old boy I only saw my small part in it. A gang of men and women in coveralls set up barricades in the hall outside our apartment. They took down the beveled mirror and exposed a rectangle of naked paint, as pale as the skin under a bathing suit. Then they hooked up their jackhammers and smashed through the wall of our apartment house.

My brother and I watched from our doorway. It was coarse surgery, with lots of noise and dust, and plenty of plaster, paint, and patching compound. When they were done, there was a new step, a new archway, and our corridor connected directly to the hallway in the adjacent building.

They worked for weeks, on every floor, on all four sides, and Adam and I watched every move. What had been solid, dissolved; what had been separate, they now brought together. By the time they had finished, we knew every one of them, even what they ate for lunch, and when they left us, we were interconnected with the rest of New York City. We were joined to an endless system of corridors and stairwells, which we explored during those long, fluorescent-lit afternoons when we had to stay out of the apartment because my father needed to sleep.

Children take what they are given. Adam and I accepted hallways and stairways as the fundamental pathways of life. When we learned in school how Pygmies had once chanted as they strolled barefoot along the moist earth of the jungle, we pictured them in some exotic form of corridor. And when we read that Plains Indians had once scrambled to the tops of buttes to search for signs of buffalo, we envisioned their dusty ascent in terms of a stairway. Our experience, the experience of the interconnected city, became the basis for everything we understood. So it was no wonder that my father's stories were difficult for me, with their airy softness, with their acknowledgment of loss, with their undercurrent of celebration for something no longer attainable.

Chapter 2

During my father's lifetime, light and space closed up like a hand into a fist, and the world became clenched. And all this happened as if it were so natural and inevitable that there was nothing to do but shrug. Once-upon-a-time people used to joke, "You know, if we're not careful, New York could turn into a single huge house." And then the time came when they laughed about how this had once been a joke.

For New York, a real but unrecognized turning point came way back in the 1960s when an airline company built a giant office building across Park Avenue in midtown Manhattan, blotting out Grand Central Station. Traffic was routed around and under it. It all seemed reasonable at the time, but perhaps it set some kind of precedent, giving buildings the right of way. As the population grew and grew, contractors in Manhattan, who had been surreptitiously narrowing sidewalks for some time, began to ignore them altogether and build to the edges of the curbs. The next step was inevitable. A local construction firm, well connected to the permit board, built between the curbs, blocking the street. Of course they were challenged in court, and around our kitchen table, we angrily challenged them as well. We slapped newspaper articles with the backs of our hands to show just how outraged we were. But it was difficult to apply vague conservationist notions to the city of New York in a convincing fashion, things being what they were. And while the case was being considered, another contractor began rapidly to excavate and build next to the first. It was easier, and certainly more politically expedient, to reroute traffic than to tear down two desperately needed modern apartment houses. No one was surprised when the court finally gave its opinion that the need for shelter was primary and more fundamental than the need for vehicle access. The building boom was on.

Those parents who picketed in the name of the family, demanding that the city preserve space for children to play, couldn't stop the bulldozers. Irony defeated them. The protesting families were the same ones who were having the children who needed the places to live.

Do you wonder why, as fast as they were built, there were never enough apartments or offices? It happens this way: a great weight, like a city, creates a depression in the field of gravity, like a sleeper in a bad bed, and everything rolls toward it, collecting there, making it still heavier. That's what happened in Mexico City, where people gathered in a great valley and poisoned the air, until birds flying above fell dead at their feet.

We children were the closest to it and the first to see it, but we had no idea what these changes meant. Even if we had, we were the last ones who could have done anything about it. Once the vacant lots were gone, the city began to give out permits to tear up playgrounds and parks for building sites. We saw our world systematically consumed. We still had gymnasiums, of course, but we had nothing outside, away from adults, where we could play our own games by our own rules. There were no more tree forts, no secret clubs in park bushes, no place for ritual and magic, or to discover sex. We were like derelicts, huddling in the shadows under stairways until we were noticed and rousted. I can still remember my mother's warnings, insistent to the point of hysteria, "Now you stay out from under those stairs!"

My mother flourished in the city. She was a natural hive-dweller, plump and placid as a honey cake. She liked all the people with their commotion and constant contact. But I watched my father become brittle without privacy. He needed space; he craved peace. He retreated, as if to some dark corner, where he shriveled but did not die. Despite the fact that he remained in the apartment where he'd lived for over a decade, he was like an animal transported from its natural habitat into an alien landscape.

These changes were probably necessary, just as it had once been necessary to dam the Nile. The logic was simple enough: Egypt needed the hydroelectric power. But as the Aswan Valley flooded, tribes that had been sheltered by remote pastures; that had lived there, off by themselves, since the time of the Romans (and daily expected them to return); tribes that, for thousands of years, had used tools and jewelry otherwise found only in graves and museums; tribes that had been farming and herding in ways otherwise known only from engraved tablets, were driven by the smothering waters, not only from their lands, but also from their customs and their ability to make sense of life. Most died. And the survivors lived on in ways that felt meaningless. My father was just such a lost tribe: a tribe of one, a stranded Ishi, a last link, a mere reminder.

 # *Chapter 3*

Margaret's eyes are turquoise, striking, her body slight, her skin pale, with pink on her cheekbones, as if they've been rubbed. But what you notice first is the long, tendriled, golden-red hair that falls past her shoulders. (What a paradox that someone so shy is such a burst of sunlight, always the most dramatic person in the room.) She doesn't use it. She doesn't toss her head or play with her hair, doesn't seem to care if it gets mussed. In this one thing, she has the confidence of someone secure in her great wealth.

Margaret is my brother's wife. I'm ashamed to admit this, but I'm obsessed with her. I wonder what she's doing. I wonder what she thinks of me. In my mind's eye, I see the quizzical expression that almost makes fun of you, or the arc of her foot as she traces circles on the floor with her toe, or the languid way she sometimes stretches, both arms reaching up and back, making visible the outline of her breasts. When she does that, it takes my breath away, and it shames me, because I know that later in the privacy of my room, I'll think about forbidden things. I'll see our bodies wrapped around each other. Then one delicious moment will follow the next. Seamless and sublime, our imaginary lovemaking is so tender and sweet, it washes away, at long last, the indelible stain of my loneliness.

I've known Margaret for years, and while I was always impressed by her looks (she's the kind of woman a successful man like my brother would naturally marry), I always took it for granted that she was his. I was polite, even warm at times, but until lately, I never meant anything by it. She was Adam's wife, after all. But gradually things changed, until now my feelings are as out of control as some wind-whipped wildfire.

I've tried talking sense to myself. It hasn't helped. More and more, Margaret and I seem drawn to each other. For one thing, in the midst of this noisy city, we're both such quiet people. And we're both outsiders, with an almost paranoid sensitivity to the misuses of power. Adam is a booming, successful insider. So when Margaret and I put our heads together at his kitchen table, I see now that it's clearly a way of allying ourselves against him. "Look at this!" Margaret will insist when she sees me, and she'll thrust before me a newspaper folded back to some article she's been reading, saving actually, in case I showed up. "Terrible," I will agree and shake my head, enjoying the pleasure of having someone to share my sense of injustice.

Margaret hates the life of the halls, so inevitably we're in some kitchen—her kitchen, or my mother's. Adam is usually there, and any number of other people. Everyone talks around us, a kitchen crowded with talk, with no one paying the slightest attention to our murmuring. Today is no exception. Adam is against the far wall romancing a member of the Board of Education about a plan to unify the district's elementary schools into a single colossal center for primary education by adding forty more stories to a midtown Manhattan high-rise. My mother, meanwhile, is whispering conspiratorially with several guests at the end of the table. Margaret is brewing a fresh pot of coffee. I saunter over to her, remove the newspaper article du jour from my pocket, and lay it on the counter beside her. The headline reads: "Mayor Cites Internal Terrorist Threat."

"Did you read this?" I say.

"Oh, yes, I read it," she says, pursing her lips and squinting her eyes in an expression I find totally charming. "They weren't satisfied with stopping us from communicating with the outside. Now, they've created an excuse to monitor communications within the city."

"So you don't really believe this stuff about new citizen-based terrorist cells?"

Margaret looks up at me and chuckles wickedly. "In my opinion, a terrorist cell is just what we need. Someone with the nerve to blow up city hall!" We laugh. We both understand that this is only partially a joke, since neither of us would grieve if some disaster were to befall the politicians who run our city.

"If they get this passed," I say, "it'll allow them to identify and squash all political opposition."

"You bet. And as usual, they're using the fear tactic," Margaret replies angrily. She's turned around now and is leaning up against the kitchen counter. I lean next to her, and place my hand a hair's breadth away from hers. I've never touched her, not since I started feeling this way, but I long to do it.

"Yeah, that always seems to work, doesn't it?" I say. I hear the coffee start to drizzle into the coffee pot, and I try my best to think of some way to change the topic to something more personal. There's a moment of silence. Suddenly shy, I can't think of anything to say.

"So, how's your life been going, Noah?" Margaret asks as though she's read my mind.

"My work's been going well," I say. "Some of my clients are making tremendous progress, but as for the rest of it…" I trail off. I really don't know what to say in lieu of the truth. Margaret waits. "The rest of my life feels like something's missing," I say finally.

"Ah," Margaret replies. She smiles, inviting me to continue, but just then my mother shows up, cup in hand, asking if the coffee is ready. Since it isn't, she stays to share the latest gossip. Did I hear that Corina up on the eighteenth floor got stuck in the elevator and had such terrible panic that now she walks up and down all those stairs? She informs me, as well, that there are real deals to be had on men's trousers down at Lord and Taylor and advises me to get down there before all the good ones are gone.

After I leave, I puzzle over whether the attention Margaret pays me has anything to do with sexual attraction and whether and to what extent she's devoted to Adam, as people often are, despite having differences. But I can't tell, and I'm afraid to ask. I'm afraid she'll see what I'm feeling and perhaps pull back, perhaps even expose me as a family traitor. So I contain my feelings, and I'm watchful, hoping to discover a clue in a glance, in a tone of voice, in what is said or left unsaid, that will reveal something of how Margaret feels about me.

I'm a psychologist, long in the habit of examining motives, so naturally I'm suspicious of these feelings I have for Margaret. What would I say, after all, if I were one of my clients, or rather ask, since leading a person to discover the obvious is so much more effective than pointing it out? "What do you make of the fact," I query myself, "that you seem to have fallen in love with the most unavailable woman imaginable? Not only is she married, she's married to your brother." And then I, as client, go over in my mind my checkered history with women. I remember the many relationships in which I've found reasons to pull back. Situations, I have to admit, where another man might have moved forward into commitment. Because rationally, I do see that all relationships must eventually chafe in some way; no two people can be absolutely perfect for one another. So I smile a bit when I find myself thinking that it is Margaret, and only Margaret, who can fill me completely.

 ## *Chapter 4*

As buildings increasingly clogged our streets, it became fashionable to debate the "metropolitan issue." Our family dutifully watched television specials that asked the question, "What are we doing to our cities?" By that time, it wasn't just us; Chicago and Los Angeles had followed our lead and were also building into the streets. The conclusion was that we were changing our cities in an unplanned manner. The implication was that it was somehow for the worse. At the very least, cities were becoming less visually attractive. They bore no resemblance to the carefully planned, two-golf-course communities of Maryland and Virginia, although there was thankfulness, as well as regret, for that. City planners and urban scientists debated the virtues and drawbacks of the neighborhood, the barrio, and the block. Commentators reminisced about stoop ball and noted that although cities might be diseased and crime ridden, there was an intensity and immediacy to life there. Condemnation was distributed cautiously and generally; it seems that we were all guilty of whatever it was that was happening, if indeed blame was in order. Obediently, we examined the issues. But they were so diffuse; there was no beginning or end to them, no place to grab a loose edge and pull. I think it all went over my father's head. And I know my mother didn't care one way or the other.

It wasn't long before all that new construction began to interfere with our travel. When we drove across town to visit friends, it now involved zigzagging about, hunting for an entrance to their neighborhood or an exit from our own. It was easier to stay home. As my father saw it, "With people jammed in on every side, why drive for hours through more people to visit still more people?" Some of the men and women in our building began to bring home boxes of work and to visit their offices only weekly. Our telephone bill went up, and we had a second line put in.

There was a brief period when it seemed as if aerial photographs might be the answer. They were taken weekly over the city and sold in neighborhood newsstands. Before we would attempt a visit to Grandma in Queens, we would gather around the latest aerials, plotting a primary and an alternate route. These family planning sessions were fun, and one quick-thinking toy manufacturer released the game of Travel in which players threw dice to advance a car through a maze or placed apartment houses to box in an opponent.

Looking back now, it all seems impossibly innocent. We still couldn't see where we were headed. Finally, automobiles became useless. Boulevards turned into cul de sacs, and cars began to rust where they stood. It was a difficult time for my father. For years after it had become obvious to almost everyone that owning a car in New York was no longer practical, barely possible even, he'd maintained his fantasy of personal freedom in the grand manner: spontaneity, mobility, privacy. But now he'd been boxed in by reality, as tightly as buildings had boxed in his automobile.

Although our city seemed to accept this transition on a rational level, it was still a shock. We were aware that countless types of animals had become extinct, but to us in New York, animals were a distant and theoretical construct. But to witness firsthand the eradication of an entire species of machine, to hear the streets grow quiet and see the parking lots go bankrupt, to have the great and colorful creatures that had always been lined up as far as we could see, like elephants on parade, vanish from the curbside, that was very real to us. Finally, that cosmic knife, which had been busily paring away pieces from our world, had actually cut the ground beneath our own feet. Men came with acetylene torches to slice up the car carcasses. Helicopters hauled away the ragged chunks of motor-meat. For a few months, dripping, dark engine blocks and the shiny tusks of chrome bumpers flew over the city. And then the great garages were turned into more apartment houses.

It would be wrong, though, to think that the great changes of that era were limited to buildings and automobiles, or that the whole thing was just some sort of colossal inconvenience. The cloth of our lives had been pulled from an odd angle, and every small interlacing of the weave had shifted. In public, only children looked directly at each other. Adults followed the etiquette of a crowded elevator; the closer the bodies of strangers, the more they must pretend not to notice each other. Among my classmates, staring now became as common a form of attack as name-calling. When privacy is available only by mutual consent, glancing carelessly about becomes a serious form of intrusion.

People compensated for their lack of personal space by drawing more deeply into themselves. And while emotional intimacy became rarer, physical intimacy became more common. With the progressive overcrowding, we were constantly forced to improvise. It wasn't unusual to open some mop closet and find two flushed friends in a jiggling embrace. Casual couplings became ever more regular occurrences: department store clerks with their patrons in fitting rooms, police with felons in squad cars, and even fellow window washers on narrow ledges high above the city, like pigeons.

The changes to our environment even altered the ancient and amazingly stable society of children. Games and rhymes had been passed down, intact, if incomprehensible, taught by five-year-olds to four-year-olds for more than a thousand years. Hopscotch and Johnny-on-the-pony are not only visible in Brueghel's paintings from the 1500s, but also in archaeological excavations reaching as far back as the time of the Roman Forum. But when Adam and I went out into the walkways that had once been streets, we milled about in crowds too dense to permit traditional games. Gloves and balls, Frisbees, jump ropes, and skateboards had ceased to be functional, but they had not been abandoned. We clung to them as ritual totems invested with a vague and adaptable magic. Patient, determined Adam once worked for a month, carefully attaching sequins, bottle caps, brass bells, and strips of velvet to a baseball bat. Materials like these were available from hobby shops in kit form to prepare the highly decorative objects, part of every child's wardrobe, that were still required to go out and play.

As time went on, people started to complain about the passageways through which we accessed other buildings and the subway stations. They were too cold in the winter, too wet in the rain. "Why do we need to go out?" people asked. They had a point. Now that there were no more streets, playgrounds, or parks, why indeed?

The huge project known as the Interconnection took years, but when it was finished, you could go anywhere in New York without having to encounter weather of any kind. Naturally, this destroyed the market for coats and umbrellas, but unless you happened to be in that business, this was a small price to pay for the extra convenience. The interior hallways of every building were joined, the remnants of the old streets were enclosed, creating a system of corridors, and the space above them was used for yet more construction. From the outside, the immense, ungainly structure New York had become must surely have been an architectural disaster, but since there was no longer any outside from which to view it, this hardly mattered.

Of course, more subway tunnels and entrances were built as well. Without the automobile, not only were the subways necessary to travel any distance, but they were also used in conjunction with handcarts to deliver goods to local stores and carry manufactured goods to the city's edge.

By the time the Interconnection was complete, everyone was sick and tired of noise and dust and disruption. And since every square inch of space on our little island was now covered, we figured we were finished with construction. Little did we know how wrong we were.

Chapter 5

My phone rings. It's Margaret. She's crying. "Can you come over?" she asks. I try to find out what's wrong, but she won't say. "Just come, okay," she says. It's late, and I've finished with my last client, so I switch off the lights and leave.

As I weave through the crowded corridors, imaginings somersault around my mind: Could something have happened to Adam? I immediately feel anxious. Thank goodness for that. Adam and I aren't close, but he is my brother; I like to believe I love him. On the other hand, if it were to turn out that Margaret is crying because she's discovered Adam's having an affair, as self-serving as this might be, I'd feel tremendous relief. It is possible, I think. Adam's a perennial flirt. I've often wondered if it ever turns into anything more. If so, he's never shared this with me. But then I've never known Adam to share personal things with anyone. Possibly with Margaret, how could I know? In any event, it's clear Margaret has called me in a time of need, and that pleases me.

When I arrive at the gates of the Central Park Community, I give my name to the attendant, and he calls up to their flat to see if I'm expected. I always feel out of place in this enclave of the rich, like I'm the brother from the other side of the tracks. About fifteen years ago, Adam joined the Liberty Party. Shortly thereafter he was awarded a lucrative city contract, and shortly after that, he was able to obtain a luxurious flat in the Community. Adam told me in confidence that joining the Liberties was purely practical, because, as he put it, it would be good for business.

"Come on, Noah," he'd said to me. "Don't give me grief about this. They win all the elections whether I vote for them or not, so my joining doesn't make a tinker's damn worth of difference." Maybe not. Nonetheless, having a brother who's a member of the Liberty Party feels humiliating. I know Margaret feels the same way, though of course, neither of us would say this in public.

I take the elevator to their flat. It's after nine. I wonder where Adam is and why Margaret called me and not him. I find myself wishing, again, that Adam is having an affair. I'm tired of feeling guilty about…about what, loving Margaret? Do I love Margaret? I shake my head. My feelings bewilder me.

When I arrive, Margaret is still crying. I want to take her in my arms. It would be appropriate, even kind, under the circumstances, but guilt throws me off balance, so I fail to reach out until the moment has passed. Margaret sinks into a chair at the kitchen table, and I sit beside her.

"What's wrong, Margaret? What's happened?"

"Adelaide is dead. I got a call from her son just before I called you."

"I'm so sorry, Margaret. How did she die?"

"A stroke. She never regained consciousness."

"So, she died without pain. That's good, isn't it?"

"Yes," Margaret says, hardly able to get the word out.

"She had a good life, and she was old."

Margaret nods but continues to cry. Just sitting quietly beside her, I feel a flush creeping through my body. Again, I puzzle over the strength of my feelings—feelings I never wished for or wanted. "She isn't yours. You can't have her!" I admonish myself. This is an old refrain, and as usual, some recalcitrant part of me refuses to accept it.

"It's so strange, so unbelievable," Margaret says through her tears. I'm struck by how young and helpless she sounds. Of course, it's understandable. For all intents and purposes, Margaret has just lost her mother. Her real mother died when she was an infant. Adelaide, a poor black woman who ran a day care center, loved and cared for Margaret throughout her childhood. I know this, because Margaret told my mother, and my mother told me.

"I feel so alone without her," Margaret whimpers. She looks up into my eyes. Suddenly I feel sad, too— for Margaret and about life, the way it rips away those we love, never caring a whit about our pain. Meanwhile, my mind takes note of the fact that Margaret has said she feels alone without Adelaide. If that's so, I think, could she and Adam be all that close? And where is Adam?

"My father would go out drinking every night and leave me alone in the dark. I was terrified." She's sobbing even harder now. I make no effort to calm her. I know this is how it has to be. "When he'd let me off there in the morning, I'd run to Adelaide. She'd hold me in her big, soft arms, and I'd feel safe again.

"I know, Margaret, I know."

She sounds small and sad and lost. I'm lost, too. My last shred of resistance dissolves. I can't help it; I do love her.

"I wouldn't have survived without her," Margaret wails.

"It's a terrible loss, Margaret, I know that." I hear the front door open. Then Adam comes into the kitchen. When he finds me there and Margaret in tears, he looks mildly shocked.

"What's happened? What's going on?" he demands. Ironically, I feel guilty, as though something *were* going on.

"Adelaide is dead," I explain. I wait to see how he'll handle this. I know for a fact he never much liked Adelaide, that he resented her coming to visit as though she was a member of the family. I suspect it embarrassed him.

"Oh," he says, his brow furrowing.

"Margaret's pretty upset," I add, as though that weren't obvious. Margaret continues to cry quietly. Adam walks over to her, puts his hands on her shoulders, and squeezes them.

"I'm sorry, honey," he says. "I know how much she meant to you." Then he sits in the chair opposite her and takes one of her hands in his. Margaret looks at him. I try to read her eyes, but all I see is sadness.

"She had a stroke late this afternoon," Margaret says. "She never regained consciousness."

"I'm sorry," Adam says. He looks deep into Margaret's eyes in a way that seems uncharacteristic, and intimate. This hurts. The way he's come in and taken over reminds me of a time during our teenage years when I brought a date home and Adam charmed her away from me. This is different, I remind myself. She's his wife, after all. I want to leave, but I don't know how to without seeming abrupt.

"Where have you been?" Margaret asks. "I got your message about not being home for dinner, but—"

"Business," Adam replies. "I was talking to some guys about a new project." Am I reading something into his tone, or does Adam sound uneasy?

"What kind of project, Adam?" I ask. Adam gives me a sharp look. He seems annoyed, which could mean either that he's lying or that he's trying to tell me that this isn't a good time to talk about his work.

"I called Noah," Margaret says. "I didn't want to be alone. Besides…" She breaks down crying again. Inwardly I end her sentence for her: "Besides, I know you never liked Adelaide, so I didn't want to be with you!" Of course, my mind is pursuing its own agenda; I have no way of knowing what she was going to say.

"Margaret," I say forcefully enough to get her to look up at me. "I'm so sorry about Adelaide. She was an exceptional woman. We'll all miss her." (I place a special emphasis on "all," knowing that she'll understand this doesn't include Adam.) I stand there a moment. I wish I could at least reach out and squeeze her hand, but Adam has now taken possession of both of them. "Now that Adam's here," I say softly, "I'm going to leave." Our eyes meet, and through her tears, I feel warmth streaming toward me. I send it back, and there's a moment, brief but precious, when I feel her heart connect with mine.

"Thank you for coming," she says.

At home in bed, I work to accept reality. Margaret is Adam's wife. I try to relax with and around this undeniable fact, and I refuse to let myself think about the way he touched her, or about the way he's probably touching her now.

 *Chapter 6*

Last night I had another of those dreams about my father. In the dream, he was old, as he was at the end, but he was crying, which I never saw, and I was hugging him tightly, which I never got to do. Well, actually, I did force a few stiff hugs on him just before he died, when he was too frail to resist and too polite to complain. But that was after all those years when neither of us had touched the other except by accident. I remember how his body felt, brittle under the hospital cotton; his smile looked forced. But in my dream, my father allowed himself to cry, and he let me hold him close at last.

There was a time when we used to laugh at him. Really, I feel sick now when I remember it. We pretended it was fond laughter, a family joke, but it was too sharp for that. We were laughing at his stories. The truth was we hated those stories. He knew it, but he insisted on telling them anyway. "We took the subway," he would explain, "from down in the Lower East Side." I could feel him wanting me to look up at him. "There were seven of us, a big family. We'd pack a picnic lunch and go to Central Park. We'd put our blanket down under some magnificent, big tree, or sometimes my brothers and I would just lie out in the sun on the grass. They had a sprinkler system, so the grass was always soft and green. I had one of those old army canteens with a canvas cover. My mother would fill it with borscht, with sour grass borscht." He would tell us this, wistfully insistent, as if these simple facts were something we must understand.

My father was a small, thin man. He seldom seemed excited, but when he told us his stories, he gestured a bit with his hands. He would sweep one slowly out, trying to suggest to us what it felt like to wander through such a large and breathtakingly beautiful expanse of open space. But nothing he said in those days could tempt me. No matter how often he described it, or with what deep emotion, I refused to picture his large family, or his park.

There were also stories about visits to my father's Uncle Harry in upstate New York. "I'd feel excited for days before we left," he'd tell us, "and my nose would be pressed against the car window the whole way. The road would wind up through the mountains." Always he'd show us with his hand the curves and twists of the road. "There were forests, and in spring they were filled with wildflowers. Sometimes we'd see deer. And when we came out of the forest and started down again, we'd see Lake Ontario glistening in the distance. When we arrived, as soon as we could wiggle free of Aunt Rachel's and Uncle Harry's hugs, we kids would run outside. There were fields that stretched as far as the eye could see." At this point in his story, my father would gaze straight ahead, as though those vast fields lay in front of him at that very moment. "And in the late summer when they'd mow the alfalfa, there was such a lovely, sweet smell—you can't imagine." He was right, I couldn't imagine. I wouldn't even try. I dug the toe of my sneaker into the shag of our carpet. And I bent my thin neck, stubborn as a bow, as I'd somehow learned from him, just as he'd learned this in his struggle with his own father.

Now I can be amazed that New York once had a great Central Park, and I can even feel pride that my father actually saw it, but in those days, I still turned my emotional back on him. If you had asked me then why I was doing it, I would probably have told you, in my ten-year-old way, that I was absorbed in my own childhood, so it was boring to hear about his. But even more important, I had accepted our own reality, so what could be gained by belittling it? His stories seemed to say, "I had something wonderful that you will never have and never even fully understand," and I resented feeling taunted by him.

I realize now that he was only trying to convey what it was like growing up in a world that was very different from the one in which we now live. But to me as a child, that was something alien and disconnected, something from the time before time itself had buckled and snapped and carried us off on a temporal version of continental drift.

My father has been dead for fifteen years. Now, after all this time, I've begun remembering his stories. I've been gathering them up from the corners of my mind, where I once carelessly tossed such things. But now I'm of an age where I need to put my life into better order. So this time, I listen.

 *Chapter 7*

I've just returned from dinner at my brother's flat, and I'm miserable. I'd vowed to myself that I would at least hint to Margaret how I felt about her. As an excuse to get close to her, I'd brought a newspaper article about some builders who had used shoddy materials in an apartment house, causing a collapse that killed hundreds.

Adam always brags about how he never cuts corners. I believe him, and I'm proud of him on this account, though I do wonder why the rich and the powerful and the politically well-connected come to his parties, and why he is never without work. Are deals made? Are there payoffs involved with my brother's success? In any event, his material success puts mine to shame. Which leads me back to Margaret. Why would she leave Adam for me? Yes, I've gone that far in my mind. I'm no longer fantasizing about some sex-centered fling. In my daydreams, I now imagine us making a life together. More and more, I believe I truly love her.

As usual, other people drifted in after dinner, and as usual, both my brother and my mother occupied themselves with these visitors, leaving Margaret and me to huddle over our newspaper article. As usual, we both expressed our righteous indignation, and as usual, I did nothing more. Any number of times I might have reached out and touched her hand. Or I might have said something corny and complimentary like, "How lovely you look tonight, Margaret." So, why didn't I? My psychologist self jumps in to answer this question. "You lack self-esteem," he says, far more critically than I would ever speak to any client of mine. "You don't think you've got a chance. You believe if she understands what you're up to, she'll reject you, that possibly she might even denounce you to your family, leaving you to wander through the dimly lit corridors like some forlorn Ishmael." I sigh, admitting the truth of this.

I could claim that I refused to act because I was too honorable to betray my only brother. But I don't believe that. Yes, I feel guilty, but at bottom, I think I'm too jealous of Adam, always the favored son, the good one, the successful one, to worry about his welfare. And I'm bewitched by Margaret. She has a delicate cat face and a cat's coolness of manner. And beautiful, slender hands that move with secret fervor when she talks. I seem to be the only one who's noticed.

Chapter 8

Perhaps it was inevitable from the start that the city would eventually have to be sealed. There were so many people and so many businesses. There was so much sweat and piss and shit, so much noxious gas from combustion, so many chemical processes, so much ash and garbage. It was a vicious cycle. The more waste was dumped in the countryside, the more the land died and the more people were forced into the city. The more people, the more there was to dump and the more expensive it became to dump it. It was starting to cost a fortune. "Why are we wasting so much money on crap?" people asked. "The funds are needed for better things." They always are.

The most obvious way to economize was to cut the transportation costs by not hauling the garbage and pumping the sewage so far away. But then how were we to protect ourselves from it? We couldn't have it seeping back. We needed a shield, something watertight, impervious to acid, long-lasting, and economical. Recognizing in these concerns an opportunity to make billions, Stratton and Hicks, a huge engineering firm, worked up a plan to encapsulate Manhattan. There was really nothing to be lost, the proponents argued. True, it was still theoretically possible to take an elevator up to several special observation roofs and stand in the sun or gaze up at the moon and stars, but given how busy life is, how many people ever bothered?

Still, there was lots of opposition, especially by the environmentalists, and the Encapsulation might never have happened, or at least, it might not have happened as soon as it did, had it not been for the terrorists. The first terrorist attack to really get people's attention occurred before I was born, an awful incident where foreigners, Muslims, crashed two airplanes into a big building called the World Trade Center. What a terrible awakening. Suddenly everyone realized that there were people, lots of them, who despised us. Given my interest in history, I went back and read the newspaper reports following that momentous event. Strangely, our President claimed that this horrendous attack occurred because the perpetrators "hated democracy." This doesn't seem credible to me. I have a hard time imagining families sitting around dinner tables on the other side of the world seething because Americans got to vote, but if there was a better explanation, no one seemed interested in discussing it.

In any event, after the terrorists destroyed those two great towers, things turned very grim. There were wars. In theory, the wars were supposed to wipe out the people who hated us so that they wouldn't be able to attack us again. But this strategy backfired. It was never possible to wipe out all those who hated us, because as we bombed cities and killed and mutilated thousands, including civilians, more and more people began to hate us. Ultimately, the whole world seemed to hate us, even those who had once been our allies. For a long time after the World Trade incident, the terrorist attacks occurred mostly in foreign countries. Eventually, though, they returned to our own soil, and New York was an exceptionally popular target.

Once bombs started going off in crowded places, once trains started to collide and the sickening horror of all this was flashed onto TV screens throughout the city, the desire to be safe overwhelmed all other considerations. Those in favor of Encapsulation used the terrorist attacks to bolster their case. If we enclose the city, they reasoned, and there is only one great highway leading in and out, we can inspect every vehicle entering the city and thus keep terrorists and explosive materials out. And as far as people crashing airplanes into buildings, we'd make the walls of our encasement so strong, nothing like that would ever happen again.

But they didn't just appeal to reason, they used fear as well, fear and hatred. In their TV commercials, they showed gory scenes—people injured and bleeding, mothers weeping over the bodies of dead children. Then the angry face of some politician would tell us how evil our enemy was and how greater horrors were sure to befall us if we failed to encapsulate the city. We were exhorted to wall out this enemy who had failed to recognize our essential goodness and had somehow mistaken us for the devil.

It's not that the politicians were wrong about the attacks, they were horrific. But there was something about the fear and hatred these diatribes engendered that was itself a poison. Racial tensions grew, as well as a fierce animosity between people with different viewpoints. When the issue finally came to a vote, Encapsulation won overwhelmingly.

It required lots of steel and lots of cement and many years, but finally the Encapsulation was complete. On our TVs we were shown aerial photographs. We were now encased in a huge, irregular, gray lump, reminiscent of that nuclear power plant that ran amok in the old Soviet Union and had to be filled with cement, except that protruding from our much larger lump were chimneys and steam pipes, as well as openings through which our wastes could be expelled. These wore pressure release valves to protect against backflow, so there were sudden emissions of hissing, the pop-pop-pop of smoke puffs, and great eruptions of vapor. Mechanical straining announced the dropping of chunks of garbage from trash compactors, and sewage oozed and plopped as it was pushed out through great oval orifices.

Of course there were celebrations and all kinds of hoopla. Our politicians bragged nonstop about how much we'd save on waste removal and how safe we were from terrorists. And protected inside our termites' nest of tunnel ways, we did feel safe. We'd reached a stable plateau. We could relax, take a deep breath (well, perhaps only figuratively), and return our attention to the process of living.

 *Chapter 9*

I phone my service. The operator repeats a message verbatim without inflection. "Hi Doc, can't make it today, suffering from arrested orgasm. Tried to come, but couldn't. See you next week."

The caller leaves no name, confident, or perhaps demanding, that I know who it was and what she meant. Her presumption implies we have an intimate connection. She's right. Of course, I know it's Amy.

I've been watching this woman die and discussing her death with her, and there's little more intimate than that. The fact that she made a sexy joke when she canceled her session encourages me. It suggests she's chosen to live for at least another week.

I call her home, but no one answers. Once again, she's disconnected both her telephone and her answering machine. Now I'm not quite as confident. I wonder if she's aware of this effect, if it could be deliberate. We have a pact. We have agreed that it's essential to maintain control over one's life, never to submit to paternalism in the name of state, religion, or even friendship. She understands, of course, that if she intends to harm other people, I am obliged to prevent it. But I gave my word that if she decides to kill herself, I will not take any action. This is so she can feel free to explore her feelings with me. But if she had answered the phone just now and admitted with slurred speech that she had taken an overdose, I would have been put to the test.

Amy misses at least a third of our sessions, more than anyone I have ever worked with. She will start for my office, sometimes confidently, sometimes barely able to drag herself down the corridor, and along the way one of her legs will become numb and then paralyzed. Or she'll experience a sensation like someone chopping her back with a hatchet. Often she has to sit down and lean against the wall until she can crawl home, or until she can call a friend to help her. Her mystery disease does a little dance: a step forward, a hop back, a pirouette—sharp little feet crushing parts of her life the way a child steps on bugs, innocently cruel, unaware of harm. She has a hoard of pills, and quite understandably, she wonders if she should kill herself while she still has the strength. I wonder too.

Amy is only twenty-four. At twenty-two she had already become the office manager for Viper Records. She dressed elegantly, had the best sound and video equipment, and had sex when she wanted it, with both men and women, entirely on her own terms. She never had moods. Everything was fine until one morning she woke up and found the lower part of her body temporarily paralyzed. Until it lifted later that morning, she was unable to call for help or crawl from her bed. She soiled her silk pajamas and her satin sheets. It was a clear statement that life would be different from then on.

The first time I met with her she told me, "Two of my friends have been to see you. I won't tell you who they are. I don't want you to have any way to know about me, except from me." Then a long pause to see if I would argue, if I had any difficulty understanding that she, and only she, would control every aspect of our work.

The first session was a series of such curt announcements and long pauses, time for weight and measurement, an attempt to see if I could live up to whatever claims her friends had made about me. "I don't want to start with any bullshit between us. I'm on to you guys. Most of what you people do is a lot of crap." Pause. "And you should also know that I hate men."

Now it was my turn to pause. She was tall and slim, auburn haired, with an oval face and a small gap between her front teeth. She looked pretty in the butch way of someone who had been on her own and at war since she was young. Her bravado clearly revealed the vulnerability it was designed to conceal, like a sheet spread over a naked body, so that you found yourself rooting for her. Which is not to say that her anger couldn't be bruising.

"If you hate men, you must have a good reason," I said.

"Damn right!" she said, glaring at me as if I were the reason.

In her second session she told me, "I'm a very closed person," as if it were a point of pride, an accomplishment of strength. "I live lies, and after a while, I forget which parts are true. I'm manipulative and I'm vicious. When people cross me, I never forget it." And again she sighted me like a target.

Her physical health is apparently a casualty of environmental poisoning. Tests show chemicals in her hair and teeth and nails that shouldn't be there. Perhaps an incompetent worker crossed some hoses, and exhaust gasses were pumped into her room instead of freshened air, or perhaps it was her water, or her food. Whatever it was, certainly Amy is a product of modern living and never had a chance to play in the green fields of my father.

The doctors don't seem to know what's wrong with Amy, or else they won't tell her. And they aren't able to face the fact that she's finished. She hasn't found a physician yet who will look her in the eye and say, "You're dying. I have no idea how to help you, and I'm sorry." Instead, they avoid her by ordering more tests, or they blame her by implying she's a crank and that their frustration is somehow her fault.

Her elegance now comes from thrift shops—colors mismatched, sizes approximate. Pain has made her face into thrift shop material as well. Her old lovers are off chasing other butterflies. Now her only admirer is a man, a poet with whom she refuses to sleep, but who is allowed to serve her. Over time he's become essential to her survival. He dresses her, he picks up things too low for her to reach, he does most of the cleaning and cooking in the small room they share. I find myself wondering if he feels blessed to be so near to his goddess, or tormented.

She hadn't begun to have moods yet when she began her therapy. Superior and in control, her only reason for being there was, "I want you to help me learn how to deal with doctors. Unfortunately, I need them. I have to have pain pills, and I can't write my own prescriptions. I need tests, and the labs won't do them for me. I might even need surgery." She shrugged. It was just how things were, just an inconvenience that she couldn't reach her own back and do her own surgery. If the world were only better engineered, she might not have to see me.

"I've spent months and months in medical libraries," she explained. "When I try to share what I've learned, they tell me I should leave all that to them. As if the medical side of my life was their property. Then they prescribe something and have the nerve to smile reassuringly at me, as if the problem has now been solved. Hooray. When I tell them I'm familiar with that medication, that it's ineffective and has toxic side effects that they should have warned me about, they turn purple. Of course, most of them are men." Pause. "But I still have to work with them. So I need help becoming more diplomatic."

Our diplomacy lessons amounted to my sitting quietly through our sessions week after week. Not because I'm a psychoanalyst, but because she wouldn't tolerate any suggestions, or even interruptions. She would critique for me the lives of various people she knew, she would complain about her doctors, and she would keep me current on the decline of her health.

Eventually it became possible to ask an occasional, brief question. "What was that like, Amy?" Or, "How did that feel?" gently steering her out of the stockade of her intellect and toward the dark swamp of her emotions. Since the only feelings she'd revealed so far were anger, or its more pastel form, disdain, I felt as if I were delicately tapping on the shell of a soft-boiled egg, hoping to get to the yolk without causing the whole thing to shatter.

The time did come, a few patient months later, when she looked at me with tears in her eyes and moaned, "God, I'm so lonely!" She who had not cried in front of anyone since taking a bitter oath at the age of eleven, she who had not imagined that people could be of any use except to get things for her and to do things to her. Now, with the passing of her innocence, there were terrible realities never before confronted: there was need and the first bleak awareness of all she'd lost.

This was the kind of moment I lived for. Can you believe it, I actually rejoiced because she felt pain? The safety she'd wrapped around herself was a shroud, her lack of moods, a numbness. I was right to be happy for her, because I knew enduring this suffering would bring Amy back to life and allow her to experience joy as well. But no matter how wonderfully significant this was for her, it remained a narrow pleasure for me. The way a seducer will enjoy provoking love without really caring, I got my thrill by provoking life without really living.

Therapists are a lame lot, you know. There's an occasional fuss when someone discovers we are really "wounded healers," as if that means we are somehow counterfeit. But that's our strength, not our weakness. There has to be some reason for doing this kind of work, and given the demands we face, it must be compelling. So however pathetic that reason may be, it's an essential part of the alchemy that can sometimes transmute fear and pain into pleasure and love.

At the entrance to New York Harbor, there used to be a great bronze statue that once cried out to the world, "Give me your tired, your poor, your huddled masses yearning to breathe free." That's our cry too. That statue was eaten away, first becoming smooth and featureless, like an elusive memory, then corroded by pollution to a bronze stump. And all this came about because she got her wish. Except for the breathing, of course. Still, it was a noble cry and not any less so because it destroyed her

Chapter 10

Once I touched Margaret, there was no hope for me. We were in Adam's living room. Margaret and I were sitting next to each other on the couch, close enough for me to catch the sweetness of some scent she used. Adam had just gone into the kitchen to get himself a cold beer. Then the power failed.

There are various types of emergencies that regularly occur in our city. When the ventilation breaks down, the air gets humid and the toilets stink. Both of these are gradual and cumulative crises. But the blackouts are as instantaneous as a hammer blow. Some of the main corridors are equipped with emergency battery-powered floodlights; everywhere else the darkness is complete. Nothing reminds us so forcefully of our special condition as a blackout.

That day, as always, it came in a burst, a flash of black, a stomach-sinking recognition quicker than any thought, and then we were blind. Margaret made a staccato sound, and her fingernails struck my arm like fangs. I could hear her breath, quick and shallow, as she held on with all her strength. My biceps went numb. I put my other hand over hers and stroked the long fingers I'd so often admired. "It's all right, Margaret, it's all right," I murmured over and over. Even in terror her skin felt sweet. I wanted to soothe her, I wanted to touch her face, and I couldn't help it, I wanted to pull her to me and kiss her so fiercely she'd know in an instant I was the one she loved.

"Are you okay, Margaret?" Adam called from the doorway.

She didn't answer, so I called out, "She's all right." For perhaps two full minutes, I sat with my hand over Margaret's while my heart pounded. I felt protective and loving and sexually excited all at the same time. When the lights came on, Adam stood behind her with his hands on her shoulders until she opened her eyes and let go of my arm.

There are some for whom the blackouts are totally intolerable. We call them "screamers," even though most of them don't actually scream but, like Margaret, freeze into an ice block of panic. But even the quiet ones have to fight down the urge to shriek, and those who do lose control are memorable enough to make up for those who don't. They can be heard for blocks as they smash themselves frantically through the darkness, around rooms or down corridors, unaware of the possibility of causing damage to themselves or others.

Our schools used to give us "panic lessons" in an attempt to protect us from this. It was well-intentioned but misguided. By law, at least two adults had to be present during blackout drills, so our principal, Miss McGuire, would come into the room to handle the switches. Light switches were kept in locked boxes high on the wall, so children had no access to them until they were old enough to understand the seriousness of using them inappropriately. There was a standard schedule for darkness exposure, from fifteen seconds in the first grade to fifteen minutes by the freshman year of high school, which was the maximum amount of time that could be spared for a nonacademic drill. In practice, however, these lessons in self-improvement were inflicted only on the helpless lower grades, and as the dark times grew longer, students and teachers found one pretext or another to skip them. The exercises were dropped completely when it was discovered that the procedure created more fears than it relieved.

For some, however, chaos means license. In the sudden freedom of dark hallways, purses are snatched, expensive hothouse fruit scooped up from grocers' stalls, breasts groped by men, crotches by women. Meanwhile, most of us press back against the walls, praying we escape the grasping of anonymous hands, listening with dread to the moans, the panting, and the blindly rushing bodies, unable to distinguish escaping perpetrators from fleeing victims.

In that pitch black, I stroked Margaret's smooth hands, the thief of a small intimacy I can't forget. The feel of her hands lingers, filling me with excitement, and with thoughts I shouldn't entertain. I imagine myself bursting into her kitchen and boldly declaring my love. I imagine whispering to her softly in the corner of a crowded room or writing her a letter (I've even started one) in which I say extravagant, romantic things. I know I have to act, and since touching Margaret, I know that I will.

Chapter 11

Twins are distinctive for their special qualities. Companions, not just from birth but from the instant of conception, they develop unique understandings, private languages, even, some claim, paranormal connections. Possibly twins have the only souls who never feel the almost universal despair that comes from recognizing one's aloneness in an infinite universe. But I never experienced any of these things regarding Adam.

My first memory is of a fight with him. We are four. He is picking up the toys and piling them patiently back in their chest while I keep pulling them out and throwing them around our room. In my recollection, he doesn't seem unhappy because he can't have his order. I'm the one who's upset, because I can't have my chaos. (Adam claims he doesn't remember this and laughs, as if the point of the story is to tease him about his neatness.)

We're not identical twins. Adam is blond and I am dark. He's larger and stronger, but with a certain softness, a layer of pudding spread over his bones. I'm more wiry and angular and, like my father, more intense. So we were different from the start, and he never provided the promised comfort. The way a bad marriage can make you feel more alone than solitude, I believe I would have been less lonely as an only child.

Not only did Adam's presence make me lonely, it also made me bad. When we were four, we played doctor. We brought a little girlfriend to a dark corner under the stairs and took turns solemnly pushing the eraser end of a pencil into each others' rectums to take a temperature. Of course, adults had taught us this game, using real thermometers, but we wanted to explore the sensation and the intrigue of the procedure further on our own.

Intuitively, I felt sure this was a secret of the highest order. But Adam told. In complete innocence, he described what we'd done under the stairs. We were scolded, and we were admonished never to do that again. My mother even felt it necessary to talk with the little girl's mother, because we were boys and, in her eyes, more culpable. So it was clear, even at that age, that Adam could not be trusted.

I had no intention of surrendering my sexual curiosity just because my parents demanded it, so I went underground. If I'd been an only child, or the only child my age in the family, I might have done the same things, but I would have thought about them in an entirely different way. It would have been simply me against my parents, and easy to see them as intrusive. But with Adam there, I was endlessly confronted by the contrast between us. Not only was I the one with the unacceptable impulses, but only I refused to give them up. Clearly I was the bad one.

I continued to be bad, and I got worse. I argued regularly with my parents. I couldn't stop myself. My behavior had the compulsive quality of a cause: the way some people have to fight injustice, I had to provoke it.

Once my path diverged from Adam's, and I chose, or was pushed onto, the low road, it seemed I had to keep putting one foot in front of the other and continue down that path. There was one advantage. Being bad helped assuage my loneliness, because I always had plenty of company.

There was a secret society of bad children. Since we didn't have meetings or special handshakes, we recognized each other by their functional equivalents: a sullen slouch, an expression of boredom, language and hair and clothing that offended adults. So we had no trouble finding each other. All through those years that Freudians primly refer to as "the latency age," I knew many moody girls who were eager to be bad with me. We undressed and played with each other, but our primary intent was defiance, not sex, and certainly not love.

Margaret had once been a bad girl. I could tell from remnants in her manner and from her bitter concern with the rights and freedoms of others. She always seemed misplaced in her do-nothing life with my self-satisfied, conservative brother. To me, she looked most alive when we whispered together at the kitchen table, as if she and I were two snipers taking turns firing from behind the same tree. So when she finally said to me one day, sitting alone over cups of coffee, "Adam is always so right about everything," bearing down on the word "right" in irritation, I finally saw how things were. She'd married him for his stability, but now resented her confinement. This doesn't, of course, mean she has any interest in me. She's always had plenty of suitors.

I imagine Margaret as a princess imprisoned by a spell in a secret cave, and Adam as the ogre who put her there, dooming her to a life of boredom. Many princes seek the maiden, but only one knows the secret of the cave where she languishes. There's some secret I must know. But I don't. I don't know the secret.

Chapter 12

Today I find myself with several unscheduled hours, so I decide to get some exercise. My office isn't far from the Great Promenade that stretches around what used to be Central Park. The great park in which my father and his family once picnicked was one of the last places to be sacrificed. People were sentimental about it, and there was a big fight over whether it should be preserved. As the buildings invaded the streets and covered over the last of the small parks and plazas, the politicians kept reminding people that they still had Central Park, and "who could want more open space than that." As a result, many came to see Central Park as a special place that should be preserved forever. When plans emerged to start building there, as well, there was strong opposition, and the Save the Park Coalition was formed to fight the developers. There were marches with banners, as well as paid spots on radio and TV. (This was back in the time when political opposition was still reasonably safe.) My father, who had never in his entire life been a member of anything, joined. I still have a photo of him marching down the street holding a sign on a stick.

Ultimately, this group did not prevail. Not only were there the usual pressures of more people trying to fit into the same space, but the crime rate was soaring, and the terrorist attacks had begun. Those with money were desperate for a safe haven, and they spent huge sums to defeat the Save the Park movement. Finally, the Save the Park people agreed to allow Central Park Towers to be built in return for a guarantee that the rest of the park would be preserved in perpetuity. But gradually over the years, the thick wall that surrounded the original high rise complex was extended and extended to allow for more high rises, until now the entire park is a huge gated community, impenetrable to thieves and suicide bombers alike. It's a city within a city, and of course, only the wealthy can afford to live there. What the rest of us have left is Central Park Promenade, a wide path that extends along the outside of the wall. The Promenade was a concession to the walkers and joggers of the city. No carts are allowed, and those walking are to stay to the right, so the runners can pass by without breaking their stride.

That my own brother now lives inside the Central Park Community quite literally puts a wall between us. He's wealthy and I'm not. But far more serious is Adam's membership in the Liberty Party. Admittedly, he doesn't defend everything the party does, but when I think about his joining at all, the gap between us yawns so wide I can't believe we'll ever bridge it.

As a young man, I was able to run the entire length of the Promenade. My current goal is to be able to do that again. For several months now, I've been working out regularly. I'm determined not to let my body turn to mush now that I'm over forty. This is one area where I feel I can best Adam. When Adam first got into the construction business, he actually hammered and sawed and carried heavy things. But success made him sedentary. Now he rides the underground from one construction site to another. He talks with architects, negotiates with city planners, and attends gourmet dinners, so that over the years, his body has grown thick and heavy.

I feel sluggish at first, but once I get started, I remember how good it feels to run. Then when the going gets tough, I remind myself how much I want to be worthy of Margaret, and I push on. I count the trees painted on the white cement wall. Today I pass by a hundred and ten of them, the most I've done to date, so I feel triumphant and even a little cocky as I saunter back to my office to begin my afternoon sessions.

Chapter 13

When it finally happens, we're in my mother's kitchen, and after all my planning, it happens without my even knowing it's going to happen. Sunday morning brunch, a tradition in our family. Myself, Adam, Margaret, and my mother, as well as the usual assortment of people my mother has seen fit to invite, are sitting around her kitchen table eating pastries and sipping coffee.

The talk is of the subways and a new camera system, which is supposed to control the rampage of crime occurring there. Adam is derisive. He doesn't see why the criminals wouldn't just send one of their gang to block the camera while the others went about their business. But Eldon, an elderly gentleman with whom I sometimes think my mother actually flirts, claims the new cameras are so cleverly concealed that no one can tell where they are. Margaret and I don't care. Neither of us has used the underground for more than a decade, not since the electricity started to fail periodically, leaving people stranded on dark trains at the mercy of urban predators. We just sit across from one another at the end of the long table quietly engaged in our own conversation.

"Is there anything wrong?" Margaret whispers. "You're so quiet." Naturally, I can't tell her the truth. I can't say, "Margaret, I've been in love with you for almost a year, but I have no hope that you'll ever chose me over Adam. I'm afraid to even speak of it." Instead, I talk in general terms, always careful to preserve Amy's confidentiality, of my client who's dying and how deeply it's affecting me. It is, actually. Margaret responds with a soft, low, sympathetic sound. Her eyes seem to say, "I understand." I feel a powerful yearning. I want to touch her. I want to lay my head on her breast. I want to take off her clothes and bury myself inside her. Then the fat woman, who's been sitting at the end of the table to my right and shouting over our conversation to express her indignation regarding the subway situation, gets up for more coffee. And suddenly, without my deciding to do it, my foot moves under the table and presses hard against Margaret's. Margaret gasps softly and straightens in her chair, her eyes locking on mine. Then I hear myself whisper, "Come to my office, I'll be there until six." Margaret doesn't say anything, but neither does she pull her foot away. She continues to stare into my eyes, looking bewildered. Perhaps she nods her head, but it's such a subtle movement, I can't tell for sure if she intended to make it or not. Then the woman returns with her coffee, and Margaret, once again the smiling, gracious hostess, asks if I would like another cinnamon twist and gets up to warm one for me in the toaster oven.

Chapter 14

As I rush through the corridors toward my office, I wonder what I'll say if Margaret comes and how she'll come if she does—angry or as a lover? For surely it could only be one of those two ways. She couldn't have imagined I wanted to chat. And if she doesn't come, what will that mean, that she's told Adam? Only then do I realize the risk I've taken. It had been so exciting to feel my foot pressed against hers, in that moment, I would have done anything. And I did. I propositioned my brother's wife!

Suddenly, a new and terrible thought occurs to me. What if Margaret tells Adam, and they both show up at my door, Adam and Margaret? If Adam finds me in my office on a Sunday afternoon, a time he well knows I don't see clients, there'll be no denying what happened. I picture the three of us standing at my door, Adam swollen with anger, the way he gets when he can't have his way, Margaret disdainful, and me at a loss for words, unable to explain my behavior. I feel nauseous, and my heart starts to pound. I try to breathe deeply and slowly in just the proper way. (I'm a therapist, after all; I know how to deal with panic.) And I try distraction. I force myself to stare into the window of a men's shoe store and decide which style I like best. It doesn't help. The panic continues to build, until I feel like running headlong through the corridors, a screamer without a blackout.

How could I have believed I could get away with making a pass at Margaret? Now I feel certain she's told Adam. Of course she has, or she will. Naturally, she hadn't wanted to expose me in the midst of strangers, thus making our family the subject of endless gossip. But as soon as everyone leaves, she'll tell. Perhaps she already has.

"Now wait," I say to myself. "You can't know that for sure. You told her you'd be there so you have to go." I'm experiencing an almost overwhelming impulse to turn around and go home. But I don't. I start walking toward my office again. I don't believe Margaret will come, but if she did and I wasn't there, I'd never forgive myself.

When I reach my office, I try to distract myself from the pounding of my heart by reading a professional journal. I read one article and then another and another. Hours pass, and Margaret doesn't come. Anxiety turns to sadness, then back to anxiety, as I wonder if she told Adam what happened. After four hours of waiting, I lose all hope. I decide to call Phillipe and see if I can talk him into coming to Leticia's and having a cup of coffee. If worse comes to worse and Margaret's told Adam, maybe I can get Phillipe to say we met much earlier and spent hours talking. Then I'd have an alibi, someone to say that I definitely wasn't there and, therefore, could not have said what Margaret thought she heard me say. It was noisy around the kitchen table. Margaret must have misunderstood. What could she be thinking? Surely Margaret must know that I would never…!

Phillipe is home and eager for diversion. He agrees to join me at Leticia's in twenty minutes. I turn off the lights and leave. On the way over there, I pass an ice cream shop with a crowd of children outside. One little boy is screaming in anger and agony; his ice cream has toppled off his cone and lies smashed on the pavement. It's then that it hits me. This is the end of Margaret. Or more accurately, I think, smiling disdainfully at my own foolishness, the end of my fantasy relationship with her. The end as well, I realize, of our friendship, of talking comfortably and cozily. Margaret knows I made a pass at her, and despite her shyness, when Margaret's offended, she can be colder than the winters of my childhood. Her icy disdain will freeze the space between us harder than the ponds I once skated on in upstate New York. But even that unpleasant prospect isn't the worst of it. Finally, I must face the truth. Margaret has never loved me, and she never will.

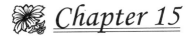 *Chapter 15*

I used to worry that if I was miserable my clients would notice, but this has never happened. Perhaps because they need to believe that the person they've chosen to help solve their problems is perfect and all-knowing, they fail to detect the obvious. For this I'm grateful, since it allows me to continue with the one thing that makes me feel I have something of value to offer.

Amy has new complaints about Appoppa, her poet roommate. (Appoppa is a chosen name; there's been a vogue among young people for symmetrical names: Iri, Mim, Alooola. The generational hiatus prevents me from understanding exactly what they're up to, but I do know it indicates a certain sense of style.) Regardless of his name, she's sick of him. She has put up with too much. True, by this time she totally depends on him, but even that will not deter her. She is through. She will not take any more abuse; his maleness is a defect from which he is too weak-willed to recover, too self-centered to even try. As if this weren't bad enough, he has no ability to communicate and lacks the capacity to face difficult truths. This is intolerable for Amy, who, as she explains, is quite stern with herself and examines herself for weaknesses as diligently as a monkey picks for fleas.

And what are Appoppa's infractions? She hates the way he makes her ask for everything. He knows that the canned food is on the lower shelves. He knows she can't bend over. He knows she has to eat lunch every day. Why can't he just get the can at the proper time and put it on the counter by the can opener? If their situations were reversed, that is what she would do. Because she pays attention, she sees what needs to be done, while he only cares about himself.

Suddenly, something interrupts. The look on her face says she's been stabbed in the spine again. Her eyes are wide, her mouth opens, but the scream is sucked inward. She refuses to let me see a tear. I have been instructed at times like this to sit still and be quiet. It's several minutes before I can see she's breathing again. Finally I risk asking, "Are you all right?" She's too weak to be furious at my noticing. She nods carefully, then closes her eyes, quiet, resting.

"Did you ever think about what happens after you die?" she asks me finally. Her voice is still weak but now bemused.

"What happens, Amy?" She takes her time, letting the image form.

"Strangers will touch my body and go through my things."

This is a new concept for me: death as a loss of privacy. She knows she's amused me. Each time I assume I've finally heard it all, something happens to remind me that there's no limit to what I don't know. This is actually quite reassuring; it relieves me of so much responsibility.

And now Amy has another surprise. She's brought a poem for me to read, written for her by Appoppa, the Offender. (In a softer mood, she sometimes calls him Pop). She's had it in the pocket of her ratty wool coat all this time, and now she hands it to me neutrally and watches to see how I'll respond. It's typed on bright orange paper and titled, "Would You Like Me to Love You?"

Would you like me to love you?
I could watch you while you slept.
I could sing while I brushed your hair.
You would never be without compliments or conversation,
Someone to hold your hand
While you walked among the foggy eucalyptus.
Your sweet sadness would finally be satisfied.
You could act knowing.
You could eat cherries, out of season, from other hemispheres.
You could wear a hat.
Everything would be right.
Everything would be right.

"Eucalyptus used to be some kind of tree," Amy explains, focusing on this exotic detail without acknowledging the obvious adoration the poem addresses to her. I tell her I've heard of it.

Chapter 16

Ever since last Sunday, I've been hiding out. For several days, I pretended to be sick. My mother came to my room and brought food and a sad, half-wilted little flower, most likely imported from halfway around the world. She was her usual, bustling self. Obviously, Adam and Margaret hadn't talked to her. And Adam never showed up on my doorstep. I'm beginning to hope that Margaret didn't tell. It is, after all, part of the code of all bad girls and boys not to tattle on one another. Perhaps this common allegiance has saved me.

Now it's Sunday morning once again. It's not believable that I'm still sick, and if I don't show for brunch, my mother will want to know why. I'm pretty sure nothing overt will happen, because as always, my mother will have extended an invitation to whoever has struck her as "interesting." And yet, as I walk down the stairs and through the corridor toward her apartment, I feel like a man headed for his own execution.

I'm late, and when I arrive, all the seats at my mother's table are taken, except for one directly across from Margaret. So I sit there and look down at my bialy, which I butter with excruciating care. My mother is telling one of her jokes. As usual, I don't find it funny, but I force myself to laugh. Out of desperation, I try to tell a joke myself, one I heard on TV and by some miracle remembered. Naturally, I do it awkwardly. I'm not a joke teller. Everyone laughs anyway. Everyone except Margaret, who is completely silent. I notice that Adam is staring at me, but not angrily. More surprised, more like, "What's gotten into you? I haven't heard you tell a joke since we were kids." Now I know for sure Margaret hasn't told. Gratefully, I glance up at her, but her eyes are so icy, her expression so accusing, a shiver runs through me. I've never seen her look so angry. My last hope shatters. In complete silence, she sends her message strong and clear: "How dare you make a pass at me. I'm married to your brother!"

Since I can't bear to sit there another second, I jump up and ask my mother where the paper is. I say I want to find an article written by one of my clients. The paper's already been thrown out, so I have to dig through the trash to retrieve it. Then I stand at the kitchen counter pretending to search for the article. Carefully, I cut something out, stuff it into my pocket, make apologies (I've agreed to help a friend move), and leave.

🌸 *Chapter 17*

I no longer fantasize about Margaret. The mind is reasonable. When it gets a definite no, it moves on, or in my case, moves backward, since I'm once again brooding about my father. I ponder how and why things happened as they did or, more importantly, didn't happen, since it's more an absence of happening that I can't seem to digest.

My father was a baker. And his father was a baker, the descendant of Orthodox Jews who immigrated from a Russian-Polish border village. His family had prospered as a result of passing down through the generations what had become an antique method of baking. Because they still used old-style brick ovens, the bread they baked was exceptional—soft on the inside, crunchy and delicious on the outside. It sold extremely well and for boutique prices.

My grandfather was a harsh, demanding man. Before he died at the age of ninety-one, he'd had three wives. My mother had seen unusual bruises on the last of the three and suspected my grandfather of being a wife beater. It was whispered, as well, that he didn't allow any of his wives to use birth control and that that was why there were so many kids. He was equally difficult as a father. He worked his children hard, not out of necessity, but because he considered it a way to build character. Perhaps his harshness was the reason my father always hated baking.

Bakers work through the night so they can deliver fresh bread in the morning. My father came home in time for breakfast, carrying baked goods that were more fragrant than an armful of flowers. There was sourdough rye—a long, heavy, oval loaf with a crunchy, brown crust, speckled with caraway seeds and still hot enough inside to melt sweet butter. There were cinnamon sticks, tacky as flypaper, with honey and pecans. There were Danish pastries, fruit squares, and challah. It all went on the table. And with it we ate a huge meal, because my father needed his dinner—half a grapefruit or cantaloupe, a plate of scrambled eggs made with fried onions, a toasted bagel or bialy covered with cream cheese and lox or slices of cheese, usually thick pieces of Gouda or port salute, and finally a bowl of cereal. He ate like this every day and remained a small, thin man. Some chronic tension consumed his food like a parasite.

Our house was quiet during the day because my father needed to sleep. His schedule was one more barrier between us. My brother and I usually played outside in the corridors, intense games of hallway tag, which left us flushed and panting from dodging in and out among the pedestrians. At mealtimes we were quiet and separate, as well. My father was hard of hearing and often too tired to talk. No, not tired, more like weary, something with a tinge of defeat to it. This sense of ruin, of a fatigue that was as much an exhaustion of possibilities as of energy, was an essential quality of my father.

His family, descended, as they were, from Polish peasant stock, was big and energetic, coarse and crafty. There were seven of them, six draft horses and a pony, my father, fine boned and sensitive. While his brothers went early to balding, my father maintained a rich head of wavy, dark hair. I always wondered how he was born into that family. Was he a mutant? Had my grandmother (the second of the three) grown resentful of my grandfather's tyranny and spited him with an infidelity? Or was he simply the runt of the litter? Whatever it was, he didn't fit, and he became his father's scapegoat.

It wasn't just his size. It was also that he was introspective: injustice made him sullen. This caused my grandfather to become self-conscious, cognizant of what he was doing. While the other children merely whined when hit, unaware that being beaten had any significance beyond their own discomfort, I think my grandfather felt accused by my father's sullenness, and he punished my father for that as well.

When he was only nine, something occurred that changed my father's life forever. He and his friends were in the habit of stopping by a construction site across the street from where the family lived and teasing the night watchman. In return, the watchman kept a bucket handy to splash water at them. One time when he threw the water, a piece of scrap metal had fallen into the bucket. The metal hit my father in the head and crushed part of his skull.

I find this story confusing. Whenever I've thrown water from a bucket, it has followed the arc of my swing and splashed back on me. It doesn't seem like a way to propel a chunk of metal some distance with force. So here's another mystery: Was this accident really innocent or a cover story for something more sinister, something my father felt we shouldn't know? Was he actually beaten by someone, perhaps with a metal pipe? Was he only teasing the watchman, or was he really trying to steal? Whatever it was, he was knocked to the ground, blood pouring from his head, a little boy bracing himself on skinny arms, aware only that something terrible had happened. When his arms buckled, he pitched forward into a coma. The watchman called an ambulance, and my father was rushed to the hospital. He wasn't expected to live, but he recovered, except for some damage to a nerve in his inner ear. Slowly, but inexorably, sounds became fainter and fainter, until in his last years, my father was completely deaf.

So some of the time when he failed to respond to my grandfather, perhaps he didn't hear and was hit for that. But knowing how quietly and passionately stubborn my father could be, at other times, I suspect his disregard was deliberate. All this is a part of why my father hated baking, and why he was tired and sad, and why he was quiet and seldom talked with us. So when he finally came to Adam and me with his stories, imploring us to hear him when he was too tired and preoccupied to hear us, we were not sympathetic.

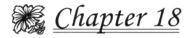 # *Chapter 18*

I don't sleep well. I make lists of things I need to do and then worry I've forgotten something. As I lie in the dark, I feel thoughts rushing through passages in my mind, as if it was a little city. I'm bothered, as well, by external disturbances. Through the walls and the ducts, I sometimes hear what sounds like people making love, mixed complexly with the whirring and grinding of machinery. I put on my earphones and listen to late-night radio until its jabbering replaces my thinking, and I fall asleep. In the morning, I forget my list.

I forget my list, not because I'm irresponsible, but because morning is so difficult. I dread the daily walk to the bathroom. Since I have no bathroom of my own, I have to put on my bathrobe and slippers, pick up my chamber pot (with so many living in single rooms, chamber pots have come back with a vengeance; every drug and hardware store carries them, along with their packets of magenta deodorizing tablets), push out into a hall, always thick with people, avert my mouth with its morning breath (not, of course, to the side on which I'm carrying the chamber pot), walk a short way along the hall, go down a full flight of stairs (a mob of children playing jacks on the landing while adults stumble over them), then along the corridor to my mother's apartment. Or perhaps I should say, my mother's "rooms." Whatever you wish to call them, they are full of strangers. I wade through the crowd, wait my turn, and finally get into the small, old-fashioned bathroom. I lock the door. I don't feel immediate relief, because I've usually developed a slight headache by this time, but now at least I can begin to relax. I can empty my pot. I can shower and shave.

This situation was brought about by my father's death. To my amazement, Adam, the good son, promptly moved out. And I, the rebel, the difficult one, remained at home with my mother. Adam was nearly done with his MBA and confident he'd finish soon. He'd been working part time selling building supplies, and he'd saved his money. Between his cash and his contacts in the building trades, he had no problem getting approved for a decent apartment.

I was jammed somewhere deep in the gears of a PhD program in psychology, making no progress on my doctoral dissertation. I had no hope of finishing for several years. I got a small stipend from my internships, but only enough for food, books, and movies. Adam offered to help me get a place, even to loan me a bit of money, but I had no idea when or if I could pay him back, and I felt too competitive to grant him that kind of power over me. I thanked him, but refused, limiting myself to secret envy whenever I visited him.

It was his home that made me realize Adam might be someone to be reckoned with. Almost immediately, his apartment became a gathering place. It wasn't fashionable. He furnished it in a solid, pleasant, conventional way. But it was easy to be there. The chairs were deep and comfortable, and you knew, without being told, it was okay to put your drink down on any surface, to put your feet up on the coffee table, and by implication, to speak your mind: you could curse the building codes, you could proposition women, you could tell jokes about minorities.

He got some of this from my mother, also outgoing and not overly sensitive. My mother had been devoted to my father, a traditional marriage, but after he was gone, she turned her attention outward in a way that seemed more natural. She got a job as a secretary for a gynecologist, and for her, the fringe benefits seemed as important as the salary. She got health insurance, she got free drugs, and she got a continuous supply of sex stories.

My mother loves the action of the city, and in her own way, she's become a player. She's parlayed her social assets skillfully. In her free time, she pulls a folding chair to the front door of the apartment, and her round little knees and her plump folded hands serve as an announcement to anyone passing in the corridors that she's open for discourse. People crowd around, eager to hear her latest anecdotes. Among her greatest hits is her story about how the adulterers got stuck together.

When I heard her tell this story, my mother was surrounded by a semicircle of older women and a single older man. The old guy was leaning forward at the fringe of the crowd, his head cocked sideways on his sinewy neck, his hand cupped behind his ear as my mother explained that she knew something interesting about a certain man and woman who lived in the same apartment house, though not with each other. Each had a spouse who was away at work, so in their free time, they decided to get together. With nodding heads, her audience urged her on, eager to hear the latest discoveries of medical science, as illustrated by the story of how these illicit lovers got stuck together and found to their horror (poetic justice, no?) that they couldn't get apart. (Stuck like dogs! Imagine!) The harder they pulled, the more tightly and painfully they became stuck, until there was nothing to do but wriggle together over to the telephone and dial 911.

According to my mother, who got it from her boss, the gynecologist, if the woman had only put her finger in the man's behind, it would have released something, and they could have separated without any fuss, no one the wiser. "Not in the woman's behind?" an older woman asked, apparently having her own ideas about just what engineering principals are involved. "No, the man's behind." My mother is quite firm about this, and her listeners nod thoughtfully, carefully filing away this bit of practical information, which, you never know, might just be useful some day.

As it was, the paramedics came and slid them onto a stretcher, threw a sheet over them, and carried them out in front of all their neighbors, still stuck together, and "their lives are probably ruined." (My mother is detached and objective about this detail, as she is about almost everything in her role as medical consultant, although when I did much less with a pencil at the age of four, she was hysterical.)

As for the drugs, my mother supplies almost everyone we know. Salesmen from the many drug companies arrive almost daily at her office, hoping to speak to the physician and convince him to prescribe their products. The fortunes of the giant companies depend on this.

But to get to the doctor, they have to go through my mother, and to stay on her good side, they are willing to leave on her desk, although it must be illegal, any drug samples she desires. So if a friend has been to a doctor and gotten a prescription, and if the matter isn't too urgent, if they can wait a week or so to start the medication, there's a good chance my mother can get it for them free. And for those with chronic conditions, seizure disorders, heart disease, and the like, my mother keeps a shopping list and regularly stocks up on what's needed.

For my mother, the hallway not only replaced our old street, it improved on it. It's always warm and dry, regardless of weather or season, and it's always safe and light, day and night. Consequently, the apartment became less important to her, and with the accelerating overcrowding in the city, it became a significant source of income. When the cousin of a friend offered to pay her good rent to run a small delicatessen in our living room, my mother immediately saw the advantages. She didn't need the space, and it would be handy to have the foods she liked so close by. Also, the greater the traffic flow, the more people there would be to advise and medicate and the bigger the audiences for her wonders-of-science stories. Ultimately, my mother created for herself a truly pivotal place in the community. Of course, the foyer had to be kept clear for the trade, so we moved the table into the kitchen and ate there. We had the archway boarded up and fitted with a door so we could have privacy during meals.

My mother was never a card player, television puts her to sleep, and she doesn't have the concentration to read for very long, so people and the life of the hallways are perfect for her. But what's balm for my mother is acid for me. I have more of my father's temperament, and the constant sight and sound of people makes it impossible for me to think. Work on my thesis came to a complete stop. I began to wake up early and have bad dreams; I lost weight; even sex couldn't distract me. This was a textbook case of depression. I knew my survival depended on change, so when the chance to rent a small room upstairs came along, I took it.

It was quieter up there because there was little traffic. This particular corridor had remained a dead end, because there were pipes in the walls that couldn't be cut. The location was much better, but now I had to go downstairs to use the bathroom. My mother rented out my old bedroom to the sister of the man who had the delicatessen, and she turned it into a greeting-card shop. No wonder my life felt frayed and in danger of coming loose.

One of my friends, noticing how tired and tense I'd become, suggested I meditate. I chose Vipassana, a Buddhist practice, which is favored by therapists because it promotes self-awareness. I meditate occasionally, but I find it difficult. When I relax and open myself more deeply to my experience, I discover the taste of soot in my mouth.

🌼 *Chapter 19*

I've been avoiding Margaret for weeks now. I've made up a series of excuses to avoid Sunday brunch, and if I find myself with her accidentally, I mumble and leave. Margaret shows no reaction to any of this. She goes about her business as usual, which makes me feel small and inconsequential. There have been no more angry looks, but also no cozy chats over newspaper articles.

Given all this, I was, of course, even more reluctant than usual to accept Adam's invitation to his New Year's Eve party. This is a yearly affair to which Adam invites all his business contacts. So each year begins with Adam at the center of things, and he continues for the following twelve months as the genial, well-oiled hub of the building trades, ever more prosperous and influential. I'm always invited, but I rarely go. To be truthful, I resent how his glibness and superficiality have made him happy and successful, while my deeper, more humanitarian values haven't done a thing for me. In addition, inevitably plenty of Adam's Liberty Party friends attend, and I always have to hold my tongue. Oddly, this year he was especially insistent.

"Come on! It'll be a fine time," he said encouragingly. "There will be some great women there. We'll fix you up." Then he threw a hearty arm around my shoulders and gave me a squeeze. I finally agreed, telling myself that I'd offend him if I continued to refuse. Since then I've admitted to myself how much I miss Margaret and that having an opportunity to be around her may have been more of a motivating factor than anything else. Not only that, I've decided to try to talk to her. I hate how things have been between us. I'll admit the truth. I'll apologize, I'll promise it will never happen again, and I'll ask if we can be friends. After I made that decision, I spent three weeks breathing shallowly.

Now that it's time to go, some stern inner voice keeps issuing warnings: "This is stupid. You're going to be very sorry if you go ahead with this." I stand up to it; I argue back, "No, I'm going. So what if she refuses my offer of friendship, I'll survive. And she might not refuse."

When I arrive, the front door is standing open, and some of the guests are spilling out into the hallway. Everyone has been drinking heavily for some time. Now that safe driving is no longer an issue, people view parties as an excuse to drink until they fall down. Music plays without a break, everyone is talking at once, and the pressure, the pounding beat, make it feel like the center of a great machine.

I stop at the door. Something feels unsafe, perhaps a shifting deep under our feet, multiple stories of weight crumpling some girder like a used paper cup. I decide not to go in after all. But as I turn away, a guy I've met once or twice grabs me by the arm and hauls me in for a boozy reunion. I feel as though I've been pulled through some membrane; I'm now standing on the other side of a decision.

When I get away, I pick up a glass of wine and gulp at it, pushing with small steps through the clotted crowd. I feel like a ghost. I've never made much of an effort to get to know Adam's crowd, so now they mostly ignore me, allowing me to pass among them as though I'm invisible.

As I walk into the dining room, I find myself facing Margaret. She's all the way on the other side of the room, but as soon as she notices me, she begins snaking her way through the crowd until she's standing directly in front of me. "I'm drunk," she says, and her blue-green eyes have a soft look, like crushed ice. "Shall we dance?" She takes my glass from me and sets it on the sofa, where it immediately spills between the cushions. She never glances back, but reaches for me with those slender, expressive hands. I can feel them holding me, touching the skin on my neck and my ears. She's so fluid that even I, with my awkwardness and doubt, can't help dancing easily with her. She draws me into her presence, where everything is clear and lovely, and there's no more need to think. So I stop thinking. I forget my agenda and surrender completely to the warmth of her body, lying upright against mine. With her breath a mist on my neck and her sleek, bright hair against my cheek, everything is smooth and soft. Then she looks up at me with those crushed, icy eyes and says, "Why did you do it. Was it a joke? Were you trying to make a fool of me?"

"No, no. I did it because I fell in love with you." I whisper this in her ear so no one can hear. "I know I shouldn't have but—"

"You stood me up because you loved me?" she whispers back. "What kind of sense does that make?" I feel disoriented. I stare at her incredulously, trying to comprehend.

"Stood you up?" I say finally.

"Of course. Didn't you say you'd be in your office until six?" Suddenly I understand, and an almost unbearable sense of joy wells up inside me.

"Oh, Margaret, Margaret, you came. I never believed you would."

"Well, I did, and you weren't there!" Hurt and anger color her voice. "I waited for hours for you."

"Noah, I was there by five-thirty! You said six!"

"I'm sorry. I'm so sorry. I lost hope. I didn't believe you'd come." Overcome with excitement, I hug her to me. Then I remember where we are, and I continue dancing. I look around to see where Adam is. Thankfully, he's nowhere in sight. Wherever he is, probably drinking and backslapping, he's well away from us. This is our first real time together, and my whole world is filled with the realization that I'm finally holding her.

"Margaret, I'm so sorry. I never thought you'd come. Actually, I believed you'd probably already told Adam what I'd done."

"No matter what, I wouldn't have told Adam," she says sounding aggrieved.

"Can I see you?" I whisper.

"Monday morning," she answers, ready for me. "I'm moving some furniture. You could drop by and help." She stops dancing, but she's still standing close, holding me in her arms. "Adam will be gone."

"We shouldn't be seen like this," I say, gently pushing her back. At the mention of his name, I immediately think I hear my brother's voice. She pouts, and I have to tug her hands from around my neck. The thought of Adam walking in makes me aware of the shame I feel about what Margaret and I are contemplating. We seem so obvious; if he saw us, he'd know everything, undeniably, immediately, but as I leave, there's still no sign of Adam.

 # Chapter 20

In the midst of almost unbearable excitement about Margaret, I'm surprised to discover that my father's ghost is once again walking the ramparts. For reasons I don't understand, he won't leave me in peace. There's something important I need to know. What? And where should I look for it? I consider again the bits and pieces I know of his life, searching for some clue.

I think about the time when my six-year-old father first saw the fields, the recollection of which would one day bring tears to his eyes. My grandfather's brother, Uncle Bert, lived in a small town in upstate New York, where he'd started his own bakery. One summer after my father's mother had become ill with cancer, she talked my grandfather into letting her take my father with her to visit Uncle Bert and Aunt Rachel while she recuperated from her treatments. It was there that my father explored a landscape even more vast than Central Park. Following the roads outward from Fulton, the houses thinned and then stopped altogether, giving way to fields that stretched as far as the eye could see. The rural atmosphere delighted him. There was so much for a little boy to see and do. He lost himself in the tall corn; he played in the streams. He had a pet frog. He was fascinated by its lightening-fast tongue that would snap out and in as it ate bugs dropped into its terrarium. And well away from her husband's stern eye, his mother allowed him sweets in order to put weight on him. While he was a stone in his father's shoe, he was his mother's pet, and she equated health with the solid thickness of his brothers.

My father was still small and thin five years later when his family moved once again, this time to Fourth Street, off Second Avenue. By this time his mother had died and been replaced by my grandfather's third wife. I wonder what her death was like for my father. It must have been crushing, since she was the only one in the family who loved him, and yet my father never spoke of it.

My grandfather had saved enough money to buy a building that had once been a bakery. It was rundown and filthy, but it still had the old-fashioned brick ovens, which would allow him to make bread using the methods of his peasant ancestors. The family spent weeks working together to clean it up, the huge ovens in the dark basement and the shop on street level, where they installed wooden shelves and shining glass cases. It wasn't long before they had a thriving trade. Word spread that they made the best rye bread. When my father spoke of my grandfather in this regard, it was with pride: "He only used the best ingredients, and he'd mastered his ovens."

To get a really crusty rye bread you have to bake it in a brick oven, directly on the bricks. "You can't get decent bread anymore," my father said sadly after he'd retired from baking. "They make everything in these big, electric ovens with Ferris wheels inside, and even the rye breads are baked in pans." Pans trap the moisture and give out loaves with square edges, the mark of the machine.

The methods my grandfather used had been passed down for generations. The old ovens were deep, red brick caves with openings twelve feet across. Bread was placed inside with a peel, a thin wooden paddle a few feet wide attached to a fourteen-foot pole. My grandfather would place several loaves on the peel, insert it to the proper depth, and then jerk it back sharply, leaving the loaves in place. Periodically, he would shift the loaves to make sure they were all evenly done. Then, at just the right moment, he'd scoop them up and slide them out, roasted brown and crunchy, like giant nuts.

When my father came home from high school on Thursday afternoons, he had to go down into the basement and break open eggs for the challah, the rich, braided cake-like bread that was baked on Fridays for the Sabbath. There are thirty dozen eggs to a crate, and he had three crates to open. Although by then most bakeries used dried egg yolks mixed with hot water, my grandfather insisted on fresh eggs. These had to be cracked one at a time and checked, because if you threw one musty egg into the pail, you could taint all one thousand and eighty of them.

I'm assembling these little pieces in order to put together the jigsaw puzzle of my lost father. As with any puzzle, there's no problem with the smooth outside pieces, but the inside is more difficult. I can picture him seated on a crate in the poorly lit basement, carefully cracking eggs one at a time in the hot flush of the bricks, a thin young man in his undershirt. But is he resenting my grandfather, angry because he cannot play basketball on Thursday afternoons with the neighborhood team, the Anchors, with their white anchors printed on black shirts and shorts, or is he careful and proud, aware that he is helping make rich challahs from the freshest ingredients? And what about the Anchors? I've never known him to play a team sport, let alone take part comfortably in any group activity. Did he have friends? Was he sociable? Was he someone else entirely from the father I thought I knew well enough to dismiss? And what about the Broadway plays?

My father claimed that as a teenager he went to Broadway shows three or four times a week, a man I never knew to attend a play or movie. Of course, by the time I knew him, the degeneration of his hearing was advanced. As a child, it never occurred to me that the loss of hearing could transform someone into an entirely different person. I believed then that he had always been the way I saw him, the way old people had always been old, and that he had been put on earth to play the role of my father.

My father said he knew a place where he could get unsold tickets to plays for less than half price. Did he really go three or four times a week, or was he being generous with himself, as we often are in memory? Did he go alone, or did he have friends or dates? And if my grandfather didn't pay him, where did he get the money?

Piecing together the past, the parts overflow the whole. Is this because of his telling or because of my hearing and remembering? It leads me to envision history as overlapping layers, rather than as a single puzzle on a single, infinite card table. In this three-dimensional jigsaw, there is a resentful image where my grandfather was unfair, and my father was angry. There is another where there was some caring, or at least respect, and still others where they were both controlled by realities larger and more pressing than their personal ones. I must first find the right level for each particular piece before I can hope to place it where it fits.

Chapter 21

It's Monday morning, and I'm terrified. It isn't that I don't believe Margaret; Adam will surely be away. But how sure is "surely," and how away is "away"? He could still return at some vulnerable moment. The unthinkable does happen; that's why we think so much about it.

When I arrive, there's no pretense of furniture moving. Margaret locks the door behind me and then just stands there waiting. So I take her in my arms and kiss her. I kiss her exactly the way I've always dreamed of kissing her. Immediately, I sense her eagerness for me, and that sweeps away all my self-doubt. I run my fingers through the marvel of her red hair; I feel the poignant reality of her thin shoulders; I slide my palms down her waist to the waiting secrets of her hips. Finally, I take her hand and lead her to the bedroom.

As I unbutton her blouse, she looks upset and crosses her arms over her chest, blocking me. "What's the matter?" I ask.

"I'm afraid."

"Why?" I'm afraid too, afraid she'll say "Adam" and stop me right there. At an earlier point, it might have been a relief to be stopped, a solution to an ambivalence I couldn't resolve. But not now that I've touched her. There's no question about what I want now.

"I'm afraid you won't like me if you see me. I'm small."

"Oh, no! No! No! Of course your breasts are small, don't you think I know that? Don't you think I know how you look after all the time I've spent looking at you? I love the way you look. I think you're beautiful." I pull her arms down and slide her blouse off her shoulders. "You're so lovely. You have such pretty breasts." Once I undress her completely, I see that her pale, thin body is just what I was hoping it would be, just the body I can adore without reservation. But she seems anxious about herself. She pulls me on top of her so I can't look and tries to bring us quickly to some resolution. But I can't enter her. She feels dry and tight. I start to worry that if Margaret was really attracted to me her body would show it. Maybe, I think, she's only doing this to get even with Adam, and the real payoff will come when she tells him about it.

But despite these terrible thoughts, the prolonged anticipation of being with her, the beauty of her body, and the touch of her nakedness are so powerful I stay hard and excited despite feeling tormented. She begins to scream at me, "Push! Push! Push!" and twist her head from side to side on the pillow.

"I can't," I moan, "You're not ready. I'll hurt you."

"No! Don't worry about me, push! Please push!"

I do as I'm told. I press as hard as I can, afraid I'll hurt her, but she's right. As soon as I push half an inch in, I feel the hot fluid, and when I draw back, it coats her lips. After a couple more pushes, I'm sliding easily inside her, and I don't have any more doubts, not even a fear that the neighbors will hear her screaming as she thrashes frantically underneath me.

Afterward, we lie completely still, our chests pressed together. I can feel the beating of her heart. Our breathing slows and synchronizes. Enveloped by silence and flesh, I have an experience I'm at a loss to explain. I feel as though some deep and insubstantial part inside Margaret and inside me melts and then melds us into a single being.

I lie there, fascinated and profoundly at peace. Then I become aware of my weight resting on Margaret's slight body, and in that instant of worry, the miraculous dissolves into the ordinary.

"Am I heavy?" I ask.

"A little, but I hate to have you move. I feel so peaceful."

"Yeah, me too."

I raise myself up on my elbow so I can see her. Margaret squirms and pulls the covers up over herself.

"I think you're beautiful, you know." Margaret smiles shyly. This is a part of her I haven't seen before.

Then I hear a noise. Perhaps it's a door slamming in an adjacent flat, but it causes me to imagine that Adam has come home, and a terrible sense of shame floods into me. I listen. Really, no one is there. Nonetheless, I vow never to make love to Margaret here again. I admit to myself that I will make love to her again if she'll let me. Even so, it's not necessary to double the offense by trespassing in Adam's marriage bed. Adam has never been the brother I wanted him to be, but that isn't his fault. It's simply a matter of who he is and who I am. No doubt I'm not the brother he wished for either. "Margaret, I need to go," I say.

"No, not yet, Noah. I don't want you to go yet. Don't you want to be with me?"

"Oh, Margaret, sweetheart. Yes, yes, I do. It's not that I want to leave you. It's that I'm not comfortable here. We shouldn't be doing this here."

Margaret sighs.

"I guess you wonder why I'm doing this at all," she says, "to Adam."

"No, I've been too preoccupied with why I'm doing it to worry about why you're doing it. But then I know why I'm doing it. I'm doing it because I have to. What about you?"

"I don't know exactly. I have this feeling, a kind of desperation almost; I feel I must have something else, something more, or I'll just die. It's hard to explain."

"But is it me, Margaret? Am I what you need?"

"Maybe. Sometimes I think so. I guess we'll have to see. If the feeling goes away, then I'll know you were what I needed."

"You're not happy with Adam?"

"I'm with Adam, and I'm not happy, that's all I know right now. I think about you. I look forward to Sunday brunch because I know you'll be there." Margaret looks earnest, and troubled. Well, why wouldn't she be troubled? Nobody in their right mind would have planned things this way. I pull her to me, stroke her hair and her cheeks, and then kiss her, deeply and slowly.

"I'm going to go now, Margaret. But I'll figure out a place for us to meet, somewhere away from here, where we can relax and talk for hours if we want."

"Okay, I'd like that."

I put my clothes on, we kiss again at the door, and I leave. I have a strange feeling as I walk away, as if there are lines of energy running through the universe, all of which are converging inside me at this moment. A sign, I think, that in the midst of what might seem an ordinary, even tawdry, affair, something extraordinary has happened.

Chapter 22

Unlike my father, I seldom go to plays, unless you count psychotherapy. To me, therapy is the smallest possible theater. There is an audience of one and a cast of one, the irreducible minimum. But which is which? And when? I watch while Amy acts unconcerned about the sequential horror of her progressive annihilation. I applaud, or I critique, or I withhold judgment, pending further developments in the plot. Then it's my turn. I act understanding. I act as if she doesn't intimidate me, as if I can handle her, as if we are both perfectly safe sniffing the fumes of her uncorked rage. I assume this is my obligation, my professional role. But I also feel an urge to pull down the curtain, burn the proscenium, and leave the theater. I wish I could find a way of practicing that was solidly in reality, no more acting. But would that be therapy? And could it work?

These are questions I discuss only with other therapists. There are two of them. One, Phillipe, is a madman; the other, Carl, is insanely lacking in madness. Carl is an analyst. Therapy for him is a minuet—precise steps in silver shoes to old music. Phillipe, on the other hand, wants to smash that music box against the wall.

"Civilization is the crowning achievement of existence," Carl tells me whenever the thought moves him. Human refinement is Carl's primary source of awe. When he speaks of it, he looks steadily into my eyes and lowers his voice. It would be tawdry to dramatize an insight of this magnitude; only understatement can supply the necessary dignity. According to Carl, it is through various forms of control, primarily self-control, that civilization becomes possible. Without limits, everything would be overwhelmed by the snarling beast we carry within us. His image of a sane and civilized person is a cage with legs, and his own blandness and tightness attest to his success in society's perpetual struggle with its animal origins.

For Phillipe, control is the enemy of life and Carl a strangler of the spirit. "Yes, we are containers," Phillipe agrees, "but not of beasts, rather of the divine. We are lanterns shielding a precious flame from the bleak wind of eternity!" He screams this at Carl. They loathe each other, these professional saviors.

I fall somewhere between them, perhaps with the worst qualities of each. I despise what Carl believes, and I find Phillipe a joke. Though Carl finished some years before me, he and I were trained at the same school. Compressed and darkened by the city, instead of producing diamonds, our university succeeded only in crushing the coal. Suffocatingly traditional, Freudian theory was taught there as though we were still in old Vienna. It's hard to believe that this antique therapy has survived pretty much intact, passed down through the generations like a religion. The lecture notes of one professor were so old and dry, they would flake from the fluttering of his hands, falling like mental dandruff. Classes had the emotional warmth of an army barracks. Teachers dominated and humiliated us, often with a smirking, Freudian sexual innuendo, and always as publicly as possible. One evil little monkey of a professor once commented on a paper I had written, "Not bad, but it's like you're jerking off, and you can't come." His tiny skull was shiny bald; the meanness of his mind had poisoned his hair at the roots. Another once leered at me and asked, "How do you like your new beard?" "What do you mean?" I replied anxiously, touching my chin. "Oh, I think you know very well what I mean."

We dreaded our Rorschach class. It was run, ironically, by a voyeur who was nearly blind. Behind the aquarium walls of his thick glasses, his eyes floated like dead fish. Much of the instruction consisted of having us associate in class to the Rorschach cards so that he could announce our unconscious sexual issues. We were young and naively accepted the notion that only the wise would be allowed to become graduate professors, so we were defenseless against his pronouncements. "You will never encounter a man who has a passive homosexual fantasy about his father, unless he is psychotic." (Upon hearing this, my mind perversely created an immediate fantasy, leaving me to wait in terror for my inevitable breakdown.) Or, "Hmm…Yes…Well, what I hear from your response (to Card IV of the Rorschach) is a struggle against unconscious homosexual impulses. See me after class, and I'll recommend a therapist."

I think my training was meant to be physician-like and intellectual. We were meant to use technique as a shield and face human pain without being shaken, or even moved. Though many consider empathy a basic requirement for any healer, if our professors ever felt concern, they never showed it. My graduate training rendered me massively unfit to be a therapist. One of my most challenging struggles has been to free myself from my education.

Phillipe has a very different story. He was born without real arms or legs. He has enough toes on each of his short bottom stubs to act as pincers, so he can hold a pen and write. And he can hold a knife and fork and feed himself. Phillipe has a single finger on his upper right stub, so that he can manipulate almost any machine that can be operated by pressing buttons or shifting levers. He rides around pretty much anywhere he wants to go on a mechanized wheelchair.

Phillipe conducts his therapy practice over the telephone, and because he takes his calls at home, he is often available on demand at any time of the day or night. This appeals to a very particular type of client, someone who would rather not be seen and known, someone impulsive, who wants attention immediately when there is pain and has no interest in it at any other time. Followed and watched by some secret organization? Strange smells seeping from your television? At three in the morning, at the very apex of your pain and paranoia, Phillipe is there to help calm you.

To numerous troubled souls, he is only a voice, but what a marvelous voice. Deep, rich, and commanding, it glides through the dark, hairy sphincter of his goatee like a muscular snake. A hooded confessor, his face is always in shadows, but instead of purple robes, he wears a Campfire Girls of America T-shirt. And instead of Hail Mary's and penance, he prescribes free thinking and rebellion. You want to sleep with your sister? Why not do it? You want to tell your boss what you think of him? What's stopping you?

Phillipe's whole life has been a struggle against limits; first, the limits of his disability and then, sending his rage out into the world like a teenage thug, any limits he could find to bash against. So you can imagine when he sees Carl seeking limits, actually bowing down to them in reverent submission, how it drives him to distraction.

Of course, Carl senses that Phillipe is a mortal enemy, but all of Carl's suits are gray, and all his ties are striped. The strongest emotion in his arsenal is disdain, so rather than risk a real confrontation, he picks at details. He snipes at Phillipe for conducting his practice over the telephone.

"Whatever works," Phillipe retorts airily. "Rules and structure are for troglodytes."

"What you do is not much better than phone sex," Carl comments dryly. He is closer to the mark than he realizes. Or perhaps he has an intuition. I happen to know that Phillipe, because he does not actually see his clients, feels he can permit himself certain liberties over the telephone. Sometimes he dials numbers at random and starts a friendly, flattering conversation with a stranger. (Isn't this an amazing coincidence? I dial a wrong number, and there you are, someone so fun and easy to talk to.) Within minutes, he is presuming they have a relationship, even though they don't even know each other's names. Or precisely because of this. (Do you realize we could say anything to each other? I mean absolutely anything. We have this unique opportunity to be our true selves, just because we've found each other in this unusual way.) If they are still talking at this point, he can safely imply that they have a bond: it is now undeniable that they must each be curious and intrigued. (I can't help wondering what you're like. I have this feeling that you're a very sensitive person. And I bet that in your own quiet way you can be quite passionate. Tell me, just how good is my intuition? Don't be shy, tell me…Oh, sometimes we just sense these things, don't we?)

Patient, spider-like, and merciless, he winds one sticky strand across another. (This is embarrassing to admit, but I'm getting a little turned on just thinking about you. After all, you and I are completely alone and quite safe. I'd be willing to bet you're not planning to tell your husband about this little conversation, are you? And why should you? I know my wife wouldn't understand. I mean it's only an innocent little talk; it's not like we could actually do anything. Still, if we were in the same room right now, I would want to touch you. You must think I'm really awful…No? Well, your cheek, first. And your neck, yes, definitely your neck. And then I might unbutton your blouse. Would you do something for me? Just so we could be a little closer for a moment? Would you unbutton your blouse for me? And would you put your hand on your breast? And now tell me exactly what you're feeling, and then I'll tell you what to do next…)

Even more than his words, even more than his soft, warm, flannel voice, it's his pace, particularly his pauses, the gaps he leaves for her to fill in on her own that make her surrender so completely. Connected merely by a thin strand of wire, Phillipe can touch her only with a tiny, persistent tickle, but he aims it with devastating accuracy. In the final analysis, he knows she didn't really give herself to him. Ultimately, what she couldn't resist were those secret images, hidden away in her own mind.

But Phillipe is not one to yield just because he has been fairly caught. "Poor Carl, you may not use a telephone, but your situation isn't really any better than mine," Phillipe sympathizes with venomous sweetness. He smooths down his pale blue T-shirt imprinted in bright pink with the face of some Catholic saint and the inspirational motto Love is the Answer. "I doubt you've given this much thought, but even you must have realized by now that the profession most similar to the therapist isn't the physician, Carl, it's the prostitute. Really, a special person to whom one goes privately, sometimes even shamefully, to pay for an intimate experience. Think about it, Carl. It might be some old whore, or it might just be little old you."

Philosophically, I live in the unresolved space between these two, like some ill-adapted amphibian struggling to crawl from the muck of Carl's Id mythology, but uncertain of how to survive on the arid rock of Phillipe's perpetual rebellion. The question of how to help people (for want of a more sophisticated word) be "happy" fascinates me. But it's a strange business to be in. My phone will ring, and someone I've never met will be on the line requesting to see me because so-and-so has told them I'm "good." Am I good? Am I worth the money people pay me? I have to trust my clients on this. What I do is so elusive, I have little else to go on.

🌺 *Chapter 23*

It's been three days since I made love to Margaret, and I long for her with an intensity that hurts. I've played our brief time together over and over in my mind, like a teenager obsessed with a new song. I savor each delicious moment and am filled with delight. Unfortunately, I'm also filled with apprehension. Margaret could easily decide that having an affair with her husband's brother is pure madness and call the whole thing off.

I've found a place for us to meet. Now if I want to see her, I have to call. I organize in my mind the reasons we must see each other, no matter what, and I dial the phone.

"Margaret, it's Noah."

"Ah, Noah. I wondered when you'd call." She pauses. "Even *if* you'd call."

"How could you possibly think I wouldn't call? Adam's not home, is he?"

"No."

"Good."

"Well, I thought you might have had second thoughts."

"I was worried that *you* might have had second thoughts. Have you?" My stomach tightens as I wait for her answer. Like a thing made of glass or ice, my connection with Margaret feels like it could shatter at any moment.

"Noah, I've had lots of thoughts about this. But no, I still want to see you. I have to know what this is between us."

"Good. I was afraid to call, afraid you'd say you'd changed your mind."

"No."

"I think about you constantly, Margaret. Being together was so wonderful."

"It was wonderful for me, too. But this is very new, we don't know yet…"

"It isn't new for me, Margaret. I've wanted this for more than a year."

"It's not good to hope for too much, Noah. It just hurts more if it doesn't work out. And this is complicated." Her voice suddenly sounds sad, and weary.

"You mean Adam?"

"Yes."

"Margaret, how is it between you two? Do you love Adam?" Margaret sighs.

"Yes, I guess I love him. He's always been good to me. But I don't feel close to him the way I feel close to you. I often feel lonely when I'm with Adam."

"Why is that, Margaret?"

"Oh, you know the way Adam is. He talks about his projects, his friends, what we should have for dinner. Never much about himself."

"Yeah, I know. I've been his brother for over forty years, and I still don't feel like I really know him."

There's a moment of silence, and then Margaret says in a different, bitter voice, "And then, as you know, it irks me that he joined the Liberty Party. It irks me even more that he wants me to entertain those people. It just feels so false!"

"Poor Margaret," I say. "I can imagine it would. He shouldn't ask that of you." It's stupid, I think, for Adam to treat her like that, but I'm glad he's doing it. I'm so desperately in love with her that I'm willing to rejoice about anything I think gives me a chance with her.

"He feels it's necessary."

"Necessary for what?"

"For his business. It's terribly important to him to succeed; he feels that this is the only way."

"I never even bring politics up with him," I say. "Does he really go in for all that patriotic talk?" I feel a pang of guilt as I realize that I already know the answer to this and am asking only because I like dwelling on how she and I are alike and Adam is different.

"Adam is a pragmatist. He sometimes chimes in if somebody important goes off on a patriotic bender, but really he couldn't care less about all that stuff."

"Margaret, regarding what you said about being lonely. You know, I'm not like Adam. I want to know you right down to your core."

"I like that. Adam thinks he knows me, but he only knows me on the outside. I'm not sure he recognizes that there are things inside me that he can't see."

"Well, I want to know you inside and out. I want to know everything about you."

"Good. That's what I want—what I've always wanted. When I was growing up no one ever took the time to see inside me, even Adelaide. Adelaide loved me to death, but like Adam, she just assumed she knew who I was." I feel a surge of warmth toward Margaret. I know so well what she's talking about. It was like that with my mother. Plenty of love, but love that missed the mark. She never asked how I felt or what I thought, so I never ever had the sense that she knew who I was. The love was for her Son, with a capital *S*.

"Yes, I know what you mean. It won't be like that with me. I'm a shrink, after all. I'm infinitely curious about what's inside people." Margaret laughs, and she sounds really happy. Suddenly I realize that there really is something important I can give her. "You know I have this intuition that, like me, you were naughty and rebellious when you were growing up."

"Oh, I was. When I was in high school, I smoked, wore tight clothes, talked back to my teachers. I spent so much time in the principal's office, it's a wonder I graduated."

"How come?"

"I was angry, I guess."

"What about?"

"Oh, lots of things. Probably I started being angry when my mother died."

"Yes, I knew your mother died. How old were you?"

"Only four months. I don't even remember her."

"When I came over after Adelaide died, you told me your father was an alcoholic. That must have been tough."

"No kidding. When I was still in my crib, he'd lock me in my room at night in the dark so he could go out and drink. I was terrified, and despite my begging him, he refused to leave a light on. I'd cry and scream for hours." Margaret is starting to sound small and scared just thinking about what happened so long ago. I wish we were together instead of on the phone. I want to hold her and protect her.

"That's terrible, Margaret. You should have been taken away from him. Didn't anyone know?"

"Adelaide knew. She tried to stop it. She threatened to report him, but he told her if she interfered in any way, he'd take me out of her childcare center, and she'd never see me again. She knew how much I depended on her, so she kept quiet. But then when my father got a new job in another part of town and took me away from her anyway, Adelaide did report him."

"Good for her!"

"The authorities came and investigated, and I was put into foster care."

I'm shocked. I've never heard anything about any of this. "Margaret, why didn't I know? You've never said a word, nor has Adam!"

"I don't like to talk about it. It makes me feel odd and different. You know how when you're a kid you want to be like everybody else. I guess it's left over from that. As for Adam, he's not much interested in the past."

"Did things get better then?" I ask. "Were your foster parents good to you?"

"They were, actually. They tried, they really did, but I was so awful they finally gave up and returned me to Child Services."

"You were that bad. How old were you?"

"Five."

"Five! What could you have done at that age to be so bad?"

"I had regular tantrums. I threw my food on the floor. I hit their kids for no reason. Really, it wasn't their fault. I was impossible."

"You must have been really angry."

"I was. Not only did my mother die, but then I was ripped away from Adelaide."

I make a sympathetic sound. "Yes, of course. Any kid would have felt that way." Then suddenly my psychologist self jumps in and starts to tot up what all this might mean in terms of my having a relationship with this woman, but I push him away. All I want is to be compassionate and here, a person, nothing more.

"What happened then, Margaret?"

"I was put in a home for emotionally disturbed children."

"But Margaret, you're so normal! It's hard to believe you could've had a childhood like that and be so normal."

"Well, I'm not normal. You know how anxious I get when I have to go out, and I'm terrified of the dark."

"Yes, I know. But given what you're telling me, I'd expect much worse."

"I was lucky. I got assigned to a social worker who somehow understood that, from my point of view, Adelaide was my mother, and I needed her. She arranged for me to go back to Adelaide's center. Gradually I got better. Eventually I got new foster parents and was able to attend a regular school."

"No wonder you loved Adelaide so much."

"Yeah, she was so good to me. I still miss her terribly. I spent part of my day with her all the way up until I graduated from high school. I'd go to the childcare center after school. When I got into junior high, it became a job. Adelaide paid me to help her care for the little kids."

"So you never really had parents?"

"I had foster parents. Some of them were nice; some of them weren't."

"That sounds so sad." We're silent for a moment. These revelations are surprising and unexpected. It will take awhile to let all this sink in. I think about how self possessed Margaret seems and how she gives the impression of a person with deep inner strength, and I have new respect for her. She's survived more than I could have imagined. "Listen, Margaret, I promise you, I'm going to make it all up to you. I'm going to give you every bit of the love you missed when you were growing up."

"That's a sweet thing to say, Noah."

"I mean it, and I can help you get over your fear of the dark. I know a technique that's surefire."

"Well, that's hard to believe. I've been afraid of the dark all my life."

"You'll see. It's not hard, and it doesn't have to be painful or scary either."

"Okay." She sounds a little dubious.

"I miss you, Margaret. I long for you so much it hurts. When can I see you again?"

"Adam has a meeting with some architects day after tomorrow. Can we meet at ten?"

"That'll be perfect. My clients don't start until one."

"Where shall I come?"

"Come to my office. I've found a place for us to meet. It's very small, but it's cozy. I think you'll like it."

"Where?"

"I don't want to tell you. It's a surprise."

"Okay. I can wait." She pauses. "Noah, you know this scares me a little."

"I know, it scares me too, but I couldn't stand not to see you. I love you."

"Noah, you are so full of feelings. I'm not used to that."

"Yeah, I got the feelings, and Adam got the good sense."

Margaret laughs. "It's incredible that you and Adam are twins."

"That was one of nature's little jokes. We're not only "not identical," we're polar opposites. Sometimes I wonder how you could be attracted to me if you were attracted to him."

"I was young and insecure when I met Adam. I needed what he had to offer. But life moves on, people change. I'm not the same person anymore."

"I'm so glad."

"Well, I ought to go."

"So, I'll see you at my office day after tomorrow at ten."

"I'll be there."

"Do you promise?"

"Yes, I promise."

"I'll be waiting for you."

"Good-bye, Noah."

"Bye."

When I get off the phone, I'm brimming over with so much excitement, I feel like I'm going to explode. I get up and walk around my office, swinging my arms and taking deep breaths. I'm seeing six clients, including someone new, so I need to settle myself down. Thank goodness my workday is about to begin. When I'm in session, I rarely think about anything else. Time passes quickly. That will be handy given how hard it will be to wait two days to see Margaret.

My new client is a middle-aged woman, thin, with quick, bird-like twitches. She seems never at rest, constantly smoothing her dress and adjusting her glasses. I wonder if she might have thyroid problems. "I'm claustrophobic," she explains brightly, "but not in the usual ways. I mean I do get panicky in stuffy rooms. And when I go to the movies, I have to sit near the exit. But what's interesting is I can actually feel much more upset about being trapped in my own body. If I let myself think about it..." She smooths the fabric over her knees and gives it a tug to make sure she's covered. "And sometimes it's almost impossible *not* to think about it. I start to feel oppressed by all this stuff that constantly surrounds me." She gestures at herself, at her breasts actually, rounded and snug under the cornflowers printed on her navy dress, and I wonder if she means them specifically. It is safest not to assume anything.

"I can also feel claustrophobic about my tongue in my mouth," she explains. "Normally I don't notice it, but when I do, I see how extremely confined it is. Did you ever realize how tightly your tongue is walled in by your teeth? And the roof of the mouth is constantly pressing down. Imagine how terrible it would be to be pushed into a little cave with no more room than that. How could you breathe? How could you even stand the sensation of being in there?" She shudders for emphasis.

Her teeth are discolored, and they remind me that mine are also. "You have the teeth of a patriarch," someone once told me. "With teeth like that you could start a tribe." That had given me a certain quirky pride, whereas before I had felt only embarrassment. Suddenly an image flashes in my mind of being in my own mouth, imprisoned by those same large, stained teeth. The moment passes quickly, but it gives me an eerie sense of what her world must be like.

I find it interesting that she doesn't seem frightened while she's telling me all this. She's quick with excitement, seemingly eager that I appreciate her very personal vision of reality. "And sometimes I become aware that my self is not really my body, but something that lives in my head and looks out of my eyes," she says and smiles. "And then I feel trapped in my skull, as if it's a tiny, bony cage."

As she explains her problems in more and more detail, I notice she never expresses any interest in how I might help her rid herself of these phobias. And she sounds well rehearsed, like someone who's been to many therapists. I wonder if I'll ever see her again. I have a hunch she may be more interested in telling her story to a new listener than in changing her life.

As my last client walks out the door, my mind returns to my own life, which seems to consist of nothing but Margaret. I've never before had this experience where someone seems to be the whole of everything. This is all new. In the past, I've been, if anything, too guarded, too reluctant to commit, and because of that, I've never been able to make anything last.

My most serious relationship was with a woman named Beverly, another therapist. We were together for five years. Four of those we lived together in her apartment. That whole time I kept paying the rent on my room, which I guess is a pretty good indication that I never gave in and really loved her. I don't know why. She was attractive, we got along well, and we had lots in common. When she finally got fed up with my ambivalence and issued an ultimatum, I left.

With Margaret, I don't feel any of the old caution. In fact, the shoe's on the other foot; I want her so much, *I'm* afraid of being rejected. It's scary, but it's also a relief. All my life I've dreamed of feeling this way about someone. Then I think about Adam and I groan. Why does the woman I finally fall in love with have to be married to my brother? I feel a little sick. I hate what I'm doing. It seems small and shameful. But scruples seem so pale next to passions, and regardless of what it may mean about me, I know I can't give Margaret up.

Chapter 24

In the corridor by my office I have a storage closet. I keep my futon there, which I occasionally move to the office so my clients can lie down for relaxation training, phobic desensitization, or certain types of hypnosis. Between a few cartons of files and a few shelves of books, there's barely enough room to spread out the futon. But now there's a lovely woven cloth from South America over the boxes. This creates a table for candles and flowers, and I've decorated the walls with expressionist prints. It's here that I bring Margaret.

This time when we make love, she screams, and I worry she'll be heard. Her shrieks have nothing to do with my physically entering her. They seem more the expression of some violent need, and whether it's her longing for me or her relief at escaping from Adam or some undercurrent in her life I can't yet guess, I don't know. Our loving seems like such a miracle, so far beyond what is reasonable, or even possible, that I'm afraid to say too much, afraid that anything so sensible as a discussion might change or destroy it, like realizing while dreaming of flying that, of course, you can't really fly. And falling. And waking. We don't ask questions; we talk of how we care and how we feel. We confess over and over, this weakness, this softness that we keep secret from the world. And of course we talk about our world, talk with relish about how corrupt the city is. I tell her about Phillipe and Carl and about how funny they are, how they behave like a pair of terriers growling over a rag, and about my practice. I'm not supposed to talk about my practice, but Margaret doesn't know the people I see, and how can I not tell her about the only other part of my life that matters, the only other part that has any redeeming value? Lying together naked, reading aloud to each other the novel of our lives, I feel young and buoyant. It's so easy, and so wonderful, to feel understood.

I'm not religious, and yet I find myself murmuring under my breath to some abstract power, "Please, don't let me lose this." At last, and for the first time, I experience myself as a member of that mythical breed, the ones who feel happy and whole and at peace with the world.

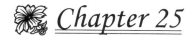 *Chapter 25*

Mmm my screamin'
Voodoo Demon
Please
Take me into Your Fire
(Whoopee)
That's where I long to expire.

This breathless little doggerel is homage to Amy from Appoppa. This time the paper is appropriately sinister chartreuse. I wonder where he finds his stationary. These children have apparently been doing some devil dancing of their own. Amy hands me the page with a blank expression, which on her looks like a smirk, and I realize that smugness in one who has so little to be smug about can be quite touching.

"I'm in love," she announces flatly, "with the most ridiculous, irritating person possible."

"Congratulations."

"Thank you. I will accept your congratulations, even though it is most probable that you are actually teasing me. I know I've complained mercilessly for months about this jerk. And in fact, I have plenty of doubts about this myself. I've never been in love before, and even while I'm in the middle of it, I keep thinking the whole thing is quite preposterous. Still, there it is." Now, for the first time, she shows a grin that lifts and widens, too slippery to hold back, until she is beaming, the gap between her front teeth revealing its special charm. I have never seen anything remotely resembling this expression on her face before, and I'm moved. It's still very new for her even to cry, but already she's gone far beyond that.

"For weeks now I've been…I don't know quite how to put it… noticing him. One day, for instance, I was just minding my own business, going along as usual thinking what a bothersome person he was, when suddenly I noticed what nice hair he happens to have." Big smile. "Really, he has the loveliest hair. Soft and light brown. You probably can't believe how stupid I'm being." I just smile back at her, completely delighted.

"And then I realize he has hands. I mean, I have no idea how he picked up things before, but I honestly never noticed that he had hands. Really, the most gorgeous hands. Perhaps he had them grafted on, you know, some kind of rapid plastic surgery, because I can't believe I wouldn't have noticed if he'd had them before. And his voice is different. He even smells better. It's amazing." She tilts her head to rest her cheek in her palm, and this posture also seems new, softer, more tolerant, almost a self-caress. She sighs, and for a moment seems lost in the wonder of it all. "And when I have pain, it doesn't seem so bad, as long as he's there to comfort me."

Of course, I'm happy for Amy, happy for her happiness, and happy because even if she dies tomorrow, at least she won't have died without experiencing love. I am relieved, as well, that she now has a reason for living. And whether I deserve it or not, I take credit for this, believing that my skill in opening her to the reality of her pain has opened her to love as well.

How strange that she and I are having such similar experiences. I have an impulse to tell her all about Margaret, just as though we were old friends, but of course I don't, since this would fundamentally change our relationship and possibly render me useless to her as a therapist.

She smiles slyly at me. "And now for the part you've been waiting for—the sex is terrific. It's tender and nasty and disgusting, just the way good sex should be. But there's something extra to it, a warm feeling all over my body, and especially here." She touches her heart. "Does that happen to other people?"

"I don't know, Amy," I answer honestly, "but I think it's wonderful it's happening to you. That sounds marvelous. A warm feeling all over your body and especially in your heart, whatever could that be?" She knows I'm teasing and gives me her "don't be a wise guy" look.

I wonder quietly why Amy seems so special, why I especially look forward to her session despite the fact that our work together is often difficult and frustrating. Is it the dark cloud of death, the ground against which I see her, that makes her seem so bright and alive, or is she just that way, making what's happened to her especially tragic?

When Amy leaves, I bask in the glow of our mutual good fortune. I don't know whether other people have experienced what she is experiencing, but such miraculous things have occurred between Margaret and me, things I never even realized were possible, I'm convinced that we've discovered things totally new to the world of love.

Shortly after Margaret and I started meeting, I bought a stereo system for our closet love nest. Not only did this allow me to add music to the flowers and candles, but it made me feel secure that we could let go completely and not be overheard. And so it came about that I made love to Bach. Not "to" in the sense of "accompanied by," but "to" as in "directly engaged with"—to Bach as much as to Margaret. This cannot be explained. I can only say that in the recklessness of our lovemaking, everything came apart. As we threw ourselves into each other and surrendered our sense to our senses, Margaret and I were juggled wildly, handfuls of breast and penis, hip and hair. And at the same time the music from the stereo became palpable, great swooping scoops of Baroque bittersweet mixed with Margaret and me. It was real and present and thrilling, a completely new perspective, this sense of how intimate he and she and I could be. This happened several times and then disappeared forever.

But the wonders were not over. Next, I lost the sense of Margaret completely. In the midst of my most feverish clinging, bucking, seeking, she disappeared without leaving so much as a scent, a taste, a hair on the pillow. Instead, I found myself in a summer field, wading waist-high through dry grass, under brilliant white clouds. I was kneeling on damp earth, smelling pine, holding a smooth stone. I was lying naked on a cot, brushed by a curtain blowing in a hot breeze. Hallucinatory, yes, but I wasn't frightened. I was thrilled. It felt as if our heat had melted some binding element, as if the universal and eternal swirl of experience had been loosened to circulate with complete freedom. We had dared to go beyond the rules, to feel beyond the limits: now we were free to feel anything, and we did.

I'm aware that all this has the distinct sense of my father's stories. Where else could I have gotten these images? Was this all buried inside me, waiting to be uncovered whenever I was finally ready for such moments of massive self-excavation? My father seemed so bland when he was alive. Why is he more and more magical the longer he's dead?

There's magic in Margaret as well. Sex has never been like this. I'd practiced it like a craft, tried to become skillful by attention to detail, by understanding structure and theory, by careful practice in reading my partner's needs and pleasures. But these experiences are completely different, they awe me; they leave me breathless and trembling. Our lovemaking is as far from technique as throwing oneself on an altar is from droning through a catechism. In this universe, pedantry and planning don't even exist. I hurl myself repeatedly off the cliff of surrender, and whether it's chance or mercy that sends the wave that saves me from the rocks below is irrelevant, because I know that next time I must leap again no matter what.

Chapter 26

I'm actually humming to myself when I open my door and retrieve the newspaper. I've been wearing a perpetual smile, which I try to suppress when I'm seeing clients so they won't feel I'm not listening to their woes with appropriate solemnity. I take the rubber band off the newspaper. On the front page is a picture of the Brooklyn Botanical Gardens. I stare at it incredulously. There are numerous jagged holes in its glass panels, and the caption reads: "Conservatory Shattered, Plants Destroyed." A group of onlookers are crowded around the front door, examining something.

The Brooklyn Botanical Gardens, of course, are no longer in Brooklyn. When the waters rose and much of Brooklyn was flooded, the exquisite art-deco glass structure known as the Conservatory would have been destroyed, along with the exotic plants inside. But New Yorkers so loved the Gardens that a work party was sent out to deconstruct this beautiful and fragile building and bring it into the city. The Conservatory was reconstructed on this site where an old apartment building had been torn down, and then a towering office building, supported on steel beams, was built above it. In what seems an unusual concession to architectural beauty, enough space was left around the Conservatory so it's still possible to appreciate the glass dome and arched art-deco entryway. At night, it's illuminated so it glows like a giant Christmas ornament.

The Gardens are everyone's sentimental favorite. Every school child has visited this strange and exotic world. Teachers love this field trip because behavior is never a problem; the children are awed by the presence of real plants, some of them actually in flower. There's even a petting garden, although it's "planted" with synthetics, which are renewed daily. Not even the toughest swamp grass can stand up to the caresses of a thousand sticky little hands.

It's a place where people grow quiet in the glow of the grow lights. It's a place to take a lover, a place to hold hands. Now madmen with crowbars have smashed the windows and hacked our last remaining real plants to death. I discover by reading the article that painted on the front door, pretty much the only panel left unbroken, is a stencil of the Statue of Liberty. Obviously this is the work of the Patriots. But why? Why would they attack the Gardens? Usually they go after people who lack "proper values." But plants! It makes no sense. My good mood evaporates. I pound my fist on my little table so hard it almost collapses. Deprived of light, these people have grown up twisted.

Chapter 27

Adam came down with the flu, which then turned into bronchitis. He was home in bed for more than three weeks. Margaret didn't feel safe sneaking off to see me. Normally she goes out very little, and when she does, Adam always asks where she's off to. It's not that he suspects Margaret of anything. It's his way of being protective. When he was in the Boy Scouts, they taught him always to inquire where a companion was going, so that if that person later turned up missing, you'd know where to search for them. This advice was meant, I think, for forays into the wilderness, but I have to admit it could apply just as well to the maze of our city. So for all that time when Adam was sick and being a good Boy Scout, Margaret and I were unable to get together.

I've missed her terribly. Her image has been in front of me every moment; my life has had to pass through it, like a filter, to reach me. When we finally meet, Margaret and I are in a fever for each other. She looks so dear. She feels so delicious. Perhaps it's our pent-up feelings that cause us to be so completely abandoned, so totally reckless in what we dare to give and take that we break through some barrier and experience the miraculous.

This time, I not only lose Margaret, I lose myself as well. I have no sense of who I am or where or what's happening. My eyes are wide open, but what I see is the sheer black backdrop of deepest space. Two enormous, spiral nebulae glitter, brilliant against the blackness. Neither one a solid entity, they swirl together, joining completely. They turn, they intermingle, one with the other, with such grace and beauty, it's breathtaking. Then they move right through one another and on out into the infinite darkness beyond.

When I return to reality, Margaret is sobbing in my arms, deeply moved by something. Did she see what I saw? I don't know. The moment seems so tender, I don't want to speak. I don't want to do anything but just hold her. She looks up. Her eyes are wide. Her tears glimmer in the candlelight. I gaze at her and wonder, "What have we done? Where are we headed?"

❀ *Chapter 28*

To understand the place where Margaret and I live and love, it's necessary to explain the events that led up to New York City's declaration of independence from the United States of America. Had it not been for the cataclysm taking place, not just in the country, but in the world, this never could have happened, but as it was, we were able to slip out of the Union practically unnoticed.

As we inched toward the middle of the century, a tipping point was reached, and the ongoing environmental catastrophe kicked into high gear. The oceans rose so quickly that dikes failed, and vast areas of coastland were flooded. At the same time, water shortages went from bad to dire, and fires raged more and more routinely through areas scorched by drought. Since under such conditions there was never enough money to go around, fights broke out among the states regarding how federal money should be spent. The states concerned mainly with fires and droughts didn't want their money used to build dikes to protect the coasts, and likewise, as great chunks of coastal land were inundated by the sea, the coastal states didn't want their money spent to fight fires and desalinate ocean water for the interior. There were even conflicts between regions. Tax strikes were organized, and people began sending their federal taxes to their local government, who they could trust to spend the money for whatever was most needed in their own area.

Meanwhile, we New Yorkers were feeling pretty smug. Since we were now encapsulated, our island was protected from the rising waters. We did, however, have one major problem. Due to the incredible expense of the Encapsulation, the city was deeply in debt. To make matters worse, with all the trouble outside, federal and state taxes rose astronomically. In addition to the financial stress of paying off city bonds, we saw yet more of our money march off to fix problems that had nothing to do with us. For a time, New Yorkers simply grumbled and paid. But then after years of litigation, the federal government won a huge judgment against our city for polluting the public waterways. That was the final straw. New York City issued a Declaration of Independence and seceded from both the Union and the State of New York.

Shortly thereafter, every region or city that had something to gain, mostly the rich and heavily populated ones, followed suit, and the United States ceased to exist in any meaningful way. Such a thing would have been unimaginable a decade before, but with all the droughts and fires and flooding, the country was in such chaos the federal government simply didn't have the will or the resources to fight its own people in so many places at once.

Following the Succession, the flag of New York City replaced the stars and stripes. We even formed a small army for the purpose of protecting our water supply and preventing bands of displaced people from storming the city gates.

Because we were now independent, the people who had campaigned for the Encapsulation, and who had profited from it in the form of huge building contracts, felt they needed a party name that was distinctly and exclusively New York. Thus, the Liberty Party came into being. In our first election as an independent city-state, a grateful New York elected them to every office by a landslide.

The Liberty Party's first move was to launch a massive campaign to engender civic pride. Patriotism became mandatory. Funds were allocated to place city flags on stubby little poles at intersections in the wider corridors, and fans were installed so the flags would wave perpetually, as if in the wind. The long-standing hatred toward the outsiders morphed into hatred as well of anyone who criticized what was now proudly referred to as "the New York way of life." There were banners proclaiming New York "the greatest city in the world," and it was strongly implied that the citizens of such an illustrious city must be pretty special as well.

In order to protect and preserve our way of life, people had to be prevented from attacking it. It's never become illegal to say anything one wishes—that is still hypothetically guaranteed by the Constitution of New York City—it has simply become dangerous. Newspapers have been ransacked after publishing "unflattering" stories or editorials, and not just about New York, but about the Liberty Party or its members as well. Licenses for TV stations, or even a business, could be revoked for a variety of reasons, and they were, though never directly because of the offending story or product.

I've never figured out why the Patriots hacked up the plants in the Botanical Gardens. Possibly they viewed plants as "foreign" entities. But now something even more horrible has happened. I've just read in the paper about a young woman whose body was found stuffed into a utility closet. She had been badly beaten, and her skull was crushed. I know who she is, and I'd been hoping this wouldn't happen.

She was a reporter from the *Times*. She had hard evidence that a high-ranking member of the Liberty Party had taken money from the Empire Paper Company and that shortly thereafter Empire was awarded an exclusive contract to supply paper and forms to all city offices. Rumor has it that the story was killed by the editors, but that the reporter was so determined to get it printed, she managed to erase another story and enter hers into the computer after the final editing for that day's paper had already been done. I saw the story, as well as the retraction printed the next day. The *Times* had apologized to the official and had said the "mentally unbalanced" woman who'd written the story had been fired. Idealism like hers is rare these days.

Most of us don't have to worry about such things happening to us. We keep our criticisms to ourselves, or we discuss them only with family or with close and trusted friends. We live our lives quietly. And as much as we admire those who get themselves into hot water by speaking out, we also consider them foolish.

I am a reader of history, so I know what we're experiencing isn't in the least unusual. Which is not to say that it doesn't seem strange. We never believed it could happen in New York City, and yet it did. Our freedoms have eroded like that poor stump of a statue out there in what used to be New York Harbor.

 # *Chapter 29*

Why is it Margaret in particular, I wonder, who stirs such passion in me? I sense a special bond between us for which there's no rational explanation. I puzzle over this, and I worry. If there are no good reasons for my feelings, might they not suddenly disappear, like some mirage in the desert, and take my happiness with them?

Ironically, it was Phillipe who helped me focus these thoughts. Phillipe, the perfect foil for tender feelings, the Antichrist of romance. As usual, we were at Felicia's. The cafe spreads into the intersection of two main corridors. Tables are pressed in on every side, and a steady stream of walkers brushes past us, so we're constantly jostled. Phillipe was drinking a cappuccino. Despite his muscular torso, he folded himself nimbly in half to swing his cup up to his lips. I had a fruit drink. It was too bright, and I wondered what was in it.

"Are you getting any lately?" He smiled at me with steamed milk in his mustache. Despite my better judgment, I told him, "Phillipe, I think I'm in love." Phillipe would never be my first choice for a confession of the heart, but I was too full of feelings to pass up the opportunity.

"I knew something was wrong. Is she pretty at least?"

"Yes, she's pretty. As a matter of fact, I think she's beautiful, but people usually think their lovers are beautiful. And that's not what it's about."

"No, it never is…" he leered at me. And then he actually licked his lips, the little pig, leaving them bright and wet behind the pubic bristle that surrounded them. "Well, who is she?" he asked.

"Phillipe, this is not the kind of thing you could understand."

"Do I know her?" he insisted.

"I wouldn't tell you if you did. I wouldn't let you sully something so delicate and magical."

"What you mean is she's married."

"That's none of your business."

"Well, isn't this interesting! Mr. Middle-of-the-Road, Mr. By-the-Book is involved with a married woman. Who would have thought it?"

"Stop it, Phillipe! Not about this."

"You're right, there's no reason for us to fight. Actually, I'm quite happy for you. For so long now you've seemed all covered over with this grimy layer of gloom, and I think a little intense agony, something like love, for instance, will cut through it and really brighten you up. Suffering is so ennobling. I expect great things from you."

"Make up your mind, Phillipe. I won't tell you a thing if you keep it up."

"Woof! Woof!" Phillipe panted and made pawing motions like a dog begging for a treat. When I glared at him, he insisted, "I'm being good! Tell me! Tell me!" His T-shirt du jour was black with a silver pout, and the words "James Dean Fan Club: St. Mark's Junior High School."

"I'm thinking…"

"You're stalling. I'll bet the sex is great."

"The sex is wonderful, but that's not it. Actually, part of it is the way we talk. After we make love, we lie around for hours just talking."

"What do you talk about?"

"Anything. It doesn't seem to matter. Art. Postmodernism. Politics, a lot of politics. It doesn't sound very romantic, but I'm deeply happy the whole time. We understand each other. Even when we argue, we still understand each other's point of view. It's wonderful."

"Yeah. It's wonderful, all right, but it doesn't make any sense. Because you talk to people all the time. You're talking to me, right now. But you're not in love with me. And that's because we don't have great sex, and you don't think I'm beautiful. There's no need to make it so complicated."

"I don't think you're ever going to understand this, Phillipe," I said tiredly, "but it's not her looks, and it's not the sex. It's really something else."

"What?"

"I don't know."

"Then either I don't understand, or I understand much better than you do."

"I don't think either of us understands. I wish I knew why I feel this intense passion. I'm completely obsessed."

"It wasn't worth being nice to you," he sulked. "You know it's hard for me, and you didn't even tell me anything good."

"I wish I knew what to tell you, Phillipe."

"Then tell me something dirty," Phillipe commanded cheerfully. "You could even make it up." I think he was teasing, but I couldn't be sure.

What Phillipe helped me start, Carl helped me finish, and that was just as unexpected. Who would have thought that either one of these two could have had any relevance for me at this time? We were at Carl's apartment. The couches and arm chairs were covered in soft, gray wool with a diagonal, blue pinstripe, so similar to the way he dressed, it suggested the possibility that he'd been upholstered. He still wore his suit pants and a white shirt, but he had hung his jacket carefully in the closet and had rolled back his shirt cuffs two precise turns. To see Carl this way was as shocking as finding another person naked. I was surprised that his forearms were muscular, that he was actually flesh under all that dry cleaning and starch.

"Do you ever think about love?" I asked him.

"All the time," he answered, surprising me again. He was making us dinner. I sat at his table while he worked at the counter by the sink. He stirred a cup of potato mix with drinking water, the water meter dinging ounce by ounce to encourage conservation. When the mix was thick enough, he patted it into irregular lumps for baking. It was traditional that baked potatoes be rolled round like dumplings. Then he took down a box of meat mix and repeated the process, only this time pressing it out and cutting it into star shaped patties with a cookie cutter, his own little touch of creativity.

"I think I'm in love, and it troubles me that I don't understand why."

Carl accepted the idea of understanding love without question. "Well," he asked sensibly, "do you have common interests?"

"Some. But we never go anywhere or do anything, so I'm not sure how much that matters."

"Does she remind you of your mother?" He had the decency to turn and smile as he said this, a reference to our ongoing ideological warfare.

"I don't think we can chalk this one up to unresolved oedipal longings, Carl."

He stirred a pitcher of fruit drink from another box. More meter-music. He let the gap in our conversation elongate gracefully. One thing you have to give to the analysts, they're good at waiting. That's what they do.

"Might you share the same fears?" he asked softly, not looking at me this time.

It was like acupressure, a small force on a point of leverage to move a large emotion. And Carl, of all people, had helped me feel it. For the first time, I wondered what his experience had been in love. He handed me some silverware to spread on the table. We went on with the meal, and in our manly way, neither of us mentioned the subject of love again. But Carl had released me from repetitious self-examination.

To understand this love, I had been going down the lists of our positive qualities, searching in the wrong places for the wrong thing. But neither Margaret nor I had special virtues, or if we did, they were irrelevant to our bond. There was something else, something very different. Deep inside her was a mixture of hurt, fear, and bitterness that matched mine with the amazing precision of a virus locking onto a receptor. That same sense of "badness," which had made me feel lonely and different for a lifetime, now bound me to someone similar in the most intimate way. It was so ironic that the very thing that had always cut me off from others now connected me; and even though I still felt as odd and unsuitable as before, I was no longer alone. Now there was another of my species.

I had been loved before, touched by caring and naive hands, and ultimately it had felt alienating. Though I didn't realize it, I must have felt intuitively that these women were not in love with me, but rather with the person I pretended to be. I had pulled the wool over their eyes, and in doing so, I disqualified their love. But because Margaret and I experience ourselves in much the same way, she knows me almost as I know myself. Finally I've been unmasked, found out, seen as the person I truly am, and that is an entirely different matter.

Chapter 30

Lately I've had odd thoughts, flashes, imaginings of Margaret and me somewhere else, somewhere outside, as though my unconscious mind is actually urging me to wonder what it would be like to leave New York. This isn't a practical idea. I have no idea where we'd go or how we'd survive. Yet, if Margaret would go with me, run away with me, we could love each other openly. No more hiding.

The last time I was outside the city was in my twenties. The four of us, my mother, my father, Adam, and I, took a family vacation to the Berkshires. Despite all the trouble outside, if you took a bus directly to a protected resort, it was still reasonably safe to travel.

We left by bus on the ten-lane highway that connects New York to the outside world. The Great Highway starts where the old Henry Hudson Bridge used to be, and for a distance it runs between two thick, concrete walls. These walls are necessary to keep the sea from inundating the roadway until it reaches a safe altitude, since sea level has risen to the point where Manhattan would be flooded were it not for the Encapsulation.

Even then travel was limited, and you had to apply for a permit months ahead. This was necessary because the road had to be used primarily to supply the city with food, manufactured goods, and raw materials, as well as for the export of goods made in New York. It couldn't handle the vacationers going anywhere they wished anytime they wished, and especially not since on the return trip each passenger bus had to be scrupulously inspected to prevent terrorists from entering our safe haven.

But then the incidents occurred. Twice terrorists infiltrated the city by murdering New York travelers, then using their clothes and identities to enter the city. Once inside, the first, a teenage woman, managed to assemble enough chemicals to build a bomb, which she then set off at the Lexington Avenue subway stop during rush hour. She killed herself as well as about fifty other people. In the second incident, the subway tracks were tampered with, and two speeding trains crashed head on, killing or badly injuring almost all the passengers.

In the third incident, a suicide bomber drove a truck full of explosives down the Great Highway and, before reaching the inspection station, crashed it straight into the wall. Sea water, polluted with our sewage and industrial wastes, poured in through the resulting hole and flowed down toward the city, sweeping every vehicle on the road with it and drowning (or poisoning) their occupants. This water would have swept into the city, filling New York to sea level, had it not been for a quick-thinking woman in a bus uphill of the breach who used her cell phone to call 911. The main gatekeeper was alerted, and disaster narrowly averted. The main city gate clicked shut just in time. Knowingly or unknowingly, Samantha Young, the woman who called in the warning, sacrificed herself and became a celebrated heroine.

Once the water came to the now closed, heavily fortified metal gate and could not continue downhill into the city, it quickly backed up and filled the uphill segment of the Great Highway until it reached sea level, drowning hundreds, including Samantha. I have often wondered whether Samantha thought things through before making that call or whether she simply acted quickly in an emergency, as we are all taught to do, and then was surprised when the water came back in her direction. The city was cut off and without supplies for a week while divers repaired the hole and the water was pumped off the Great Highway.

As a result of these incidents, which unfortunately occurred in close succession, there was quite an uproar. Blame, of course, fell heavily on the official who had decided to put the inspection station at the city gate rather than at the beginning of the Great Highway, and this error was quickly rectified. But while people were still upset, the Liberty Party quickly introduced a bill to prohibit citizens from traveling outside the city, except when absolutely necessary. It was too dangerous, they said, and besides, they argued, who would want to go out there anyway, since out there one could be murdered by a terrorist or killed in an automobile accident. (City officials see to it that grotesque pictures of automobile accidents and other disasters are published regularly in the papers and shown on TV to help us keep in mind how much better off we are here in New York.)

The law passed as a temporary emergency measure, but periodically it was quietly renewed on the grounds that the situation hasn't changed. It didn't seem to matter to anyone that the most serious incident, the one involving the wall of the Great Highway, had nothing at all to do with a traveling New Yorker. People were upset. It would be safer for everyone, they reasoned, if the only ones allowed to go outside were those responsible for delivering supplies. If someone felt the need to leave New York, well fine, they said, let them do it, but we won't let them back in. This "love it or leave it" attitude is part of the patriotic fervor that arose after the Succession. And now that the Encapsulation has saved us not only from terrorists and rising waters, but also from a deadly pandemic, I'm convinced that our right to travel outside will never be restored.

The ban against travel was the last nail in the coffin of my father's spirit. Until then, he had looked forward to traveling outside the way Adam and I had once eagerly anticipated going out to play. He'd apply for a new permission as soon as we returned from our last trip. And even though my mother complained a bit, we never went anywhere near another city. It was always a mountain, a lake, a forest, a river; once we even visited a glacier, one of the last in existence.

When the travel ban was proposed, my father railed against it in the privacy of our apartment, but due to the charged atmosphere in the city after the terrorist attacks, he didn't dare express his opposition publicly. If anything, things are worse now. Expressing a desire to leave the city is tantamount to treason. Yes, some people sometimes have to go out—members of the army to protect the water supply or business people to examine goods for import, but it's customary to treat this as a necessary evil, something to be endured, certainly not a pleasure. In our society, there is no place like home, and you'd best not say that there is.

So leaving New York would be no small thing. It would mean leaving never to return, going someplace I can't even visit first. It would mean leaving my mother and brother, neither of whom would ever consider living anywhere else, leaving my friends, my clients, everything I've ever known. In addition, it would mean facing a host of unknown dangers. It's really unthinkable. Nonetheless, this idea has entered my mind. I want to be free to love Margaret, that's a big part of it, but it isn't the whole thing. I feel a strange desire to live somewhere where things still grow.

I think again of my father. Did I inherit some gene from him, or is it his stories and his love of natural places that are responsible? Despite my childish determination to shut him out, did my father's attitudes seep into me anyway, setting me apart from those who love the safety and coziness of our great hive, and who are, as we are daily exhorted to be, "proud to be New Yorkers"? This feeling of being a misfit and an outsider has been with me as long as I can remember, and I'm so tired of it.

Chapter 31

When I was in the third grade, I fell in love with a tiny red-haired girl named Jennie. I simply held her hand and walked her home from school. But we soon learned. The other children teased us so viciously that we avoided each other from then on. Now, because Margaret and I are no longer so innocent, we know how to communicate our desire in more careful ways. She and I can flash signals in public, in front of her husband, my mother, her family and friends. If I look full into her eyes, if I brush her shoulder as I pass, if she stretches in that slow, bored way because she is enjoying the thin tightness of her body, shortly afterward I will be in the closet, waiting impatiently. If it is she who signals, usually the wait is short, since she is privy to Adam's schedule. But if I signal her, sometimes I have a long wait, and sometimes she doesn't arrive at all, since it's not always possible for her to get away.

Today I'm lucky. It's not long before I see a flash of light from the hallway and my cat-woman slides into the dark closet. I've been entertaining myself with fantasies of what we will do when she arrives, and I'm impatient to touch her. I pull her down onto the futon along side me. But Margaret doesn't melt against me as I expect, and when I try to touch her breasts, she says, "Don't, not now. I want to tell you about something. Did you see the clowns on TV?"

She's chattering away excitedly about some clowns who were featured on the morning news. It seems that a group dressed as clowns has been showing up on streets, in subway stations, or in parks and doing some kind of guerrilla theater. They appear, enact a mystifying little scene, and then disappear, all in a space of minutes. This morning they showed up in Times Square Plaza. They skipped and cavorted around, and then one of them fell down as if dead. The others crowded around and mimed grief and horror, then another fell, and then another, and another, until they were all dead. Then they all jumped up and ran away. A video of this was sent by courier to the TV station.

For the life of me, I can't figure out why Margaret is so excited by this, and I'm hurt that she prefers talking about such silliness to making love to me. When she arrived, my body was aching for her. Now I feel annoyed. "What," I say, "is so great about these clowns? If these people have so much energy, why don't they do something useful, like cleaning the hallways, fighting corruption, or caring for the sick?" My voice is sharper than I'd intended, and Margaret looks startled.

"No, no, you don't get it. I think it's about the people who are becoming ill and dying, like your client. I've been hearing rumors—"

"Is that what they said on the news?"

"No, of course not. They could never say anything like that. They'd be afraid of losing their license."

"Margaret, please let's not talk about this now." I pull her close, then slip my hand under her blouse. Her sensitive nipples usually bulge into raspberries at the slightest touch. They are vessels where an erotic devil hides, who I can release by gently rubbing or kissing them. She doesn't wear a bra, so when I raise her blouse, I do so with reverence. I'm exposing a shrine, lifting her last veil. I'm not so ceremonious with my own shirt. Usually I just jerk it to my armpits. Once I tore it open, ripping off the buttons, which shocked us both, thrilling us the first time, but it felt rehearsed after that. Often we deliberately hold ourselves apart while we kiss, knowing that she is about to bring her sensitive, fruity nipples to my hungry chest, picturing all that is about to happen. Then when the tension becomes unbearable, we thrust our bodies together.

But today it's different. Margaret doesn't seem eager. For the first time, I have to resort to seduction. "She's still preoccupied with those damn clowns," I think. I feel hurt, unwanted. I need her to yield to the same hoarse, demanding voice from the groin that makes me desire her so desperately. I kiss her face and neck. I run my hands up and down her back and gently stroke her buttocks. Margaret still feels unresponsive, and I'm starting to feel uneasy, tense. I pull her blouse up and start to nurse on her nipples. After some minutes of this, she finally catches fire. She presses her body hard against mine, and we slide into that delicious place where nothing exists but mindless swimming in a river of flesh. I'm reassured. I relax and allow this bliss to build and build. When I enter her, she wraps her legs tightly around me, and her moans grow louder and louder, until finally she and then I explode into orgasm. Lying in stillness afterward, we hear voices in the hallway, a door opening and closing, then silence.

Margaret says no more about the clowns, but later back in my room, I tune in to the evening news to see if I can learn anything. By switching around the dial, I find a channel that's playing the video. All the clowns are identical—fright wigs, big red noses, white painted smiles. They gesture broadly and make faces, happy and smiling in the beginning, then filled with alarm and despair. The reporter links them to a number of other odd, theatrical events in the city and speculates on a possible resurgence of Dadaism. I can't seem to get involved. I'm still feeling stung, I suppose, by Margaret being so enthralled with them when I wanted her to be enthralled with me. In my current mood, people who act silly are an irritation.

Chapter 32

It's my birthday, and when Margaret comes to our closet hideaway, she takes a covered cake plate and a brightly wrapped present out of a shopping bag. She's baked the cake herself, and on top she's inscribed "Happy Birthday Darling" in bright pink. As much as I like her to call me "darling," the idea that she might keep something like that around the house where Adam could find it worries me. Then it strikes me, and I have to smile at this, that since we're twins, he would naturally assume the cake was for him, though I imagine he might wonder why it was spice cake, my favorite, and not the dark chocolate he prefers.

I advise myself to stop worrying and let myself enjoy having Margaret make a fuss over my birthday. Growing up, I always had to share my birthday with Adam, and to make matters worse, to avoid jealousy my mother always got us the same gift. I unwrap my present. It's a rich-looking, leather-bound appointment book. I'm delighted. But of course my real birthday present is Margaret. I pull her to me, and we make love, slowly and sweetly at first, then fiercely.

When we're finished, I feel deliciously content, but Margaret seems restless. I wonder what's going on. She sighs deeply, sits up, and looks directly into my eyes. "When are we going to tell him?" she says. It takes me a moment to comprehend, but then I know that she can only mean "tell Adam about us." My heart does a little dance. I've never thought about telling Adam, only about how to keep it from him, and the image I have of what that would be like is deeply disturbing.

"You want to tell him?"

"Yes."

"But, Margaret, that would end your marriage. Where would you go?"

"Where would I go? Where would I go?" She seems incredulous.

"Margaret, Margaret, what's wrong, sweetheart?" I try to take her in my arms, but she pushes me away.

"I guess I thought I'd move in with you!" Suddenly I feel over-whelmed. It's the first time Margaret has ever been angry with me, and so much else is happening. I try to imagine Margaret and I crowded into my little room. It seems a bizarre notion.

"Don't be angry, Margaret. I love you."

"Do you? Well then, why do you let things go on this way?"

"I didn't know you didn't *want* things to go on this way. I assumed…"

"You assumed that I like coming here and making love with you and then going home and making love to Adam."

"I never think about you and Adam…maybe I haven't wanted to. And now when I do think about it, I can't imagine it's anything like what we do."

"I'm his wife. I sleep in the same bed with him. Don't you care?"

"I didn't know I had any right to care."

"What is this to you, then, a back-alley romance, an affair that runs its course and ends?"

"No!"

"Well, what did you think, then, that we'd just go on like this forever, or until we slip up and Adam finds out? Then what, he drags me home by the hair or kicks me out into the corridor?"

It's a fair question. What did I think? I didn't. I was busy being thrilled about what we had, and I didn't think. Not about the future. Margaret looks flushed in the candlelight. I hate having her angry with me. "Margaret, I didn't know you felt this way. But I don't know how you can even consider moving in with me. I live in a room with a hot plate. I don't have a kitchen. I don't even have my own bathroom. I use Mom's." Suddenly I feel ridiculous. I'm a successful middle-aged professional, and I'm living in the same single room I've had since graduate school. Even though I could have afforded it long ago, I've never bothered to go through the complicated process of applying for a better place to live.

"I know where you live."

"And you'd seriously consider—"

"We'd just have to make do until we could get an apartment."

"You know that would take a long time, at least a year, maybe even two years, and I doubt that Adam would feel much like using his pull at city hall to help us out."

"You don't love me. You say you do, but—"

"I do love you!"

"Then why don't you do something?"

"I didn't know you wanted me to do something. And now that I do—"

"Now that you do, you're scared."

I weigh this for a moment. I do feel scared, but of what? "Yes, okay, I am scared. Scared of how guilty I feel, scared of my mother and brother never speaking to me again, but—"

"If you really loved me, none of that would matter."

"But even more, Margaret, it scares me to think of spoiling what we have. Which is probably what moving in with me would do. Think what it would be like to leave your huge flat and share a ten-by-twelve room with me. You hate being out in the corridors. What would you do? What if you ended up thinking it was all a mistake…and got bitter…and—"

"What if, what if!" Margaret looks at me intensely. She seems to be trying to read my heart. It's clear I've disappointed her. She wanted a prince, someone to carry her away, and apparently she's been waiting for me to do it for some time.

"I had no idea you felt this way, sweetheart. But it's not as simple as you think. I've had lots of clients forced by the housing shortage to make do with a room or two. As often as not, when they're crowded together like that, they start to hate each other. The last thing I want is to spoil things between us. You're the best thing that's ever happened to me. I don't want to lose it."

Margaret has softened, but she looks sad. I reach out and stroke her face. "I love you, Margaret. I do love you." Some sort of melancholy has settled over me as well. I feel I've failed, failed in some way that's very deep and very old. We lie in silence for a few minutes, then Margaret says, "I guess we'll have to talk more about this later. I have to be going. It's Adam's birthday too, you know, and we're going out to dinner."

"Margaret, tomorrow I'll go down to the housing authority and apply for an apartment. I'll tell them I'm getting married." This seems weak compared to what was expected of me. And yet, when I think about Margaret and me trying to live together in my room, it doesn't seem sensible. We kiss good-bye. We listen for voices in the hallway, and she slips out the door.

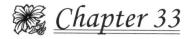 *Chapter 33*

I was surprised when I found out that Phillipe's most passionate commitment was not to sex or to therapy, but to the AngelBeasts. The AngelBeasts came into being shortly after World War I. During that war, an opera singer, serving as a soldier on some European battlefield, heard the shrieking of torn and dying men. In the dark reverberation of his trench, he suddenly realized that his voice training had covered only a very narrow range of the human expression, only the polite, proper, and pretty sounds. Concert singing was merely a tea party and excluded most of what was real. The man pledged to himself then that if he survived to sing again, he would take off the white gloves and grab hold of life with his bare hands. He did survive, and he kept his word. His work has evolved into the AngelBeasts, which still continues his quest.

When Phillipe found the AngelBeasts, he discovered a home for his dispossessed spirit. As much as I find him relentless and abrasive in everyday life, to watch him in a workshop is stirring: his one finger on the toggle, steering his electric wheelchair in swoops and staggers around the floor of the dance studio, his image multiplied by the walls of mirrors, his long, dark hair trailing him like a comet's tail, his stumps waving, his voice shrieking and growling. He looks like the very essence of life, a person trimmed down to the bare essentials, clipped as close to the heart as you could get without destroying it. The voice is the key, not only to manifest the most secret self, but also to discover it; not to create a sound, but to unleash it at any cost, no matter what it reveals.

There are about fifteen or twenty men and women, old and young. The leader might divide them in half and tell one group, "Be sweet," and the other, "Be foul." And the first group will begin the sweetest noises they know and the sweetest expressions, and they'll sway and stretch, addressing each other or the others or the heavens. The other group will crouch and growl and sneer, stamping and clawing. The leader, gesturing with arms and face and voice, will play them like an organ, bringing the foulness down to a hiss and the sweetness up and up until there are tears, an agony of sweetness, exquisite to the point of pain, and then the foulness up like a storm, rolling over and over, filling the room, dancing like devils delighting in doom. It is thrilling to watch them. Cleansing. Even though I've never had the nerve to join in.

Logic says that I can do anything they can, that I could step out on the floor and become one of them. And Phillipe, eager for defectors, for lapsed rationalists who will come into the hills and take up arms with him, has invited me so many times. But I hear a voice in my head that weakens my knees, so I never stand when Phillipe beckons. The voice that threatens me says, "This will break you!" I suppose I fear that to be really myself is more than I could stand and more than anyone could tolerate from me, that I must live as I do: closed in, shut down, folded up because there is actually no choice. So far the voice has been convincing. I live in a way that takes it so totally into account, I rarely even hear it. It is as if I, too, have some pinched nerve that has led to some deep incapacity, some atrophy of vital responsiveness. Or as though, rather than dismissing him as I had thought, I've absorbed some killing lesson from my father.

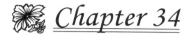 # Chapter 34

Margaret no longer hurries to meet me. When she does arrive, and I see the flash of her thin silhouette slipping through the door, and she lies beside me, a breath in the dark, and when she finally kisses me, she does so with prim lips and tight shoulders. She is not ready. She is not certain. She feels vague in my arms. I feel lonely in hers. The message from her hands is troubling and equivocal. Even though we both wait for these moments, now we always struggle first.

All this began on my birthday. I understand what's wrong, but not what to do about it. Margaret is hurt. She feels I've failed her by not sweeping her away to my room. She's not sure I really love her; in fact, she believes I can't really love her if I'm willing to let her continue living with Adam. I've told her again and again that I do love her, and that it is, in fact, because I love her so very much that I'm not willing to jeopardize our relationship by acting foolishly. I've showed her a copy of my application to the Housing Authority and my number on the list. I try to joke with her. I ask if she would like me to go out and murder several thousand people so we can get an apartment sooner. Margaret is not amused. From her point of view, not being loved is nothing to laugh about. After weeks of this, I find myself starting to feel resentful. I don't like having my love dismissed just because I'm not willing to do what she wants, and the way she holds herself back from me hurts.

Today I've been waiting for two hours, and still no Margaret. I wonder if this delay is necessary or if it's punishment for my bad behavior. I think about going home, but I don't; I want to see her. When she finally arrives, she's sullen, and the space between us feels tense.

"So how have you been?" I say.

"Okay. How about you?"

"I missed you."

"Really. Well, you didn't have to miss me. I was willing to come live with you!"

"Margaret, please don't."

"Don't what?" She says this with an innocent tone, even though I feel sure she knows exactly what I mean.

"You know what. We've been over and over this. I'm doing what I think is best."

She sighs. I pull her down onto the futon beside me. She lets me, but there's no enthusiasm, no reaching out on her part. I can see that if we are going to make love, I will once again have to play the seducer. I put my arms around her and hold her quietly for a while, then begin to stroke her face and lightly kiss her lips. She kisses back a little and holds back a little. It's a delicate balance. She won't reject me completely, but she won't give in to me completely either. I kiss her again, more deeply, testing. When I feel her lips soften, I slip my hand a little way under her blouse. I keep kissing her and move my hand bit by bit toward her breast. I know from experience, if I can reach the summit of this small mound, her defenses will crumble. Just when I'm almost there, Margaret grabs my hand. "Don't," she says.

"Don't what?" I say.

"Don't make love to me like that."

"Like what?" I ask, though I'm pretty sure I know what she means.

"I don't know. Sneaky, like you're trying to get away with something."

"I *was* trying to get away with something," I say, my tone purposefully light and teasing. "I was trying to get away with making love to the woman I love."

"I don't like you touching me that way," she says. She's angry, accusatory, and despite my determination not to, I feel myself starting to get defensive.

"I'm beginning to wonder if you like me touching you at all. What exactly do you want me to do?"

"I want you to touch me like you love me."

"I do love you!"

"Then make me feel it."

"I'm not sure I can. I tell you I love you, and you don't believe me. You wouldn't believe me no matter how I touched you."

"I don't know. Maybe you're right."

I make myself take a couple of deep breaths. "Sweetheart, please try to trust me."

"It seems like it'll be so long. And I don't like deceiving Adam this way. It's not right."

I can't argue with this, but still, taking Margaret from her luxurious big flat and trying to live with her in my little room seems like a bad mistake, one that could mean the end of everything. "I'm sorry," I say. "I know how you feel. I don't like deceiving him either." We lie quietly for a while. Then I feel Margaret slip her hand into mine, a signal, I realize, that she'll now allow me to make love to her. But I'm not sure I can. I feel nervous, afraid I won't touch her the way she wants to be touched. Of course, I realize that in part she's being critical because she's angry and hurt. But it isn't just that. She has a point. Things have changed. Now that Margaret is holding back, I've gone back to the kind of lovemaking I know most about. This kind of lovemaking is strategic and as mindless and relentless as some smart bomb. It aims to render my "lover" helpless, to overwhelm her resistance and take pleasure, even if it's not freely given. Its roots go back to my troubled childhood.

I take Margaret in my arms and hold her. "Sweetheart," I say, "let's not make love today. I want to think about what you said, you know, about the way I touch you."

"Okay," she says. We fall silent, and I feel as though the train in which I've been riding has derailed and is hurtling through space.

"So how's your work been going?" Margaret says.

"Okay. Good," I say. We continue like that for a while, making small talk. Then Margaret leaves, and I go back to work, but I have a sick feeling in the pit of my stomach. This is the first time we've ever gotten together and not made love.

Chapter 35

It's past midnight. I can't sleep. I've been thinking about Margaret's objection regarding how I touch her. Unfortunately, I understand what she means only too well. The bad way, the old way, was there from the beginning, even before I was caught and punished for playing doctor under the stairs. It's related to my preverbal intuition that sex was a forbidden pleasure, that it was dirty. Like sugar-coated candy dropped on the sidewalk, sex glistened alluringly, yet everyone skirted around it like it didn't exist.

By the time I was ten, I had read a marriage manual and the more than five hundred pages of *The Complete Illustrated Encyclopedia of Sexual Fact*, both of which I had borrowed surreptitiously from a high shelf in my aunt's closet (I had developed an uncanny sense for where sex might hide itself), and a book of Chinese erotic stories, supposedly more than a thousand years old, which preferred the dark space under my father's bed. I kept my sexual explorations completely secret from Adam, since by that time he had firmly established himself as the "good" son, and I thought he'd disdain my prurient interests, or even use them to make me feel worse about myself. So while Adam was off earning merit badges at the Boy Scouts, I was hiding in closets reading forbidden books by flashlight. I could explain in detail the "right of the first night" (a medieval lord's claim to the first intercourse with all the peasant brides on his estate) and clitoral circumcision and Kraft-Ebbing's anecdotal research into the aphrodisiac qualities of underarm sweat. Nonetheless, when it came to the simple, everyday reality of sex, there was an anxious void. For some reason, my mind refused to close that gap, to visualize how male and female actually came together and what they then did. Just realizing that it really did happen somehow was enough to overload all my circuits.

When I finally stumbled onto masturbation at the age of eleven, I wasn't surprised. All of my life I'd been receiving reflected signals, like radar, so I knew something was out there; and by the size and intensity of those beeps, I knew it had to be something great and terrible. And it was. The first few times I exploded into orgasm my heart stopped. I really thought it might kill me, and yet I never turned back. I couldn't. But I felt terribly guilty. Masturbation became a horrendous secret, as if while fooling with my chemistry set, I had accidentally discovered some terrible explosive. It was so forbidden, I never considered talking to anyone about it. And since it wasn't something I wanted to do in our bedroom, where Adam could walk in at any moment, I locked myself in the bathroom for this experience, and that cold, tiled privacy, and the associations with excrement and cleaning up, unavoidably stained my sense of my sexual self.

For all I know every child in my classroom was a similar little self-contained reactor, supercharged with secret energy, volatile with guilt and self-consciousness, and hyper alert to any sexual signal that might confirm that he or she wasn't alone in the universe. Perhaps, but I couldn't see it. I felt as if I was the only one, some secret freak, not immediately recognizable from the outside, but with access to dark powers that suggested some unwholesome deviance from the right and normal ways of growing up.

When I think about it now, I feel sad. It seems so natural that, as a lonely child, I would give myself whatever solace I could. But at the time, having no such capacity to be sympathetic with myself, my obsession with masturbation filled me with shame.

Then there was the incident with Miss Murray in the seventh grade. Miss Murray taught math. She was a gangly woman in her mid-forties who was always dropping her chalk or knocking things off her desk. But she redeemed herself with a talent for sarcasm. It was a tool that could be used offensively to make you ridiculous and laughed at by the others or affectionately, teasingly, so that you blushed with self-conscious pleasure at being singled out for torment. We could have ridiculed her for her awkwardness, but we didn't; she had our attention and respect. She was protected by our affirmation that she was a "character."

Above all, one thing set Miss Murray apart from all the other teachers: she touched us. As she passed down the aisles during the silence of an exam, any one of us might feel a comforting pat on the head. What a fine signal that her tests were merely tests and not the Day of

Judgment come to deal with the ungodly. And as we filed out of her room after a class, she would stand in the narrow doorway, so we had to brush past her. She might have a few words of approval or a warning about our work, and she would pat some of us on the shoulder, rumple some hair, and every now and then grab someone's head in the crook of her arm and give it a quick hug. It felt mildly embarrassing, too babyish, and a bit disrespectful for people of our advanced age, but it was tolerable. She was after all a "character," so no one complained.

And then one day I suddenly saw it differently. She hugged only the boys. And she pressed their heads to her chest. I had never questioned this before. I had automatically accepted the idea that girls were innately more dignified, and it would not have been permissible to fuss with them in this way. But now it occurred to me that maybe this had less to do with dignity than with sex, that brief contact between the boys and her breasts. I had no way of knowing if sexual titillation actually had anything at all to do with it, but once I began to think of it that way, this small, affectionate gesture became supercharged, breathless, overwhelming in its implications. Sex was happening right in my classroom, and sometimes it was even happening to me.

I had never seen sex before. Movies didn't count; they were obviously pretend. In fact, we had it from some vague but irrefutable authority that movie stars secretly slipped a hand between their faces before they kissed so they didn't have to share germs with strangers. So when I got it into my head that Miss Murray was being covertly sexual with the boys in our class, it exposed me to a feverish range of possibilities. I would ask her to tutor me. I would say I really liked her math class, but needed more help to do my best.

My fantasies weren't very cooperative, and even in my own mind, she looked incredulous when I said I liked math, which was a transparent lie, or when I said I wanted to do extra work. In my imagination, I tried to find a way around her skepticism, but I never could. In the end, my solution amounted to pure courage: I would stand there and insist, all the while knowing full well she disbelieved me, until she acquiesced. And then I needed double courage—no, at least triple— because when she finally offered, despite her doubts, to stay with me for a few minutes after class, I would have to say, "No, couldn't we go somewhere more private?"

"Couldn't we go somewhere more private?" Even now when I repeat those words, I can call up some of the thrilling audacity of being eleven years old and plotting to seduce my math teacher. And knowing how profoundly naive and frightened I was, I'm amazed I could, nonetheless, sense the basic structure of seduction, as if it's inherent, an instinct in its own right, independent of understanding, just as an infant knows how to suckle without having the faintest concept of nutrition. "Couldn't we go…" In those days, just thinking those words was enough to send me racing to the bathroom, where I would lock the door and risk my life.

My plan was that she would invite me to her home. I had once heard that Miss Murray lived with her mother, but in my daydreams, the older woman was never around. I had a mental picture of her residence. She had a place remarkably similar to the last apartment we had lived in. Her couch was also familiar, almost identical to our old one. My imagination was evidently so strained by the possibilities of our drama that I had little energy left for anything new and interesting in the way of stage settings.

And what might happen when we were finally at her home alone on the couch, collaborating in the obvious fiction that I wanted to learn more math? The ultimate in bad sex: something so intense it was frightening, so forbidden it was delicious, so pent up it was a colossal relief.

I'm not sure if I actually meant to go ahead with this scheme, or if by fantasizing so intensely and repeatedly, I lost the contours of reality and simply drifted forward, just as if I was moving through another daydream. But the next thing that happened was that I touched Miss Murray.

One day, when we were filing out of her class, running her gauntlet, I could see from the activity up ahead that she was in a hugging mood. So when I came alongside her in the doorway, I made a motion with my head, partly a ducking down and partly a moving toward her, putting myself more within reach and reacting as I would if she had already hugged me. And she did. It felt as if I had drawn her to me, provoked her to reach out reflexively to the head that bobbed up in front of her. And when she squeezed me briefly against her, before I lost my nerve and while we were still in a close if sideways embrace, I pressed the back of my hand between her legs and up until it stopped against something spongy, something rounded and resilient. No one could see. It was possibly an accident; when she had pulled me suddenly against her, perhaps I had lost my balance and moved my arm only to right myself. But I looked up at her face, and that could be no accident. Her mouth opened, and her eyes went wide. I had surprised her, and she had seen me look up to measure that. And then the instant was over, and I walked down the hall. When I looked back once, she was still watching me.

You must realize what this did to me. There was nothing in my entire life to match it for significance. I replayed that brief moment over and over in my head, keeping myself in a perpetual sexual frenzy. In her class, I tried to behave in a way that seemed normal, but I smoldered, like one of those underground fires that starts in a coal mine and burns out of control. I think this must have been visible to her in some dark smokiness I couldn't completely wipe from my eyes. I didn't notice any change in her behavior, nothing I could take as an acknowledgment, but whenever she looked at me, I felt a crackle of current jump between us.

One day I was late for school, and when I arrived at math class, the room was empty except for Miss Murray. The other students had gone off on a field trip, which I hadn't known about because I'd been out sick for several days. She asked me if I was feeling better and how my school work was going, and I gossiped with her about my classes, the first time I'd ever talked with a teacher the way I talked with my friends. I sat down on top of a desk in the front row, and after a few minutes, she got up, came around her large oak desk, and sat opposite me, but only a foot away. For some reason, it was harder for me to talk that way, and where originally I'd felt relaxed and comfortable, now I strained and stumbled. After another minute, she sat next to me, on the same student desk, and put her arm around me. Now I couldn't talk at all. I sat stiffly and looked straight ahead. "It's all right," she assured me softly and stroked my shoulder. But for some reason it wasn't, and I got up and moved to the next desk and sat there alone. I could feel her looking at me, but I couldn't look directly back. After a minute, she sighed and returned to the work she'd been doing at her desk.

That was the end of my first sexual encounter. It's significant to me now for a number of reasons. I think it's remarkable that she risked so much. I could have destroyed her, either out of some childish frustration or by a few bragging words to my classmates. I never did. I remained steadfastly loyal to her, but could she really have been able to predict that?

I regret to this day that I couldn't respond to her. I think the fear that overwhelmed me was a basic part of bad sex, which is inherently full of conflict. I didn't love her; I was propelled by intense curiosity and by the excitement of an adventure I couldn't yet understand. But I think it's possible that if I could have let her initiate me, I might have come to love her, and she might have loved me. We both needed that; I'm sure of it. And it could have been a wonderful turning point in my life.

Ironically, that may have been what stopped me. Even then I realized she was lonely and that she offered the possibility of real and gentle contact. I felt so lonely too, cut off from other people by my belief in my oddness and my badness. I don't think it was the possibility of sex that frightened me that day; I think it was more the sense that if I were cared for and treated tenderly, I would feel intensely vulnerable, and the pain I had dealt with by ignoring it might be released. I might cry; I might even reveal how needy and lost I felt, how hungry I was for comforting. And since I was trying so hard to grow up and be a man, and believed I was failing so miserably, such behavior was unthinkable, a terrible threat rather than a promise of nourishment.

So I lost a chance, very early on, to take a different path. I went on to have bad sex for most of my life: to think that the sweaty torment of sneaking into a friend's apartment to screw with his wife was the real excitement of sex itself; to work with numb, clumsy hands, full of tricky little tricks and no real meaning, efficient hands obsessed with production quotas; to enjoy getting a woman to do things we both thought were vile so there was the thrill of piercing our reluctance, even though we sometimes felt sickened afterward and glad to be away from each other once it was done. I sought sexual accomplices, not lovers, and the thought of sex with someone I really liked seemed bland, impractical, disconnected from the only source of power I understood.

With Margaret, in the beginning, I felt released from all this, as if by grace. What happened between us then was so extraordinary it defied classification. But slowly, in the absence of those miraculous experiences, and especially once Margaret's reluctance made seduction necessary, "bad sex" crept back in. When Margaret said she didn't want me to touch her "that way," I felt like a kid caught with my hand in the cookie jar. She was right; I hadn't been touching her with love (though I do love her). I had been playing out a calculated strategy to break down her defenses and get what I wanted. No, more than wanted, what I desperately needed. Because ever since the first time I actually made love my last year of high school, I've felt a kind of desperation with regard to sex, as though sex is a kind of nourishment I must have or die.

I'm puzzled and I'm worried. The old way, the bad way is back. I know that there's something better because I actually experienced it with Margaret. But since it came of its own and went the same way, how do I get it back?

🌺 *Chapter 36*

Amy has missed a long string of sessions. There's no suicide watch yet, because each week she cancels a full day in advance. Her tone is curt, which I choose to interpret as vigor; she is still far from the limp hopelessness, which in her would signal the greatest danger. When I call my service, I find her anonymous messages: "Just tell him, no way." Of course I hold her hour open. And when she finally does come in, I understand why her health and her mood have declined so seriously. Amy is once more estranged from Appoppa. Once again, she's wrapped in self-protective bitterness. She utters not a single word of grief; she will not even admit she's suffered a loss. If life could snatch away what she wants so soon after she finally gets it, then life is a bully, and she knows that bullies must never be appeased.

Amy will not consider the possibility that she has any part in creating these fights with Appoppa, or that she may have something to contribute to the healing of them. She's too hurt. So instead of using this as an opportunity to understand more about herself, she focuses on him. Once again he is only "thoughtless and self-centered, a profoundly hopeless example of a human being." There are no more poems to show me. And they are clearly not making love. But they still live together; she certainly would have mentioned it if they did not. The time has passed when either of them could lightly walk away. They've been married by her disease.

The only odd note in the session comes when Amy stares at me silently for a moment, reminding me of the measuring and testing of our very first days together. "Do you like clowns?" she asks. Warned by her eyes, I am particularly cautious. "If you're referring to the article in the paper today, I saw it. What about the clowns?" It is not my style to play the classical therapist, to answer every question with a question, but this is a hard time in my life, and I'm not at my best.

According to today's *Times,* a group of people dressed as clowns crowded into a subway car at rush hour, silent and deliberately mysterious. It seems obvious they're the same people Margaret was so excited about a few months ago. Amy wants something from me, and since I'm not clever enough to understand what it is, I dodge her with a clumsiness uncharacteristic of our relationship. Of course she sees this; I can tell from the scornful flicker of her eyes. She immediately abandons whatever she was after and goes back to trashing Appoppa.

I am depressed by this lovelessness between Amy and Appoppa, but even more I'm depressed by my own. Strangely, Amy and I seem to be living in tandem. When she first experienced Appoppa as a god, Margaret was my goddess. No longer. Things have continued to deteriorate between us. At first I managed to be patient and reassuring. But Margaret's behavior toward me became more and more intolerable, wearing my patience so thin it finally broke. I felt hurt by the way she held herself back while I continued to give myself completely. And I hated the way she'd insist I didn't love her and was just "using her for sex."

Lately I've started finding fault with her, and over the most ridiculous things. To be embarrassingly specific, I can't bear the way she washes dishes. I feel like a complete fool, but regardless, watching her pour quantities of detergent and hot water down the drain, when a drop or two on a scrubbing pad would do, when we all know that conservation is so important, irritates me. And when I express my irritation over her wasteful dishwashing, or about the way she interrupts me before I have a chance to finish my sentence, or how she leaves sticky stuff all over the counter tops at my mother's, Margaret—shy, pale, contained Margaret—fires back at me angrily, letting me know that I haven't the right to tell her how to live.

Our quarreling has to be the bitterest joke possible. Even in the midst of my self-justifying irritation, I hate what I'm doing. Nonetheless, I pick at her as if she has faults that reflect badly on me. I seem to be acting out a caricature of a bad marriage.

Since lately there has been little warmth or tenderness in our feelings, we see no need to hide them. We argue openly in public. Adam is amused by our squabbling. He pulls a long face, with wide, amazed eyes and looks from one of us to the other and then to any visitors, "What's this? Please, children, please. Play nicely now."

In the quiet of my room when I reexamine my nagging, my insolence seems amazing. I see that my need to complain comes first, and the pretexts follow. I know that far beneath this foolishness is something I don't understand. Unfortunately my expertise as a therapist hasn't helped me see what it is, and my sincere desire to act differently hasn't enabled me to control my behavior. Time and time again my irritation gets the better of me. So I'm chagrined when I find myself thinking that Amy is largely responsible for her own misery. Physician, heal thyself.

Chapter 37

This city is never silent. Sometimes it's reasonably quiet, and I can hear nothing more than the humming vibrations of the great pumps and the giant fans, sounds that are conducted for miles through pipes and girders, as well as the occasional subliminal groan of something deeply shifting, something that should be solid but perhaps isn't completely. But the city is never absorbent enough to suck the static from my head and smooth the wrinkles from my brain. I imagine people used to be soothed by nature, although since my father never actually said any such thing, perhaps this is just an idealization. Still, there must be some reason why he's always crying in my dreams. I wonder what he would think of my life if he could see it now.

In such an environment, it's hardly surprising that we struggle with sleep. I have a new client, a civil-service architect, who's as haggard as I am. (I've asked her about the unsteadiness I sometimes feel, as if the city shuddered from secret dreads, and she assures me that these are only "harmonics," one area vibrating in sympathy with another, and that everything is as solid as it needs to be.) She has come to me because she has lucid nightmares. In her sleep, she compulsively adds more dark passageways to the city. Then terrible creatures come and chase her through the hallways and up the stairways of her imagination. Her only escape is suicide, to throw herself down some elevator shaft she has created. But even though this wakes her and saves her, she finds this solution terrifying; she can never be completely certain she's dreaming. What if one time the grotesqueness she fled from wasn't a dream?

How can I quiet her fears and let her sleep? Her weariness and talk of suicide remind me of Amy. Once again, Amy has missed several sessions in a row. I worry about her. I know that any one of these absences could turn out to be permanent. But I can't just call her up any more than my dentist could call me because he missed me and felt like doing a little work on my teeth. But I do miss her, her endless jumble of problems, the vividness of her reactions. Her life, less than half lived, seems more interesting than mine at full strength. I wonder if my patients ever guess how much I get from them.

When I finish with my last client, I realize I can't go back to my room yet, but I don't know where else to go. I stop at Felicia's and order a beer and a vegetarian burrito. (Rumors I've heard about how we get our meat are beginning to make me gag.) The beer comes first, and it goes right to my brain. I look at the people around me. There's a woman in front of me, bisected by the man she is with. On one side of his head, I can see her hair, and it's smooth and young; on the other side of his head, her hands hold each other on the table, and they are old and red. I can't see her face. It seems important to know if she is young or old and how her hands and her hair came to be together. I'm a little drunk by the time the burrito comes, and I feel a wave of gratitude that someone in the kitchen has put in so many mushrooms. I like mushrooms; they're one of the few vegetables that are not reconstituted, since we can grow them here in the dark. Some benevolent soul has placed an extra handful of these fresh treats in my burrito. Then the beer-glow begins to fade, and I'm tired and sad again.

I've finally had to admit to myself just how much things have changed between Margaret and me, and every time I think of this, I feel heartsick. My name is still on the waiting list for an apartment, but I now doubt we'll ever live together. My list of Margaret's faults has grown. I find her defensive, so defensive I wonder how Adam has put up with her all these years. If I have a complaint, instead of dealing with it, she counterattacks. She claims she has every right to do this because I'm not talking to her "nicely." No matter how angry and frustrated I feel, she insists I follow her rules of talking etiquette. If I don't meet her standards, if my tone is not correct, if I raise my voice, if I use what she calls "blaming words," she won't listen; she doesn't, in fact, feel any obligation to listen, because she "won't put up with being mistreated." This leaves me feeling unheard and uncared for; she's obviously far more interested in how I talk than in under-standing and alleviating the pain I'm feeling. Beyond this, Margaret interrupts me constantly, which I hate. In addition, she will not admit to having said things I know very well she did say.

Most of the time lately, Margaret is sullen and withdrawn. Yet when we make love, she wants me to feel loving toward her, not just sexual. So in addition to the talking standards, she has another set of standards by which she judges whether I am touching her lovingly or not. If she feels I'm not touching her in a sufficiently loving way, she'll suddenly pull away, leaving me feeling like a teenager whose date has taken him to the brink but won't go all the way. And while she may correctly sense that my heart is not filled with love, how could it be, given what's been going on between us?

We still meet, of course. For some reason, neither of us is ready to give up. But our meetings are infrequent, and I don't think either of us really looks forward to them. I no longer buy candles or flowers, nor do we bother with music. After we've made love or not made love, depending on how things have gone, we lie on our backs, facing up, trying not to touch, though the space is so narrow that that's not completely possible. Without candles it's completely dark, but I can tell by the point of her elbow that Margaret has her arms crossed over her chest, the same defensive gesture she made the first time we made love, only now she is protecting more than her breasts.

We lie there and ask each other, "What's the point? Why do we do this?" We feel each other's shoulders shrug, conceding nothing. There are long silences in which we fire off sighs like artillery shells, exhalations that insist, I am the one who has been hurt and misused. No, it is I. Sometimes it strikes me as comic how we struggle for the lowest position, each of us wanting to be the one who is more injured and less to blame.

A year ago we were explorers of the cosmos. Now I wonder how I could have sighed over her, how I could have dreamed that she would be the first and only person to truly know and love me.

Chapter 38

Since my dream of love has evaporated, I'm depressed; there's no doubt about that. This morning that annoying entity inside who seems to think he's my therapist asked me to come up with an image to represent the current state of my life. (I sometimes ask my clients to come up with an image that represents their childhood, a troublesome feeling, a particular person or relationship, any aspect of their life I want to bring into sharper focus.)

For a while when I was a kid, before it escaped to God knows where in this skyless city, Adam and I owned a parakeet. I was squeamish as a child, and I hated cleaning out the cage. (I've even wondered if I might have let the bird escape "accidentally on purpose," just to get out of this loathsome job.) The image my mind chose to represent the current state of my life was the bottom of a birdcage.

At times like these I'm thankful for my profession. Therapy is the most absorbing work imaginable, endless storytelling, a constant sideshow, wonders and horrors far beyond what I could ever imagine on my own. For instance, that this slight, balding man with the gray, plastic-framed eyeglasses and the overly polite voice was once a flaming transvestite, a leader of orgies, a speed freak who was repeatedly jailed for outrageous behavior. Or that this earnest young fellow is the devoted lover of a famous woman politician more than twice his age. Or that this young woman's mother repeatedly tried to drown her in the bathtub. They are all seeking peace, they are all seeking love, and it touches me how trusting and earnest they are, and how much faith they seem to have that I can help them. If I'm unhappy when I come to my office, after hours of concentrated effort, I often leave feeling much better.

Today I'm seeing Amy for the first time in several months, and I'm very much looking forward to that. But when she arrives, I'm shocked to see how radically she's changed. She's as pale as a saint. I don't think it suits her, and I don't like the hint of phosphorescence in her skin, a kind of light that suggests dampness and decay. Poor little Amy. Or perhaps more poignantly, poor big Amy, because it is more unnerving to see the mighty fall than the meek.

"It's strange," she says, making my skin crawl with her new softness, "but nothing bothers me much lately. I used to be so afraid of vomiting, but I'm not anymore." She's found herself a pretty little blouse, pale blue, with a label stitched on the outside of the pocket: "Good Girls."

"You never liked to feel out of control," I say.

"No. I never wanted anyone to see me helpless. But Appoppa sees me, and he mops up after me. He's really kind." I add her appreciation of Appoppa to the list of things that distresses me about her.

"Amy, why are you throwing up so much?"

"I don't know. Probably one of the new medications they're giving me." Add that to the list: no diatribe against the doctors.

"Have you gotten the results of your tests yet?"

"No, I'm not interested."

I sigh. Blood seeping from various places, lumps here and there, coughing up earth tones in her phlegm, all this in addition to the everyday transitory paralyses, stabbing pains, weaknesses, and yet she has no interest in her tests.

"Don't you see?" she continues. "It's not what really matters."

"How do you mean that, Amy?"

"There's something about being this sick that is actually peaceful. I've been fighting all my life. And now…finally…enough." She sits there glowing pale green. It's as if I've awakened in the middle of the night and faced the dial of my clock and wondered, "Is it really that late?" Yes, it really is. Death is with us. It leaves a smudge on the wall as it hovers behind her. The ultimately uncompromising parent has decided it's time for her to go to bed, and nothing either of us can say will alter that judgment.

She hugs me as she leaves, and that's it, after all these many months of talk.

Chapter 39

Then the inevitable happened. Margaret phoned and said she wanted to meet. When she entered the closet, she snapped on the light. I scrambled to my feet from where I'd been lying on the futon. We stood for a moment, looking at each other in the unaccustomed brightness. Then Margaret made her announcement. "I won't be coming here anymore. What we've been doing is wrong, and it's not working."

Even though I'd been expecting this for some time, the words hit like a knee to the groin. But what could I say? I couldn't beg her to change her mind. I knew she was right. Things hadn't worked out the way we'd hoped. For a long time now, we'd been making each other miserable.

"Oh, Margaret…" I said, and then I just stood there, not knowing what to say. I didn't feel angry anymore, just sad. I wondered how we could have made such a mess of something that once had been so wonderful. "I'm sorry," I finally said. "I'm sorry things couldn't have been different."

"So am I. But no harm done. We'll just go back to the way things were. I don't think anyone even suspected."

No harm done? I wasn't so sure. To me, our failure felt like yet another blow to my heart. I was ending another relationship. (What number was this? I'd lost track.) I had to wonder if it would ever be any different.

"No," I said. "I don't think anyone ever suspected. That's good anyway."

"Do you think we can forgive each other?" Margaret said, looking wistful yet self-possessed, a woman who'd thought things through and then done what was sensible and right.

"I've already forgiven you," I said. "I've more than forgiven you. I really care about you, Margaret. And now that we won't be locked in some foolish struggle, it'll be like before. We'll be friends. We'll cut articles out of newspapers and commiserate about corruption and injustice." Tears welled up in Margaret's eyes. I had an impulse to take her in my arms, but I stopped myself. That would only have made things harder, and the truth was I no longer had any faith that she and I could be good for each other. Even though it hurt, I wanted it to be over, and I was glad that she had been the one to make the decision.

Since there was nothing more to be said, we said nothing. We stood for a long moment, trying to come to terms with what was happening and surrender our tarnished hopes and dreams. Then Margaret said, "Well, I have to be going." She carefully checked the hall, as she always did, for passersby, and slipped out the door.

"Good-bye, Margaret," I said, but by the time I said it, she was already halfway down the hall.

Chapter 40

Life after Margaret is grim, but I'm handling it. When I went to brunch on Sunday, Margaret greeted me pleasantly, even warmly. To reassure her I was going to keep my part of the bargain, I'd brought a newspaper article. It described a new bill introduced by the Liberty Party, which made the punishment for defacing a city flag expulsion from New York. Exile, in other words. Banishment. History must be some kind of circle. We live in a walled city-state, and now we're about to return to a form of punishment commonly used by ancient civilizations. Back then to be cast out was a fate so terrible some people committed suicide rather than endure it. I wonder, would it be a tragedy to be forced to leave New York or a blessing, especially now that I no longer have Margaret?

Actually, I do have Margaret, but it's the old Margaret, the one who's married to my brother. When I showed her my article, she responded the way she always had. "How dare they! Who do they think they are! I wish we could *do* something about them!" (But of course we knew we couldn't do anything. Ever since the Encapsulation had succeeded in protecting us not only from terrorists but from rising waters and deadly epidemics as well, the Liberty Party had won every election with ease. Now, more often than not, no one even bothers to oppose them.)

I've been avoiding Carl and Phillipe, especially Phillipe who will, if he gets the chance, poke at me and make jokes about how I had finally found "the love that was going to last forever." Carl, of course, will be more circumspect; he'll merely probe in his soft, gray flannel way in the hope that we might catch a fleeting glimpse of my unconscious mind. I don't want either, so I stay in my room and occupy myself with my art books.

Sometimes I spend hours browsing through paintings. There are so many interesting things to see: men in top hats and women with bustles and parasols walking arm in arm, gazing at the Seine flowing blue and bright in the sunshine. If these paintings are to be believed, there was once a time when people actually glided across snowy landscapes in horse drawn sleighs and bathed outside in streams.

Of course, I do believe them; who could doubt the precision of Seurat? But it's more as if the painter is depicting a fantasy world than something real. Deep down I think we New Yorkers naturally assume, "Everyone has always lived like us. Our ways are the real and inevitable ones."

I still sometimes wonder what it would be like to live outside. I can't actually believe that the Great Plains, the Rocky Mountains, or the Pacific Northwest are real in the same way our rooms and corridors are real. (This is particularly so, I think, due to a law passed ten years ago by the Liberty Party forbidding the showing of positive pictorial representations of the outside world on TV or in movies.) If I try to imagine myself actually being in one of these far-off places, I feel a little queasy.

Chapter 41

My role as a therapist is to help people live happier lives. But what about me? Am I happy? Following the demise of my relationship with Margaret, not very. There's a heaviness in my chest. It feels very old and never seems to go away. I have no idea why. If I were my client, I'd wonder if I hadn't suffered some terrible loss in my early childhood, but as far as I know, I never even had a pet die.

My investigations regarding my father were put on hold during the Margaret era. I was deliciously happy, so none of that mattered. Now, once again I've dreamt of my father, a turbulent, scary dream, the meaning of which is a mystery to me. In my dream, it's night and my father is feverishly piling up baked goods: bagels, bialys, loaves of bread, cinnamon sticks, every wonderful thing he used to put on our breakfast table. He makes a huge mound and then, like some crazed arsonist, pours gasoline over it and throws a match into the middle. It flares up into a great, blazing bonfire. Strange, dancing shadows are reflected on my father's face. I'm standing a little way off watching everything, but either my father doesn't know I'm there, or he's ignoring me. I feel small and lonely and frightened. These feelings have lingered, weighing me down for the better part of the day.

Again, I feel sure that there's some mystery regarding my father I've never been able to unravel. I've avoided talking to my mother about this, because I know if she suspected I was unhappy, she'd worry over me and nag me to let her bring home antidepressant medication from her doctor's office. But after this dream, I've decided I have to question her. She was there after all. She knew my father long before I did, and she knew me before I was old enough to really know myself. I won't mention the dream or my unhappiness.

I find my mother, as usual, in her kitchen. After she's fed me dinner and is washing up the dishes, I start at the periphery. I ask her if she knows whether my father really went to the theater as often as he claimed and where he got the money if he did. She doesn't. Then, since I can't think of any way to lead up to it, I come right out with it.

"Ma," I say, "when I was little, did I ever lose anything or anyone important?"

"Yes, of course, you did," she replies without hesitation.

"I did?" She seems to feel that this is a topic we should discuss face-to-face, so she dries her hands and sits down beside me.

"You certainly did. You lost something very precious." Her eyes look tragic, and I begin to feel a little crazy. How could I have had such a great loss and not remember anything about it?

"What? What precious thing did I lose?'

"Your father, of course."

"Ma, I don't mean that. I mean before Pop died, long before, when I was very young."

"This was long before. You didn't lose him because he died, you lost him because he went back to work at the bakery."

"What do you mean? I thought Pop always worked at the bakery."

"You don't remember? I'm surprised. You were four years old. I remember things from when I was four, even younger than that, I remember."

"Well, I don't remember. Where was Pop working?"

"When you were born, he was working in an appliance factory. As a foreman. People looked up to him. He made a decent living. He worked normal hours like a human being, and we were happy. You were happy." She gives me a meaningful look. "You know the way you're always telling those stories your father told you when you were a boy? Why do you think you do that? It's been more than thirty years since he told those stories. You know what I think? I think you're trying to mend a quarrel you had with him when you were a little boy. And you don't even know it, do you?"

"Ma, please, just tell me what happened. I need to know."

"Well, you and Adam were always different. And right from the beginning there was a special way you loved your father. If you were crying and he'd pick you up, you'd get quiet. So he'd take you up a lot. Then he started singing to you. I don't know how it started, but you loved it. You'd look up into his eyes, or you'd watch his mouth.

You were just a tiny little thing; you couldn't even hold your head up. He'd sing, 'Little Sir Echo, how do you do?' Or, 'There'll be blue birds over the white cliffs of Dover.' Your father didn't know many songs. Before he sang to you, I never heard him sing, because the man certainly didn't have a singing voice. When he was in high school and had to be in the choir, the director told him it would be all right if he just moved his mouth. After he stopped singing to you, I never heard him sing again."

I struggle to picture this: my father holding a little baby, me, and singing off-key about bluebirds. "Why did he stop?"

"It was a crazy thing. It certainly made me crazy. And the more I tried to fix it, the worse it got. It started, as I said, when your father left the factory and went back to the family bakery."

"But why did he do that? Pop always hated the bakery."

"I don't know. He never should've done it. But after a while his family began to nag at him. They were still together in the bakery, and they wanted him back. Why, I don't know. They told him there was no future in what he was doing, and that now that he had a family to take care of, not just himself, he needed something secure. Maybe they didn't like him being different. Maybe they were insulted that he didn't want to have anything to do with the bakery. I don't know. I argued against them. But I was careful; I didn't want to put myself between him and his family. And they could be right, I thought. But if I'd known what would come of it, I would have fought it with all my strength. Anyway, he went back to the bakery. Right away he knew he'd made a mistake, but now his old job was gone, and he couldn't get it back. He went looking for something else, but there was a slowdown, and nobody was hiring. Then his hearing got worse, and he wasn't so confident anymore. After a while, he gave up. He felt trapped in that bakery for the rest of his life."

"I never knew all this."

"It was awful, but that wasn't the worst part." She shakes her head. "All of a sudden your father wasn't around for you. He worked nights and slept days. He was always tired. He was unhappy. It was a terrible change for you. For years he'd been reading to you every evening. Adam was always restless and would get up after only a few minutes, but you'd sit on his lap like it was your throne while he read aloud to you for half an hour every evening, the first thing after he changed his clothes. Sometimes it would be a children's book, and you two would look at the pictures together and point at things. And sometimes it would be one of his books, whatever he was reading. You looked so peaceful together; it made me so glad. Then, he wasn't there anymore. When he went back to the bakery, he had to work nights and sleep days. You didn't like it, and why should you?"

As she explains, I feel a clenching in my stomach; something is creeping closer and closer, and then it pounces: a ferocious grief, a rage at my father for pulling his lap from under me, for taking away his books and our evening time, the time when he washed me with his voice, like a bear licking its cub.

"You were too young to understand. There was no way we could explain it to you."

But I am understanding. Finally.

"So your way was to act up. Now I realize you were just trying to tell us how unhappy you were. But at the time, it wasn't so clear. Of course, we knew you were upset, but we thought you'd get over it. And we had other problems. Your father kept trying to change jobs and was always failing. And I didn't get to see much of him either. I needed him too. The whole house was upside down with him working nights. And you had spoiled us. You'd been such a happy, easy baby that when you became difficult, we weren't prepared. Maybe we were even a little impatient. I tried. I gave you extra attention. It worked all right with Adam, but it only made you meaner. You needed your father. But when he came to you, you'd run away. Now I see that you wanted him to chase after you. You wanted him to pick you up and make you be his little boy again, to prove he loved you and ignore the things you said. But that wasn't his way. When you were loving him, he was so happy, and when you were angry, he was very hurt. He thought you didn't like him anymore, and he pulled back. And the more he pulled back, the angrier you got. It just got worse and worse. I talked to him, and I talked to you. It didn't do any good."

I remember how furious I used to feel when my mother would tell me how much my father loved me. "It's a lie!" I would scream at her. "If he loved me, he'd tell me, not you." But suddenly I can see how it was, how events beyond either of our control inexorably carried my father and me further and further from one another. I feel overwhelmed by sadness; my stomach clenches even tighter. I'm not willing to cry, not in front of my mother, so I sit silently trying to digest all this, and for a change my mother is quiet as well.

Those wonderful times sitting on his lap could have continued if only he and I had understood. And that would have made my entire life different. I never would have turned to badness as a way of expressing anger and getting attention. And I never would have come to believe that I was bad, bad past redemption.

Of course, my father did talk to me. He told me those stories, trying over and over to contact me after he became too hurt simply to reach out and gather me into his arms. But I refused to listen. In those days, I still felt he had too much to prove to be let off that easily. It all fit. Everything I'd experienced as chaos when I was little now made sense.

"Ma, why didn't you tell me all this? Why didn't you tell me before now?"

My mother looks sad and confused. "Well, I don't know exactly. You were there the whole time. I guess I assumed you knew." Again she looks puzzled. "Or maybe it was that at some point, I just gave up. Accepted there was nothing I could do. And remember, I did try to tell you your father loved you all through your childhood, and you just got mad." A defensive quality has crept into her voice, as though I'm accusing her of not having done enough.

"I understand, Ma. You tried your best. I wouldn't have understood all this. Not until I was grown, and by then it was ancient history. I remember how hard you tried. You tried and tried; it just never worked."

She seems mollified. For this I'm thankful. I desperately need to be alone. Such intense feelings are churning around inside me that once I leave, I barely feel able to negotiate the short distance back to my room.

Chapter 42

When I arrive home and close the door behind me, I feel relieved. Sinking into my easy chair, I focus my eyes on the shadowy wallpaper at the far end of the room. I've never remodeled, so my wallpaper is practically antique, a peach background crowded with repeating patterns of green vines and large, white trumpet flowers, all of it quite faded.

I need to rest. I need to absorb all this. I always believed having the pieces of my puzzle finally fall into place would be a good experience, but now that it's actually happened, I feel sick and dizzy. I need to calm down. To sit quietly for hours, or days. As I stare at the ancient wallpaper, gradually my breathing slows and deepens, and I find myself lost in a strange daydream.

It's as if I'm standing at the doorway of my office watching myself. I see myself in session with some anonymous client who has his back to the door. I'm seated in my armchair, pleasant looking, serious, perfectly routine. This image is so vivid in color and detail, bland as this instant is, it absorbs my complete attention. Spread across the far wall from me, larger than life like a giant billboard, I sit half-facing myself, conducting my daily business.

This whole scene has unfolded before me without my doing anything to make it happen. Suddenly my father is with me. Not in front of me where I can see him, but behind and underneath me, as if I'm very young, and the chair is his lap, and the pillow I'm leaning against is his stomach. My sense of this is so compelling, I feel little and weak, and I'm able to experience how I once trusted my father to hold and protect me. For a moment, I can even smell him. Then his large hand reaches out over my shoulder, as if to turn the page of the book from which he's reading to me. But instead he reaches for my image. It's twelve feet from where I'm sitting to the far wall, but his arm stretches like chewing gum all the way to the other side of the room; his fingers grasp the huge, bright picture of my life by the corner and peel it back. It curls over easily, just like paper, and it's no thicker, nor any more substantial. And behind it? No wallpaper with faded flowers and vines, not even the scaffolding for a billboard…nothing. Behind my life, which I see now has no more depth than a sheet of paper, is absolute emptiness, a cold, whistling void, the feeling of outer space beyond the last star.

I'm crushed. I once visited this same darkness at the peak of my love for Margaret. But then it had been the background for two magnificent spiral nebulae that intermingled and filled the sky with light and beauty. I realize with a stomach-sinking sensation that the whistling emptiness I'm now experiencing is what remains once love is gone. I feel myself groan as the blackness of that void flows into my heart. And then suddenly I know. I know beyond all doubt that I've made a terrible mistake. I've somehow been asleep. I've been unconscious, blind, lost. I've allowed the most precious thing I ever had, or ever will have, to slip through my fingers. I begin to cry. I cry for hours. It's dawn before I finally fall asleep.

When I wake hours later, the image of that awful blackness is still with me. I'm convinced I had a vision. That may sound too exalted for something that could happen to a credible person, but this had an impact that absolutely demands some special word. Perhaps mechanically it was nothing more than a daydream, but this daydream had tremendous pressure behind it, the need to finally face some truth so essential that it erupted with hallucinatory intensity.

Like some poor victim of post-traumatic stress syndrome, I keep reliving my collision with that image over and over. Wherever I go, whatever I do, there it is. It isn't an argument I can debate. It isn't an accusation I can deny. It's a realization. A direct perception. I've been blind, and in my blindness I've destroyed my relationship with Margaret, leaving me with a life as empty as outer space beyond the last star.

I've always been scornful of people who believe it's better to leave some illusions intact because they make life bearable, but then it never occurred to me that I had any illusions. I was a realist, and whether life was pleasant or not, I faced things as they were. Now I see that this view of myself was itself an illusion.

I also believed that my life had purpose and that my work was meaningful. Now I see that one of the main purposes of my life is to keep busy, and one of the meanings of my work is to avoid real contact. Becoming a psychotherapist was a perfect choice, since it allows me to be close to people without taking the ultimate risk of surrendering my heart to anyone in particular. I love all my clients, some more than others, but in the end, I send them all off into the world to live their lives. By its very nature, my profession sets up boundaries, which I now see are quite convenient. I can be close but not too close. To do my job well, I can't become too personally involved.

I've succeeded as a therapist. But outside of that very special kind of relationship, I've failed at love over and over again. In subtle ways, of which I was never consciously aware, I stuck a knife into the heart of anyone who threatened to love me. Now, thanks to my mother showing me how the jagged pieces of my puzzle fit together, I understand why.

I've had an "ah-ha" experience of colossal proportions. I should be delighted. If this had happened to a client, I'd be dancing on air. But given what I've done, I feel nothing but despair. I've destroyed the one thing that could have made me whole and happy, and I'm doubtful I'll ever get it back.

Chapter 43

The next morning when I go back to my office, I do everything in the usual way, but nothing's the same. When I sit with my clients, I can't concentrate. I constantly see the void of my life before me and feel the gut-shock of revelation. When I run into colleagues from neighboring offices, I can't follow what they're saying. Like someone who's been in an accident, I repeatedly hear the screech of the brakes, repeatedly brace myself, and over and over again I feel that terrible thud.

I've had a head-on collision with the truth. Of course I loved Margaret. I never stopped loving her. My refusal to let her live with me only meant I had no confidence she could love me and I lacked the courage to take the chance. I was blinded by fears I didn't even know I had, and so I believed my own oh-so-sensible story about how it would be better to wait until we could get an apartment. The irony of it! It's this kind of unconsciousness I've spent my life trying to help my clients recognize and overcome. With myself I completely missed it. And just like my clients, now that I see the truth, I'd do anything, anything at all, if only I could roll back time and make different choices.

I marvel that Margaret was actually willing to leave her luxurious flat and my well-off brother to live with me in one room. And I refused her. Unbelievable! Now, too late, I can sympathize with her thinking I didn't love her. Surely I would have thought the same had our positions been reversed. I would have been deeply wounded, just as she had been. To offer oneself and be rejected, put off, given excuses, what could be worse?

I long to see Margaret and admit what a fool I've been. I want to explain about how what happened with my father made me afraid to risk loving. Of course, I have to try to get her back! I couldn't live with myself if I didn't. But I'm very afraid that nothing I say will make any difference. After knowing Margaret for as long as I have, I know that once she makes a decision, she rarely goes back on it.

Finally, I finish with my clients and start home. The walk to my room is eight buildings long and up three flights. The most direct path is also the least crowded, but I'm feeling too awful to face that maze of dark, twisty corridors, so I take the longer route, which allows me to walk part of the way along one of the main thoroughfares. These have the largest shops and the most bustle. And the light is so much better. In the regular halls (narrow and oddly-connected passageways constructed from the original apartment houses), city maintenance uses standard fluorescents, and not enough of them. The tubes give off a bluish light, the ceilings are low, and I don't like the damp cave-like atmosphere. In the main corridors, the fluorescents are color balanced, so people and things don't look green. The businesses insisted on it. They found it too difficult to sell their clothing and food when everything looked as though it had been overgrown by fungus. And because the main corridors tend to follow the old streets, they are straighter and wider, with higher ceilings. You have more of a feeling that you can stretch and breathe out there, and people naturally collect in these places. There's always someone I know in the cafés. Sometimes I join a friend, but often I prefer just to sit alone and watch. It gives me a rest from the quiet intensity of my office and the quiet loneliness of my room. I feel shut-in if I shuttle back and forth between room and office without spending any time outside in the corridors. Tonight, however, I keep my head down and look straight ahead. In my current state, having to make small talk with anyone would be excruciating.

Back in my room, I sit in my big chair and stare at the wall, where only last night my devastating vision unfolded. Tonight there's nothing except trumpet vines on faded peach wallpaper. An eerie sense of silence surrounds me. It reminds me of an old-time space movie I saw as a child. In it, the protagonist figured out how to enter an advanced but alien society. The aliens were humane, so they placed their uninvited guest in a room and provided him with all the necessities of life. Like a strange animal carefully placed in its natural habitat, he was to live out his remaining days there. I remember a shot of him sitting at his table eating. The clink of his silverware against his plate in the otherwise soundless room was chilling. My room seems no different. Surely I'll live here alone forever, my footsteps echoing as I cross the room.

I think about how Margaret might at this moment be sitting up in bed across the room from me, reading a book. How I might join her there. How we might read peacefully side by side. How at some point, we might turn off the light and snuggle down in bed together, her body warm against mine, her lips sweet against mine. All that could have been mine. It's almost more than I can bear.

Chapter 44

I spent several days trying to decide exactly how to approach Margaret. I wrote out everything I wanted to say, so no argument would go unmade. I considered all kinds of extravagances: having dozens and dozens of roses delivered to her house (which of course I can't do, because how would she explain it to Adam, and surely after what I've done, I have no business destroying her relationship with him) or sending musicians to serenade her with love songs (that I could do when I knew Adam would be away) or buying her the beautiful, blue-green silk sari, the exact color of her eyes, that I saw in the window of an import shop. Ultimately, I decided against any of this. I know such things won't impress Margaret. What I need to communicate is a lot more personal than a sari or a serenade. I have to convince Margaret that I've changed. But how? How do I get her to take a chance on something only time can prove?

Armed with a story about needing to borrow a tool (in case Adam's home), I head toward her flat. The minute she opens the door, I can tell she knows why I've come. She stands there, hand on hip, giving me a wry, "been there, seen this" look without even asking me to come in.

"I'd like to talk to you, Margaret. It's important."

She continues to stand there as though she expects me to speak to her from the doorstep.

"May I come in, please?"

She steps aside, allowing me to enter. Already things feel hopeless, and I realize with dismay that the warmth and friendliness I've experienced from her was for me her brother-in-law. For me her ex-lover, there is no warmth.

She gestures for me to take a seat on the sofa, then she sits in an easy chair several feet away. This isn't how I imagined things. I'd intended to take her in my arms and look directly into her eyes as I spoke, but clearly she won't allow that. It feels hard to say the things I've come to say from such a distance.

"Okay, what is it?" she asks. Her voice is so cold my courage falters. I feel like a schoolboy giving a speech.

"Margaret, I've realized I made a terrible mistake. I was afraid to love you, and that's why I said no when you wanted to move in with me. I know I hurt you, and I'm sorry. And if you'll let me back into your life, I promise nothing like that will ever happen again. You can move in tomorrow. I'd love it. We don't need an apartment. We'll make it work the way it is."

Margaret pauses. She gives herself time to think, and she looks sad. "No, it's too late. I took a chance with you, and it didn't work out. I'd have to be a fool to walk back into that. It was awful."

"I know it was. But it doesn't have to be that way. I've learned some incredible things about myself. I understand now why I did the things I did. And that will make it possible for me to be different."

"How can you promise that? Remember back in the beginning when we talked so much? You told me about all the clients you'd had who'd decided only after they'd made a shambles of their relationships that they'd lost the love of their lives."

"Margaret, I know what I said, but—"

"And didn't you tell me that in every case they begged to be taken back and that a couple of times their lovers took them back and that then, despite your best efforts, your clients did the same thing again?"

"But this is different! Something extraordinary has happened to me. My mother laid some things out for me…things that happened when I was only four. Things that I should have remembered, but didn't, maybe because they were so painful. And I saw how it all happened. I saw how hurt I'd been, and how I came to feel I was inherently so bad that if I let myself love, I'd just be found out and abandoned, just as I believed my father abandoned me."

"And now you don't feel bad about yourself anymore?" Margaret's no dummy. Hadn't I myself explained to her that insight doesn't necessarily equal change?

"Fair enough. But this isn't just some kind of temporary emotional breakthrough. I know this sounds strange, but I had a kind of vision. I actually experienced how meaningless my life was without love, without you, Margaret! It hurt a whole lot, but it changed me.

I'm different. I'm not the same person! I know I can do it now, Margaret. I know I can love. I won't hurt you again."

"You may believe that, but I don't. You're a middle-aged guy who's never been married. Never even lived with anyone for more than a few years. And what do you do? You fall in love with your brother's wife. I should have known from the start how this would turn out."

"You sound angry."

"Of course, I'm angry. Do you need a degree in psychology to figure that out? You're a no-show, that's what you are. You were that right from the beginning. Remember how you propositioned me? Asked me to come to your office? Then when I did, you weren't there. I was a fool, and I'm not going to be a fool again."

"I know, Margaret, but I'm not the same. Today I would have handled everything differently. I—"

"And worst of all, after telling me how wonderful I was, you turned around and started criticizing and picking on me."

Margaret looks close to tears, so I get up and go to her. I kneel in front of her chair and try to put my arms around her, but her body stiffens. "No! Go away!" I retreat to the sofa, where I sit quietly trying to think. I can hear the clock ticking. I'm afraid she'll throw me out soon if I don't find some way to get through to her, and who can say if she'll ever give me another chance?

"Okay, Margaret. Everything you say is fair. But what about you?"

"What about me?"

"I did find fault with you. And I see now that the faults I saw were mostly excuses because I was afraid to love you. But when I told you about something I didn't like, your response was to get angry and scream at me. You weren't willing to look at yourself at all. What does that say about you?"

"Oh, I see. Now that I won't do what you want, you're going to criticize me some more."

"I hope you'll listen to me, Margaret. Don't you want love in your life? Do you have it? You've been married to Adam for sixteen years. Maybe you think that puts you on the high ground. But what kind of relationship do you have? Adam's my brother. I know him well. You've admitted yourself that he's not the kind of guy you can have much of a personal conversation with. Does he ever really listen to you? Do you think he really knows you? Adam keeps everything simple and on the surface. That's how he feels safe. Is he the person you want to spend the rest of your life with?"

Now at least Margaret is listening. She looks stunned, and I don't hear anything from her for quite some time. I wait. Like Carl, I too have learned to wait.

"You're right about Adam, I admit that. But if I left him, which I well might, why would I want to get involved with you again?"

"Maybe you wouldn't—"

"I don't believe in miraculous transformations. And neither do you. You told me—"

"Just give me a chance to *prove* I've changed!"

Margaret is silent, but she doesn't look convinced.

"Anyway, we were talking about you. You know, back when things were good, I was puzzled about why I was attracted to you in particular."

"I told you why. I was married. I wasn't available, or so you thought. And then when it turned out you could have me, suddenly you didn't want me."

"As you know, Carl asked me if possibly you and I had the same fears. That was another revelation. I realized immediately he was right. And what is the number one fear we both have?" Margaret looks at me mistrustfully, like I'm trying to pull something over on her. "Come on, Margaret, we've talked about all this. I misbehaved when I was growing up. I gave my parents and everybody else a lot of trouble. After Carl put me on to this, I asked you, and you told me that the same was true of you, that you behaved very badly."

"You know, I'm not sure I'm in the mood to play psychology. I loved you a lot once, then things got bad, and after a while, I didn't anymore. I stopped loving you. It's over. I don't love you anymore!"

"Margaret…"

"We can be friends. We're good at that. But that's all."

"But Margaret, I love you. I love you more than I've ever loved anyone else in my whole life."

"You'll find somebody else."

"I don't want anybody else. I want you!"

"I can't help that. And I'm not sure I believe it, either."

"Have you ever given any thought to why you chose my brother? You must have had some idea what he was like before—"

"Look, I'm not angry anymore. I really hope what you say is true. I hope you are different. I hope you find someone to love and that you have the life you want. But you have to go. I'm tired, and Adam will be back any time now."

"But Margaret—"

"Please go! Now!"

I leave and wander through the corridors, unable to face going back to my room. Then I can't face being out in the corridors, so I go home. Once there, I start crying. Now, hours later at my office, I'm managing to move my arms and legs and mouth. My clients seem to believe I'm in my chair as usual trying to help them, but somewhere deep inside, I'm still crying.

# *Chapter 45*

After several weeks of constant pain, I've begun to consider dying. I'm not actively suicidal. I don't have a plan or a means, but I no longer see any point in living. If I were to find myself in some serious danger, why not accept it? Why not refuse to hand over my money if I felt a knife at my throat? Why not just let myself drop if I tripped in front of a subway car?

I pass the florist each day on the way to my office, and every time I think about the roses I used to buy for Margaret. They were so beautifully crafted: a fresh drop of scented oil in a coil of pale pink silk. I always bought the most romantic kind, the ones where the perfume faded quickly, the glue crumbled, and the silk unrolled. Appreciate these moments, those flowers tried to warn us; they are fragile.

I can't go into my closet anymore. When my clients need hypnosis, I make excuses not to use the futon until they stop mentioning it. For one thing, it's no longer suitable; there are spots on it. And I don't want to find any more strands of red-gold hair. At first I saved them, then I threw them away, and now I don't know what to do.

When I walk to and from my office, my mind plays tricks. I see Margaret over and over again, but always out of reach. A red-haired woman comes out of a music shop, and my heart lurches after her. In a main corridor, I lose her in a crowd, or it turns out only to be someone with a red shawl. Or I think I see Margaret, and it turns out only to be an adolescent's flirtatious eye peeking around a door. Or even a bent back, which straightens into a man with long, reddish hair. And a beard.

I haven't heard from Amy, and given how she looked the last time I saw her, I believe she's dead. If she weren't, she'd at least call to cancel her sessions. Worst of all, my work, which always functioned as a kind of sanctuary from my personal life, has become agonizing. I struggle to get through each hour, and I can't even rest for the few minutes between sessions. Instead I wait with dread for my next client, as if my office were a cell and some personally dedicated torturer was goose-stepping toward me down the corridor, some fascist with a hand-crank generator and a pair of brightly colored alligator clips.

If I had a desk job, I could deliver my body, put on a polite mask, and keep safely to myself until I was fit to be with people again. But not in therapy. There's no place to hide. I'm on stage, and my audience sits only three feet away, peering at me without a shred of costume or scenery between us. It's incredibly claustrophobic, and since therapy is the only part of my life that's ever worked and made me feel worthwhile, I worry that in my current state, I'll fail my clients.

Sometimes I go to my mother's. "What's the matter?" she always asks. "You look sick to me," she says, and she feels my forehead. This familiar routine gives me some comfort.

"Nothing's wrong," I assure her. "I'm just tired."

"I should get you some antidepressants," she will announce, as though it's the first time she's mentioned this. "If I got you a few, would you give them a try? They have some wonderful medications; they work like magic."

"No, Ma. I'm just tired," I tell her again. I know I'm deeply depressed and that antidepressants might be a good idea, but some perverse stubbornness won't permit me to take them. As I brood at her table, my mother brings me hot tea and this and that from the bountiful bosom of her kitchen. I snack mindlessly, not really caring that for the first time I'm starting to put on weight.

 # *Chapter 46*

Standing in my office, the aftertaste from my last session still in my mind, like something I regretted having eaten, my schedule for the day is done, and I don't know what to do with myself. I've felt at home in this room for years without ever giving it a thought, but now my office seems desolate. The light is chalky, the chairs look embalmed, and I'm struck by the conspicuous lack of equipment. I have no microscope, no cyclotron, not even tweezers. A beautician has a more professional setting than I do. The most substantial element, the only real element, is atmosphere, blatantly comfortable chairs, walls painted a warm cream, a heavy door that closes with an insulating click. I put my elbows on the mantle of the nonfunctioning gas fireplace, which until this moment I've always found charming, and peer closely into the mirror to check the condition of my face. As expected, I look awful.

On my way home, I refuse to walk the extra two apartment buildings to get to the main corridor, to the longer, brighter way home; tonight I want the dark, direct path, which kinks slightly each time the hall passes to an adjacent building that's not quite aligned. I want the route that leads past the grimy bins of used parts, the chunks of handcarts and wheelchairs, the tattered racks of the cheapest of the used clothing stores, used and reused, last chance of the poor, before these rags are grabbed and baled by the re-processors, soaked free of grease and smell, shredded and rewoven into fresh, expensive garments for those who can afford the luxury of new clothing. Tonight the glitter of the main corridors would be unbearable. I have no patience for pretense. All I want is the sullen privacy of my room. But as it turns out, even that is too much to ask.

Since I've been avoiding my friends lately, Carl and Phillipe have taken it upon themselves to come find me, and since I was out, and since in my absentmindedness I forgot to lock my door, they've let themselves in to wait for me. They're drinking my coffee and arguing comfortably to pass the time.

"At last," Phillipe salutes me with a raised mug. "Back from the lists of love, I see."

It is not the right thing to say, given my agony over Margaret, and they sense it. They're quiet while I pour myself a coffee. Even though I know I'll be up half the night, and despite the fact that I keep it only for guests because it makes me so tense and talkative, tonight I don't care. Carl has taken the easy chair, not crossing his legs in order to preserve the creases, sharp as chefs' knives, pressed into his pants. Phillipe has rolled himself to the middle of the room, center stage as usual, so I sit on the bed, where I must slouch because it's so far to lean back against the wall. This discomfort adds to my irritation and suits me perfectly.

"Yes, I'm back from love..." I say bitterly after a long pause, "but not with some slimy crotch, which is what you probably think, Phillipe. I'm back from the only kind of love I know how to hold onto: love of humanity, psychotherapy, the Great Answer. What a weird way to earn a living!"

I've stunned them. I may have some of Phillipe's cynicism, but I also have a lot of Carl's tightness, so they're not used to my bursting out like this. Their faces become professionally sympathetic, their eyes canny; they automatically calculate the depth of my pain, perhaps even whether there's a chance I might become violent.

"It's like some dream of flying," I say, and then remember, painfully and too late, I once had this very same image about loving Margaret. "You're up there, soaring around, thinking you're doing just great, and then this nag comes in the back of your mind that says maybe nothing's holding you up but faith, and once you doubt, you crash to the earth." Their composed faces are watching me from an impartial distance. "Don't you ever have any doubts?" I challenge each of them. "Aren't you ever afraid what we do might be a hoax? That perhaps we might even be fooling ourselves?"

This is too much for Carl. "You've lost your perspective," he sputters, genuinely offended. "We're not just some quacks off the street. We all have doctorates from good universities. Years of study. Very challenging study! I can assure you that my degree is not a hoax."

"Ah, Carl, you're going to have to do better than that," I reply. "My fat leather armchairs, the grand new APA headquarters, those constant, self-congratulatory professional conferences—right now all that, as well as your righteous indignation, just seem like additional proofs of what I'm feeling."

"It's not the possibility that it's a hoax that makes me frightened," Phillipe snaps back. "It's the fact that there are still therapists who refuse to even consider such a possibility." Without bothering to look at him, Phillipe flips a grenade into Carl's lap. "There are therapists who actually believe that any sort of doubts are breaches of the faith."

"You certainly don't mind having doubts," Carl counters, jerking his lapels straight in irritation. "In fact, I think you actually like having them. They save you from having to believe in anything. And the fact that I'm not afraid to commit and that I have a practice based on a long, honorable tradition of knowledge, that really irks you."

Carl has put it too mildly. Phillipe is not irked. Irking wouldn't make his face turn that color. "Freudianism may have a long tradition in the history of psychology," Phillipe growls, "but as far as knowledge goes, it's a laugh! It's smug, it's sexist, and it's so utterly lacking in scientific support that you can't possibly understand the meaning of the word if you refer to it as knowledge. Tradition is the only thing it has going for it." Waving his mug in his toes as he speaks, Phillipe is sloshing coffee blindly on my rug, but there's no point in interrupting him. His mug is already almost empty. "Why don't you admit it? Your precious Freudianism is no more than the psychological equivalent of religious fundamentalism! And like all the fundamentalisms, it has zero trust in our humanity: we're bad, little more than instinct-riddled

animals. We're talking, here, about a therapy so negative, so guilt-
and shame-inducing, that it can actually make people worse!" Phillipe
spits out this last word with such vehemence that Carl is stunned.

Their fights always end this way. Carl invites Phillipe to a chess
match, one move at a time. And Phillipe responds with all the games-
manship of a vandal sacking Rome. And it never hurts Phillipe's
argument that he's willing to speak twice as loudly as Carl.

Now that Carl has been predictably overwhelmed, Phillipe can
afford to lower his voice to a gravelly sneer, drawing out his words
dramatically, relishing his domination. "If only it would die and stay
dead." He arches his eyebrows; his eyes are huge. "If it were merely
the quaint chapter in history that it should be, then we could just be
amused, as we are about corsets and about fainting at the mention
of sex, which are all from the same antique period as your beloved
Freudianism. But unfortunately, Freud's dismal picture of life has not
gone the way of ladies' fans."

His soliloquy is so scathingly delivered I almost applaud. I can
appreciate it as grand opera. But tonight, beneath the broad caricature, I see something in what Phillipe is saying. Lately, too many of the
bright, young therapists who come to me for training are completely
enthralled with Freudian theory. "It's the most powerful perspective
ever formulated on the human mind," one recently told me. He was
clearly thrilled at the thought and had not the slightest awareness that
"power" refers to real effects in the real world, not to intellectual conversation over coffee. But how was he to know? There is no real world
left for these poor students. There are no poisonous snakes or plants,
not a chance of crossing a desert or of being caught in a small boat in
a rough sea. In here, nothing tests a thought but another thought, and
like that woman who felt trapped in her skull, we live together like
a composite brain in a huge box, each of us merely a single neuron,
and we know only level after level of inside: inside the theory, which
is inside the head, which is inside the city, which is totally and termi-
nally inside.

Chapter 47

That night when Carl and Phillipe came uninvited to my room, none of us ever dreamed that what we were observing was Phillipe's final triumph over Carl, nor did we suspect how much Phillipe would come to regret it. At the end of the evening, Carl had accepted an invitation from Phillipe—a dare might be a better word—to come see the AngelBeasts. Carl had asked me to come along, and I'd agreed. Perhaps he'd felt nervous about attending what he rightly suspected would be a no-holds-barred orgy of the Id. The AngelBeasts invitation had been Phillipe's last salvo, an attempt on Phillipe's part to demonstrate to Carl the beauty of the unleashed human spirit.

Carl never showed up, so afterward, Phillipe insisted we go over to Carl's place and confront him about his cowardice. The whole way over there, Phillipe railed about how closed-minded Carl was. "That pin-striped pollywog missed a terrific opportunity," Phillipe declared, pounding a flipper against the arm of his wheelchair, "to witness firsthand how enriching it can be to let go completely, to soar, to fly!"

When we arrived, we found seven different notes stuck to Carl's door. This was strange and a little alarming, so we decided to take a look at them. Five were from the same patient. The first note, "Dr. Sigelman, why did you miss our appointment? Please call," escalated over six days' time to "Dr. Sigelman, call or I swear I'll kill myself." Phillipe looked stricken. We both knew that Carl would never ignore a note like that. We debated whether to break down the door ourselves or call the police. Phillipe felt we had to do it ourselves, reasoning that if Carl were lying inside direly ill, every second could count. "Ourselves," of course, meant me, since Phillipe couldn't help.

I hurled myself against the door from across the corridor several times, but succeeded only in hurting my shoulder and making enough noise to bring several neighbors out into the hall. One man, a weight lifter, fetched a barbell from his apartment and proceeded to batter down Carl's door. Then he returned to the TV show he'd been watching, just as though breaking down doors was routine in his hallway.

When we entered Carl's small apartment, we immediately smelled something foul. Carl wasn't in his living /dining area, so we continued into his bedroom. There we could hear the shower running. "Carl," I called out, but there was no answer. As we entered the bathroom, the bad smell became stronger. Phillipe used his single finger to slide back one of the door panels to the bathtub and shower.

What I saw then has been burned so deeply into my consciousness I'll never be free of it. Carl, or at least what was left of him, lay crumpled on the shower floor. His skin was completely gone, and his flesh was eaten away, right down to the bone in some places. He'd been there for days, and his body had started to rot, which accounted for the smell. The shower was running full blast, washing some sort of smelly, reddish, yellowish liquid out of what remained of his internal organs.

We stared for a moment in disbelief. Then we ran and rolled from Carl's apartment as quickly as we could. On my way out, I noticed what looked like the suit that Carl had been wearing at my apartment the night we'd last seen him. It was neatly folded and draped over a chair, as though he'd carefully placed it there before stepping into the shower.

After I'd called the police on my cell phone, we waited down the hall, numb with shock. For quite a while, neither of us could manage to speak. Tears were streaming down Phillipe's face. I felt like my legs were going to buckle, so I pressed myself back hard against the wall for support. Meanwhile my brain was racing, trying to come up with some sort of explanation for what I'd seen.

"I don't understand," Philippe finally said, almost in a whisper. "What happened?" I just shook my head in bewilderment.

"The only thing I can think of," I said, "is that something other than water came out of that showerhead."

"Don't be crazy," Phillipe said. "How could that happen? What else but water comes out of a shower?"

After the police arrived and a crew had removed Carl's remains and mopped up, one of them came over and asked us if we were relatives. When we told them we were very close friends, they said they couldn't give out any personal information about the deceased unless we were family and told us to go home. Phillipe was so emotionally distraught he swore at them and demanded an explanation. That, of course, made them angry. When they threatened us with their billy clubs, Phillipe finally agreed to leave.

It took more than a day for them to figure out how Carl had died. During that time, we were constantly in touch with Carl's sister, who had promised to tell us as soon as she knew anything. My theory turned out to be correct. When Carl turned on the shower, instead of water, a strong acid came out of his shower head and hit him directly in the face. There was evidence he'd fallen in the tub, and because of that, and possibly also because he'd been blinded, he was unable to get out of the tub quickly enough to save himself from the acid that relentlessly poured over him. The authorities told Carl's sister that there had been an "unfortunate malfunction in the plumbing."

The pipes that carry water and waste can under certain circumstances turn into siphons that suck up instead of pouring out. This phenomenon is called backflow, and it's not uncommon. That's why we must have check flow valves on every sewage outlet on the city's sides, so if for any reason there's a drop in the pressure, pollution can't be drawn back into our system. There are backflow valves at all industrial sites, as well. These are required by law; the environmentalists made sure of that. But the law doesn't require that they be regularly inspected; the industries made sure of that.

Several floors below Carl's apartment, there's a plant that manufactures electronic equipment. The workers use strong acids as cleaning agents, and they have vats where these fluids are mixed and stored. Water pipes, used to dilute the formula, lead into the vats. On this particular occasion, for what reason no one seems to know, instead of delivering water into the vats, these pipes sucked up the acid, like soda through a giant straw, and then spit it out through Carl's shower head. Given the size of the vat, fifty gallons of the stuff must've poured over Carl before it was used up and the pipes filled again with water.

It could have happened to anyone on the line, but Carl was unlucky enough to be the one who had first opened his tap and allowed the chemical to escape. No one else was affected, since the entire fifty-gallon vat had emptied out onto Carl.

Phillipe and I never talk about this part, but what we both believe is that Carl, feeling sweaty after their last argument, decided to shower before bed. Phillipe feels responsible. It's totally illogical. Phillipe didn't make Carl take a shower, and he certainly couldn't have known that the shower would kill him. Still, Phillipe believes Carl would be alive today if they hadn't argued, which may be true. And he imagines that everyone now holds him at fault, which isn't true.

Of course, I don't blame Phillipe. If he's responsible, then so am I. I could have interrupted their argument. In fact, even though I didn't say a word out loud, I was siding with Phillipe in my mind and feeling irritation with Carl for his conservative beliefs.

I've seen my clients blame themselves for the death of someone close to them. Now I'm experiencing firsthand the seductiveness of guilt, as though it would be better to be responsible than to be helpless. Worse still, the pain Carl must have suffered during his last moments haunts me when I try to go to sleep at night.

Phillipe really misses Carl. They spent so much time together arguing, which Phillipe enjoyed, even if Carl didn't. Carl could always be trusted to rise to the bait, struggle feebly, and then succumb, thus giving Phillipe the opportunities he so craves to lecture and scold. He's clearly depressed, and that isn't at all like Phillipe. As for myself, I can't tell yet how much Carl meant to me. Like a leper, I'm growing numb to my losses.

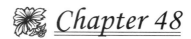 # *Chapter 48*

Carl's gruesome death seems to have broken something open inside me. I suffered terribly as a child, but instead of crying, which for me was something only girls did, I became angry and unmanageable. Now I have to struggle to keep from weeping during sad sessions with my clients. And sometimes, while I'm groping my way down a dim corridor with a blur of blue-gray faces pushing roughly past me, I cry for no reason at all.

Now I understand something of what my maternal grandfather went through in his later years. An earnest man with a great ruff of white hair, he sometimes wrote to the newspapers about the need for more city colleges or the importance of art in education. When his letters were published, he passed them around with pride. We considered my father's parents blue collar, but by our standards, my mother's were intellectuals. We thought this spoke well of the family.

Like my other grandfather, he had been stern with his children. But he was gentle and indulgent with me, and I loved him. It was a terrible thing for him, and for us, when in the middle of his eighties, his mind "began to go." He began doing strange things. Most particularly, he began to cry. He became less hard-edged and more sentimental, and much more interesting to be with. At dinner, for instance, instead of being preoccupied with the correctness of our table manners, he might tell us stories about his boyhood in Poland. Like the time he sat bareback on the old plow horse, and together they wandered through an orchard one warm afternoon. As they passed under the trees, he reached up and picked an apple, and when he bit into it, it was so sweet that he ate and ate, just letting the juice run down his chin. "They don't have apples like that anymore," he said. And then he cried. He was embarrassed that he couldn't stop, and that we could all see him holding his hands in some awkward middle space, unable either to admit to his tears by raising his fingers to wipe them away or to drop his palms to the table and surrender completely to his feelings.

I remember especially the time when Adam noticed his violin case behind the glass doors of the sideboard and asked him what it was. Before retirement, he had earned his living as an insurance salesman, but his rolltop desk was still cluttered with broken bits of pastel chalk from many years before when he had drawn portraits professionally. Now we discovered he had also played the violin, and we pleaded with him until he took it down. He was so vulnerable to his grandchildren that it overcame his sense of self-protection. It had been too many years since he'd held the instrument. He scraped the bow a few times, and it was immediately obvious, even to us, that there was no possibility of music. When he started crying, Adam and I felt responsible. All we could do was to leave the room so that he could cry in peace.

Now, at a much earlier age, I find tears running down my face at odd times. I'm not mourning the loss of music, and I never had orchards in my youth. My tears come when I think of people who are afraid to say that they care for each other and then drift apart, and so lose their chance at love, as Margaret and I did.

Except for the crying, which is accompanied by some sensation, I feel dead inside. As I move through my days, I feel like a ghost. I stay in my room a lot, then when I can't stand that anymore, I go out and wander in places where I don't think I'll run into anyone I know. Drifting as I do, I see what others are too busy to notice: our walls are scraped and pocked from the carts carrying goods, and the corners of the halls are chipped away. The paint crews have apparently exhausted themselves, leaving the hard institutional enamel that covers all public spaces free to scab and peel. (What malevolent bureaucracy chose those dull greens and light browns anyway?) Ceilings are buckling and walls discoloring, pipes drip. Garbage chutes are clogged; they back up into the halls. At times I've seen cracks travel along a wall, and despite the architect's assurances, I'm convinced I feel a subtle shifting under my feet.

One day as I'm out wandering aimlessly around the city, I decide to sit for a few minutes on a bench near the Freedom Tower. This plaza is one of the few places so sacrosanct that no matter how much pull you had, and no matter how crowded the city became, no one was ever going to build there. There's a memorial wall on which the names of the dead had been inscribed. Not far from that, an especially large New York City flag waves in the breeze of several big fans.

When I arrive, a troop of Boy Scouts stands in a circle around it, pledging allegiance. When they finish, the fans are turned off, "Taps" is played, and our flag is lowered and folded. Even though the light within the city never changes, exactly as sunset occurs (according to a carefully calibrated clock in city hall), this ceremony takes place all over the city. Just as was the case with the flag of the United States, leaving the New York City flag up at "night" is considered disrespectful.

The Boy Scouts are no sooner gone when a group of about fifteen people dressed as clowns suddenly emerge from all four sides of the plaza and gather at its center. One clown, a tall, skinny fellow, steps out from the group, blowing a whistle and waving his arms to clear a space. From a small suitcase, another clown plucks a folding cot and snaps it open. She sets the suitcase next to the cot as a nightstand, and on it she places an antique alarm clock and a candle in a quaint holder. Then she lights the candle. It's a clown cartoon of bedtime. She pulls on a tasseled red and white striped night cap over her wild orange wig, yawns, and lies down to sleep, all in less than thirty seconds of jerky motion like some old silent film. The rest is even quicker and sharper. One of the other clowns pulls a long thread to tip the candle onto the cot, which explodes into real flames. Gasps and screams from the crowd. The rest of the clowns jump up and down, crying out, "Wake up, wake up, wake up." The sleeping clown jumps out of bed, and at the same moment, another clown leaps forward with a fire extinguisher and puts out the flames. These two kiss, pack up the suitcase, and the clowns disperse. They are done in under two minutes, instant drama, as compact as their suitcase; such a brief, intense flash that you almost wonder if they've really been there, or if possibly you've just imagined them. Before anyone can ask a question or call the police, they've vanished.

Everyone around me is chattering about them, but all I can think about is Margaret. I remember how excited she'd been after she'd seen the clowns on TV, and I wish she could have been here with me. I know she would have been delighted. Suddenly the pure fact that she wasn't there seems so terribly sad, I start to cry, just like my maternal grandfather, even though I'm not yet old, and even though I have no good excuse for my behavior.

Chapter 49

As the weeks pass, I'm surprised that life has begun to change without any conscious effort on my part. At times, in the midst of all the deadness, I feel some sharp slivers of sensation. When I drink a glass of water, for instance, there is an instant of bright, cold smoothness before the gray flows back. These sensations attract me because they feel good. I've never noticed such subtle things before, and I've become curious. Now, I purposefully look for ways to create sensation in my body.

The city's no help. Now that I need such small pleasures, I realize how few there are. The breeze from an air vent seems promising, but then when I hold my face in it, my pleasure is spoiled by the rancid odor of lubricating oil from the fans. There's nothing in the hallways, almost nothing in the rooms, and that's what we have, hallways and rooms. I can rub my scalp or stroke my arm. I can take a shower. I feel as if my skin has been peeled, and anything more than such small wisps of experience would gouge me and make me bleed. Sex, which would previously have been at the top of my list of entertainments, seems incredibly complex, and when approached with complete openness, even monstrous.

Clients regularly come to me complaining that they're having a breakdown. They say this with horror. But what they actually mean is that they can no longer make themselves continue in a direction that now sickens them, but that they believe is normal, or honorable, or god-fearing. They are terrified of change, and those close to them usually agree and want them to be familiar and predictable again. So what they are actually asking me to do is help them overcome the revolt of their own bodies and the repugnance that makes it impossible to proceed, so they can return to the very existence that caused them to break down in the first place.

I had the good luck to be miserably alone at this time. There were no sympathetic friends, nor any lover, to urge me to pull it together and get back on track. So I got off the track. I let myself go. I collapsed. And after days of darkness, I was surprised to find I hadn't perished. The great effort I'd always assumed was necessary to keep myself together apparently wasn't required. I laughed. I was still somebody; I just didn't know who it was anymore.

So instead of first knowing who I should be and then forcing everything to conform to that abstraction, I decided I'd get to know myself the same way I'd get to know anyone else: by noticing what I did and how I felt. This time, instead of starting from the top down, with great ideals and grand ambitions, I started my mosaic humbly from the ground up, and absolutely nothing was cemented in place, no matter how desirable or attractive, until I was certain it was a bit of the real me. A drink of cold water, a nap on the couch, I assembled myself from small specks of experience as babies do, before they're taught what to think and feel.

🌺 *Chapter 50*

"Hey, Doc, long time, no see. Tried to die, but couldn't. See you at three today." A woman who wouldn't give her name left this message with my answering service. I'm stunned. This has to be from Amy. Not only is she the only client who would leave a quirky, anonymous message, but her regular appointment time was Tuesday, at three, and today is Tuesday.

Amy alive! Hard to believe. I haven't heard a word from her for three months. Believing she was dead, I gave her time to another client. As memories of Amy flow through my mind, I start to smile. It's such a rare thing for someone we care about to come back from the dead, and it makes Amy seem even dearer. I make an excuse and switch the client in her spot to another time.

When Amy arrives, she's angry as ever with Appoppa. They're "not talking and not fucking, and not necessarily in that order," but that's okay because she has decided she "will not be made into a victim and will not be made into an invalid, not by some vague disease, which doesn't even have the decency to have a name, not by the dubious tests of incompetent laboratories, and not by the pompous male medical establishment, whose cerebral circulation has clearly been impoverished by perpetual penis erectus."

Appoppa has kept right on writing poetry to her during this gap in their affections, but he's adjusted his attitude accordingly. Amy reads me his latest, "Homage to an Asshole," typed on suggestively beige paper, and offers it as evidence of how low he can stoop, while at the same time appearing pleased by the amount of effort he's putting into their latest fight.

With her renewed determination has come a more ambitious program of rehabilitation. She will limp through the hallways every day to build up her stamina until she can walk for a full hour. She will pay more careful attention to nutrition and sleep. And she will avoid men who drain her energy and tarnish her moods.

She offers no explanation, nor any apology, for being absent for so long. I gather she was too ill to get out of bed for quite some time. But somehow Amy has rallied and is once again ready to challenge the seemingly unbeatable forces that oppose her. She isn't the kind to take death lying down.

I have to admire her. But in admiring her, I'm critical of myself. My problems seem inconsequential compared to hers. Now that I'm feeling a bit better, I should be looking for someone new to love, not living in the past, not continuing to hope for something that obviously can't be.

I didn't after all just give up that day when Margaret refused to take me back. All through the depths of my depression, every single day Margaret received an e-mail notifying her that she was free to download a different composition by Bach. When I'd exhausted Bach, I sent other classical music. Finally, I sent anything I thought she might enjoy. It was the only thing I could think to do that Adam wouldn't be likely to see or know about. Each of these daily gifts was accompanied by a graphic, a red heart with "I love you" written across it. I've told Margaret I love her every single day for months now, and she's said nothing, not "thank you," not "leave me alone," nothing. At family gatherings I've caught her gazing at me with a sad, wistful expression, but with the exception of the usual polite pleasantries, she's never actually talked to me.

The Buddhists would call what I'm doing clinging and advise me that my behavior is unwise. I don't disagree. I just haven't been able to manage to let go. I move right to the edge of it, I sense the magnitude of the pain, and I retreat. Perhaps Amy and I should switch places one day. Perhaps she could teach me a thing or two about courage.

Chapter 51

When you listen to national and international news, it's more understandable why New Yorkers chose encapsulation. I know, of course, that we're being manipulated, but still the photos of the flooding, the fires, the fighting going on between different factions in this or that country, the bloody wreckage of human bodies after a terrorist attack, and so forth, look quite real. I would have thought that when things got so hard, that grudges would be forgotten and people would be preoccupied with simply trying to survive. Instead, hatred seems to be what gives meaning to life for those bent on destroying others.

It's hard to avoid seeing such things, because even if I'm watching the New York City Ballet, it will be interrupted for a special news flash if something particularly horrendous happens. People are out there killing each other. So if New York is a little drab and its politicians are corrupt, should we not still count ourselves lucky to be here?

When I don't want to risk being exposed to images of warfare, death, and devastation, I read, most recently an anthropology book about native tribes. Last night I came across something that sounds like a children's story. Once there was a tribe named the Mehinaku. They lived in the Amazon Basin near the Xingu River and swam in the warm water, wearing nothing but colored bands around their waists and necks, not to cover their bodies, but to decorate them. In their society, killing was unheard of. When they met with their neighbors, it was for trade, not war. They resolved their rivalries by wrestling, then they laughed and roasted fish, feasted, and told tales. But before the wrestling came the most exciting part, the ritual teasing. They'd squat down in a long line, directly facing their opponents, and hurl outrageous insults at one another.

"You're cheap. You give nothing to your brothers!"

"You can't use a spear. The fish laugh when you try to kill them!"

"You're lazy. It's lucky your family hasn't starved!"

As each of these barbs struck the heart of an opponent, the tribes would cheer, "Whoo! Whoo! Whoo!" and slap their thighs in appreciation.

"We were only feathered arrows," the Mehinaku taught their children, "before the sun shook us and woke us up and made us human." When, I wonder, will something shake us and wake us. Now that I've learned to be more deeply in touch with my feelings, sometimes the evening news feels unbearable.

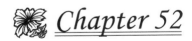 *Chapter 52*

It was inevitable that sooner or later Margaret and I would find ourselves alone again. I had no idea what would happen then. But given the decisiveness with which Margaret had rejected me and her total lack of response to months of gifts and love notes, I felt sure it wouldn't be anything like the 1940s movie endings of my fantasies.

We're in my mother's kitchen, my mother, Adam, Jon, Margaret, and I. All that's left of my mother's apartment is her kitchen and her bedroom, since even the bathroom is shared with the shops that inhabit the other rooms. But the kitchen still works as it was meant to, and people are always up and down from the family table for fresh cups of coffee and big pieces of flaky, brown bobka. There's bustle inside and out. We can hear the foot scrapes in the hall and the complaints and gossip of those passing by.

Jon is a contractor, a man who does business with Adam and apparently owes him favors. Adam, always a careful keeper of ledgers, is ready to collect what's owed by getting Jon to replace the countertops in my mother's kitchen.

"Tile is not all that practical," Jon insists, allowing his voice to sour with annoyance.

My mother is not intimidated. "And why is tile not practical?" She nudges me, pointing to the plate of bobka, indicating that I should take the last piece. I notice how her own appearance is distinctly dough-like as well: a hand full of ladyfingers, baguette arms, and a bun of a face.

"It's not up-to-date," Jon says, changing his tack entirely. "They have beautiful counter materials in all kinds of colors. We could find something that would go with your table." Jon has easy access to a standard line of upscale prefab countertops, can trim them to size, slap them in place, and get this problem out of his hair quickly. But my mother has developed an unwholesome interest in tile.

"I don't want something up-to-date," she says. "I want something cozy. Tile. Creamy white with little pastel flowers in the trim. And my table is another story entirely." Her table has its origins beyond the limits of my memory, part of the original stuff of life, like rock and water. It's been sanctified by use and is associated with my father and their marriage. Its coziness is not up for discussion by some contractor. Adam smiles at Jon. It's no skin off his nose. Jon has made the mistake of agreeing to complete the job without realizing that my mother may not be willing to settle for what he has in stock.

"Well, we'd better get on with it," Adam says cheerfully. "You two want to come down with us and help pick out some tile?" I've been watching quietly, but his question jerks me from the safety of the sidelines as I realize I'm supposed to tell everyone whether I'll leave with them or remain alone in this room with Margaret. I'm not ready for my forties movie endings, let alone for real life. My biggest challenge to date has been to appreciate a cold glass of water. I look down at my coffee to avoid having to answer first.

"No, you go on. I'll clean up," I hear Margaret say easily.

"Okay, we'd better get going." Apparently no one expects me to respond. They gather themselves, put their cups in the sink, and take a comfortable and interminable time leaving. Meanwhile I face the risk of suffocation, the air now unbreathable while they're still in the room. On their way out, my mother dumps the last piece of coffee cake on my plate and sets the platter tidily in the sink. I can't begin to think until I hear the kitchen door finally click shut, and then my mind is crowded with an expanded sense of Margaret. Washing dishes at the sink, she has her back to me. I hear the water run, the crockery clack.

"How have you been?" she asks without turning. How have I been? The computer that ran my life has crashed, and all the data was lost. My little boat came unmoored and drifted over the falls, and I don't know yet if I've hit bottom or if I'm still falling.

"I'm okay, I guess."

"Good, I've been worried about you."

"You have?"

"Of course I have. You've looked…well, not good."

"How should I look, Margaret? I've been telling you every day for I don't know how long that I love you, and you don't even really speak to me."

"I'm sorry, I couldn't!" She turns to face me. Her delicate skin is unusually bright, her golden-red hair flared at the sides like some signal of animal warning. "You have to understand that I didn't know what to say. And it seemed better not to say anything than to create false hope."

"I know. What could you say? You probably said it all that day I came to beg you to come back."

Margaret is leaning back now, and where her hands rest gracefully on the counter edge, there will soon be flowers, as if flowing from some goddess of spring. There's a wet splash below her waist. I know it's only dishwater, but it reminds me of sex, and I wish she'd walk over and let me press my cheek against it and warm it and feel her reassuring flesh underneath. Now that would be a movie.

"I've been in therapy," she says. I frown at this news. At a time like this, naturally she would be easy prey for some therapist who despises men, some woman eager to work out her resentment through her clients. What is she doing to my Margaret? This is a completely new perspective for me. From here therapy looks threatening, a long, dark alley with the menace of uncontrolled change crouching in the shadows.

"Is it anyone I know?" I sound like I'm asking about an infidelity, and I realize now how my own clients' lovers must have asked anxious questions about me, the intruder in their lives.

"As a matter of fact, I decided I needed to talk with someone who actually knew you. How you really are."

Why are the most terrible insights the most effortless? "You're seeing Phillipe!" I'm not equal to this. I feel too new to the world, soft, and not yet steady on my feet.

"Not seeing him exactly. On the phone."

Phillipe! This is impossible. It's unethical for any friend of mine to see her in therapy. But of course Phillipe has no ethics. How could they do this? Probably they've been amusing themselves at my expense. I saw Phillipe only yesterday, and he was oh-so-cheerful, the bastard!

Now that I'm obviously helpless, a turtle flipped onto his back so his tormentors can enjoy him at their leisure, Margaret has softened. She drifts over, but it's not to hold me, not my movie. She sits down next to me. She doesn't look at me and doesn't talk, but I can feel the aura of her warmth, and the scent of her body is painfully familiar. She takes my plate and slowly slides it over. She tips it and lets the bobka fall onto the table. There's a bowl of sliced peaches, and she picks one of these fleshy crescents up with her fingers and sets it in the middle of the plate. This is her sand tray. She's making some spell, and I am hers, bewitched and at her mercy. Watching her hands, her fingers as slim and supple as a dancer's legs, her whole naked beauty in miniature, I miss her so much, and I realize, at last, what she's been telling me: even though she has been angry, she's been thinking of me, talking about me, all these months.

There is a chessboard on the table, and she transfers pieces, one at a time, to my plate, pickets guarding the peach. Then she crumbles a buttery crust of bobka over the scene like glossy brown snow. I am crazy with longing for this witch of the chess-forest. I take her hand. I see the cool blue-green of her impossibly crystalline eyes. I see her stand and step toward me. Unbelievably, overcoming all of my hopelessness, we have actually come to my movie, to the place I've practiced over and over in my mind, image and reality combining at last. I take her hips and pull her to me, so I can rest my head on the small fullness of her belly, and yes, the wet spot is cold and dear and easily warmed between us. I feel her thighs on my chest, the puff of her pubic hair under my chin, and I sigh. She brushes the hair back from my forehead with a slow stroking, her hand calm and soothing. I'm at peace. I let myself relax completely as my body rests softly against hers.

The door opens, and Adam sticks his head in. "I wanted to let you know that Mom and I will pick up some Chinese take-out for lunch." Then the door slams shut. My body goes rigid. How could we have been so careless!

"It's all right," Margaret tells me soothingly, continuing to stroke my head. "It's all right. They know."

"What?"

"I told Adam. And Adam told your mother."

"When? How could you do that?"

"I told him more than a month ago. And I told him because… because I needed to tell him."

"Phillipe made you do that."

"Don't be stupid. Nobody made me do anything." She's irritated, but reassuringly she doesn't let go of my head. "He only encouraged me to face myself."

"And this morning, all the time I was sitting here, they both knew?"

Now she laughs at me. "Not this morning. This whole month."

"And no one said anything?"

"Adam didn't say anything, because I asked him not to. I wanted time to think. And your mother…as it turned out, she knew about us all along and never said anything anyway."

"You've been talking to my mother? About me?"

She pinches my nose and gives it an impatient tug. "Grow up."

"And she wasn't outraged that we've been having an affair?"

"It turns out that your mother never thought that Adam and I were right for each other, and she said she could see that you and I were in love way before we started our affair."

"Really! And I always thought the subtleties of human feeling went right over my mother's head."

"Adam's not the type to pine away over anyone, she said, but Noah's been suffering terribly."

I feel a surge of love toward my mother. That she could see and understand me so well and support me in something so unacceptable amazes and touches me.

"And Adam just takes all this?"

"Adam was furious at first. He yelled and stamped; he even threw one of our lamps against the wall."

"Wasn't he furious with me? He never said a word. I never suspected."

"Remember that morning when Adam didn't come to Sunday brunch, because he was busy with a new project?"

"Yes."

"That was right after. He didn't think he could face you without showing his anger, and I convinced him he shouldn't do that. He was still hoping, then, that I wouldn't leave him." I'm speechless. "And there's something else you don't know."

"It seems there's a lot I don't know!" I say, looking up, but without loosening my grip on her. Her head is tipped to the side, and she's smiling mischievously, obviously enjoying her power to shock and amaze me.

"Adam has had affairs of his own, quite a number of them as it turns out."

"No!" I feel as if the elephant that's been riding me piggyback has finally decided to support its own weight.

"I had him followed. Caught him with a sexy brunette half his age. So you see, he doesn't have grounds for outrage."

"No kidding? Margaret, I feel so relieved."

"Me too."

"So we're not the only bad ones!"

"No."

"Margaret, wait a minute. Let's get back to the part where you said that Adam was still hoping you wouldn't leave him. Are you going to leave him?"

"Yes, of course. I'm coming to live with you."

"You are!"

"Yes. You'll probably get scared now, poor thing. After all, why would you pick a married woman and have a secret affair if you were really available? But I have confidence in you; you'll figure it out sooner or later. We've both been afraid, but I think we're getting ready not to be."

"What do you mean, '*we've* been afraid'? I'm the one who refused to let you come live with me."

"Yes, but the minute you did, I felt I'd been abandoned again and threw up all my defenses. I became impossible to deal with. You had a point about the room, and you kept telling me you loved me. Phillipe helped me understand how my mother's death and my father's deserting me night after night caused me to have abandonment issues. What happened wasn't all your fault. I could have been a lot more patient and understanding."

"Sweetheart..." I just look at her. It's all I can do not to cry. All through that bad time, I longed for her to take responsibility for something, anything, but she never would. "Thank you so much for saying that."

"I'm going to try harder to trust your love for me, Noah." Suddenly I feel a twinge of anxiety.

"Margaret, how do you know I can do this?" I demand. She just sighs. I can't tell if it's about me or about our relationship or even about life, the whole confusion of it. But I don't need an answer. There's something magical between Margaret and me, and I'm going to pursue it for all it's worth. I won't let her down this time.

"When will you come? I can't wait. How about tonight?"

"No, I can't. I needed to see you again before I could know for sure, so I haven't told Adam anything definite. He deserves a little time with me to work this through. I won't be more than a week. If he's angry and wants me gone, I'll come right away."

"You're sure you'll come?" I ask. "You won't change your mind? What if Adam begs you to stay?"

"You know Adam. He won't do that. But even if he did, I couldn't. I want to be with you." As she looks into my eyes, hers fill with tears. "I love you," she says. "I love you." We gaze at each other, and then slowly our lips come together and we kiss. We have now surpassed even my 1940s movie script.

"I love you, too, Margaret. And I will never hurt you again. Never, never, never." I pull her into my lap. I can almost hear lush, orchestral music playing in the background as I hold and kiss and stroke her. She feels delicious in my arms. That, more than anything else, makes me know we belong together.

I don't feel ready to face Adam and my mother yet. Being found out will take some getting used to. I want to escape before they return, but it's hard to let go of Margaret now that I have her. I make her promise again not to change her mind and leave.

At home I sit for hours in my big chair, listening to my heartbeat and experiencing my life as something golden and delicious, like that apple my maternal grandfather ate long ago while riding a horse through an orchard.

❀ *Chapter 53*

Early the next morning, I'm awakened by a loud knock at my door.

"Who is it?" I say.

"Don't worry, I'm not going to kill you." These are the first words out of Adam's mouth. Apparently hiding in my room hasn't protected me from him.

I pause, then open the door.

"Adam, I'm sorry," I say quickly. "Can you ever forgive me?"

"You're a shit." As he pushes by me, he punches me in the chest hard enough to send me reeling. Then he continues over to my bed and sits down. His bear-walk looks more shuffling and bent than usual, and I wonder how much losing Margaret is affecting him.

"I never meant for it to happen." I hear Adam groan, and then there's a thud. He's thrown himself back on the bed with his hands over his head, as if he's surrendering.

"All the women in the world and you have to go after Margaret. Why her?"

"Because I fell in love with her. I know it's strange after so many years, but—"

"The two of you carrying on right in front of my eyes, and I never suspected. I feel like such a chump."

"I think it happened because Margaret and I are so alike. We understand each other in a way other people can't. It doesn't mean anything bad about you."

"Yeah, well, I don't guess that she's so pretty had anything to do with it."

"She is pretty, but that wasn't why it happened. Have you ever thought about how different you and Margaret are?"

Adam has propped his head up on his hand, and the look he gives me is full of resentment. "You always get what you want," he says.

"What do you mean? You're the one who made all the money."

"And you're the one who got the PhD."

"You could've if you'd wanted."

"Ma and Pop never encouraged me. They never cared enough."

"What are you talking about? You were the one they loved most. You were their favorite, the good one."

"Are you kidding? It wasn't me they loved, it was you. I was good because I had to be. I could never compete with you at being bad. And they wouldn't have stood for it. You know what Ma told me when I was little? 'One bad boy is enough, Adam!' Can you believe that? 'One bad boy is enough!' What if I needed to be bad?"

"But I didn't want to be bad. There was something wrong with me. They told you that because they couldn't stand to have any more like me. They doted on you."

"You can't believe that. They used to sit up late at night talking about you! What did you need, how could they help you, what could they get you? You got all the attention. You were the original one, the creative one, the one that needed sensitive guidance. I was just a plow horse. I was just trudging along, doing my work, being the good boy, not causing anybody any trouble. I didn't dare. Because they didn't care enough to let me."

I'm amazed at Adam's perspective, and I'm even more amazed that he doesn't seem all that angry about Margaret. I pull my armchair around from its place by the radio and sit across from him. I put my hand on Adam's knee and give it a squeeze. I want him to look at me, talk to me. I ask him directly how he feels about Margaret leaving, but he just shrugs. "Ah, what can you do about women?" he says, as if this were a class of problem, not a particular one.

He could be saying it was too painful to talk about. Or he could be telling me that he and she weren't really that close. I don't know. But he obviously doesn't want to talk about it, so I don't press him. Nor do I bring up the issue of his infidelities. He seems to have resigned himself to losing Margaret, that's the important thing, and with far less rancor than I'd anticipated. I put on the coffee pot, and as it gurgles and hisses, we go back to arguing over who was the most despised and least loved son, but now it's more a competition than a lament.

After he leaves, I continue to think about Adam's viewpoint regarding our childhood. Those few minutes of looking at the world through his eyes have changed the way I see him. For the first time in memory, I don't feel resentful. In fact, I feel protective. I want him to be okay. He's my little brother, after all, if only by eight or ten minutes.

Chapter 54

Aweek after Margaret and I talked in my mother's kitchen, she came to live with me. And she was right; apparently we both were ready to stop being afraid. Even in the cramped quarters of my room, we haven't been fighting.

Our time together has been blissful. Yet being with her is also a constant emotional challenge. I always thought of successful love as something static, a goal achieved, a conclusion so ideal it seemed boring. Now I see that loving is not like that at all. It's a journey, as frightening as it is joyous, and so mysterious it can be disorienting.

Love is a risky business; there's no denying that. Can I know Margaret won't betray me? Not for certain. And even if she doesn't, something could happen to her. Something slow and agonizing, or sudden and shocking. Sometimes I feel afraid. But I'm determined to take these risks, to place my undefended heart in Margaret's hands, because I've come to the point where I'll risk anything, risk everything, rather than die without experiencing love. Though what exactly love is, I couldn't say. Only now as I explore it do I begin to experience its shape and substance. I have, of course, been in love before. But never like this, never this feeling of being permanently, irrevocably joined, mated for life. For me, this is shiny and new and miraculous.

Late at night Margaret and I lie in bed together, shoulders touching, holding hands as I read her novels or poetry. Her favorite is Appoppa's first love poem to Amy, "The Eucalyptus Poem," she calls it. I recite it slowly, secretly imagining the words as my own: "Would you like me to love you? I could watch you while you slept. I could sing while I brushed your hair…" And as I read, I can feel her exquisite hand resting peacefully in mine.

I'm surprised to discover, as time goes on, that what moves me most isn't her beauty. The ways in which she seemed so striking from a distance have become commonplace very quickly. What touches me more now are the things that force me to recognize her as herself: the fine wrinkles, the slight droop of her breasts, the beginning of a belly, small signals of aging, warnings of more to come, messages I cannot deny that say, "You will not have her forever."

Like many men, sex has always been the most direct expression of my need for intimacy. We make love no less wildly than before, but now it's more personal, if that makes any sense. It's no longer woman I make love to, it's Margaret. I press myself so deeply into her that I can't hold back. I have to let go, give in, need her. Recklessly I say, "Hold me, please hold me," and I hear Margaret answer, just as recklessly, "Yes, I will, I will." Then she wraps her arms around me even more tightly, and does some womanly thing with her legs that welcomes me more generously and holds me nearer than I could ever get to her by myself.

I've always been a person for whom sex was of paramount importance. Before I became so smitten by Margaret that other women ceased to be of interest, I almost always had something going with someone. I'd had many orgasms that rattled my bones, but these were more the product of clever fingers than true passion. Myths and fairy tales are full of stories about gifts that turn against you if they're used for the wrong purpose. That's what happened to me. The search for more and better sex ultimately led to disappointment, frustration, and boredom. I'd failed to understand an essential truth: it is love that is the fiercest and most terrible of aphrodisiacs. It is intimacy that is the most thrilling and inexhaustible risk. Infidelity and seduction and debauchery have their pleasures, and certainly their perils, but they're superficial ones: the delight in a nice patch of skin, the novelty of a new partner, the danger of a jealous spouse. But love requires you to risk everything, the essential self, to risk being known for whom and what you actually are, and then be taken in or shut out. And neither one of these is a small or easy thing.

Chapter 55

I've forgiven Phillipe for seeing Margaret, even though according to the rules of our profession, it was unethical. In fact, I can't help feeling grateful. I see now that his challenging Margaret to "face herself" led her to discover it was me she truly loved.

In Carl's absence, Phillipe and I have become closer. We go for walks in the corridors (though for Phillipe, I guess they can hardly be called "walks") or we meet for coffee. We've even invented a little game, which we like to play from time to time. I will stop down at Felicia's between clients, and at some point will mention offhandedly to those slouching around my table that I've just met a most unusual man, a wizard with telepathic abilities. This excites even the most bored little group. "A wizard? Telepathy? Don't be such an idiot."

I let them scoff. I antagonize them if I can, a matador exploiting the simplicity of the bull, and then at the proper moment, I say in the most arrogantly dismissive tone possible, "All right. Look. The wizard is a very busy man, and usually I wouldn't think of disturbing him. But the depth of your ignorance is more than I can bear. If we could agree on a simple, straightforward experiment, I'll call him right this minute and let (and I choose the loudest skeptic there) speak to the wizard himself and have his mind read in front of all you. Would that satisfy you?" It's interesting that no matter how much they scoff at my claims, no one ever turns me down.

The experiment I maneuver them into agreeing upon is for the skeptic to pick and tell us a number from one to ten. Then we go to a phone, and surrounded by the group, I dial a secret telephone number and ask, my voice suddenly humble, "May I speak to the wizard?" After a few seconds I say, "Hi, Wizard, there's someone here who doubts your powers. Would you mind terribly giving a brief demonstration," and I hand the telephone to the skeptic. Then Phillipe, in his deepest, most wizarly voice, tells him his number and hangs up.

The trick is simplicity itself. When I ask to speak to the wizard, that's a signal for Phillipe to start counting slowly out loud. As soon as he says the correct number, I say hello. Phillipe was born to conspire, and his enthusiasm for this adolescent game makes it fun.

It's a surprise to discover I can actually talk to him about Margaret, who he is no longer seeing as a therapist. Probably in part because he feels that our relationship was his doing, Phillipe is delighted about Margaret and me. He actually asks serious questions and gives sage advice, all without a hint of sarcasm. He's especially pleased about Margaret's new aspirations, for which he, of course, takes credit.

Apparently as an outgrowth of her therapy with Phillipe, Margaret has decided to start a completely different kind of existence. She's not willing, she says, to simply be an appendage as she was with Adam. She's now determined to do something that "really matters," though exactly what this will be is still an open question. She's considering becoming a teacher, or a social worker, or perhaps a therapist. (This particular option is more ironic than it might appear, because it was knowing me and seeing my weaknesses close-up that brought being a therapist within reach of her bruised self-esteem.)

She's also considering becoming a structural engineer and working as a building inspector. This concerns me. She seems to think that as a structural engineer she'd be able to put a halt to the kind of shoddy building that so often results in deaths and injuries. I've told her that I believe graft, not lack of expertise, lies at the bottom of this problem. Adam has told her the same, and he's in a position to know. She'd never get hired as an inspector if our building department believed she was going to cause trouble, and if she tried to buck the system, she'd be fired, or worse. But given how long it will take her to get through school, I'll have years to talk her out of that crazy idea. Meanwhile, Margaret is filled with hopes and dreams. She's vivacious and happy and a delight to be around.

Chapter 56

Death may be an Angel
But we dread its Song
That huge Black Mosquito
Filling the room with Impatient Wings
(how did it find
and enter so exactly
that small gap
in our bravado?)
The Unwelcome Guest took our Last Snack
Those moments we set aside for Ourselves
Leaving me only my Little Carcass
A scrap of crumpled Adoration

Amy died two nights ago in pain and sorrow. I thought you should know.

—Appoppa

When the note slides under my door, I'm in session with a young man who's been abused as a child, and who still wakes at night in a panic, crying, "What? What do you want?" Normally I wouldn't interrupt a session, particularly not a session with someone so vulnerable, but the note is a ghostly pale blue; I'm almost certain what it is as soon as I see it. I excuse myself, get up, and read it. It's hard to finish the session, but my client is fragile and in pain, so I feel I must.

Now that he's gone, I sit facing the empty chair Amy inhabited only a couple of weeks ago. I gaze at the delicate sheet of paper in my hand, trying to comprehend the finality of death. Then, I cancel the rest of my appointments for the day and leave to look for Appoppa.

When I arrive at her room, she's already been carted away, but he's there. We shake hands and stare at each other, acknowledging that we aren't really strangers. We've been peering at each other for quite some time through the long tube of Amy's perspective.

"So you're her shrink," he says smiling wanly.

I hadn't realized I'd already formed an image of him until I notice it surprises me that he's so tall and good looking, and that he's obviously younger than she was. He has long, dark blond hair and a rakish mustache, and nothing about him is subdued or subservient. I hadn't pictured him as her equal. Appoppa motions to a table and chairs and offers to fix some tea.

They may have been poor, but their room is more interesting than mine. It's larger, the former living room of an apartment, and better lit and more cheerful. They've painted one wall a soft rose, and in front of it, they've placed a row of chromed stovepipes splashed lightly with pastel paint, like some fantasy of a pipe organ. The effect is both orderly and free. The other walls are papered in a light mauve, with silver flecks that glitter down like rain. The space is uncluttered. A large bed (large enough so that Amy could withdraw, as if to another country, and sleep without touching Appoppa for eons), the table and chairs where I sit, and some good quality sound equipment, the only fragment of her former life Amy had managed to preserve, fill the rest of the space.

Appoppa returns with tea in two brightly colored, irregularly shaped mugs.

"Thanks for letting me know about Amy," I said. "It could have been weeks before I found out. She never wanted me to call to check up on her—too paternalistic."

"Yeah, she always wanted to be her own person."

"I'd hoped to get here before they carted her off. I was really fond of Amy. I wanted to say good-bye."

"Not a good idea. She died in pain. You wouldn't have liked the way she looked. Not peaceful. It wasn't a peaceful death."

"I'm so sorry."

"I was holding her when she died. I told her not to be afraid. I told her that she was going to splinter into a million billion shiny little pieces and expand and expand until she filled the whole universe, and that she'd feel joyful and free."

"That was a lovely thing to say, Appoppa. I'm sure it gave her comfort."

"When I was stoned one time, I had an image of death that was like that. You just got bigger and bigger until you were one with everything."

"The Buddhists see it something like that," I say. "They call it becoming one with the Deathless." We're silent for a moment, contemplating the mystery of it all. Finally, I put my hand on his knee and squeeze it. "I know she loved you a lot, Appoppa."

"I think she did. She could be pretty hard on me, but she loved me in her own backward, hard-assed kind of way. Despite the things she'd say, I always knew that."

"She'd been hurt so much, it was hard for her to let herself risk loving. But she did, she loved you a lot."

"She could be some bitch," Appoppa says with pride. He nods at me solemnly. "Did you know we used to talk baby-talk? When we were talking, that is."

"No, I never knew." This makes him smile, either from the memory of it, or because she'd kept something of theirs private from me and special for him.

"After she was dead, I held onto her for a while, but she made me promise to call them right away. She didn't want anyone staring at her once she was dead. So after a little while, I got up and called them, and they were here with that cart so fast, it almost seems like they were right outside just waiting for her to die."

"I'll miss her."

"She thought a lot of you, man. She'd quote things you'd say, which was pretty amazing for Amy. Never heard her do that with anyone else."

This makes me tear up, and too late I realize I've shattered Appoppa's brittle composure. We sit in silence for a couple of long moments with our mutual tears, and with our discomfort at having them. Then Appoppa gets up, hurls his lean body across the bed and dissolves into grief.

At times of terrible loss, people make a unique sound. I first heard it when I attended a play by Euripides, and the women of the town were keening for husbands and sons killed in battle. It comes from a deeper place inside us than we normally even know exists, and it's frightening to hear, since it reminds all who dare to love of the suffering that we, too, almost certainly will have to endure one day.

I don't know what to do. Should I play therapist, sit beside him, and say something wise and comforting? Or should I just quietly slip out the door? I decide on the latter. I'm not his therapist, after all, and whether I am or not, I know there's nothing I can say that will make it hurt any less.

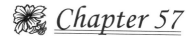 *Chapter 57*

Walking home, I feel shaken by Amy's death, by Appoppa's pain, and by my own vulnerability. Why, just when I've finally accomplished loving, do I have to be confronted so starkly by love's dark side? But I can't turn back. Come what may, I can't stop loving Margaret. Already I'm longing to see her, to have her comfort and soothe me.

"Maybe I'll die first," I think, and I immediately wish for this. But then I feel guilty, because am I not wishing to avoid pain at Margaret's expense? If I really loved her, wouldn't I want to let her die first, so I could be there to comfort her in her last moments? The perfect solution, I think, would be to die together. Not likely though, since all the ways that used to occur—car crashes, airplanes going down, and so forth—are no longer possible. Possibly, I think, we could be simultaneously murdered by a mugger.

I still feel disappointed at not having arrived in time to see Amy before they took her away. These days if you want a final contact with the deceased, you have to outrun the people with the body carts. There seems to be a conspiracy to banish death. Perhaps this isn't true. Perhaps it's only a practical matter. Burial in the earth hasn't been an option for a long time. No earth. So everyone is cremated. In a city of this size, how can we possibly give the dead a private room just for themselves and their mourners when there isn't even enough space for the living? So maybe they have to grab them and whisk them away.

Phillipe disagrees. "It's not practical, it's political," he said the last time we had this discussion. He's convinced that the frantic haste of the body carts and the ban on funerals are an attempt to keep us cut off from the natural consequences of the way we live and so to buffer the authorities from outrage. "If you don't believe it," he said, "just look at what happened at our last funeral."

Phillipe had been there. He'd known the man. And no doubt about it, the last funeral ever held in our city had been a scandal. It had been for a man named S. Jacobi, a performance artist who'd died of AIDS. He'd known for some time he was dying, so he'd had plenty of time to think things over, and he was determined not to have his death glossed over or prettied up in any way. He wanted to make an example of himself. So he made an arrangement with his mortician that instead of making his corpse look as if he had died peacefully in his sleep, as was the custom, he would aim for quite the opposite effect. When you looked into his casket, what you saw staring back at you was anything but pretty. The make-up was mostly black, white, and gray, with a few harsh, red accents. His eyes were not demurely shut, but opened disconcertingly wide. His mouth was stretched, teeth and gums exposed, his tongue protruding in a frozen scream.

His friends were satisfied, Phillipe said, that Jacobi, wherever he was, was definitely enjoying this. It was the final performance of a really rebellious (aren't they all?) performance artist, and the very first truly posthumous work. A voice, a shout actually, not from the muffled distance of the grave, but from much closer, right from the bier. No final curtain for him, no embalming, no disposal of the remains. He decreed that he be left in his open casket until that terrible look rotted off his face, and beyond that, until his bones collapsed in a heap, and even beyond that. He wanted to be left there permanently, forever in the middle of his message, impossible to interrupt. But of course this was merely vanity, Ozimandius on his way to the trash compactor.

When word got out, the police were sent in, clubs swinging, and Jacobi's friends were unable to prevent them from seizing the body. The corpse was officially declared a sacrilege, and it was stuffed without ceremony into a furnace. The provocative presence of one S.

Jacobi, performance artist, occasioned the first mandatory cremation. Ninety-seven percent of him blew out some stack, exiled from the city forever, and the remaining cup of ashes was flushed down the toilet.

After that, funerals were outlawed. A fleet of covered carts rushed through the halls, snatching bodies before they were cold, before anyone could get upset. Death was silently decreed a form of pollution, a dirtiness to be cleansed as rapidly as possible from the hearts and minds of those left behind.

When I arrive home, Margaret is preparing dinner on the little two-burner plug-in appliance I had purchased so we'd have some way to heat canned food when we didn't want to go out or over to my mother's to eat. When I tell her about Amy, she takes me in her arms just as I'd hoped she would. "It's as though I knew her myself," she says. "And Appoppa, too."

"He's suffering," I say. "I didn't know what to do. If he'd been sitting in one of my chairs, I'd have known, but in the real world, I'm useless."

"Don't blame yourself. There isn't anything anyone can do. Tomorrow I'll make food for him at your mother's, and we can take it over there."

"Better than nothing, I guess. At least he'll know we're thinking of him."

"Does Appoppa have family?" she asks, as she turns away and starts dishing out our food: canned beans and franks, and some reconstituted seaweed salad she insists we eat for the sake of our health.

"Beats me. Amy never mentioned any family, but then whenever she mentioned Appoppa, she was either adoring or hating him, mostly hating, unfortunately."

"Poor thing, how can he stand it? Why does life have to hurt so much?"

"I don't know, sweetheart, it just does."

As a therapist I see so much pain, and I've had my share of it too. But my luck has changed. As sad as I feel about Amy, deeper down, I feel buoyant and light. Miraculously I've washed up on some enchanted island, and I feel a little guilty knowing others, like Appoppa, are still out in the dark sea, struggling to keep their heads above water. What have I done, after all, to deserve happiness?

That night when Margaret and I go to bed, I light a candle, and I stroke her hair back from her face so I can see her more clearly. You can look at someone quite differently in candlelight. It's soft and warm, and it moves, so you can get closer and peer more deeply into them without seeming to stare. I'm trying to make a picture in my mind, so if Margaret ever disappears, as Amy has, I'll be able to remember her face forever.

At that moment, as if for our consideration, the couple in the next room begins to make love. They're like us, I think. People have always lain in the dark and listened to sad, wild sounds. To coyotes, at one time, or even wolves. To train whistles. And this is what we have left, two neighbors moaning in the dark, so we can hear them for a little while over the rushing of the vents and the distant hum of the great machines.

Margaret and I gaze softly into each other's eyes, while the voices go on and on. The woman is freer. Her call is sharp: a bird, a small animal running in a pack, the nest has been raided, there's never enough food, the night is full of hunters. The man is heavy and slow, reluctant to cry out. Sighs escape him unawares; low groans force their way past his determination. How can he go on? Is there ever an end to the worry? Their rhythm becomes relentless now. They have gone too far to turn back, their seeking has trapped them, and they have to finish what they've started. Even if their path goes over a cliff, they have to go on. Their sorrow is loud, a rough rope; their voices are braids of crushed and twisted wishes. They've reached the point of confession; they have to admit what they've always kept hidden: that they need one another, that it's too hard to face it all alone, that their love, and only that, makes their struggle worthwhile.

Lying there together in the dark, understanding how things ultimately are, there seems only one decent, human thing to do. Margaret closes her eyes as I lean toward her and touch my lips to hers. Her mouth receives me softly. Her body welcomes my weight, the needs of my hands. And our nakedness speaks: "We, too, can do that for each other. We can make the struggle worthwhile."

Afterward there is such peace. Somehow I always knew this existed, that it was waiting for me somewhere, if I just tried long enough, if I wouldn't let the pain turn me back. We know some things the way plants know growing, before the seasons, before the reasons.

"Would you like me to love you?" I ask this woman who has woven her arms and legs so sweetly between mine. We've made ourselves into a basket that can hold our lives. "I could watch you while you slept," I whisper, and I mean it. I feel no restraint. If she lets me, I think, I'll love her completely. "I could sing while I brushed your hair. You would never be without compliments or conversation, someone to hold your hand, while you walked among the foggy eucalyptus…" We're not alone, I realize. We're connected to all the Appoppas, and to all the Amys. "Your sweet sadness would finally be satisfied…Everything would be right…" The grip of her body answers me, and in my ear I hear an infinite echo, like the ringing of a Buddhist bowl. "Yessssss…"

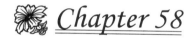 *Chapter 58*

Several weeks later there was a knock at my door, and when I opened it, Appoppa was standing there. Of course, I invited him in. We now had two straight chairs, in addition to my big easy chair, as well as a small table. I made tea for the two of us. Margaret was off at class.

"I wanted to thank you guys for the casserole. It lasted me days. I never even had to open a can." He said this last with the faintest glimmer of a smile.

"How are you doing, Appoppa?" I said. "I know it's hard."

"Yeah, it is," he said and shrugged his shoulders.

"It won't feel this bad forever."

"It had damn sure better not." Appoppa looked down at his sneakers. Again I was struck by how handsome he was. Amy never lost her special attractiveness, even during her illness. "Listen," he said, "I didn't just come here to thank you. Before Amy died, she asked me to talk to you." He paused, giving me a once over with his eyes. "She said you could be trusted." Appoppa, himself, looked dubious.

"I'm a therapist," I assured him. "I'm used to keeping all kinds of confidences."

"Well, this one's pretty important. It's a rule not to tell anyone unless you know them inside and out, and I don't know you hardly at all." He looked woeful, a man caught between mistrust and the desire to fulfill his lover's last wish.

"I would never betray Amy's trust, even if she's dead. I promise you that."

"And do you promise you'll never tell anybody about this unless I say it's okay?"

"I promise." Then I thought about Margaret and how I didn't want there to be any secrets between us. "Wait. What about my…" I almost said wife, but of course, Margaret wasn't my wife. She wasn't even divorced yet. "I'm living with a woman. We're very close. It would be hard to keep a secret from her."

"Then I can't tell you."

"She's very trustworthy."

"Well, I still can't. One wrong person and it could all be over just like that," Appoppa said and snapped his fingers. "And bad stuff could happen to the people involved." I thought this over. I didn't like the idea of keeping a secret from Margaret, but I wanted him to tell me whatever it was Amy had wanted me to know.

"Okay. I promise."

"You won't tell anyone, not even your girlfriend."

"No one, not unless you say it's okay."

"Have you heard about the clowns?" Appoppa asked, with a sly little smile.

"Yes, I have. I've even seen them. On TV, first, and then when I was at the Freedom Tower one day, I saw them in person."

Appoppa looked pleased. "Which piece did you see?"

"The one where the clown goes to sleep and the bed catches fire."

"I'm in that one," he said, now full of excitement. "I blow the whistle to clear a space."

Suddenly I remembered the tall, skinny clown, the one who stepped out of the group and blew the whistle, and I realized I'd actually seen Appoppa before. "Yes, I remember you."

"What did you think?"

"I really liked it. It was crisp and concise. Everything happened so fast that after you disappeared, it almost seemed as though I'd just imagined it, like it was a hallucination or something."

Appoppa smiled broadly. "Did you understand what it was about? Did it make you think?"

I felt chagrined. I'd been impressed with the theatricality, but if it had a meaning, I had no idea what it was. From the start, I'd seen the clowns as some kind of lunatic fringe. It was Margaret who'd taken such an interest in them. "I'm sorry. I never gave it much thought."

"You and how many other people! That's what it's all about. We're trying to wake people up."

"Wake them up to what?"

"To what's happening, man. Amy's not the only one. People are getting sick."

"Yes, well, I have heard rumors."

"You don't read about it in the newspapers, but that's because they don't allow such stories to be printed. After Amy got sick, we started finding out there were others like her. You'd be surprised how many. The city's not exactly safe, man. People are dying."

I thought about Carl. He had died, and you would have thought the newspapers would have been interested in such a bizarre freak accident, but there was never any mention of it in the papers.

"And there are other things," Appoppa continued.

"What kind of other things?"

"Graft, corruption, bad stuff." Well, that didn't surprise me. Finally, I was getting it. The clowns were political. Their pieces were meant to mean something, just like Margaret had said. "Amy thought you might be interested in joining our group," Appoppa went on. "She said you cared about people."

"Well, I…"

"She thought you were a real straight shooter."

Suddenly I realized I was being invited to dress up in a clown suit and do guerilla theater. Of course, I couldn't do that any more than I could become one of Phillipe's AngelBeasts. Besides, Amy had misunderstood. I cared about her. I cared about all my clients, but "people"? I wasn't sure I cared about "people." But then why was I so concerned about injustice? Why had I fumed and fussed for so many years about the things I read in the papers? That's all I'd ever done, though, I reminded myself. I'd fumed and fussed, but I had never actually *done* anything. I sighed.

"Appoppa," I said, "I don't think I could dress up like a clown. It's not that I don't admire what you're trying to do, or that I don't think a lot of things that go on around here are truly awful, but—"

"No, man, you don't have to dress up like a clown. The people who do that, most of us are actors; the majority of people in our group don't do the clown thing. But everyone is concerned about the stuff that's coming down, and we're trying to figure out what to do. The clowns, we're just a small part of it."

"So, what do the rest of the people do?"

Appoppa hesitated. It seemed clear that he didn't completely trust me yet. "Well, right now we're mainly trying to gather information. You know, understand the situation, so we can see what to do."

"Was Amy involved in this?"

"She sure was. She went to the meetings whenever she was well enough. She was one tough bitch. Always had lots of radical ideas, too radical for a lot of them. But that was Amy." He smiled proudly; then remembering her, he had to fight back tears.

I imagined Amy limping through the corridors to protest what had happened to her. I felt touched and inspired. If she had wanted me to take her place, I should at least try it. "Okay," I said. "What do you want me to do?"

"Thanks, man. You know, I think Amy was right about you. You're okay." And with that he gave me a manly slap on the back.

Appoppa and I spent the afternoon together talking about the city and its problems. We had a few beers at a nearby bar, and he told me a lot more about his organization. They called it the Club. This name was meant to sound innocuous, so no one would suspect that its members had serious intentions. If anyone was overheard saying that they'd "gone to the Club last night," people were intended to think bridge, not politics.

Appoppa gave me a blow-by-blow account of how our rights had gradually, but relentlessly, been stripped away, starting way back in the days just after the World Trade attack. I had been aware of most of what he told me. They were the very things Margaret and I had often talked about with outrage, but having it all laid out before me in chronological order made me realize just how complacent we New Yorkers had been. The very fact that we had to sit in a far corner and make certain we weren't overheard made the point that even though the right of free speech theoretically still existed, it didn't actually, given what could happen to you if you tried to exercise it.

With the erosion of rights came the erosion of democracy. What had begun as scattered election irregularities had mushroomed into a situation where no one believed anyone but a member of the Liberty Party would be allowed to win, even if the vote went against them, which we had to admit probably hadn't happened all that often. Everyone realized that the Liberties were the same group that had campaigned for the Encapsulation, and since the Encapsulation had protected us from terrorist attacks, the rising sea, and most recently the flu pandemic, the Liberty Party was hugely popular. This is what people seem to care about above all else. But Appoppa put into words what I'd already started to feel deep in my gut: "At what price safety?"

Appoppa moved from the loss of rights and the erosion of democracy to the corruption rampant among our politicians and business people, and from there to the environment, ours in the city, as well as the degradation that had taken place in the rest of the world. I already knew that entire coastlines were under water. And I'd seen pictures on TV of fires raging through areas that no longer received much rainfall. Appoppa talked as well about pollution, expanding deserts, and dwindling supplies of food and water, the consequences of which even we in our protective shell wouldn't be able to avoid forever. He said that if the flu pandemic hadn't come along and wiped out a third of the world's population, we'd already be experiencing mass starvation.

He was too young to have ever seen a tree, save in the arboretum. Nonetheless, he'd developed a love for the natural world to rival my father's. The Club had been smuggling nature movies into the city, and Appoppa was an avid fan. He knew about species of animals I'd never heard of, a great number of which, he said, no longer existed.

Currently the Club wasn't focusing on any of these problems. Something bigger and scarier had to be taken care of first. According to Appoppa, in the last two months alone, there had been at least 786 unexplained deaths. That's how many the Club had been able to document. The real number was surely much higher, since they were being disguised as normal illnesses in medical reports. "Something real bad is coming down, man!" he said, "and the authorities don't want anyone to know about it." We were silent for a moment. In the stillness, it seemed to me that Amy's spirit was there with us. Appoppa must have read my mind, because just then he said, "Amy sure was one tough bitch."

After we'd talked for a long time, and while we were still immersed in a fog of mutual tipsiness, I reintroduced the subject of Margaret. I told him how excited she'd been about the clowns, and how she'd understood the meaning of the piece where they all fall down. Finally, he agreed to allow me to tell her about the Club. A little while later, we gave each other a brotherly hug and parted.

I hurried home. I was dying to tell Margaret about Appoppa's visit, but she wasn't home from school yet. When she did arrive it turned out she was eager to tell a story of her own, one that had been buzzing around her school all day.

An instructor at the medical school, a physician who was only in her thirties, had stopped off at the X-ray lab that day and had taken a quick picture of her chest in order to provide her class in thoracic surgery with a real-life visual aid. But when she clipped it to the light panel in her classroom, what she and her students saw was an illumination of her own death, a picture of a silent avalanche about to crush her. The X-ray revealed that her lungs were clotted with cancer. She'd left without a word, and the members of her class knew they'd never see her again.

She hadn't gotten cancer from smoking, that was certain. We'd banned smoking years ago, had had to, ever since we started recirculating our air. From then on, anytime anyone lit up a cigarette, everyone in the city would have had to share it.

"Some people are saying there's contamination at the school," Margaret said. Suddenly I felt uneasy. After being with Appoppa and finding out that people were falling ill and now hearing this story…

But it was all so vague. As Appoppa had pointed out, no one really understood why so many people were getting sick. It could be something in our food, in our air, in our water. It was even possible that it was some new kind of virus or bacteria. Nobody knew.

 ## *Chapter 59*

The next day, Phillipe called and asked me out for coffee at Felicia's. I wanted to tell Phillipe about the mysterious illnesses, but I'd agreed not to talk to anyone about the Club or what they'd discovered. Still, if anyone was born to be a member of the Club, it was Phillipe. I felt more than a little smug about having discovered this band of revolutionaries before he did, and I made a mental note to talk to Appoppa about inviting Phillipe to join.

I dropped by Phillipe's apartment. Together we struggled though the crowded hallways toward Felicia's. Phillipe steered in and out around the handcarts, and I stepped over the children's games. No matter what direction we went, it always felt against the current. Phillipe grunted something low and annoyed that I couldn't make out over the gabble and clatter.

"What did you say?" I asked.

"I said, sewer rats!" he snapped, waving a flipper at the teeming hallway. He was wearing a crimson T-shirt (where does he get these things?) with a large black-winged skull and the proud motto Dr. Darkness.

"You know," I said, "if I wanted to describe this city, the first thing I'd mention would be darkness. But except for the blackouts, it's never really dark here. It's like a subway station. No matter how well you light it, it always feels underground."

"Yes," he agreed. "The old city was full of contrasts, bright light and sharp shadows. I used to love those dark alleys." We looked around us. Our fluorescents didn't beam, they diffused. A greenish gray crept over and around everything; nothing was obscured, but nothing was distinct. Nothing distinct. Perhaps that's what I really meant by darkness. Fresh paint was dingy, right out of the can; washed faces dull; new clothes drab.

Phillipe seemed deep in thought and not at all interested in my musings. We reached Felicia's and wedged ourselves in. "Did you know that Rachmaninoff once went to a therapist?" he said suddenly. He squinted at me as I waited stoically for his punch line. "And it ruined him," he finished, triumphant. Good old Phillipe, one-man fifth column, attacking the establishment from within. When the proverbial revolution finally comes, that ultimate secular Day of Judgment, when the heads of therapists are impaled on spikes and our guts are strewn in the corridors, Phillipe will be cheered by the masses and paraded on their shoulders.

"He was having trouble with his music," Phillipe continues. "He didn't feel recognized, not with his first symphony or his first piano concerto. So he went to a therapist. Can you believe it? And do you know what happened? He became popular! Yes, his second piano concerto was a bombshell. The second symphony, the rhapsody, they did fine. They're famous. So I went back to listen to his pre-therapy music, and do you know what? It was much better! It had some real guts to it. Not all that background music for movies he churned out later. The early stuff, you really should listen to it. It was great."

For Phillipe, popular acceptance was the ultimate curse, a sure indication that something essential was lacking. When I considered where the popular sentiment had brought us, I had to wonder if he didn't have a point. I challenged him anyway. "I don't remember the early Rachmaninoff, but I can't buy that crap about therapy ruining artists."

"The pain," he explains. "It takes away their pain. They have no more soul."

"Oh, please spare me, Phillipe! There's so much pain. There's more than enough to go around. Therapy just skims off the excess. And as for stealing souls, I thought photographs did that."

Phillipe was always looking for a straight man, someone more conservative to poke at, but I resented being pushed into that role just because Carl was no longer available. Phillipe seemed surprised that I didn't want to play with him. After all, he was merely looking for the right kind of conversation to go with his coffee, a little biscotti-talk, something crunchy, with a few almonds. But he responded good-naturedly to my impatience and even placated me. "Actually I'm not certain the man he saw was a therapist. Sometimes he's described as a hypnotist."

I tried to imagine the world back then, full of horse carts and early automobiles, and I tried to picture what it might have been like to visit a therapist. Like an appointment with a psychic? Or with a scientist in the old-fashioned, romantic sense? Or like a dreaded trip to the dentist, to some mechanic of the mind with rows of drawers full of sharp little instruments for various painful purposes, whose deep probing must be endured for one's own good? Not only are the horses gone now, but the automobiles are gone as well. And if it is Phillipe and I who have survived them, like some life form with superior adaptive capacity, evolution has clearly lost its way.

Phillipe rolled his wheelchair up close to the table and sipped his cappuccino. Always intuitive and companionable, he grew somber along with me. "Nothing interests me anymore," he complained.

I didn't take his mood seriously. He might be mimicking me. And I know he would put on any face that was necessary to draw me out for a little amusement. "This fantastic thing happened to me," he continued. "About a month ago someone sold me a complete model train set-up—tracks, houses, trees, tunnels, little red lights and bells, everything. They haven't made this kind for years, and it must be worth thousands. All she wanted was fifty dollars. Fantastic luck."

Something about the way he said this made me wonder if it was luck or if it might have been a gift from one of his clients, a gift he should have refused.

"So I ordered a big sheet of plywood, and I hired a guy to cover it with green felt, nail the track down, and glue the village and the hills and the little people in place. It was beautiful, better than what I had when I was a kid. So I run the engine around the track once, and then

I leave it. That was a month ago. I haven't touched it since. I don't know what's wrong with me."

"Why does something have to be wrong with you?"

"Because I'm not like that. I used to love trains. And women, too. When I was fifteen I would travel all the way across town to see a girl. Down corridors, up elevators, long subway rides, and then all the way back again, late at night, with the constant risk of getting mugged. Yet I couldn't wait to do it. Today I wouldn't cross the hall to see a woman."

I grunt. Phillipe has more sex than anyone I know. He has developed a teasing, taunting approach that makes some women angry, then defensive, and finally curious. The next thing they know, they're rolling around in bed with a little rubber ball of a man with a cock like a horse and the ethics of an alley cat.

"I don't think you've changed," I told him.

"How can you say that?" He made a face like a schnauzer.

"I think it's your situation that's changed, that's all. When you were ten, trains were a challenge. When you were fifteen, girls were a challenge. All you need now is another challenge."

"What do you mean?" I've piqued his curiosity, and he's uncharacteristically attentive. He's even leaning forward a bit in his chair. It's flattering to receive this kind of response from such a habitual cynic, so I find myself less resentful of his games and more willing to take pains to express myself.

"How about this? How would you like to have a date with Rachmaninoff?" I asked him. "Imagine I could arrange for you to spend an evening with him, that I could bring him back somehow, and you could ask him about his therapy. You could discuss his music before and after treatment and tell him what you thought of it. Would you like that?"

"Of course!" he exclaimed. It was like telling a bedtime story to an eager child, and I wanted to make it good.

"Let's say I have a way of tapping into the brain waves of famous people, dead people, and bringing their consciousness forward into the present. It isn't easy, understand? There are problems." He smiles and nods. He can understand there might be problems resurrecting the minds of the dead. "For instance, there's no telling where this consciousness is going to land once we bring it back. It could plop into anyone. You could be sitting around, having a conversation with the spirits of Einstein, Gandhi, and Heckler, and all anyone passing by would see would be a high school cheerleader and two little kids with chocolate on their faces.

"Now as it turns out, Rachmaninoff has landed in the brain of a welfare mother with six kids who lives all the way on the other side of town. It's going to be very hard to get to her. Are you still game?"

"Is it dangerous?"

"Not very, just a little bleak. You have to go all the way over to her place by subway, up elevators, down corridors, take her out to some little restaurant where you can find out all the secrets of a Russian composer, then take her all the way back again, then come home late at night with the risk of getting mugged. Would it be worth it to you?"

"Of course. I'd kill to be able to explain to Rachmaninoff just how therapy screwed him up," he assured me enthusiastically.

"Then you see? You haven't changed." I'd made my point quite neatly and was pleased with myself. "That's exactly the kind of thing you used to do when you were fifteen. All we did was raise the stakes to something new and exciting, to something that suits your age and experience better than a train set."

"That's great. You're so right. I never looked at it that way." Phillipe was beaming. Much too late, I realized why he was enjoying himself so much. He'd manipulated me just as deftly as the women he seduces. He'd provoked me to talk to him while he drank his coffee, when I didn't feel conversational, and more than just talk, to lecture and explain and make up interesting examples, while he looked up at me, wide-eyed and ingenuous, and totally corrupt. To his credit, he never once stepped out of character. He was still telling me enthusiastically, "That was great. I won't forget that," as he rolled away from the café.

Chapter 60

W e met Appoppa at the entrance to the underground the following Wednesday night. We were going to our first Club
meeting. Neither Margaret nor I had used the underground for years,
and her hand felt damp and cold in mine. Despite Appoppa's assurances that trains nowadays had emergency backup lighting systems in
case of blackouts, Margaret was terrified. But afraid or not, she was
determined to go.

The meeting of the Club was to take place near the loading docks
in a warehouse slated for demolition. We went up a lift and into a big
room, empty except for some folding chairs and forty or fifty people
seated or standing in clusters. Everyone seemed to be talking, and the
voices ricocheted around the empty room, creating an excited hub-
bub. A glint of chrome tubing suddenly caught my eye—Phillipe's
wheelchair. Phillipe! I should have known! There he sat enthroned on
one of those elegant tapestry cushions he collected for his use. He had
positioned himself right smack in the middle of the largest group and
was holding forth and waving his stumps around. He didn't notice us
at first, but when he did, he came rolling over.

"Hello, Wizard," I said.

"Well, well, well, what a surprise. Never dreamed you'd get
involved in something like this, or I'd have invited you myself." He
was right, of course. As a revolutionary, I was an unlikely candidate. A
distinguished-looking Asian man entered, and everyone started moving toward the chairs. As he sat down and faced the group, Appoppa
whispered, "That's our leader. He's a professor at NYU."

"What's his name?"

"No idea," Appoppa said. "Everybody just calls him the Leader."
A slight man with wire-rimmed glasses, white hair, and a beard, he
seemed extremely self-possessed. I liked him immediately. "Maybe it's
for safety," Appoppa continued, "so people don't use his name where
it could be overheard."

"Safety? What do you mean?"

Before Appoppa could say anything more the Leader began to speak.

"Welcome everyone," he said. "Let's begin with the committee reports." His voice was calm and unpretentious, yet he spoke with authority.

A tall, thin, middle-aged woman named Geraldine, head of the Medical Committee, stood and began to speak, and after her, Howie, head of Intelligence, and then several others, including Appoppa, who spoke for the clowns.

There was an avalanche of unsettling information. The number of unexplained deaths documented by the Club had now risen to over a thousand. In addition, they had uncovered evidence that the cancer rate had increased 23 percent during the last ten years. Since neither the suspicious deaths nor the increase in the cancer rate had been made public, it seemed that our politicians, and possibly our corporate leaders, were suppressing this information and that they might even know why the illnesses were occurring. For this reason, some Club members were engaged in spying on those in political and corporate high places. I couldn't believe it. While pretending to service air conditioners, they had bugged the offices of several high officials. When I heard that, I realized that this group really was subversive and that just being here put Margaret and me in danger. It made my stomach queasy. The clowns had seemed so fanciful, and the Club such a ridiculous sounding name, I hadn't imagined anything like this was going on. It seemed foolish, I thought, to speak of such things in a meeting attended by people they didn't know well, such as Margaret and me.

Just before the end of the meeting, all of us who were new to the group were asked to stand up and give our first name only. Margaret and I stood, along with a woman named Betsy, who looked seventy-something, and a guy named Brad, who later told us he was a construction worker. We were all sworn to secrecy and warned that the entire fate of the Club and the safety of its members depended on our keeping this pledge. Then the Leader asked us if we wished to join. I hadn't expected this, and before I could make apologies and decline, I heard Margaret's voice ring out loud and clear, "Yes, I want to join." Then the other two said yes, and then I said yes. After that, one person after another came up and thanked us and hugged us, and Appoppa stood there looking like a proud parent, and I felt like a big wave had come along and swept me somewhere I didn't want to be.

Margaret, who from the outset had loved the clowns, decided to join them. Before we left, she chattered excitedly with Appoppa about ideas for possible new scripts. As I watched them together, I realized that despite Margaret's being my age, there was something very youthful about her. I've added this to the ever growing list of things I love about her.

As we traveled home, I was filled with apprehension. I had no illusions regarding what could happen to people intent on sticking their noses into things those in power wanted to keep secret. My anxiety was probably pretty high, because while I was just sitting there listening to the clicking of the train running along the track, I had a vivid fantasy. In my mind's eye, I saw a man stepping out from under a dark stairway and pointing a gun at Margaret. The image rolled forward like a movie. I saw myself throw my body between her and the bullet. I saw the bullet hit me in the back. I heard Margaret scream. Then the image disappeared, and I was back on the subway feeling shaken and amazed. Did I love Margaret so fiercely I'd be willing to die to save her? It was like something out of a book, yet it was also me, this strange new person I'd become, and who I was still just getting to know.

When we got home, I made Margaret face me directly. "Do you understand that being a member of this group is dangerous?" I said.

"Of course I do. Do you take me for a fool?"

"No, I'm the fool for having gotten us involved in this. I wanted to do it for Amy. I wanted to be courageous for a change. But the truth is, I'm frightened. I'm afraid for myself, but even more, I'm afraid something will happen to you."

"But don't you see how bad things have gotten? We wouldn't be afraid if we actually had any of the freedoms we're supposed to have. We're afraid because of the kind of things that happen to people who speak out."

"I know that. But why us? For the first time in my life, I'm happy. I don't want to lose that, not yet. It's too new and too good."

"You don't have to be a part of this. I won't stop loving you if you don't go with me. I'll still love you." With that she pulled me onto the bed, climbed on top of me, and covered my face with about a hundred little kisses. My heart felt like it was going to burst, I loved her so much.

"Margaret, if you will promise not to involve yourself in this, I'll be a clown, or even a spy. I'll fight for us both, but I don't want anything to happen to you. I couldn't survive it."

"Shhh. Don't talk." She started to unbutton her blouse and gave me a playful, sex kittenish look. But I couldn't make love to her. Not until we got this settled.

"So will you drop out if I go?" She stopped and looked directly into my eyes, suddenly serious.

"No, I can't. My life hasn't meant much until now. All those years sitting around showing each other newspaper articles. We got angry, but we never did anything. Well, these people are trying to do something, and I want to try too."

"I'll try. I'll try for us both."

"No, we'll do it together. If we go to jail, we'll both go to jail."

"What do you think, that they'll put us in the same cell, and we can continue our love affair there?"

"Well, maybe."

"Don't be silly. You know very well if they considered us a threat, the best we could hope for is that they'd dump us down the same garbage chute."

"Don't be negative. Nothing has happened to any of the others."

"Yet."

"And besides, it doesn't sound like we're very safe the way things are now. We could become ill and die, like Amy and the others. We've got to find out why people are getting sick!"

I tipped Margaret over onto the bed beside me. I held her tightly and tried to concentrate on my breathing. Fear and confusion were starting to overwhelm me. I wanted to calm down so I could think clearly, but Margaret kept talking.

"They've whittled away our rights until we don't have any, and now they won't even tell us the truth about why people are dying. They've falsified death certificates. They've kept it out of the papers. I think they know something they're not telling us. Doesn't it make you mad? Don't you want to fight for our right to know the truth?"

Of course it made me mad, but I didn't want to fight. I wanted to be left alone. I wanted to live my life simply: to love and be loved, read history, visit my mother's kitchen, think deeply about things, and continue to do my very best to help my clients. I hated injustice, but I wasn't a soldier. I couldn't march into battle waving some banner, buoyed up by some high ideal, ready to sacrifice my life or the lives of my loved ones, if that's what it took. That's what they were like, the people who'd taken control of our city. They were fighters, and I figured that that's why they'd probably win. They didn't seem to mind fighting for power and for money, and supposedly for "our way of life," though at bottom, I wasn't sure all that patriotic talk wasn't as much a way to manipulate their followers as anything else.

"Why aren't you saying anything?" Margaret demanded.

"Because I'm thinking. A lot of upsetting things have happened. I'm trying to calm down, so I can decide what to do."

"What do you suppose is making people sick?" Margaret asked.

"I have no idea. Exposure to something toxic would be my guess. But where, how, I don't know."

"Well, we've got to find out."

"Margaret, let's not talk for a little bit, please." A long minute passed. I could hear the faint whir of the machines and the sound of a TV in the next room. I closed my eyes and tried to connect with myself as deeply as possible.

"I want to ask you something, something important," I said finally.

"Okay, sure."

"Sweetheart, have you ever thought about leaving New York?"

"Leaving?"

"Yes, leaving. Going somewhere else to live, somewhere outside." I could tell by the look on her face that she hadn't. She was quiet for a while, trying to comprehend what living outside would mean.

"No," she said. "And I really don't think that would be a very good idea. Outside are terrorists and tornadoes, and lots of other things even more dangerous that the threats we face here."

"Oh, Margaret, that's what they want us to think. But Appoppa says that tornadoes and tidal waves and things like that don't happen nearly as often as they make out. And as for terrorists, we've got plenty of those here. What else are those so-called patriots who roam our streets in bands?"

"Well, at least they don't set off bombs."

"There are places, Appoppa says, where terrorists never go. Small places where they don't bother to set off bombs, because there just aren't enough people to kill."

"Well, what about the droughts and the fires and the flooding?"

"Apparently there are still places that are okay to live out there. Appoppa says that since so many people died in the flu pandemic, for the time being there's still enough water and food for the survivors. If there weren't, we'd starve too, because nobody would be willing to sell us the food we import."

"How does Appoppa know so much about the outside?"

"He talks to the truckers at the unloading docks. They tell him what it's like. Many of them wouldn't live in New York for anything. Some think we're crazy to stay here."

"There are people starving out there, Noah," Margaret says emphatically. "I've seen pictures of them on TV."

"There have always been people starving in the world. They're poor; they don't have money to buy food."

"Noah, you really don't know what we'd have to face out there. Besides, New York is my home, and I want to fight for it. If we could clean it up and get rid of the Liberties and their thugs, things would be fine."

I could tell Margaret was frightened, so I didn't say any more about leaving. Clearly it was an idea that would take some getting used to. And, of course, I wasn't sure we could survive outside. Margaret might be right.

"Come be here with me, sweetheart," Margaret said, and she gave me a cute "come hither" look. Suddenly I didn't want to think about any of it anymore. Margaret and I were together and in love, and for the time being we were safe.

"Okay," I said, taking her face in my hands and kissing her. We took off our clothes and snuggled under the covers. Her body felt delicious, an ice cream sundae made of flesh. Later, inside her, with great torrents of feeling surging through my body, I knew the truth. I knew I'd rather die than let anything happen to Margaret.

🌸 *Chapter 61*

The next week Appoppa, Phillipe, Margaret, and I all piled onto the underground together. We planned to arrive at the meeting a half-hour early, because Margaret and I wanted to meet some of the other members. Rush hour was under way, and the underground was so packed that some of the people waiting at the stops weren't able to board. I prayed there wouldn't be a power outage, because emergency lights or no, it would be awful to be caught down there all squeezed in together the way we were. It was hot, and the man next to me had clearly neglected to use deodorant. Phillipe treated the whole situation as a lark, but then his wheelchair provided him with a little extra breathing space.

Phillipe's function within the Club seemed to have been tailored especially for him. It made Margaret and me laugh every time we thought about it. Technically he was a member of the Intelligence Committee, but he didn't spy in any of the usual ways. Instead, the Club had provided him with the unpublished numbers of high-up members of the Liberty Party or, in many cases, the spouses of members—female, of course. Phillipe would pretend he'd dialed them by accident and had no idea who he was talking to. Then he'd use his seductive powers to engage them in a "personal" relationship, which whenever possible, he'd carry on long-term in the hopes of winning their confidence and finding out something important. He now had three such relationships going, which he figured was about his quota, because otherwise he wouldn't have time to talk with his paying clients.

The part that amused us most was that Phillipe would pretend to be an avid patriot, a flag waver of the first order. He never uttered the words "New York," except in a tone of utmost reverence. Phillipe! He also pretended to live within the Central Park Community, so his contacts would consider him "one of them."

Only two people had arrived at the meeting before us, Howie, the head of Intelligence, and Betty, the old woman who'd joined the same night we had. What a contrast. Howie was a fiery liberal, a one-time member of the Green Party, while Betty, a sweet little grandmother type, had never been a member of anything more subversive than a sewing group. Margaret asked Betty how she'd come to join the Club.

"Well," she said, "I lost my granddaughter to one of those strange illnesses."

"I'm sorry," Margaret said, putting an arm around her shoulder.

"She was a cute little thing, just four and a half. Had terrible pain. Just withered away to nothing, and no doctor could tell us why. When her mother found her dead one morning, I nearly died myself. Imagine having your little granddaughter go before you do!" She paused; her gray eyes hardened to stone. "I'm old," she said. "They can do what they like to me, but I have to see to it that nothing happens to my children or the rest of my grandchildren!"

Death was involved in Howie's story as well, or so he believed. He'd been campaigning hard against the Encapsulation when a close friend, also prominent in the Green Party, disappeared. The authorities investigated. Eventually they said she'd been seen boarding a bus headed for Canada. They claimed she'd chosen to leave the city. Howie never believed this. She'd had a fiancée, he said, with whom she was very much in love, and she'd never said anything about leaving. He believed she'd been kidnapped and killed as an example to the rest of them. The strategy had worked. After that, he and a lot of others were just too scared to continue fighting. I watched the little twitch in Howie's jaw and wondered if it was a sign of anger gone underground.

By now the room had filled with people, and it was time to start. The Leader came in and took his seat. Again, I was struck by his unusual sense of calm. I made a mental note to ask Appoppa more about him.

Chapter 62

I've been pacing, sitting down, standing up, trying to read, standing up, pacing. On the hour, I turn on the TV to catch the local news, but so far there has been nothing. It's Margaret's first day with the clowns. They're performing a new piece. Margaret came up with the idea, and because she's such a good dancer, they chose her to star in it. I saw it for the first time yesterday in rehearsal. Appoppa blows his whistle to clear a space. Then a female clown (Margaret) enters and dances. At first she's happy and vivacious. Gradually her movements become slower and slower. She just seems to run out of steam, like some wind-up toy, until she's barely able to move. Finally, her legs buckle, and she collapses. The other clowns run in carrying a folded stretcher and a gas mask. One clown puts the gas mask on her, two others load her onto the stretcher, while the rest make alarmed faces and jump up and down. They carry her off, fold up the stretcher, and run away. With luck, they then duck under a stairway, remove their clown outfits, and melt into the rush of the corridors.

I wish I shared the prevailing belief regarding the stupidity of those in power. They aren't deep, and they're certainly not wise, but in my mind, they are smart—smart enough to manipulate the majority of New Yorkers into electing them to office over and over again. And they're cunning. The bill they passed that cut welfare to our poorest citizens was called the Work with Dignity Act. The bill that raised the level of pollutants allowed in our food was called the Fair Competition Act. (Since no one is against working with dignity or fair competition, and since the voters don't actually read the bills, they passed handily.) They've consolidated the media into a couple of papers and a few TV stations, all of which are owned by their cronies, and they've been in power so long, they've appointed all the judges. Worse yet, if anyone should dare to criticize them, he or she is likely to be intimidated by bands of patriot thugs whose violence the Liberties abhor, but do nothing to stop. I hate the people who govern our city, but I do not think they're stupid. So how long is it going to be before they figure out what the clowns are up to and decide to silence their silence?

Finally on the six o'clock news, they show the video. (Each time the clowns perform, one member makes a video. Copies are then dropped off at the TV stations.) This time they've chosen a space near the old wharf. The station has apparently cut the beginning, because Margaret is in the midst of her dance. Lots of people are crowded around watching. Margaret's almost to the part where she sinks to the ground. The camera pans in on a little girl's face. She's totally entranced, and so am I. Margaret is so graceful, and so brave. Margaret is wilting now. She's beginning to sink lower and lower toward the ground. Then the camera pans away from the clowns and focuses on a group of hulking men with flags printed on their shirts. They're pushing their way through the crowd toward the performance space. "Run! Run!" I scream at the TV screen. But apparently the clowns have planned for this. Appoppa starts blowing his whistle over and over, and in a split second, the clowns disappear. The crowd moans as they depart, unhappy to be deprived of this entertainment. But when the spectators notice the Patriots moving toward the spot where the clowns had been, they quickly shrink back. Then the TV newscaster speaks: "The mysterious clowns, who've been popping up all over the city for months now, cut short their performance today when a group of Patriots tried to join the audience. The crowd was disappointed to see the clowns go." On the screen, I see the Patriots moving into the crowd in the direction the clowns disappeared. Are they looking for them? I pray that they aren't.

During the two excruciating hours before Margaret finally walked in the door, I made a decision. As incredible as it seems, I'm going to put on a fright wig and a big red nose; I'm going to learn to make faces and jump up and down. I'm going to behave in ways I never thought I could or would. It's the only way I can be there to protect Margaret. And I must be there. I can't live through another day like this.

How strange life is. I sit in my little boat and am carried along. I can paddle with all my might, and sometimes it seems possible to make my boat go wherever I want, but ultimately the current is always stronger. Against all odds, I'm going to become a clown.

Chapter 63

In order to achieve my goal, I had to convince the others I'd had a change of heart and really wanted to help "wake people up." Naturally, given all I've said, Margaret remains skeptical. I still don't think she believes me. But just as I once planned to insist to Miss Murray that I liked math and wanted to do extra work, I continue to insist to Margaret that I've changed and sincerely want to be a clown. If I admitted the truth, she'd feel she had to tell the others, and then they wouldn't want me.

The clown training has been excruciating. I've always been reserved, and wearing a fright wig, making faces, all the simple everyday things any good clown does, make me feel foolish. But the threat of having them see the truth has caused me to throw myself into my clowning to such an extent that the others seem to think I'm great. Appoppa even told me I was "a natural."

As if all this weren't enough, now when my sense of humiliation is at an all-time high, something strange and equally embarrassing has happened in my work life. Over the past couple of weeks, I became aware that some new quality had come into my therapy sessions, something I was at a loss to explain in the attitudes of several of my clients. My first reaction was guilt: I was afraid the stress I was under was making me distracted and that I hadn't been giving them my full attention. But that didn't really fit; they didn't seem upset. They just watched me with an interest that was off-key somehow, though not unpleasant. It was almost as if they knew that after hours, I dressed up as a clown. But they couldn't know that, so I was completely puzzled.

Then yesterday afternoon an older woman smiled shyly at the end of her session and told me I was "certainly a sweet-looking baby." I was shocked and insisted she explain, keeping her there as we ran over into the next hour. She confessed to me hesitantly that she liked my mother.

It turns out that lately my mother, overflowing with pride in her son, has been devoting her lunch hours and her evenings to sitting in my waiting room and discussing me with my clients. She soon developed some regular appointments of her own. She brought in the family photo albums, plumply padded with white vinyl, and showed pictures while she told her favorite stories: the clever things I'd said, my cute mistakes, the terrible problems I had when I was growing up. She was quite pleased with her intuition, because she couldn't have hit upon a more receptive audience, particularly since I've been so scrupulously reserved about my private life. And with her marvelous instinct for survival, my mother excuses herself just a minute before the hour and pops out into the hall, so that she's vanished before I, like a tin saint in a Swiss village clock, march out of my office and into the waiting room with perfectly predictable promptness.

When I confronted her, my mother sniffled and said that she didn't see the harm in letting my clients know a little more about me. Naturally, I forbade her from ever entering my waiting room again, and from talking to my clients anywhere else either. But I can't undo what she's done. My foibles have been paraded before my clients. Now I feel like a clown, both in and out of my sessions.

Phillipe, of course, thinks my mother's right and that my professional reserve is ridiculous. As I often do when I'm having some emotional difficulty, I consider what I'd tell a client if he or she came to me with this story. Clearly I'd say that my sense of humiliation indicates that I think what's occurred somehow changes my value as a human being and that this is an error. I'd point out that it's irrational to believe that an external event, like my mother telling my clients stories about me, or a particular kind of behavior, like jumping up and down and making faces, could actually diminish my human worth. I am, after all, still exactly the same person I was before these things occurred. Amazingly, just seeing the truth of this does make me feel better.

Chapter 64

When we attended the Club meeting tonight, Margaret surprised me. The discussion turned to the various tactics certain civic pride organizations use to intimidate people and what we could do to stop them. Those who indulge in this flavor of political bitterness take it personally if you disagree with them. The Patriots, by far the largest and scariest of these groups, has adopted the Statue of Liberty as the symbol of their way of life. Of course, the real thing had been permitted to erode to an unrecognizable stump long ago, but on city holidays when big parades are held in the main corridors, the Patriots ride Liberty on floats or carry her on platforms supported on poles, like a patron saint.

If some individual or some business, such as a newspaper, for instance, is seen as guilty of criticizing "our way of life," the paper may find a stencil of the statue sprayed on the door as a warning, along with the Patriots' favorite motto, "If you don't like it here, why don't you leave!" They seem to consider the status quo their birthright. People have even been found beaten with a stencil of the liberty symbol spray painted onto their skin or clothing. In this graffiti, the torch Liberty carries is always painted a bright red, a purifying, avenging flame, while her book is not colored at all.

In the midst of this discussion, I noticed that Margaret had raised her hand. When the leader nodded in her direction, she stood, so all eyes turned toward her. When she spoke, she kept her voice low and even. In fact, she was so remarkably even, so surprisingly steady and clear, that everyone listened. "We would be foolish," she said, "to give up that lovely image to these people, who so totally misuse her. We don't have to let them defile her with their hate. We can use the statue as our emblem, too."

"But they spray it on people's doors. It's become a threat of violence," someone objected.

"We can spray it too. It can become a reminder of freedom, just as it used to be."

"But people won't know the difference between us and them. It'll be confusing."

"Good," Margaret said. "Maybe the confusion will wake people up. Maybe it will force them to think."

A motion was made to adopt the Statue of Liberty as our symbol, but in order to distinguish our Liberty from theirs, underneath ours would be the words, "Remember What Liberty Means." The motion passed unanimously.

As we rode home on the subway, Margaret seemed especially tired. Then, as we walked the last couple of blocks toward home, we found the corridor ahead blocked by a group of children. They were running and shrieking, and it took us a minute to realize that they were more excited than frightened. They were chasing a rat. The ones in front, the older ones, had small nets on long handles. They were shoving each other as they ran, competing to make the capture once the fleeing animal found itself cornered. A plump little girl with a bobbing ponytail stumbled behind them. "Don't leave me," she cried. "Don't leave me." She was carrying the cage, which was covered with a mesh so fine it made the cage look like a solid gray box. Our rats make fierce pets, snarling and gnashing at the mesh with yellow teeth, but they don't live long in captivity. That cage will be its death chamber.

Suddenly Margaret tore her hand out of mine and ran all the way home. I ran after her. Once there, she threw herself on the bed and sobbed for almost an hour. This made me understand anew what it costs her to venture out into the world. When she was with Adam, she hardly left the house. Now that she refuses to be controlled by her anxieties, their power over her has diminished. She walks to school, rides the subway, participates in the clown activities, and speaks her mind. But these things are still hard; they still require courage, and sometimes it all just gets to be too much. I wrap her in my arms. I want to protect her from all life's hurts. Of course, I know I can't, and that my heart will ache again and again for her, as it does tonight.

Chapter 65

Something is trickling. I can hear it at night, lying in bed when the halls are quiet. I've looked around when the lights are on; there are no spots yet on the ceiling, no mold on the walls. I should report it, that's my civic duty, but then they'll come and hack holes and make dust, and why should I let them before it's absolutely necessary?

Tonight as I lie awake listening to the water, I'm filled with a kind of inner effervescence that's both pleasurable and disorienting. Things are shifting inside, and just like the time when that strange vision revealed my life to be empty and paper thin, this change has come without my trying to make it happen, or even conceiving that such a thing was possible.

As I continued to go to the clown rehearsals, I gradually started to feel less and less self-conscious. Then slowly, I started to actually enjoy clowning. Now, I can't get enough of it. I love the physicality, the exuberance, the thrill that comes when I get the timing exactly right. Unbelievably, I can now do just about anything without discomfort. This is so different from my former buttoned-down self, it almost seems like I've become someone else.

Margaret's thrilled. Not only does she have a partner in clowning, but there have been other benefits. She used to beg me to dance with her. I tried a couple of times, but I was stiff and awkward, and then so shamed by my awkwardness and by the comparisons I made between myself and other people, that despite wanting to please her, I couldn't continue. Now, thanks to the clown training, I've discovered I have a magic genie inside who's far more creative and graceful than I could ever hope to be. I let the music pulse through me; I let go completely and trust it to move me in ways I couldn't even imagine.

I add clowning and dancing to my list of things that feel good. Like the sensation of cold water sliding down my throat, they are part of the real me.

I lie awake, listening to the trickling of water and the hum of machines. Somewhere in the city, water has escaped from its prison of plastic pipes and is finding its own way. I add that to my list. More and more, I find I love the sound of water running freely.

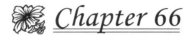

Chapter 66

When I unveiled my idea, everyone crowded around me and slapped me on the back and congratulated me. They loved it, and it didn't seem to bother anyone that we wouldn't need to wear our clown suits. I named it Operation City Day.

City Day is our newest holiday, sort of a Fourth of July for our cities, complete with parades and speeches. In the same way our dried and packaged products are labeled "fresh" and our manufactured goods described as "natural," it's been decided that the way to combat the growing disenchantment with contemporary city life is to have a holiday to celebrate it. What a fresh and natural idea.

Since I'd never even contemplated, much less done, anything like this before, I was surprised how well it all came together. I chose the elements from things I'd seen around me, and I tried to imitate the playful, quirky feel of the clown performances. But I thought it also had some of my own personal flavor, and a taste of Margaret as well.

As usual, Phillipe "knew a guy" who could get the small battery-operated TVs we needed at wholesale prices. In New York, no one pays list, not even revolutionaries. We had no treasury, so we took up a collection to buy what we needed.

On the eve of City Day, we worked through the night. Choosing the site was easy. I picked the bathrooms at the Grand Central subway stop. After the Encapsulation, security there became almost non-existent, so I figured if we were careful and someone kept a lookout, we could get away with it. I wanted to use the subways because that was where the sleepwalkers streamed past in great numbers every day. I chose Grand Central because according to legend, that was where it had all begun. Of course, that's not really true; it didn't begin in any one place. It began everywhere, but Grand Central Station was where, for the first time, a building had crossed a sidewalk and invaded a street. Certainly that deserved to be memorialized in some way. I chose the toilets for reasons that will become obvious.

At 3 am, we entered the bathrooms and worked quickly. I felt the thrill of being part of a group on a mission, and I wondered why I'd resisted for so long. Taking action felt so much better than hunkering down and hoping things would change. As a finishing touch, we spray painted our new liberty emblem with our motto, "Remember What Liberty Means" in each stall.

Unfortunately, it was too dangerous to linger there to enjoy the effects of our handiwork, so we phoned the TV stations to report the improvements we'd made, and then we went back to my room to wait for the response. It made the news, of course. It was a perfect item for the holiday. They referred to us as Dadaists again. They analyzed us to death, tying everything into intellectual knots. But I had faith that most of the viewers would see past that.

It was quite simple, really. When City Day dawned, what our citizens found as they flowed through the subways on their way to the parades and the speeches, and into the men's and women's toilets by Grand Central Station, was that the official celebration had followed them, even to these intimate moments. Peering up at them from the urinals and the commodes were the porcelain smiles and shiny white reassurances of the politicians. We had opened up each tiny TV and carefully split the speaker diaphragm so that the speech-makers all sounded as if they had kazoos stuck in their throats. The sets, which were waterproofed with a thick transparent resin, were epoxied firmly into the bottom of the toilets, so those commuters who didn't enthusiastically embrace the opportunity that presented itself were stuck. If they had come into the bathroom with any sense of urgency (and who goes into a subway toilet unless it's urgent?), the only way to relieve themselves was to let fly directly at the smirking face of the government.

Back home we played one news show after another. Margaret was beside herself, clapping her hands and jumping up and down each time the TV cameras panned in on the oh-so-dignified faces of the politicians talking up from within the toilet bowls and sounding like ducks. The stations were too delicate to show pictures of any of our officials covered with excrement, but one of our Club members, who regularly went to Grand Central Station on his way to work, checked it out and reported back to us—and yes, some of our officials definitely had shit-eating grins on their faces.

We clicked around the dial and found a news show where they were interviewing experts and asking the opinions of people on the street. These were no more enlightening than you'd expect. They were speculating regarding whether the people responsible for the toilet TVs were Dadaists and, if so, whether they were the same or different Dadaists as the clown people. Then one of their experts explained that the Dada movement began in Zurich in 1916 and idealized the behavior of children. This was not as silly as it might seem, I thought, since it occurred at a time when adults were enthusiastically gassing and chemically poisoning enormous numbers of each other in the trenches of World War I.

We were getting a lot of press, and we couldn't have been feeling more jubilant. Then an announcement came that smashed us flat. A newscaster with a stern face suddenly came on and reported that the mayor's office had issued a statement saying that "the terrorists who perpetrated this obscene act and defamed our city and its officials" would be tracked down and punished. They showed pictures of our liberty symbol and motto, which they claimed was the emblem of a new terrorist organization, and they asked anyone who saw such an emblem to report it immediately.

I spent the rest of the day feeling morose. The clown performances had never raised any official ire, but now, because of me, we had been classified as terrorists and were being tracked. I began to wonder if we'd left any clues. Had anyone dropped a personal item that could be traced back to them? We'd had the foresight to wear gloves (who wants to root around in a public toilet barehanded anyway?), so surely there wouldn't be any fingerprints. And how would they distinguish our hair or flakes of skin for DNA tests from those of the hundreds of other people who had passed through there? Still, considering what could happen to people classified as terrorists, everyone is frightened.

She was right, of course, that woman who felt so proud of her discovery; claustrophobia can be contagious. The proof is she's made me much more aware than I want to be of how confined I am. Wandering through the corridors, I feel caught in a maze with no exit. New York is a dark weight. Like the roof of a great mouth, it presses down on me.

There are to be no more clown performances, possibly ever. The clowns are suspects in the "terrorist activity" that occurred on City Day. Our clown suits would make us easy targets for arrest. Margaret is grieving, too; she loved the clowns. It was our way of trying to speak out.

Chapter 67

Wouldn't you know, it was Phillipe who finally succeeded in discovering the cause of the mystery illness. He had been talking intimately with a woman named Angela, the wife of our so-called public defender, for over five months. Shortly after he'd called her during their mutually agreed upon "safe" time, Angela broke down crying and told Phillipe that her five-year-old nephew was deathly ill. The symptoms she described sounded like Amy's: stabbing pains, weakness, nausea. Then Angela had gone on at length about how hard she'd been trying to get her sister and nephew an apartment inside the Central Park Community "where the air filtration system is so much better."

"But now it's too late," Angela wailed.

Phillipe, realizing this could be very important, pursued the subject. "Yes," he said, "I feel really sorry for all those poor people who live outside where the air is so polluted. I hear more and more of them are getting sick."

"Yes, I know," she said sorrowfully. "But we just can't put those filtration systems in everywhere. They're so expensive."

"No, no," Phillipe commiserated. "I know we can't. The city would go broke."

That was the sum total of it. But now we knew that a special, very expensive air filtration system had been installed for the benefit of those who lived behind the Great Wall and that this woman believed her nephew would not have become ill if he'd been protected by it.

Geraldine, the nurse in charge of documenting suspicious deaths, was called and asked if any such deaths had occurred in the Central Park Community. She checked her records and didn't find a single case. I wondered why we'd never looked at that before, but really who could have imagined that the rich and powerful were secretly providing themselves with cleaner air than they provided for the rest of us?

Then I remembered that about five years ago, City Hall had been moved to a location inside Central Park. This, despite the fact that the original facility had been nicer in every way. The Liberties had made a big fuss over how they were allowing the old City Hall to be turned into a hospital, while they would inhabit a more modest building "as a cost-cutting measure."

All those vents spewing wastes outside our protective shell. It figured. Especially when there was no wind, the city would be enveloped in a thick cloud of pollution. And where did the vents that brought air into the city get that air, except by sucking this same air in through holes in our cement husk?

That much was obvious. We'd felt safe because we'd been assured our city was equipped with such an excellent air filtration system that our air was actually much cleaner than the air in those unfortunate cities that hadn't yet been encapsulated. Bad air was one of the things our protective shell was supposed to protect us from. Because of our advanced filtration system, our air was said to be "fresh."

To be honest, most people knew this wasn't entirely true and that our air wasn't totally clean, but then air pollution had existed since way before the Encapsulation. We'd gotten used to the idea of the air having chemicals in it, so even if there was a little more of this or that in the air this year than last, no one worried all that much about it. Apparently we'd finally reached a tipping point where the most sensitive among us had begun to sicken and die. We had no idea exactly what was in our air. Funding was cut for those kinds of studies years ago. Such studies weren't needed, we were told, because our air and our water were filtered.

The Great Wall that surrounds the Central Park Community goes all the way up and intersects with our shell, completely walling off the Community from the rest of the city. Within two days, we were able to confirm that very elaborate air filtration systems had been installed at intervals all along the Great Wall. These weren't filtering air drawn in from outside New York; they were further filtering the already filtered air from other parts of the city—our air.

The Leader found a chemist at NYU who analyzed samples of air from inside the Great Wall, as well as samples from the rest of the city. Our air was found to contain the usual pollutants: nitrogen dioxide, carbon monoxide, sulfur dioxide, ozone, volatile organic compounds, and particulate matter. The concentrations of these chemicals were about the same as they had been when the last recorded analysis was done over twenty years ago. Even though our city still consumed a great deal of fossil fuel, except for the trucks that delivered goods to the loading docks, we'd eliminated automobiles. The surprise was that there were several new chemicals in our air, chemicals that didn't even have names, and about which we knew nothing.

The air within the Great Wall contained, along with the usual pollutants, the same new chemicals, but they were 87 percent less concentrated. Without studies, who could say what effect these new chemicals had on the human body, but you didn't have to be a genius to figure out it couldn't be good. Outside the Great Wall people were getting sick and dying, while within it, so far as we knew, there hadn't been a single unexplained death.

Suddenly I found myself trying to take shallower breaths, and I became hyperaware that our air didn't smell good. I watched Margaret breathe in and out, as she did every minute of every day. I'd joined the clowns so I could protect her, but how was I to protect her from the air she breathed? And it was because of me that Margaret was no longer tucked safely away in the Community with Adam.

Club meetings had been suspended because they seemed too dangerous while there was a manhunt going on for those who had perpetrated the City Day Caper. Now, however, we felt we had to get together regardless of the danger, though in order to make this safer, we changed our meeting place to the studio where the AngelBeasts performed.

It was a difficult situation. We all agreed that we couldn't go to the papers. That would only result in us being silenced through violence, or apprehended and locked up for the rest of our lives in a hospital for the insane. Howie suggested that we organize a rebellion and storm the Great Wall. We should, he said, march the Liberties off to jail, charge them with crimes against humanity, and then sell their personal assets to pay for the expensive new air filtration devices that apparently were now necessary to protect us from our own toxic exhausts. As bizarre an idea as that seemed, we actually considered it. Potentially there could be a lot more of us than there were of them. But how would we convince sufficient numbers of people that a serious problem existed? It wasn't anything you could see or feel, and the majority apparently believed that the Liberties could be trusted. Even if we were able to recruit a large enough army, we had no weapons, whereas they did.

Jill Ellington suggested that we start a drive to collect money to improve the air filtration system. We could do that, she said, without ever having to embarrass the Liberties by disclosing what we knew about the special filters in the Great Wall. We batted that idea around for awhile, but it was difficult to figure out how to motivate people to give money without disclosing specifics about the air problem. It always came back to the same thing. Since the Liberties apparently wanted to keep the air quality problem secret, we'd be scooped up and neutralized before we could garner enough support to force a change.

The meeting went on for over two hours. There were many suggestions, and a lot of anger. "How could they do this?" everyone wanted to know. As a reader of history, to me this just seems like business as usual. How could Marie Antoinette have said, "Let them eat cake"? Finally, we all went home to think things over.

Chapter 68

The next night while Margaret was off at class, I went to my mother's for dinner. Adam was there, too. My mother had made borscht using the old family recipe. It tasted pretty good even with dehydrated beets, and there were powder gefilte fish dumplings as well. We chatted about Adam's latest construction project. He was building a steel frame around an already existing apartment building so that thirty more stories could be built on top, thus utilizing the area all the way up to our shell, and even helping support it. More people, I thought, more waste, more pollution.

I tried to focus on my food. I ate slowly, trying to savor each bite. But as I noted how pleased my mother looked as Adam told about his latest exploit, I felt an old familiar bitterness invade my heart. Regardless of what Adam thought, it still seemed to me that he'd always been the favorite son and that achievements made of concrete were valued more than achievements involving improvements in mental and emotional health. In their minds, things that couldn't be touched or pointed at might not even exist. My jealousy kept getting in the way of my intention to concentrate on my food. Finally, when I couldn't stand it any longer, I interrupted Adam's gloating and my mother's cooing responses.

"Don't you ever miss the weather?" I said to my mother, trying hard not to sound the way I felt. She looked shocked at first, but then I think she understood somewhere deep in her mother's heart that I wanted her attention. She stopped and thought a while, trying to remember those long ago times.

"Oh, sometimes I think about the seasons," she said finally. "I always liked spring, but you never seemed to get enough of it. And winter just went on and on until you were completely fed up. I think it's better this way."

"Weather is for kids," Adam said gruffly. Contractors tended to be negative about weather. Their attitude was self-congratulatory, the implication being that they'd saved us from it.

"Well, I miss it," I said. "Some days I'd be happy to have any kind of weather, just to have some change."

"Oh, I bet you don't even remember the rain and snow," my mother said teasingly.

"I do too!" I insisted. "But it's hard to keep them straight when everyone talks about them like they were biblical plagues."

My mother laughed. "Yes, it made you blind," she mocked. Snow was so bright, according to the hushed stories now told to children, that it made you blind, and it was so cold that you couldn't help yourself; you'd just numbly lie down in it and go to sleep and die.

"And it made you do stupid things," I added.

"Yes," she said laughing, "every street was lined with foolish children who froze their tongues to iron fences and metal flag poles." In the right mood, my mother would sometimes make fun of the things we were told, and this gave me some gratification, as though, for a change, I had her on my side.

"Of course, the heat was no better," I said.

"No, that led to race riots and heart attacks," she said sarcastically. We were all old enough to have seen some real weather and, of course, understood what our weather legends were meant to teach us: that the world was a dangerous place, that we were lucky to have our city, and that it would be terrible if we ever had to go out *there* again.

"Pop always hated the Encapsulation," I said. "He hated it even more when they stopped letting us go outside on vacations."

"Yes," my mother said, "your father had a kind of obsession with trees and grass, God rest his soul. But me, I don't know what I'd do with a tree if I had one. Sure, it's hard to get a good Jewish rye bread these days, now that everything comes from factories, but we have a fine delicatessen right next door, which is very convenient, so things could be a lot worse."

Adam grunted, his way of letting me know he agreed a hundred percent. My brief time of having my mother on my side was apparently over.

"Well, you know things could be a lot better as well," I said testily. "Have you noticed the hallways, how grimy they are, and how the garbage doesn't always make it all the way to the chutes?"

This time Adam responded with one of his "my brother the black sheep" looks. But he had to tolerate this kind of thing because we were family.

"And it's not just the corridors," I said. "I wonder if you two have noticed that there have been a lot of people getting sick, and not with ordinary diseases." I had to be careful here. Adam wasn't a Patriot thug or anything like that, and he was my brother. I knew he'd never turn me in, but he did feel strong loyalties to those who helped feather his nest. (Strange that we still used this expression despite no longer having birds.)

"Well, sickness has always been with us," my mother replied.

"Some people think it might be caused by some kind of pollution in the city."

This time Adam snorted dismissively. "That's nonsense," he said.

"Even if it is," my mother replied, "it's a lot better than the flu pandemic they had out there. Do you know how many people died from that!" She had a point. Since people had not been allowed to leave the city, we'd had little problem with imported diseases. If anyone picked up anything from the truckers at the loading docks, they were immediately quarantined, and when the pandemic broke out, stringent measures were taken to make sure it didn't enter the city. Still, toxic air was hardly an acceptable alternative.

"Is there nothing you two feel was lost?" I found myself sounding a little shrill. I was feeling like an outcast again, as I always had, the bad one, the one who never fit in.

"Rain. Snow. Bombs. Traffic jams," Adam said sarcastically, but my mother looked sad and wistful.

"I remember one time your father took me rowing on a pond in Central Park," she said finally. "It was a beautiful, warm spring day, everything blooming. So sweet and romantic." She smiled, remembering, then dismissed the memory with a wave of her hand. "But that's all over with now. Your father's dead and gone. No need now for romance, or parks."

When I left, I went looking for Appoppa. I needed to talk with a kindred spirit. Sadly, I didn't think my mother or my brother would believe me if I told them what we'd found out. I felt grateful for having Margaret and Phillipe and Appoppa and the rest of the Club members. Finally I belonged somewhere. Then I thought about my father and felt sad. I'd been afraid of being like him, so I'd never let myself see how much we had in common. We could have been close. Instead I pushed him away almost until the end, and by then he was so hurt and shrunken inside that when I tried to hug him, he couldn't even hug me back. I whispered a silent apology, just in case in the grand scheme of things, he could hear me.

 *Chapter 69*

That night Appoppa showed me the nature films he'd bought on the black market from the truckers. I watched with rapt attention. The first thing I noticed was how sunlight made everything vivid and bright. Memories flooded in. I remembered how warm and good the sun could feel on your skin, and how on a hot day it felt too hot, and you went looking for shade. There was a shot of a stormy sea with gulls riding the crests of giant, wind-whipped waves, then an open expanse of sky split by jagged flashes of lightening. The thunder that followed seemed to strain Appoppa's sound system. In our city, if you're on the top floor of one of the tallest buildings, you can sometimes still hear thunder, but it's muffled and indistinct, nothing like these great cascades of sound. Even small, delicate things in nature seemed to radiate, not just beauty, but a kind of power our cement and steel lacked.

I thought about my father's wistful insistence that something important had been lost, and I wondered why he had stayed, and let us stay. Why had he not picked up his family and left the city? Had the hardships of his life so broken his spirit that he passively accepted whatever came?

I thought of my own lifelong passivity, and I realized how thoroughly his attitude had become mine. I've lived what could well turn out to be more than half my life without really liking it very much. I've devoted myself to helping others achieve happiness without believing in my own. Was it a stroke of luck I'd come to love Margaret, or was it something inside me, some spark of life finally asserting itself?

Since the ban on travel, the only images I've seen of the outside world have been horrific: people injured in bomb blasts, mangled in car accidents, frozen in the snow, and then whipped around by tornadoes and dropped to the ground. Appoppa's films showed a totally different side of things. Ironically, it was almost shocking to see that there are still people living peacefully in towns and on farms, still fields and mountains and rivers and animals, though the narrator kept pointing out how there were many fewer wild ones than there used to be. Land has been lost to the sea, there are violent storms, vast areas have turned into deserts, but human beings are still out there carrying on as they always have, as they always will, until the day comes when carrying on is no longer possible. It's Appoppa's opinion, and apparently many others agree with him, that that day may well come.

After I left, I wandered in the corridors for hours. At one point, I stopped at a pay phone and told Margaret not to wait up for me because I was with friends at Felicia's. As the hour got late, the corridors seemed increasingly desolate and ghostly. Left and right, backward and forward, up and down, New York is a maze that extends endlessly in every direction. Behind countless doors are countless people, mostly now asleep. I imagined myself running down the corridors knocking on doors, trying to wake them up, a mad Paul Revere. Then it struck me that, in truth, the only person I was capable of waking up was myself. It was I, as much as anyone, who had been complacent.

Things had evolved so gradually. There had always been time to get used to one degradation before the next came along. When the signs went up in the supermarkets warning us to limit our consumption of certain kinds of fish because of the dangerous chemicals they contained, we'd already been hearing about this for years, so even though we may have felt a heaviness, a subtle sense of hopelessness about the way the world was going, there was no shock, no public outcry. So many things moved along this way, gradually, yet inexorably, like the hands of a clock. So exactly when should we all have abandoned our busy lives to say, "Stop! This must stop!" Was it at six minutes after two? Was it five twenty-three? Ultimately, we'd come to a place where it felt frightening to breathe. What now? But in truth, somewhere deep inside I'd already decided what now. It was just difficult and frightening to face it.

 *Chapter 70*

A week later I stood up at the Club meeting and announced that I thought I knew the only possible solution to the toxic air problem. "It's not feasible," I said, "to complain about the problem and demand it be fixed, since that would be seen as unpatriotic and as complaint against the Liberties. It's also not feasible to overthrow our government. We'd all be slaughtered, if not apprehended and disappeared in the process of convincing others to join us. So what we must do is leave New York and go somewhere where toxic air isn't a problem. Of course, we won't just allow everyone else to be slowly poisoned by the bad air. By leaving we can warn others without sacrificing our own lives. We'll devise a way to leave a message behind. We'll make sure everyone knows about the special filtration system in the Great Wall. Then perhaps there'll be a rebellion that will force the Liberties to do something about the problem, or perhaps enough people will follow us out so the party will be stripped of their power by not having anyone left to rule, and stripped of their wealth by not having anyone left to work in their factories and buy their goods." I stood looking around the room for a moment. I wanted to impart to them the courage I'd miraculously found. Then I sat down.

There was complete silence. Many Club members were born after the Encapsulation and had never experienced the outside world. Probably they couldn't even fathom what I was suggesting.

After a moment, Betsy stood up. At ninety-two she had to support herself with a cane. "Yes, yes," she said. "We must gather our loved ones to us and leave. No need to be frightened. I lived out there for many years. It's a good place. It's not like they say it is."

Next Margaret stood. "Until a week ago," she said, "I was terrified of leaving. Somehow I'd allowed their negative messages about the outside to seep into me without even knowing it. But Appoppa has videos that show what the outside is like. Maybe it isn't completely safe, but what is? Considering that we're being poisoned by the air we breathe, it's safer than here. We can survive outside. And we can be happy. And we can be free."

"Yes, let's go," Appoppa said. "Me, I would have gone a long time ago, except for Amy. No way I'd leave her. Just didn't understand, didn't know...damn air making her sicker all the time." Tears welled up in Appoppa's eyes, but his voice remained strong and defiant. "Remember Amy. Amy believed she and I should try to do something, so we joined the Club. And I became a clown. But the clown messages, they never really got through...and now we can't even do that. So let's leave. Let's just fucking leave! Let them keep their poisonous city!"

"I know it's frightening," I said. "But we can get maps from a trucker Appoppa knows. We can decide where to go before we leave. And we can all go together. People have always done this. They've always ventured out into unknown places and settled."

"You're all invited to my room," Appoppa shouted, like a minister preaching the gospel. "I'll show you pictures of the outside, and you can see for yourselves. Those fucking horror stories they tell us aren't true. Who do you think grows our food? Who do you think brings it to us? People who live outside, that's who. They survive, and so can we!"

The room dissolved into confusion. Suddenly everyone seemed to want to speak at once. The Leader, who'd been listening quietly, spoke at last. "Stay calm. No decision needs to be made tonight. Go home and consider what these people have said. Take a look at the pictures Appoppa's invited you to see. Think about what's best for you and your family. Then, after a time, those who want to go can go, and those who want to stay can stay." Calm descended on the room. The

Leader had said what people needed to hear. "You don't have to go if you don't want to." I should have said it myself. Now even the most frightened seemed willing to consider my idea.

After the meeting, almost everyone came up to Appoppa and made an appointment to see the films. The Leader himself wanted to see them. And he wanted to see me. He'd been thinking along the same lines, and he hoped that he and I together could formulate a plan to present to the group regarding what preparations we'd need to make and what we'd do once we got outside.

When I got home, I felt shaken. I was going to leave my family and, despite all my complaints about it, my home. I'd have to abandon my clients, and there was no guarantee I'd ever have the opportunity to work as a therapist again. A lot of feelings were churning around inside me. Mostly they were old and familiar, but there was one brand-new one: I felt proud. I was ready to undertake an incredible adventure. I was ready to take Margaret by the hand and go in search of a new, better, brighter life.

Chapter 71

Howie stood up at our next Club meeting, raised both hands high over his head like a candidate for political office, and said in voice that rose up from the roots of his revolutionary soul, "We will be the biggest whistle-blowers since time began!" The entire Club jumped up and down, clapped, whistled, and cheered. "We will see to it that those who would filter their own air while they leave others to be poisoned are not only dragged from office, but put behind bars!" He was in his element. Finally power seemed to be shifting to our side, and a much deserved comeuppance for the Liberty Party seemed at hand.

We had a plan. A group of us were going to go to the loading docks, sign away our citizenship, and leave New York. Leaving would enable us, in essence, to become the whistle-blowers, because once we were gone, our computers could then be used to send out the e-mails.

Since the time of the final terror attacks, no one in the city was allowed to e-mail anyone outside New York, nor could we access any web pages that weren't either internal or officially approved. The Liberties had insisted that these limitations were necessary to prevent outside terrorists from communicating with inside terrorists. Telephone connections to the outside were also cut, though you could get a permit to make calls to an officially approved outside number if this was necessary for business purposes. E-mailing within New York, however, had continued. Hundreds of thousands of people regularly communicated that way.

Once those of us who were leaving had reached safety outside the city, whistle-blowing e-mails would be sent simultaneously from our personal computers. In a single instant, far more citizens would become informed of the skullduggery that was going on than could possibly be rounded up and silenced. Of course, the authorities would trace the e-mails and come to arrest the senders, but they'd find no one home. When we'd come up with this idea, we were really pleased with ourselves and had chortled like adolescents.

Howie would not be leaving the city. He wanted to stay behind to organize the enraged recipients of our e-mails into a cohesive political force and was busy recruiting others from the Club to help him. Howie figured the first thing the Liberties would do when they found out about the e-mail would be to try to remove the special air filters from the Great Wall. We, however, knew exactly where they all were, so we'd make certain that people with video cams were on site to film the action should they try to remove the filters and patch up the holes. Everyone was helping to collect e-mail addresses. Some were able to get long lists off computers in businesses where they worked. It was a real team effort, and there was a lot of smiling going on between us as we imagined those e-mails entering thousands of computers all over the city, a virtual rain of revelation.

Meanwhile, Howie was working with a small committee to compose the e-mails. We wanted to make them as convincing and infuriating as possible. After a good deal of persuasion, the scientist who'd done the chemical analysis of the air had agreed to leave with us, which meant he could sign his report. This would, of course, be included in the e-mail.

Margaret and I are both disappointed that we won't be here to witness the demise of the Liberties. Could this happen? Might freedom actually ring? Might we become decent world citizens and stop dumping our wastes into the waterways? Might there even be a restoration project for the Statue of Liberty? Nothing is impossible. New Yorkers might even vote to tear off the upper part of the shell and let the sun shine in. Every time the Club meets, excitement bounces off the walls. The sky's the limit.

In a dark part of my soul, though, I'm not totally convinced that these wonderful things will happen. The citizens of New York got us into this mess by blindly supporting the Liberties. Maybe the scales will now fall from their eyes, but isn't it also possible they'll believe whatever tales the politicians make up this time?

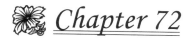

Chapter 72

The Leader, Appoppa, Margaret, and I have become the steering committee for what the Club decided to call the New Frontiers Project. We're to help our group prepare for departure and decide where out there we'll initially settle. Appoppa's job at the loading dock allows him to gather information and get maps and even pictures of possible places we might go. He asks each trucker about the place where he or she lives. What does it look like, are there places to live and jobs for new people, what's the climate like, and so forth. He also asks if, for a price, they'd be willing to smuggle in pictures of the place they live.

We in turn bring this information back to our group, where we discuss the pros and cons of each possible destination. We've become aware that brand-new settlements are being founded in the wilds of Canada. These sound promising, but we decide we don't want to travel that far until we know more about them.

Of course, many who are leaving want to tell their loved ones in the hope of convincing them to come along. This has to be allowed, since our members can't be expected to desert their families, but it's worrisome. We are constantly emphasizing the rock-solid trust that's necessary before sharing our plans even with family members, since a single small breach in security could have disastrous consequences.

We all have a lot on our minds. First, there are all the practical arrangements. We must sell everything and close out our bank accounts, and since we won't be able to take more than a suitcase or two, we must decide what is truly important and what isn't. In addition to some clothes and toiletries, I'm taking a few family portraits and some recent snapshots of my mother and brother. They looked at me strangely and asked a lot of questions when I took them, since I don't know how long it's been since anyone in our family has taken photos, but they went along with it. I took my mother in her kitchen where we'd so often gathered and sitting in her chair out front in the corridor telling one of her stories. I took some candids of Adam supervising one of his jobs and one full frontal portrait. I noticed that his eyes looked tired and dull, and I wondered, with a pang of guilt, how much he'd been affected by Margaret's leaving him.

After about a month, we reached a consensus. We plan to go to an ideal-looking little community called Preston, located high in the Adirondacks. The temperature and rainfall are still pretty good there, and due to its location, we figure the air is as clean as air gets these days. There's an old hotel and a couple of motels where we can stay until we find jobs and permanent housing. It's small enough that terrorists aren't likely to be attracted to it and big enough that we can find something to do, though we accept that we may have to take any kind of job we can get.

Margaret and I are feeling nostalgic about these last weeks in our room. In spite of being inadequate in so many ways, it's been a cozy home and a cradle for our love. I find myself cherishing every moment.

I listen to Margaret as she talks about her classes—she's determined to keep them up until the very last—and I'm aware when we have dinner together at our little table that life as it now exists is about to end. It seems so dear, so precious.

This evening we're watching television before climbing into bed. Margaret's in a good mood. She keeps up a running commentary all through the news. She does battle with the faces that pop up everywhere like targets. I don't care that I can't follow the official version. Margaret interests me more. "Okay, now smile," she says, frowning at the bland composure of some politician. "That's right, look sincerely into the camera. That's it. Oh, this is terrible! I've seen plastic flowers with more feeling. They're trying to look so very casual, but they really look nervous and shifty." She's more fun to watch than the TV, as she sits barefoot in her long, white flannel nightgown dotted with little hearts, her red hair loose on her shoulders. I wonder how it is that I can keep on loving her more and more. In previous relationships, the intensity always faded after a while, but not with Margaret. When her energy finally starts to fade, I scoop her up and carry her over to the bed, where we snuggle together and go to sleep.

Chapter 73

Then, once again, the completely unexpected happened. For years a piñata for a death-day had loomed over our city. Now finally it's burst, showering us with its dark gifts. We should have known this would happen, but it was so unthinkable we refused to let it enter our minds. Our waste products, when ejected from the East Side, flowed down into that thickness that had been the East River. On the West, it oozed over the sloping banks and into the Hudson; on the South, into the harbor, then out past the stump of the Statue of Liberty and into the Atlantic. But there was a problem in the North: beyond the Bronx, a ridge of hills blocked escape and caused this effluvium to puddle, and then to pool, and finally to form a lake, which slowly rose along the northern wall of the city.

It's obvious now that something should have been done. But at the time, given the extreme unpleasantness of the problem and the fact that no government agency had a clear and unavoidable responsibility for it (the first department head foolish enough to acknowledge it would certainly have inherited it), everyone looked the other way and hoped for the best. In all fairness, this approach did not seem as blatantly irresponsible then as it does now; the city had been run this way for years, and we'd gotten by.

At 9:37 this morning, pressure from the rising lake slowly buckled the North Wall. First, there was a terrible creaking, and if people had remembered what thunder sounded like, they might have compared it to that. Next, there was a shifting of planes; walls slid at odd angles and rooms twisted a kilter. Then, in accelerating sequence, the rivets popped from girders, pipes snapped and gushed, and with a sound even louder than thunder, the wall was breached, allowing a tidal wave of heavy, greenish-black slime, a blend of human waste, industrial waste, and the products of combustion to flow into our city.

Seventeen crowded blocks were flooded by the muck and had to be abandoned forever. And even that was a victory of sorts, considering what could have happened if our engineers hadn't moved so quickly. To save the core of the city, they sacrificed a double row of buildings, using them to create a barrier. Teams of carpenters frantically nailed doors shut, covered them with heavy sheets of plywood, sealed them with silicone caulking, and finally pumped them full of cement.

Those unlucky souls who had been down in basements died instantly. Those higher up fared better, but the young, the old, and the weak quickly died from exposure, and thousands have been hospitalized. We don't know yet what the final death toll will be. Anyone who touched this toxic slime developed chemical burns. Anyone who smelled it puked. Anyone who was even near it later became sick from inhaling the fumes. The construction workers are our heroes; many of them sacrificed their health, and in some cases their lives. Every time one team of carpenters would become too ill to continue working, a fresh team was sent in. They're still out there now, reinforcing the wall with more cement so that this will never happen again. The city is in mourning. The Club is in mourning. One of our members is dead. Four are hospitalized. Three of these, including the dead woman, Katherine Holmes, were planning to leave with us in only two weeks time. We're all asking ourselves why we didn't move more quickly, but then how could we have known?

 # *Chapter 74*

In the wake of this disaster, many of my clients have gone into crisis, and I'm in a fix. Some have relatives who were killed or seriously injured. Some are simply deeply affected by the pain of others, and the more depressive types are questioning the whole nature of existence and wondering whether it's worth living in a world where such things happen. And I'm about to leave them.

I told my clients weeks ago that I was going to close my practice. Naturally I couldn't tell them the truth regarding why. To have it get around that any of us were planning to leave the city would open us to harassment, possibly even to actual investigation. We'd be viewed as a foreign element within the city walls. The Patriots would consider our desire to leave unpatriotic. They might surround any one of us on a dark street, or one of us might return home to find his or her house turned upside down and everything of value taken. A person known to be planning to leave New York would be subjected to special scrutiny. The authorities would want to be certain that such a person was not talking to others in a way that would "damage public morale." They'd also want to assure themselves that this person was not capable of committing some atrocity on the way out. Any one of us could be questioned by the police. This could be dangerous and unpleasant under any circumstances, but the fact that the clowns are suspects in the City Day Caper makes it absolutely essential that we not draw attention to ourselves.

I couldn't tell my clients I was leaving New York. Yet, I had to tell them something. It's my responsibility to help them deal with my departure without feeling betrayed and abandoned. So I made up a story. I told them I was discontinuing my practice in order to write what I believed would be a very important book about psychotherapy.

Even before this tragedy, most of my clients found this explanation less than satisfactory. They were hurt. The more fragile ones responded by feeling desperate and frightened. Many cried. A few responded with hearty support, saying they understood and wishing me the best of luck with my book, but underneath I felt, or thought I felt, something else, a silent accusation: "You took me on, why can't you finish with me? Don't you realize how much I've invested in you? I've come to trust you, and I've spent hours and hours telling you things another therapist wouldn't know." Of course, they're right. I have no defense. Already my heart aches nonstop, and now, what now?

I can't afford to be left behind. Those e-mails must go out. To delay telling people they're breathing seriously contaminated air could result in more deaths. (And what the air must be like now, with the addition of the fumes from that toxic goo, I hate to imagine.) Given my close association with Appoppa, from whose computer some of those e-mails are going to emanate, if I stay behind, I'll surely be apprehended. Margaret wouldn't go without me, so the same would happen to her. I've preprogrammed Appoppa's computer to send a personal e-mail to each of my clients, explaining the truth. I can only hope they'll understand and forgive me.

This hour I'm working with a young woman named Stacey. She has soft brown hair that flips under in a pageboy, and when she sits her hands grip the arms of the chair. Stacy is agoraphobic. She's been able to come to my office only if accompanied by a safe person, usually her mother. She was already angry that our next session would be our last. She's particularly aggrieved because she spent several years talking to a psychodynamic therapist about her painful childhood and made zero progress, while now as a result of a very pragmatic program of desensitization and cognitive therapy, she's been able to venture farther and farther outside her apartment all on her own. In the wake of this tragedy, she's crying, and she tells me she can no longer take a single step outside her door without holding her mother's hand. She wants to know if in view of what's happened, I'll delay my departure. I say yes even though I know I can't. In my judgment, telling her this lie will be better than allowing her to think I would leave her in this state simply to work full time on a book. When she receives my letter, I hope she'll understand that I would never have left at a time like this if there had been any other way.

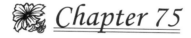 *Chapter 75*

Two days later when I was again in the midst of telling my lie about not leaving my practice for another month, I heard the door of my waiting room click open and closed long before my next client was due to arrive. Then, a piece of bright red stationary slid under my office door. My heart started racing. I knew it had to be from Appoppa, and I knew he wouldn't interrupt a session unless it was urgent. "Come home right away," was scrawled across the page. "Margaret has been injured." I hastily excused myself and ran out, not even taking time to leave a note for my next client. As I rushed through the halls and up the stairways, I willed Margaret to be okay, prayed actually. I knew there was research proving that somehow prayer worked even if the person praying was an atheist. When I burst into our room, it was full of people. My mother, Adam, Phillipe, Appoppa, the Leader, Geraldine, all of them crowded around our bed. Everyone moved out of my way as I approached. Margaret lay on the bed, her proud hair wilted like a sick plant, her eyes shut, her face devoid of expression. She looked like a dead person. On the left side of her head, just above her temple, was a bloody gash. I stared at it with horror.

"Margaret," I said, hardly able to get the words out. Geraldine returned to the bedside and gently placed a cold compress on Margaret's wound.

"Margaret," I said again more urgently. But she didn't respond.

"She can't hear you, man," Appoppa said. "She's unconscious."

I embraced her, and I continued to pray, though to whom or what I wasn't sure. I just knew Margaret was in terrible danger, and I had to do something to keep her alive. I could feel her frail body in my arms. I could feel her breathing. At least she was breathing. "Let Margaret be okay," I repeated over and over again. "Please let her be okay."

"What happened?" I finally stammered. "And why isn't she in the hospital?"

"We just brought her from the hospital," Phillipe said. "She was lying on the floor in the hall. The hospitals are overwhelmed. Thousands of people were injured when the North Wall ruptured. There aren't enough doctors or nurses or beds."

"Geraldine has come to help us," my mother added. "She's a registered nurse, and you can't do too much better than that." I looked up appreciatively at Geraldine.

"But what happened to her?" I asked again. "What's wrong with her?"

"She has a concussion," Geraldine said, "and she's in a coma. We're waiting for her to regain consciousness."

"And then she'll be okay?"

"We hope so," Geraldine said. "I'm sorry, but there was no way we could get her a CAT scan, so we don't know how bad the damage is. There's every reason to hope she's going to be just fine."

"What did the doctor say?"

"No one would look at her," Phillipe said. "They were all too busy dealing with critical cases."

"But what about Margaret?" I said, bewildered. "If nobody's looked at her, how do we know she's not a critical case? She's in a coma, for God's sake!"

"I got a doctor to listen to me for about two minutes," Phillipe said. "He told me that unless there's internal bleeding, she'll probably wake up in a day or two."

"*Unless* there's internal bleeding!" I shouted. "But they don't know…they don't know if there's internal bleeding because they didn't give her a CAT scan!" I felt frantic.

"I'm so sorry," said Geraldine. "There wasn't anything more we could do. The operating rooms are full; the doctors are exhausted."

"I rolled around the halls for an hour trying to get someone to look at her. No luck. Finally an intern came by checking everyone in that hallway, and he said it was an excellent sign that Margaret was able to breath on her own…"

"CAT scans are like beyond them now, man," Appoppa said. "You should've seen that hospital. Things are primitive; people lying on the floors. Some of them had peed on themselves; no one to give them a bedpan."

"I don't care. Margaret needs a doctor!"

"Shhh. Speak softly," the Leader said. "She needs peace. She needs to trust that all will be well. It's best not to upset her."

"Can she hear us?" I asked.

"Maybe," Geraldine said. "Many people who've been in comas report that they could hear everything."

I turned to Margaret. She looked so fragile and exposed lying there unconscious. "I'm here, Margaret. I'm with you. I love you, and I'm going to take care of you until you're well again." Then I kissed her lips. I thought about the buckling of the North Wall and all the chaos out there, and I knew they were right. Things had changed. We were no longer members of a sophisticated society capable of delivering state-of-the-art medical care on demand. I was indeed lucky to have a registered nurse standing by Margaret's side. And yet the sense of helplessness I felt was almost unbearable.

Geraldine placed a stethoscope under Margaret's pajama top and listened to her heart. "Her heart sounds good," she said, smiling at me encouragingly. Then she took Margaret's blood pressure.

"Relax. Trust. All will be well," the Leader said reassuringly. I looked into his eyes. As usual they were kind and infinitely calm. But I didn't have his faith. I didn't believe, as he did, that the universe is necessarily basically good. I looked around the room. Everyone's eyes were on me. My mother especially looked as though she understood how frightened I was.

"How did it happen? How did Margaret get hurt?"

No one seemed eager to speak. Finally, Phillipe rolled over closer to me. "Did you know Margaret was having lunch with Jill today?"

"Yeah. She said they were going to a place near the Freedom Tower."

"Right. Well, after lunch they decided to sit on one of the benches in the plaza and talk. They noticed a crowd of people on the other side. So they went over to see what was happening. Some young guy was standing on top of a box and talking. You know, the kind of thing that used to happen long ago, but doesn't anymore. Somebody actually standing on a box giving a speech! The guy on the box was angry. He was shouting about how irresponsible the government had been to allow our wastes to pile up against the North Wall and about how they're all just a bunch of damn crooks anyway—all sorts of stuff no one in their right mind would say, especially not in public standing on a box. So he's going on like this, and of course the inevitable happened. A group of Patriots came marching in, pulled the guy off the box, and started using him as a punching bag." Phillipe stopped. He looked teary. "The crowd scattered...except for Margaret, who stood there and shouted for them to stop. She screamed and screamed at them at the top of her lungs until one of them turned around and grabbed her and hurled her across the plaza. Her head struck the corner of a concrete bench. Jill saw it all."

I felt an almost unbearable urge to hit someone, to tear them limb from limb, but there was no one within reach but my friends. I saw alarm reflected in their faces and realized I was quivering all over. I started clenching my fists, trying to regain control. Adam threw an arm around my shoulder and pulled me gently, but firmly, over to my big easy chair where he made me sit down. Then I put my face in my hands, and a strange howl came out of me, the sound of an animal caught in a trap.

After everyone left, I fell asleep while sitting by the bed. My head rested on my forearm and made it numb. I was confused when I woke, and my hand felt like a stick. I looked at the clock. It was after one in the morning. Margaret still lay as if asleep. I got up and gently tried to arouse her as Geraldine had recommended, but nothing happened. Then looking down at her, I had an idea. I called Edith, a Club member who'd once worked as a nurse's aide, and I asked her to come over and stay with Margaret. She agreed immediately. It was new in my life to have such a large and supportive group of friends, and I felt extremely grateful.

About a half hour later, Edith, a stocky, bustling woman in her mid-forties, arrived carrying her cat, Xanax. She assured me that Xanax would be good therapy and placed him on the bed beside Margaret, where he snuggled up beside her and went to sleep. I thanked her and left.

When I arrived at Philippe's apartment, his door was unlocked and he was talking on his speakerphone. When he saw me, he mumbled something into the machine and clicked off. For once, I'd caught him in a plain white T-shirt. "Phillipe, you're the only wizard I know," I told him, "and I need you to get me some magic."

He went off without a word. As I let myself out, his phone started ringing. It was getting late, we were sliding down into the catacombs of insomnia, and I wasn't the only one who needed his help that night.

When I returned, Xanax opened a sleepy eye as I entered our room. Edith was reading in the chair. I went over to Margaret and stroked her face, hoping she would wake when she felt my touch, but she didn't.

"She's been resting quietly," Edith said. I went over and squeezed her shoulder. "Thank you so much for coming," I said. "I'll take over now. I need some time alone with Margaret."

When Edith had gone, I lit candles by the bed and turned off all the lights. Margaret's face seemed almost natural in the candlelight, but her hair looked freshly bronzed and static. I could imagine her as a statue in her own memory.

I waited for Phillipe. The candles were only thimbles of melted wax, their flames sputtering in their holders, by the time he rolled in. He was breathing hard. A twisted paper bag lay on his lap. I uncoiled it carefully until I found the small vial. I uncorked it and passed it under my nose. It was the real thing, and finding it in the middle of the night in this sealed city truly was a kind of magic.

When Phillipe left, I took Margaret's face in my hands and turned it toward me. She seemed so vulnerable without the shield of consciousness. "I'm here, watching over you while you sleep, just as you always wanted," I said. "And I need you to come back and be here with me. I brought you something special right out of your favorite poem." Then I rubbed a couple of drops from the vial directly under Margaret's nose. The acrid menthol mist of real eucalyptus oil enveloped us. I was hoping that by speaking to her in the language of the senses she'd hear me. I think I half expected her to sit up and put her arms around me. When she didn't, I felt terribly disappointed. I kissed her eyes and her lips then sat down in the chair beside the bed to wait through the long night.

Chapter 76

The next day at a special meeting, the members of the Club voted to delay our departure for a week. Appoppa, who came to tell me this, said that everyone felt certain Margaret was going regain consciousness, so we could all leave together. In addition, they made a schedule so that one or another of them came to sit with Margaret while I slept.

But I couldn't sleep, not much. I'd lie on the bed beside Margaret, and sometimes I'd doze off, only to wake shortly thereafter filled with anxiety. It would take me a moment to remember what was wrong. When I did, a terrible sadness would flow into my heart, my face would crumple, and I'd want to cry. I would know without even turning my head to look at Margaret that she had not awakened. Otherwise Edith or Appoppa or Jill or Geraldine, whoever it was who had come to sit by us, would have awakened me. Even so, I wouldn't be able to resist glancing over at Margaret, just be sure. Then I'd roll over on my side to hide my face until I could regain my composure.

Except for these short rest periods, I'd sit beside Margaret in the big easy chair, watching her sleep. My longing to have her eyes open sometimes filled me to the point where I felt like I was going to break open. I prayed constantly. Not to God exactly, since I'd never really been acquainted with God, as such, but to some great, vibrating, enormously powerful energy that I was determined, through the sheer force of my will, to influence.

I studied every detail of Margaret. She looked so peaceful it was unworldly. Sleeping Beauty. I tried over and over again to be the prince, and kiss her, and wake her. I would lean over her with great ceremony and touch my lips to hers, softly, reverently. But she didn't wake.

Three days passed this way. Then, after I uncorked my little vial of eucalyptus oil yet again and passed it under Margaret's nose, what had now become nothing more than an unbelievable fantasy actually happened. Margaret opened her eyes.

It wasn't at all like the moment I'd imagined. Suddenly Margaret's hands clutched the side of the bed, and her face contracted in a look of horror. I called out her name. When she saw me, she looked bewildered. (Later she would tell me that what she had seen in her mind's eye as she woke was the image of an enraged Patriot rushing toward her.) It took her a moment to realize she was at home in her own bed.

I felt blissful. I gathered her up in my arms and felt her cling to me as she cried. In that moment, I vowed that no matter what happened in the future, I would never complain, because I'd been granted this. I'd been granted Margaret's life. As we held each other, my edges softened and dissolved until I experienced Margaret's heart beating inside my own body as though we were a single being.

I don't know how long we might have stayed like that had Geraldine not showed up to check Margaret's vital signs. Then what had been private joy became a communal celebration. At some point over the next couple of days, every member of the Club showed up, alone, or as part of a group, to visit Margaret and share in the glow that came to surround her recovery. There was something about this time that reminded me of when we still had spring, of those first warm days after a long winter, when everyone suddenly felt good and glad to be alive.

Adam came, and for the first time, I felt jealous. He brought Margaret flowers, and I could tell that he, too, was terribly relieved that she hadn't died. In some way he loved her; I had to accept that. And it seemed to me, as I saw them talking, that in some way she loved him, too. Rationally, I know this isn't a threat to what she and I have together, but given my childhood, when it comes to Adam, it's hard to be rational. And when it comes to Margaret, it's even harder.

By the next day, Margaret was out of bed and sitting in the big chair. The following day, we started taking walks in the corridors to build up her strength. She's recovering quickly, and soon we're going to get the hell out of this damn city! After what they did to Margaret, I can hardly wait.

Chapter 77

It was eleven o'clock at night. Margaret and I had already gone to bed when there was a knock at our door, and Phillipe rolled in. I noticed immediately that the carry box attached to the back of his wheelchair was full to the brim. He looked ashen and tense.

"Hey," I said. "What are you doing here? Isn't this your busiest time?"

"Yeah, but they'll have to get along without me tonight. Something kind of important has come up."

"Oh?"

"There's a problem at the North Wall. It's very bad."

"But I thought they had a concrete barrier out there now."

"Right, but the concrete barrier is only eight blocks long."

"So?"

"So, what about the rest of the wall?"

"Is there a problem with the rest of it?"

"You could say that." Phillipe laughed, but he sounded more bitter than happy. "We should have expected this," he said. "For years we've dumped every kind of crap imaginable out there. Well, finally we hit the jackpot. It's merged and become something totally new, some sort of hyper-acid. Probably worth millions on the world market. First, it ate its way through the portion of the wall where the construction company cheated and the wall was thinner than it was supposed to be. That caused the break a couple of weeks ago. Now it's steadily eating its way through the entire North Wall, so we have a bit of a problem."

"Phillipe, how bad is it? We can stop it, can't we?"

"We don't have time."

"Are you saying that we're going to lose even more of the city than we did last time?"

"I'm saying that we're going to lose the whole fucking mess. We've finally done it. New York is history."

"The whole city! No, that can't be possible!"

Phillipe simply stared back at me. It's the only time I've ever known him to refuse to argue.

"What makes you think this, Phillipe?" Margaret said. Her voice sounded calm. I could tell she didn't believe what he was saying. Did I? I didn't know, but when I saw how Phillipe was gripping the wheels of his chair and rolling himself back and forth, apparently too agitated to sit still, I was convinced this wasn't one of his jokes.

"Well, you know, don't you, that Howie and his team finally managed to bug the mayor's office?"

"Yes, we know," Margaret said.

"Well, there was an emergency meeting at the mayor's office tonight. The city engineers needed to report a problem at the North Wall. A small leak was discovered a quarter of a mile from where the wall collapsed before. They plugged that up, reinforced it with lots of cement, no problem. But that gave someone the bright idea of testing the whole wall to see where it might need reinforcement. They drilled little holes to test the thickness and the condition of the cement all along the wall, and they found that the whole damn North Wall is a fraction of the thickness it used to be. That stuff out there, that slime, is eating right through it. Concerns were expressed, serious concerns, that there wouldn't be enough time to reinforce such a big expanse of the wall before it collapsed. There isn't nearly enough cement in the city. It would have to be imported. That would take days. And the collapse is thought to be imminent."

"Imminent?" I said. "When?"

"They think it's going to collapse sometime before morning."

"Before tomorrow morning?" I said, completely aghast.

"Why haven't they warned us?" Margaret said. "Why haven't they started evacuating the city?"

"Yeah, right, just ask everybody to line up in neat, orderly little rows, women and children first. If word about this got out, there'd be panic. There'd be a stampede."

"Well, what *are* they going to do?" Margaret demanded.

"I'm sure you'll be pleased to know that our mayor stayed very cool during this crisis. He ordered the engineers to begin repairs immediately and expressed confidence that they'd complete the job in time. But my hunch is that those engineers packed their bags and headed for the loading docks as fast as they could. The mayor and his family have no doubt done the same, and that's exactly what we're going to do. Grab your stuff. Let's go!"

"The other Club members? Do they know?" Margaret asked. Her tone told me that she was starting to believe the unbelievable.

"Howie's group called everyone. Each member was instructed to bring only their immediate family and say nothing to anyone else. But you know people will. They'll want to save their best friend, and that friend will want to save someone else. Word will spread, and when it does, it'll be impossible to get out. So come on, let's go!"

Margaret and I looked at each other, our eyes communicating our mutual decision. Then we began preparing to leave as quickly as we could. Fortunately, except for toiletries and the like, we were already packed. In less than five minutes, we were moving out the door.

"We're all supposed to meet at the loading docks at one thirty," Phillipe explained. "We'll sign away our citizenship and pay any truck driver we can find whatever we have to pay to take us out. Anyone who doesn't make it by one thirty can follow later and join us in Preston."

It didn't look like word had gotten out. The halls and the subways were practically empty. No one would believe this, I thought, if it came secondhand from some friend. So the majority of New York would be sleeping, literally or figuratively, when the wall collapsed. I thought about my mother and felt sick. I didn't forget her. I thought about begging Phillipe to make enough of a detour to go by her apartment and get her, but I didn't think she'd believe our story. And I was certain even if she did that she wouldn't leave without Adam, who wouldn't believe it and wouldn't leave.

When we reached the subway station, we had to wait an interminable five minutes for a train. As I continued to think about what Phillipe had learned, I became more and more convinced it was real. After what had already happened, why had any of us believed that the rest of the wall wouldn't collapse? That was the amazing thing. Yes, there'd been explanations—a limited section of wall, built by a corrupt company long ago out of business, which had not been properly reinforced. But why had we believed them? Perhaps, because this ever-so-official-sounding explanation, authoritatively delivered by the head of the engineering corps, had felt reassuring, and we very much wanted to be reassured. When he said it was limited, hadn't that implied that they'd already checked the rest of it? As children, we trust and believe our parents. We want them to reassure us when bad things happen. Perhaps we never get over that.

Finally, the train arrived, and we boarded. It seemed to take forever for the doors to close though, of course, it must have only been seconds. As the stations flashed past, I was aware that we'd never see any of this again. This was our last subway ride.

At the end of the car, a couple of guys were singing a beer-drinking song. Across from us sat a glum, heavyset man in work clothes, probably on his way home from cleaning some office building. I thought about warning our fellow passengers about the North Wall's imminent collapse. Immediately an image struck me of myself doing that, which was almost comic. I'd surely come off like one of those religious nuts predicting Armageddon. They'd never believe me. I squeezed

Margaret's hand and thought once again how lucky I was to have her with me. If she'd died, I might not have given a damn, but now I very much wanted to live.

As we approached the Columbus Circle Station, we prepared to get off. We'd transfer to the A train, which would take us all the way to the loading docks. When the tunnel opened into the broad, brightly lit platform area, we stared out the windows in amazement. The platform was crowded with people. They were standing in neat, straight lines on the opposite side of the platform, directly in front of where the doors of the incoming train might be expected to open. And they all had suitcases. Roaming between the lines, dressed in their characteristic shirts, were Patriots.

"What the...?" Phillipe said.

"Oh! Oh, no!" Margaret exclaimed.

"Well," I quipped, "I guess word got out."

"Yeah, I guess so," Phillipe said. "That's a lot of people. And what do you suppose the Patriots are doing here? Why aren't the police keeping order instead of those goons?"

As I watched the Patriots striding around, waving their arms and giving orders, I felt myself getting angry. I couldn't help wondering if it was one of those very men who'd injured Margaret.

As we headed toward the door, Margaret pointed and said, "Look, there are more people waiting on the stairs. See, they're holding them back with a big rope."

"Wait," Phillipe hissed. "Don't get out. I have a better idea. We'll stay on this train until we get to the next stop, then we'll cross over the platform and take it back as far as Lexington Avenue, take the number 4 up to 161st Street, take the B train over to the A line, and get up to the loading docks that way."

When the train pulled out again, Margaret and I looked to Phillipe for an explanation, but he just shrugged.

"It looks like they're evacuating New York," Margaret said.

"Hard to believe. Hard to believe," Phillipe said, shaking his head.

"Well, if so, they've probably arranged for trucks and buses to take everyone out," I said.

"Do you have any idea," Phillipe said, "how long it would take to evacuate New York City? It won't be possible."

"But maybe those who get there early, the first wave…" Margaret said. She was trying to keep our hopes up.

"Yeah, that's the positive side," Phillipe said. "If all those people are lined up, they must be doing something to get them out, so if we get there soon and if the wall holds for a while, we'll still be okay."

We had to hop on and off four more trains before reaching the docks, but we didn't run into any more lines, so we figured we were still ahead of the game.

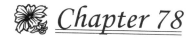 # Chapter 78

When we arrived at the docks, we saw more lines and more Patriots, but that didn't surprise us. We knew some of those people we'd seen on the platform would get there before we did. The good thing was that there were six trucks and three buses already there and in the process of loading. Margaret threw her arms around me and kissed me. I clapped Phillipe on the back and congratulated him on his subway scheme. It looked like we might be leaving within the hour.

"Which line looks shortest?" Phillipe asked, scrutinizing our choices.

"Maybe that one second from the end," I said, "and it's moving. See, they're getting on the silver bus."

"Okay, let's go for it," Philippe said and started rolling himself toward the end of the line. Margaret and I hurried after him.

"What about the others?" Margaret asked. "What about Appoppa and Geraldine and…"

"Don't worry," I said. "They're probably here, or will be soon, but we could never find them among all these people. Everyone knows our destination. We'll see them in Preston."

"Well, I guess we're not going to have to sign out," Phillipe said sarcastically. "Giving up our citizenship doesn't seem to be an issue anymore."

"No," I said. "I bet even the Patriots have decided to give up their citizenship. What surprises me is that they aren't crowding to the front of the line. Would you believe it, they must actually have principles."

"Somebody must be paying them a lot of money," Margaret said bitterly, "and they're just stupid enough to think they can get out with it. I don't believe those people have principles!"

Shortly after we reached the end of the line, the silver bus pulled out. There were still maybe a hundred people in front of us. We started hoping a truck would pull in, because probably all hundred or so of us could crowd into a big truck. In this situation, comfort was hardly the issue

Directly in front of us was a family of five. They were stylishly dressed, as though they were headed out for a Sunday matinee. The youngest child, a little girl of about five, was in a cranky mood. Probably she'd been awakened in the middle of the night. She kept tugging on her father's suit coat and whining about wanting to go home. Phillipe struck up a conversation with the wife.

"I could hardly believe it when I heard about this," he said.

"I know! I still can't believe it," the wife replied. "But Jay, that's my husband, he says we have to go, that we just can't take the chance."

"No, well, I think that's right," Phillipe said. "It's probably not true, but we can't afford to take the chance, can we?" The woman shrugged indicating that it was all beyond her. "How did you hear about it?" Phillipe said as casually as possible. (That's what we'd all been wondering. How had these people found out?) Suddenly the woman's whole demeanor changed. She smiled broadly.

"Oh, well, you see, Jay, my husband, is one of the mayor's top aides, practically his right-hand man. So of course, Jay was one of the first people to find out."

"And all the rest of these people?" Phillipe asked.

"Well, our mayor had a truly clever idea. He e-mailed a list of his staff and his supporters to the Patriots, and he asked them to set up a telephone tree. The way it works, you see, is that the first person calls ten people and asks each of them to call ten people, and so forth. So all you have to do is call ten people, and then you're free to go. Wasn't that clever? Because, of course, no one would want to get caught having to call everyone in this situation." Phillipe nodded and murmured appreciatively. "I guess you all must have been pretty close to the top of the list," she said, "or you wouldn't have gotten here so soon."

"Yes," Phillipe said, "I'd hate to tell you how much money I've contributed to the mayor's campaigns, and these two have been party faithfuls practically forever."

"Yes," I said, "we go way back. When my wife and I were teenagers, we demonstrated in favor of the Encapsulation." Margaret said nothing. I couldn't see her face, but I hoped she wasn't glaring at us. I was sure she disapproved, whereas Phillipe and I saw our behavior as merely practical. The woman glanced over at her husband to see if he was listening. When she found him deeply engrossed with the children, she leaned in our direction and spoke softly.

"You know, after Jay finished calling his ten people, while he was busy packing, I called my sister and told her what was going on. She and her family are probably here somewhere, but I'm worried they won't let her get on the bus."

"Why not?" Margaret asked.

"Because her name isn't on the list."

Blackness poured into my heart.

"Is someone checking a list?" Margaret asked. I have to give Margaret credit. She must have been feeling what I was feeling, but she didn't let it show.

"The Patriots. The mayor asked them to take charge."

Tears welled up in Margaret's eyes, which the woman mistook for sympathy, since she reached out and touched her arm. "Well," Margaret said, "I wish your sister luck. Maybe they'll take pity on her."

That was that. The woman turned away to help her husband with the kids. None of us spoke for a while. Then Phillipe started muttering under his breath, "Damn them. Damn the power-hungry bastards." Meanwhile, I was trying to think of a way out of this. "It's all about power," Phillipe continued. "They still don't want to lose their power, so they're taking their political base with them! They're probably planning to found New New York somewhere out in the Great Plains. And they'll no doubt encapsulate New New York in order to protect it against terrorists or buffalo or whatever."

"Don't waste time, Phillipe," I said. "We have to come up with a plan. Think, Phillipe. Think, Margaret."

Thinking was anything but easy with the stakes so high. And now, just when we needed more time, another bus pulled in. At least it was a bus rather than the big truck we'd wished for, so we weren't likely to reach the front of the line quite yet. When the bus finished loading, there were only about fifteen people between us and the guy with the clipboard. I wondered if we should go to the end of the line to give ourselves more time, but when I looked, the line had grown so long I couldn't see the end of it. Damn them, I thought. What an injustice. The Liberties are responsible for this disaster, yet they're the only ones allowed to escape!

"I can't think of a thing," Phillipe groaned. "It's not like me."

"Wait, I have an idea," I whispered. "Do we know the names of any people who are sure to be on the list? People they wouldn't be likely to recognize?" We all thought. People active in the government wouldn't work. They'd be known. But big contributors…

Margaret signaled for us to huddle around her so she wouldn't be overheard. "About two years ago," she said, "Adam insisted we invite this couple over for dinner. The guy was a big developer; I mean really big. He did these multibillion-dollar projects. Adam told me that they literally contributed over a million dollars to the Liberty Party every single year. Their names were John and Joan Hurley."

"Do you think they're still active?" Phillipe asked. "With the Liberty Party, it's almost certain to be a question of 'What have you done for me lately?'"

"Well, the guy is still getting big contracts, I know that," Margaret said. "You know that huge redevelopment project Adam's working on? That's his."

"Good," Phillipe said. "When we get up to the front of the line, if they ask for your names, tell them you're John and Joan Hurley."

"Okay," I said. "Now what about you? Who are you going to be?" Phillipe shook his head. It was apparent to all of us that this strategy was going to be difficult when it came to Phillipe. He was just so unusual, and since he had been unaware that he'd have to look like anything other than an undesirable citizen ready to sign away his citizenship, he'd worn his Doctor Death T-shirt. Margaret rooted around in the stuff he'd thrown into the carry box and came up with a crewneck sweater that didn't say anything.

"Here, put this on," she said to him.

"But I'll be too hot," Phillipe objected, putting on a mock expression of one too beleaguered for words.

Who could we possibly think of who would be big enough in the party to be on the list, and yet obscure enough that no one would be aware that he had no legs, practically no arms, and rolled around on a mechanized chair. I felt downhearted. This was going to be hard.

"You know who I'm going to pretend to be?" Phillipe said. "Garth Undon!" Garth Undon was a famous, ranting, raving, political commentator. He supported the Liberties in everything they did while preaching hatred against anyone who dared dissent. "If you're going to tell a lie," Phillipe said perkily, "a really big lie is often the most believable. And, hey, I can even imitate the guy." To prove his point, Phillipe launched into a Garth Undon imitation, but Margaret shushed him.

"Phillipe," I said, "Garth Undon is famous. What if they know what he looks like?"

"Do you know?" Phillipe asked. "He's on the radio. Nobody sees him. He's probably deformed like me. That's why his mind is so twisted."

I didn't know what he looked like and neither did Margaret. There was a chance that Phillipe's "big lie" strategy would work. Besides, none of us had a better idea.

"Okay, Phillipe, go for it," I said.

"Listen," he said. "With regard to me, this is going to be chancy, so you two have to pretend, starting right now, that you don't know me."

"Oh, Phillipe," Margaret said, and I could hear an agony in her voice, which pretty much summed up how I felt too. But he was right. If either he or Margaret and I were caught in a lie, it would be better if we didn't appear to know one another. Phillipe turned his wheelchair away from us and rolled up closer to the people ahead.

I took a deep breath and tried to relax. I kept repeating the names Joan and John Hurley over in my head, so I'd be sure to be able to say them without hesitation. Margaret pressed up against me. I put my arm around her waist and squeezed her close. I could tell she was really scared.

Behind us was a couple with two small children. I whispered to Margaret, so she'd know what I was going to do, and then I offered to let them go ahead "for the sake of the children." They moved in front of us without hesitation. It seemed safer to put some distance between us and Phillipe, just in case, but I felt like a hypocrite. Margaret turned to me and whispered, "All the others, what are they going to do?"

"I don't know, sweetheart. We can only hope that they think of something."

"I don't think Appoppa will get through no matter what name he gives them. He just doesn't look like one of them."

"I know," I said sadly, wishing there were something I could do. A big truck pulled in at our dock. I went back to praying. I hadn't done that since Margaret recovered, but it had worked then, or at least it had seemed to, so what better time than now. The line was moving forward, and I could see people ahead giving their names to the guy with the clipboard. Then Phillipe reached the front of the line. With his chin held high, his voice strong and firm, he said, "Garth Undon." The guy with the clipboard paused, looked at him, and then broke out in a huge guffaw as though he'd never heard a better joke. "Sorry, Jack," he said. "You aren't Garth Undon. Garth Undon is one of us. He's a Patriot. In fact, he's right over there. Hey, Garth," he called out in the direction of a group of Patriots who were standing on the next dock. "Come take a look at this. This ugly blob here is claiming he's you!" The Patriots came over, and they all had a good laugh. A short, stocky man stepped out from the group. "I'm Garth Undon," he said.

"Oh, Mr. Undon," Phillipe said, "I admire your show so much. I listen to you every Friday night. Never miss it."

"Really?" Undon was obviously enjoying this.

"You are sooo eloquent."

"So why did you tell Chuck, here, that you were me?" Undon scowled at Phillipe. It was clear he wasn't taken in by Phillipe's flattery.

"You know why," Phillipe said, staring directly at him.

"Yeah, I guess I do. Name's not on the list, right? Well, I might not have minded if you was prettier, but somebody ugly as you, that offends me, does damage to my reputation."

"What should we do with him, Garth?" the Patriot with the clipboard asked.

228

"Why not detain him over at the Visitor Center?"

They all nodded, and one of the Patriots grabbed Phillipe's chair and rolled him off. I kept my face stony and squeezed Margaret even harder. I didn't want her to make a sound or a face.

The guy checking names turned his attention to the people in front of us. They gave him their names. "Would you mind showing me some identification," he said. "It seems some people may be trying to leave without authorization." The husband pulled his wallet from his back pocket and showed his ID card, and the family climbed into the truck. When he turned to us, I said, "John and Joan Hurley."

"Could I see some identification please?" he asked as he checked off the names on his list.

"I'm terribly sorry," I said, "but we had to leave so quickly, I never thought to bring it."

"You didn't bring your wallet," he said suspiciously, "and she didn't bring her pocketbook? What's that?" he said, eyeing the bag slung over Margaret's shoulder.

"I have a pocketbook," Margaret said, "but this isn't the right one. I have so many. I just grabbed the first one I saw, and I guess my ID is in another."

"I'm afraid in the rush I must have left my wallet on top of my chest of drawers," I said.

"Don't you think we should hurry?" Margaret said. "You know, it could happen any time."

"Don't worry, ma'am," he said. "The mayor said we had at least two weeks." So the mayor had lied to them. That's why they were acting so casual and unafraid. That's why they were here doing this! "I'll have to ask you to go home and get your identification," he said.

"No!" I said. "Where is the mayor? He knows us." I felt sure that the mayor was long gone, but I hoped this would impress him.

"Sorry, but the mayor's not here. Hey, guys," he called out to the same group of Patriots who were still standing around nearby. "Any of you know John or Joan Hurley?" The group strolled back and looked us over.

"Listen," I said, "I'm John Hurley the developer. I'm doing that huge redevelopment project up in Jackson Heights. I'm a major supporter, so please let us pass."

"Hey, isn't she the lady who was screaming her head off at the Freedom Tower a week or so ago," one of them said, "the one who was trying to defend that traitor?"

"Looks like her to me," said another. "I remember the hair, that bright red hair."

"Yeah, that's her. I'm sure it's her," said the first. "Those people are traitors!" he said angrily. With that, they grabbed Margaret and me by our arms and marched us away.

🌼 *Chapter 79*

When we reach the Visitor Center, we're locked in a large room used to receive VIPs from the outside. Our jail cell is luxurious. It's plushly carpeted and has an assortment of expensive-looking sofas and chairs, a wet bar, and a large table suitable for hosting a banquet. Phillipe's already there, as is Appoppa, Howie, Edith, the Leader, and several other Club members. Edith is crying because they took Xanax from her and tossed him down outside.

Periodically, more Club members are shoved into the room, as well as a few people we don't know. Some were told that in several days, when the evacuation of the general public begins, we'll be released and allowed to take our "proper place in line." But what does that matter? We have good reason to believe there won't be any tomorrow, much less a day after.

We all mill around, looking for a way to escape. Since the Visitor Center was built after the Encapsulation, there aren't any windows. But there are two large, ornate wooden doors that meet in the middle and swing outward. That seems hopeful, since the middle part might be weak. We push against them, as many of us as will fit up against the doors, with others in back pushing to add more force. The doors hold. They feel solid and thick and securely bolted.

We check around, looking for something to use as a battering ram. About the only thing we find are some wooden dining chairs from around the banquet table. They're thick and strong-looking. Possibly, we think, by ramming the two separate sides of the doors simultaneously, the bolt will break, and the doors will fly open. Howie and a big guy I don't know each pick up one of the chairs and position themselves far enough away to get a good run at the doors. The rest of us crowd around like spectators in a sporting event. Howie and the other guy charge. As the chairs crash into the doors, the men go sprawling. Suddenly there's a deafening sound, like a machine gun, and a spray of bullets rips through the door. Then we hear a gruff voice say, "Stay away from that door, or I'll come in there and shoot every last one of you!" We stand stock still, frozen with shock. Some people start crying while others take on the task of comforting them. Margaret is right beside me, so I know she's all right. I look around. No one seems to be hurt. Hope is the only casualty. If they have a guard with an automatic rifle stationed outside, how can we possibly escape?

Margaret takes my hand. "You know, it really doesn't matter," she says. "What were we planning to do if we did get out?" I hadn't wanted to think about that part of it. Perhaps no one had. Armed Patriots are out there guarding the loading docks, as well as long lines of people who wouldn't be inclined to let us step in front of them and get onto a waiting bus or truck. What good would it do to escape from the Visitor Center unless we could also escape from the city?

We move to the far end of the room away from the door and try to think what to do. Collectively, we're able to come up with only one idea: we should try to reason with the guard and convince him that the mayor lied to the Patriots when he told them the wall wouldn't collapse for at least two weeks. If we can convince the guard that the collapse is imminent, maybe he'll let us out before the Patriots load themselves onto the next available vehicle and leave. Then we'd at least have a chance. Depending on how many people are out there, how many trucks and buses come, how long it takes the North Wall to give way, well, who can say?

We have no proof of what the engineers said, not here. The tape of the meeting with the mayor is in Howie's room. If they won't believe us, we can try to convince them to get the tape and listen to it. If they heard that, they'd be out of here in a split second.

Phillipe is unanimously elected as our spokesperson. We wish him luck with what could well be his most important seduction ever. He sits for a moment thinking over his strategy then rolls off toward the door. We stay where we are. Given what's just occurred, it seems dangerous to go over there. Phillipe starts to talk through the door. Within seconds the guard opens fire. He aims precisely where Phillipe's legs would have been, had he been standing at the door. The bullets rip into Phillipe's wheelchair, knocking it out from under him. Phillipe goes flying and lands hard on the floor. Appoppa and I run over and drag him from in front of the doors as the guard yells in a loud and nasty voice, "I told you people to stay away from the door!"

Phillipe's upper left appendage looks badly twisted, possibly even broken. He tries to be stoic, but I can tell he's in pain. "Sorry," he says. "The guy didn't seem to be in a particularly good mood. Maybe later." We sit him up on one of the chairs, and Geraldine binds up his flipper.

We stand around, trying to come up with a new idea. Time passes, then more time. Our mood darkens as we gradually realize we don't know anything else to do. People start to drift away. They sit alone or in small groups. Margaret and I lie together on one of the sofas, wrap our arms around each other, and cry softy. It seems so terribly sad. A lifetime of longing for love, and now when we've finally found it, already our lives are about to end. We can hope, of course, that the engineers made a mistake, but this doesn't seem likely.

Then something long forgotten comes to mind. I remember roaming the corridors shortly after joining the Club, feeling terrified of the pain I'd feel if I lost Margaret. I'd wished then that we could somehow die together. Well, here in a place where cars no longer crash and planes no longer go down, it looks like my wish is going to be granted. Neither of us need suffer the gut-wrenching pain that inevitably comes to one member or the other of every couple who dares to love. I recall the day I visited Appoppa right after Amy's death. The agonized sounds he'd made chilled me. Yes, this is terrible, I think. It isn't at all what I want, but I'm grateful I won't have to survive Margaret. I remember, as well, my solemn vow not to complain about anything if only Margaret could live. Surely I owe it to the universe to keep that promise. Ever since Margaret opened her eyes, I've felt so happy. I wouldn't have missed this time for anything.

I'm feeling a little calmer now, and I'm determined to find a way to face this situation courageously. As if on cue, I remember an old Zen story, the one where a monk has fallen over a cliff and is hanging by a fraying vine when he notices a strawberry growing within his reach. A moment before he falls to his death, he reaches out, picks the strawberry, and savors its sweetness. Well, if these are going to be my last moments, I think, I want to savor whatever sweetness I can find.

I try to relax and let myself fully experience holding Margaret. I let myself love her. I feel sadness and fear and gratitude all at the same time. We're the lucky ones, I think. At least we have the luxury of examining our lives through the lens of our death. Most people will have only an instant to realize how they've been betrayed, when they hear screams in the corridors and feel the thunder of our sewage returning home. I feel life more intensely than ever before. I visualize mine as a bright spot surrounded by infinite darkness, a luminous thing, sparkling against the backdrop of oblivion. Oblivion, is that what we face? Well, given the mystery of it all, who can say? Maybe we'll survive death. Maybe we'll expand, as Appoppa once imagined, into some vast, vibrating, luminous energy.

Margaret is quiet in my arms, nestling there. She feels so incredibly sweet, tears come to my eyes.

"Sweetheart," I say. "Look at me." She gazes into my eyes and smiles. She seems calmer now, as though she, too, has started to come to terms with our approaching death. Her blue-green eyes, damp with tears, are exquisite. "There's something I want to tell you, Margaret. I want you to know that I feel so lucky to have had love in my life. Thank you." She reaches up and gently strokes my face.

"Me, too," she says. "Thank *you*."

After a while, we get up. We want to say good-bye to our friends. Appoppa gives us a big smile and me a punch in the arm. When we reach Phillipe, he extends his uninjured fin, and when I reach back, he hooks his single finger over my hand and pulls me toward him. His finger is strong and calloused, a talon. I realize that in all these years I've hardly ever touched him. I put my arms around him. Tight, this muscular teddy bear, who's been such an unexpected and vital part of my life. I feel his goatee rub coarsely against my cheek.

We go around the room hugging everyone, plump little Cecil, gentle Edith. We thank Geraldine again for having been so good to us when Margaret was unconscious. We thank Howie for his bravery, for marching straight into the den of the lion and setting up his recording equipment. We hug them all, including a few people we don't know. We even hug the Leader, who until now had always seemed too dignified to hug.

How do you wait for death? From time to time we sing, mostly folk songs and spirituals. It's hardly even singing, a private sound, but we share it as we share our waiting. The Leader goes around the room, the soft lamplight glinting on the gold wire of his glasses. He touches every face. Then he stands in the middle of the room and speaks. "Don't be afraid. Life and death are only an appearance. We are all part of a Great Oneness. We knew that before we were born, and we will know it again once we have separated from our bodies." Well yes, maybe, I think. Even in the face of death, I stubbornly refuse to pretend my mind can penetrate such a great mystery. "Embrace the inevitable," the Leader continues. "The time for struggle is over, and you can be happy that you did what you could. Be peaceful. Our journey is ending, and there is nothing left for us but rest."

But I have an unquiet thought. I wonder if we really did do everything we could. This is more than just the sum of our individual deaths. A city is an adventure, an experiment, and this is the end of one of the greatest cities of all time. Perhaps somewhere people will start again. Perhaps they'll learn from our example. But for now, for us, we can no longer escape the consequences of our actions.

People hold hands. They tell what their lives have meant and what dreams will go unrealized. For the most part, Margaret and I keep to ourselves, hungry to experience each other for as long as we can. Eventually, we grow tired. Despite the occasion, our bodies go on in a very ordinary manner. Sometimes we doze off. The singing doesn't wake us. The sound of our friends' soft voices soothes us.

I dream of my father, and he isn't crying. We're in Central Park. In my dream, the park has risen like some long-vanished rain forest. Flowers bloom everywhere, floating on ponds, strung along vines, flashing from the exotic trees. I recognize only the eucalyptus, so graceful with its long, thin leaves emerging tentatively from the warm mist. We're surrounded by the soft sound of water dripping and the peeping of tiny yellow birds, busy in the branches.

My father emerges like some old man of the forest. He welcomes me to his home. He's frail and unsteady, as he was at the end, but we hug each other, and his arms feel fierce with a father's love, strong enough to reach me at last. There in the heart of the city, I tell him I love him.

The sun pierces the mist and spreads over the meadow like a benediction. I smile. I feel a spaciousness I haven't known since childhood. There are no walls. The ground is uneven; my feet are surprised; they come alive. The air is alive, too, sliding against me in scented streams. The depth of the sky and the drifting of the clouds are beyond understanding.

Then with trumpet and drum they burst through the trees, the Leader leading, dressed as a drum major in scarlet and braid, baton waving, as he high steps and kicks up his shiny black boots, marching into the crowd, because now there are people everywhere, an outdoor tavern, tables with food and wine. Margaret is there, radiant in her silver stretch jumpsuit, almost a blur as she cartwheels through the crowd. They cheer the miracle of her momentum, but the sight makes me ache. I need to reach her; I want to hold her, to touch her hair. She spins away so fast.

Appoppa is a harlequin, juggling poems of fantastic colors. Above him, Amy, ironic angel, swoops and soars in satiric circles on tiny, fleshy wings. Carl has come as a clown with a funny hat, a red nose, checked pants, and huge shoes. It's so good to see him enjoy himself. Even my mother, the skeptic, is there, her plump form now classic in a flowing white gown. She's come as a May maiden, scattering petals from a basket. And for the grand finale, of course, Phillipe roars in. He has on a black T-shirt with a red mushroom cloud and a cheery "Hi!" printed on it. He wears a wizard's long black cape and a wild, blond wig. He's soaked his wig in lighter fluid and set it on fire. Oh, crazy Phillipe! Too extreme for combustion. The flames and his cape trail behind as he zooms like a comet in and out among the tables, wheelchair at full tilt, all of his passion in his magnificent voice. "Wake up! Wake up, you fools!" The rest of our troop takes up his cry. "Wake up! Wake up, you fools!" And here's the most amazing part: the crowd isn't insulted; they love it. They stand up and clap wildly. They get it! They join in our chant, and together our excitement ripples along the footpaths, between the graceful trees, and out toward the distant horizon: "Wake up! Wake up!" we chant.

"Noah! Noah! Wake up! Wake up!" I open my eyes. It's Phillipe. He's smiling, beaming actually. "There's hope!" he says jubilantly. "There's hope!"

"What is it? What's happened?" I ask.

"They've gone after the tape, and if they get back in time, just maybe they'll take us with them when they leave the city."

"How did that happen?" I find this hard to believe, and I don't want Phillipe jerking us back into hope only to have it dashed again.

"It's true," Phillipe says, sensing my skepticism. "While you and Margaret were sleeping, I went over to the door very quietly so that hothead outside wouldn't hear me. I sat there waiting. I figured sooner or later they'd send someone to replace him and that then maybe I could convince the new guy that the mayor had sold them down the river. Sure enough, a couple of hours later, I hear the hothead talking to some other guy. After a bit, the conversation stopped. I figured old hothead was gone, so I struck up a conversation with the new guy. I kept my wheelchair to one side of the door, just in case he decided to shoot through it like the other one did, and I chatted to him very casually, not mentioning anything this time about the mayor. I asked him how the evacuation was going, and so forth, and we talked about how sad it is that the city's going to be destroyed. We went on like that for a while, and then I said, 'Well, not much time left now; by morning we'll all be dead.'

"'No, no,' he says. 'The mayor said we have at least two weeks before the wall collapses.'

"'No,' I say, 'it'll be much sooner, probably before morning.'

"'What makes you think that?' he asks.

"'That's what the engineers said.'

"'And how would you know what the engineers said?'

"'Well, if you really want to know,' I say, 'I'll call my friend over here, and he can explain how we know.'

"'Okay,' he says, 'that'll be a good story.' So I call Howie over, and Howie tells him about the hidden microphones. He describes in detail the inside of the mayor's office and the exact place the microphones are concealed. He tells the guy he can go check all this out for himself, because the mayor is long gone. The mayor, Howie says pointedly, certainly won't be in his office, because he knows the wall's about to collapse. That's why he got the hell out of here. Then, Howie asks him why he thinks the mayor left so quickly if the city's safe for another two weeks.

"'Dunno,' he says, 'could've been a lot of reasons.' But he's starting to worry, I can tell that.

"Suddenly I get an idea how I can make our story even more convincing. The Patriots are close to the mayor, so I'm betting they know about the special air filtration system. So I tell him that we know about that, too, but instead of telling him the truth about how we found out, I pretend we learned about the filtration system by taping conversations in the mayor's office."

"Phillipe, you are such a clever wizard!"

"'We have a tape,' I say, 'that proves the wall could go any minute. Sorry to tell you, but the mayor lied. You see, he wanted you guys to handle the evacuation of his precious party faithfuls.' The guy is quiet for a bit; then he says, 'So where is this tape?'

"'Well,' I say, 'if I were to save all your lives by telling you where it is, would you promise to take all of us in this room out of the city with you when you Patriots go?'

"'Dunno about that,' he says. 'I'd better tell this story to the guy in charge. Now listen up, I'll only be gone a minute, and if you try anything with that door, I'll shoot all of you when I come back. You understand?'

"'Understood,' I say. So he goes off, and in a little bit, he comes back with some big Patriot poobah.

"'Okay,' the new guy says, 'Joel tells me you think the North Wall could cave in anytime now. Says you say the mayor lied about the time frame.'

"'That's right,' I say. 'And I can prove it.'

"'Yeah, yeah, I know. Joel told me about the tape you say you have. So, where is it?'

"'I can tell you that, but first I want you to give me your word that if you find out what I say is true that you'll take all of us with you when you leave the city.'

"'Okay,' he says, 'if it's true, we'll take you out with us, but if you send us on some wild goose chase, when we come back we'll shoot all of you. That a deal you want to make?'

"'Fine with me,' I say. So Howie explains where they can find the tape, and the big poobah sends Joel off on the double to fetch it."

"How long will it take?" I ask. "The wall may not hold out that long."

"Subways are fast. He could be back in forty-five minutes."

"Will he keep his word?" Margaret asks. "Can we trust them?"

"Who can say?" Phillipe says, raising his flippers in a "what else can we do?" sort of gesture. "At least there's a chance now that we'll get out."

By the time we join the others up by the big table, Howie's already told them the news. Some people are crying. Others look elated. The stress is taking a toll on everyone.

"I don't know if I can stand this," Margaret says. I pull her close, but how can I reassure her? She knows what we all know. It's 4:00 a.m., and the engineers said the wall might not last the night.

"All right, everyone," I say like some lying politician, "we're going to get out of here. The wall's held this long, and it's going to hold a little while longer." A cheer goes up.

"Let's talk about our dreams," Appoppa says. "Let's talk about what we want to do once we get out of here."

Everyone is quiet for a moment. Then the Leader speaks. "My dream is to be able to meditate under a big tree in the middle of a forest, like my ancestors in Tibet used to do. There won't be machine noise, like here. There, it will be perfectly still, except maybe for songbirds."

"I want to build my own house. It'll be off all by itself and have a beautiful view, like ones I've seen in books." It's Betsy's son, whom I've just gotten to know.

Geraldine speaks next. "I want to do just what I've always done. I want to be a nurse. There are always too few of us and too many people who are sick."

"I want to be a farmer," Cecil says. "I don't know a damn thing about it, but I'll find somebody who does and learn from him. Maybe in the process," he says with a laugh, "I'll lose some of this flab."

"I've been closed away in this city all my life," Appoppa says bitterly. "But once I get out, I'm going to study the plants and animals we still have and work to save as many of them as possible."

The voices continue, sometimes with long silences in between, while we consider what calls to us.

"It won't matter what I do," someone says, "it will just be wonderful to be alive!" I look at my watch. It's 4:30 a.m. I wonder if Phillipe should have tried to convince the Patriots simply to believe us instead of encouraging them to go after the tape. I feel nervous. Unless we get out of here soon, these lovely dreams will surely go unfulfilled.

Howie speaks. "I regret all those years when I gave up fighting for what I believed in. Look where it's brought us. I won't do that again. It doesn't pay. Who will stand with me out there against the greed for power and the greed for money that's brought us to this terrible place?"

"I will," I say. This time I don't hesitate. I've learned the hard way just how bad things can get if you stand by passively. Then all around the room, one after another, here and then there, the "I wills" ring out until everyone has pledged to fight the forces that have brought us to this sad place.

At last, we hear voices outside the door. The Patriots have returned, grumbling and swearing, mad as hell at the mayor. They unlock the door.

"All right," the head guy says. "Come with us." That's all he says, and he sounds gruff, so we're not sure whether we're to be saved or shot. When we get back to the loading docks, the lines are even longer. There's a baby crying and a little girl whining about how she has to go to the bathroom. People in nice clothes are sitting on the dirty cement dock. There's a sense of weary perseverance, but no fear. Apparently they still believe they've got plenty of time.

The Patriots leading the way stop and confer among themselves. Then one of them goes over and talks to one of the guys checking off names. He then continues down the loading dock talking to the Patriot at the front of each line. I feel uneasy. Nobody is smiling at us reassuringly, and I still wonder what they're up to. Then there's an announcement on the PA system saying that the loading will stop for ten minutes to allow the Patriots to take a short break. The remaining Patriots join our group, and we all start walking toward one of the big trucks. I squeeze Margaret's hand and smile at her as we approach a big, silver freight truck. Only when we finally step across the small gap between the dock and the back of the truck do I let myself believe it: they've kept their word; they're actually taking us out with them.

As the door at the back of the truck slams shut, I hear a lot of yelling. Then there are hands pounding on the back of the truck. Those still out on the dock must realize we're deserting them. I wish the driver would start the truck and get going. It's total pandemonium out there now. Finally the motor starts, and the truck jerks forward. A big cheer goes up from our group. We're safe, I think, we're safe.

We can't see anything because the sides of the big freight truck are solid, but I know we must be out on the Great Highway. The air has turned hot and humid, but no one cares. Everyone is smiling; people are hugging each other. Margaret throws her arms around me, "Oh, Noah, we're going to live!"

"It looks like it, sweetheart." My relief is so intense I feel weak, yet I'm tingling with excitement. Having narrowly escaped death, I'm convinced our future will be a grand adventure, shot in glorious Technicolor. Appoppa comes over, and we do a high five.

"We're out," he says. "We're out!"

"Yes," I say, "thanks to Phillipe, our very own wizard." I look for Phillipe. He's in a corner at the front of the truck, and as usual there's a group of people crowded around listening to him. We're bumping at high speed along the highway now. We all sit down to keep from falling. I put my arm around Margaret and try to calm down, but that's pretty hard given what we've been through and what we're leaving behind. We've struggled to survive, and through a combination of ingenuity and luck, it looks like we will survive. But if the engineers were correct, there are millions of people who won't. A guilty feeling settles into the pit of my stomach. I know I don't deserve to live any more than anyone else, and I feel somehow responsible. We did, after all, fail to accomplish our mission. We set out to discredit the

Liberties and sweep them from power. They were the bad guys, and we were the good guys, the ones who were going to save city. But as history clicked forward, a different scenario unfolded; ultimately our only choice was to flee or die. But really, I think, even if we had accomplished everything we set out to do, what difference would it have made? That chemical concoction was eating its way through the wall, and the time when anyone could have done anything to stop it was long past.

I'm still mulling all this over when the truck jerks to a stop. We hear the crunch of the driver's feet as he walks around to the back. Then the big doors swing open, and we scramble out as fast as we can so the driver can return for others.

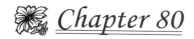 *Chapter 80*

We're in the hills north of the city. It's barren and ugly. There are some tough, scrubby looking bunches of grass, but no trees. Apparently the pollution emanating from our shell has poisoned pretty much everything. Still there's a moon and stars and a gentle warm breeze, and all of us, especially those among us who've never seen the sky before, are transfixed by the large, glowing disc and sparkling bits of light. The moon, almost full, allows us to see well enough to clamber up the embankment by the side of the highway. Four guys are carrying Phillipe in his wheelchair. It's going to be a lot harder for Phillipe now that he no longer lives in a paved environment.

Hundreds who were evacuated before us are spread out across the top of the hill. We stop halfway up, already eager not to be with so many people and to part company with the Patriots, who much to our relief continue up to the top. Those who've brought jackets spread them out on the ground. Below us the enormous concrete dome of the city with its array of vents and portals shines ghostly white in the moonlight. We say little as we sit contemplating the fate of millions of our fellow New Yorkers. My mother and brother are down there, my friends and my clients. Someone suggests we pray, and we do; even those of us who aren't religious pray.

By the time we see light in the East many are curled up on the ground fast asleep. Gradually the cool grey light on the horizon warms into a swirl of delicate pinks, yellows, and oranges. There's a chorus of oohs and ahs. The sunrise looks delicious, like sherbet. I'm suddenly aware of how dismal the city was. Not that I didn't know that and complain about it when I was there, but only now do I realize what we were missing.

Once up, the sun is brighter than anything any of us had remembered or imagined. Unaccustomed to so much light, we blink. I remember about sunglasses. Probably they're still in use here on the outside. Then Cecil says hopefully, "Well, everyone, it's morning. The wall has made it through the night." A wave of optimism sweeps over us. We talk about how the engineers may have been wrong and how the wall may well continue to hold until everyone gets out. Meanwhile, our hill has become more and more crowded as busloads and truckloads of people have been hauled from the city and deposited here.

We start to feel restless, and some of us walk off to explore the other side of the hill. It's hot, but I advise Margaret to keep her long-sleeved blouse on and her face turned down and away from the sun. The Liberties always exaggerated the power of the sun to burn, but sunburn does exist, and we're all extremely pale. We need to buy hats at the earliest possible opportunity.

When we get back, everyone who has brought food is snacking and sharing with those who didn't bring anything. I get out the fruit drinks and meat patty sandwiches Margaret packed with our stuff. The bright, warm light of the sun has made us feel hopeful. A debate starts among us about whether it isn't time to move on, since we don't actually know when or if the wall is going to fall. It could be days or weeks or never. This line of reasoning cheers us further. The issue is never completely resolved when people start chattering about other things, what they forgot to bring and what we should do first when we arrive in Preston. Unfortunately it's a decision we never have to make, because just then a loud cracking sound splits the air. We jump to our feet, and when we look down at the shell, we see a jagged line, maybe half a mile long, extending across the North Wall. It's then that we know, we know without a doubt that the unthinkable is about to happen. There are groans and screams. Someone shouts, "No! No!" as if through the force of will alone he could stop it. An instant later, the North Wall crashes down with a thunderous roar, leaving a rim of torn cement and a giant maw of an opening in the city's shell. Then we hear a great whooshing sound as the sea of sludge rushes in and floods the city.

A moment later, all is quiet. The only sound now is the gentle lap of water as it sloshes around the huge piles of grey rubble. But we know that all is not quiet inside the city. None of us wants to think about what's happening there, but how can we avoid it? In my mind's eye, I picture millions being drowned in the toxic slime or being gassed as its fumes rise and concentrate under the giant dome of the capsule. I feel sick all over. Margaret turns and bolts from the group. She runs headlong downhill toward the highway. I run after her, and when I catch up with her, I pull her to me and we hold onto each other so tightly it hurts.

After a time, the others come down and join us. Some people are clearly in a state of shock. Others are crying. We start walking up the highway. I figure a truck is bound to come along soon on its way to save people who are already dead from a city that no longer exists. We can flag it down, and once the driver recovers from our news, possibly we can hire him to take us to Preston.

We've survived, I tell myself; that's all that matters. Yet, over and over I reexperience the cracking and crashing, see the image of the wall crumbling, and imagine the horror of death by drowning, death by asphyxiation. Margaret squeezes my hand and gives me a hard look. "Don't think about it," she says. "Just don't!"

I look at this woman whose life is now inextricably entwined with mine, and my heart practically splits in two realizing how horrible and how beautiful life is. "You're right," I say. "Let's talk about the future."

"We've seen pictures of Preston," Margaret says, "and it's beautiful. It still gets enough rainfall, and it's in the mountains, so it'll never flood. We can live there and be happy."

"Yes, we can, and we will."

As Margaret and I walk along we try to imagine what life in Preston will be like. We wonder if our savings will be enough to buy a small house and what sort of vegetables we can grow in a garden. We talk about seasons and rain, how wind can sometimes actually howl, and I try to describe that special time when the leaves turn scarlet and gold.

Then we fall silent. Once again I have to struggle not to think about what's happened, about my mother and brother and everyone else I know who didn't get out. There will be a time to grieve, I tell myself, but this isn't it. I purposefully turn my attention to a happy memory: the time my family rented a cabin in the Adirondacks over Christmas and I saw snow for the first time. I was four. I got up one morning and looked out the window, and I thought a fairy had been there in the night and covered the entire world with sugar. Margaret was never taken out of the city, so she knows snow only as dirty, slushy stuff that makes your feet wet and cold. I imagine us waking up the morning after the first snowfall and looking out to see the trees all splendid, the meadows perfect and untouched, except perhaps for the tracks of some small animal that's skittered across, and I don't know which will be better: experiencing that again myself or watching Margaret, who'll surely be so thrilled she won't be able to contain herself.

"Why are you smiling like that?" Margaret asks.

"Oh, nothing. You'll see. It's a surprise."

Then someone up ahead shouts. It's Appoppa. He's climbing up the steep incline at the side of the highway and pointing at something. Those of us who are able scramble up to see what it is. There growing out of the barren earth we see a cluster of bright blue flowers. I examine this miracle with care. Each delicate blossom has five rounded petals, a splash of white at its center, and a ring of tiny yellow stamens. It's May, so this is an ordinary thing, I suppose, but to me it seems wondrous, a sign perhaps that against all odds nature might still pull through, even if we humans succeed in destroying ourselves. I whisper to my father, just on the off-chance he might be listening. I tell him I finally understand what he was trying so hard to tell me.

Reading Group Guide

In the questions below, page numbers are given to indicate where in the book specific statements are made that are relevant to a specific question. However, there may be other portions of the book or, in many cases, conclusions based on the entire book which may also be relevant. No page numbers are given when the question must be answered based on material that is widely spread throughout the book or if the answer depends on your own personal opinion. Try to answer the questions without checking the references. They are there to help you if you get stumped or if there is disagreement between members of your group.

Questions for Discussion:

1. How does the stanza of the poem by Edna St.Vincent Millay cited at the front of the book relate to the content and the theme of this novel? (Pages 199, 244-245)

2. Noah, the story's narrator, is a psychotherapist by profession. After his breakup with Margaret, Noah realizes that his work has helped him avoid true intimacy in what way? (Page 118) Does Noah seem to be talented and skillful as a therapist? Why or why not? Did you gain any new insights regarding what it is like to be a psychotherapist from Noah's description of his work life?

3. Noah has a fraternal twin brother named Adam. Compare Noah and Adam. In what ways are they different? According to Noah, what is the single most important circumstance that makes it difficult for him to feel close to his brother? (Page 30)

4. Noah falls in love with his brother's wife, Margaret. Did you sympathize with Noah, or did you feel he should have exerted more control over his feelings and behavior? What factors do you think lead Noah to develop such intense feelings toward Margaret? (Pages 5, 79-80)

5. Why might the author have named this novel *In Memory of Central Park*? Do you believe that New Yorkers would actually destroy Central Park in order to build more housing? If you look at Central Park as a symbol, what might it represent?

6. Noah's two colleagues, Carl and Phillipe, have very different personalities. Describe these two characters. (Pages 54-55) What circumstance led Phillipe to become the kind of person he is? (Pages 55-56) Who are the Angel-Beasts, and what do they represent for Phillipe? (Pages 89-90, 131) Where does Noah stand in relationship to his two friends? (Page 58) By the end of the book, do you feel Noah has changed so that he has become more like Phillipe, more like Carl, or neither?

7. Describe the political situation in this imaginary mid-twenty-first-century New York City. Discuss the Liberty Party and the Patriots. What is one of the main strategies the Liberty Party uses to continue getting elected? (Pages 6, 110, 167) Do you believe that a political situation even remotely similar to the one described could ever occur in the US?

8. As a child, why does Noah resist listening to his father's stories? (Pages 1, 16, 40) Do his feelings about these stories change? (Page 16, 199, 245) What kind of relationship does Noah have with his father as an infant, (Pages 112-113) later in childhood, (Page 114) as an adult, (Page 14) and after his father's death? Why do you believe Noah spends so much time ruminating about his dead father?

9. The Encapsulation not only makes umbrellas obsolete, but the politicians are also originally able to convince New Yorkers to vote in favor of Encapsulation because it will benefit the city in what important ways? (Pages 18-19) Of the original benefits touted by the politicians, which one turns out to be a very bad idea and eventually leads to the city's destruction? (Pages 207-208) Two additional benefits become apparent only after two catastrophes occur in the outside world. What happens outside, and how does the Encapsulation protect New Yorkers from these two catastrophes? (Pages 74, 198, 82)

10. Most people would consider the idea of a city seceding from the US preposterous. According to the author, what makes it possible for New York to "slip out of the Union practically unnoticed"? What is the advantage for New Yorkers of becoming an independent city-state? (Pages 73-74)

11. Where does Noah's mother work, and how does she use her job to achieve "a truly pivotal place in the community"? (Pages 41-43) Contrast the personality of Noah's mother with that of his father. (Pages 3, 41-43) Which of his parents is Noah more like? (Page 43)

12. Discuss the clowns or mimes. Why do they not speak? Appoppa states that the clowns are trying to "wake people up." What does he mean? Wake people up to what? (Page 165) What is the City Day Caper, and how does it result in the clowns being forced to go into hiding? (Pages 189-192)

13. It is stated that Margaret and Noah share "the same fears." What information does Noah find out from his mother regarding what occurred in his early life that he has forgotten, suppressed, or repressed? (Pages 112-115) What similar events occurred during Margaret's early

years? (Pages 60-61) How are Noah and Margaret alike in the way they react to their respective childhood traumas as children and adolescents? (Page 124) What fears do they share, and how do these fears help cause them to break up? (Pages 122, 148) In what way do their shared fears ultimately have a positive effect on their relationship? (Page 80)

14. Why does Noah originally join the clowns? (Page 183) From what dangers is Noah ultimately unable to protect Margaret? (Pages 194, 214)

15. What has happened to the actual Statue of Liberty, and how is the statue used differently by the Patriots and the Club, both of which adopt it as a symbol of their organization? (Pages 24, 186-187)

16. How does Phillipe violate the ethical standards psychotherapists are expected to follow? (Page 145)

17. What are some of the ways the Liberty Party tries to manipulate the citizens of New York to feel appreciative of the "New York way of life" and to be fearful of venturing into the outside world? (Pages 82, 110, 197)

18. Describe Noah at the beginning of the novel and at the end. What factors help him evolve as a human being?

19. It seems unlikely that the dome encasing Manhattan is technologically feasible, but if viewed in terms of current US foreign policy, what might it represent?

20. How did the Club finally solve the mystery of why so many people were dying from mysterious illnesses? (Pages 192-193) Do you feel that pollution-caused illnesses are a problem in the present-day world?

21. While the members of the Club intend to warn and save their fellow New Yorkers both from poisonous air and political oppression, when it becomes apparent that disaster is imminent and that they must flee or die, they flee. Do you feel critical of them for not selflessly sacrificing their own lives in order to save others? What would you do in this situation? What important purpose do the members of the Club still hope to serve in the outside world? (Page 239)

22. Does *In Memory of Central Park* contain social satire? If so, who and/or what are the targets of this satire?

23. *In Memory of Central Park* combines a modern love story with environmental and political issues. Did you enjoy this combination, or do you feel that the author should have stuck to one thing or the other?

24. When in the final line of the novel, Noah whispers to his dead father that he finally understands what he was trying so hard to tell him, what does Noah mean by this?